Praise for previous Frankie MacFarlane Mysteries

A twisted tale of greed, revenge and murder plays out against the gloriously spooky stone towers of the Chiricahuas . . . Susan Cummins Miller proves once again that she understands Arizona right down to its rocky core.
—**Elizabeth Gunn,** author of *Cool in Tucson*

Field geologist Frankie McFarlane is hard and beautiful and fragile—like obsidian. Fracture either and you'll find an edge sharper than steel. Miller's writing cuts the page like a scalpel. *Hoodoo* is pure gold! —**J. M. Hayes,** author of *Broken Heartland* and the Mad Dog & Englishman Mysteries

Well-developed characters, a lyrically drawn sense of place, a budding romance, and the importance of family and friends distinguish this mystery series. —*Booklist*

Fast-paced, yet lyrical and evocative. —**Wynne Brown,** author of *More Than Petticoats: Remarkable Arizona Women*

A rollicking pentimento of fieldwork gone afoul! —*Geotimes*

Assured and erudite. —*Publishers Weekly*

A gripping thriller, exciting and eager to lure the reader into a labyrinth of human deceit. . . . Attention Hollywood-- this is the stuff from which blockbuster movies can be made! —*Midwest Book Review*

Hoodoo

Other Frankie MacFarlane Mysteries

Hoodoo

Susan Cummins Miller

Texas Tech University Press

A Frankie MacFarlane Mystery
Copyright © 2008 Susan Cummins Miller

This book is typeset in Sabon. The paper used in this book meets the minimum requirements of ANSI/NISO Z39.48-1992 (R1997). ∞

Library of Congress Cataloging-in-Publication Data

Miller, Susan Cummins, 1949–
  Hoodoo / Susan Cummins Miller.
    p. cm.
    "A Frankie MacFarlane mystery."
  Summary: "After an environmental lawyer, a copper mining executive, and an ethnobotanist are killed, geologist Frankie MacFarlane becomes a suspect. Frankie must decipher interlocking puzzles to clear her name and to find the killer in a mystery that involves the conflict between mining and land values in the Southwest"—Provided by publisher.
  ISBN-13: 978-0-89672-623-9 (alk. paper)
  ISBN-10: 0-89672-623-1 (alk. paper)
  1. MacFarlane, Frankie (Fictitious character)--Fiction. 2. Women geologists—Fiction. I. Title.
  PS3613.I555H66 2008
    813'.6—dc22   2007039944

Printed in the United States of America
08 09 10 11 12 13 14 15 16 / 9 8 7 6 5 4 3 2 1

Texas Tech University Press
Box 41037
Lubbock, Texas 79409-1037 USA
800.832.4042
ttup@ttu.edu
www.ttup.ttu.edu

For my father, Justin "Jim" Miller, Celtic storyteller and closet historian—the world is less colorful without you
And for Wynne and Hedley, Mike and Liz—you know why

Hoodoo:

(geol.) A fantastic column, pinnacle, or pillar of rock produced in a region of sporadic heavy rainfall by differential weathering or erosion of horizontal strata, facilitated by joints and by layers of varying hardness, and occurring in varied and often eccentric or grotesque forms . . . Etymology: African; from its fancied resemblance to animals and embodied evil spirits.

—R. L. Bates and J. A. Jackson, eds.,
  Glossary of Geology, 2nd ed., 1980

(n) 1. Voodoo. 2. Something that brings bad luck.
(vt) To cast a spell on . . .

—*Webster's New World Collegiate Dictionary,*
  G & C Merriam Company, 1979

Chiricahua Mountains, southeastern Arizona
Friday, May 12

"If it is any point requiring reflection," observed Dupin, as
he forbore to enkindle the wick, "we shall examine it to
better purpose in the dark."
"That is another of your odd notions," said the Prefect,
who had a fashion of calling every thing "odd" that was
beyond his comprehension, and thus lived amid an
absolute legion of "oddities."

—Edgar Allan Poe, "The Purloined Letter" (1845)

1

I noticed the vultures first. One shadow slipped over the van. The second bird took off from a point maybe thirty yards away, just beyond an outcrop of welded tuff poking through the island at the center of the parking lot.

Joaquin Black was at my elbow. "What do you think it is?" I said.

"Something big." He pointed to the southwest and north, where two more vultures were homing in as if to a dinner bell. "A deer, maybe. Or a bear. No cattle up here."

Neither of us wanted to mention the other possibility, especially within earshot of my students, who were still unloading their backpacks. Joaquin dumped his coffee on the ground and screwed the cup back on the steel thermos. "I'll check on it, Frankie," he said, and loped off around the parking loop.

I turned to the students, now clustered around the nearest picnic table. This was a makeup field trip for my Geology of Arizona class. The class was over, the final exam given yesterday. But I had till Wednesday to turn in the grades. Because I'd planned to scout locations for future class trips to the Chiricahuas, I'd given students the option of joining me. Three had joined me out of necessity. The fourth, because she loved to explore new country.

Joaquin, my godparents' younger son and my childhood playmate, had volunteered to drive so I could concentrate on the rocks. This was Joaquin's backyard. He was Chiricahua Apache on his father's side. Their ranch lay below us on the east slope of the range.

We'd gathered at dawn at Foothills Community College, piled in the minivan, and driven east on I-10. A few hours later, four sleepy students stumbled out into the warm morning air at Massai Point, the end of the road in the Chiricahua National Monument.

I'd planned to introduce them to the geologic history of the Chiricahua Mountains, to peel back the layers of rock, metaphorically speaking. I was beginning with the young layers of rhyolitic ash-flow tuff, formed from compacted fragments of volcanic ash, glass, and rock that had exploded out of the Turkey Creek caldera nearly twenty-seven million years ago. In Chiricahua National Monument the tuff layers had weathered and eroded into phantasmagoric pillars of rock called hoodoos.

"Why'd they name this place after an African tribe?" said Wyatt Cochran. He was reading the sign at the Massai Point trailhead. "Because of the hoodoos?"

"Good guess, but no. The Maasai both spell and pronounce their name differently. Massai," I pronounced it *Mah-see,* "was a maverick Apache who escaped into the Sierra Madre of Mexico after Geronimo's capture."

"They made a movie about him back in the fifties," said Harriet Polvert, without taking the binoculars from her eyes. The glasses were trained on a mountain spiny lizard, sunning on a nearby boulder. "*Apache,* with Burt Lancaster."

"Way before my time," Wyatt said. "Though old Burt was pretty good in *Field of Dreams*. Did Massai ever come back?"

"Ranchers spotted—"

Joaquin was beside me. He didn't say anything, just held up one finger.

2

I asked my four students, aged twenty-one to sixty-something, to stay at the van. I followed Joaquin onto the ellipse of dirt and rock dotted with thickets of manzanita. A clean-shaven tanned man with graying blond hair lay faceup in a small clearing.

The vultures had been at work on his hands and face. So had the ants and flies. Sightless eye sockets stared into the cloudless blue sky. A bloody loaf-shaped stone supported his head. One shot had been fired from close range through his right temple. Both the wound and his mouth gaped open.

I felt cold, as if my own body were shutting down. My mind hovered somewhere above, tethered by a hair-thin line.

"Frankie? You okay?" Joaquin's voice seemed to come from a distance.

I reeled in the line, forced the detached scientific observer to take over. Feeling detached was good. Detached would work. I took a couple of deep breaths. My hands tingled as warmth returned to my fingers. "I'm fine."

"Definitely not suicide," Joaquin said.

I saw what he meant. No weapon. Hands crossed on his chest. And a dead man doesn't slip a stone pillow under his neck. "But there's no sign of a struggle, either. You think he knew whoever shot him?"

I trusted Joaquin's observational skills. He was a tracker. His father, Charley Black, had begun teaching him to read sign when he was still drinking juice from a sippy cup. And a human, alive or dead, leaves more sign than most animals.

"Maybe," he said.

To avoid disturbing the site, Joaquin stepped to a patch of exposed rock near the victim's feet. He hunkered down, pushed his straw cowboy hat farther back on his head, and studied the body. The man wore a blue Oxford-cloth shirt, its long sleeves rolled up to the elbows. Charcoal dress pants. Expensive black leather shoes. His legs were together, elbows close to his sides.

"Know him?" I asked. Joaquin knew everybody in these parts.

"He isn't local."

It was, at best, half an answer. But I left it and said, "When?"

"Body's stiff, but it hasn't begun to decompose. Last night, I think. Had to be—otherwise someone would have noticed." He looked up at me. "You going to make the call?"

I tried my cell phone. No signal. Why is there never a signal when I need one? I turned off the phone and returned it to my pocket. "I'll drive down to the ranger's station."

Joaquin stood and made the sign of the cross over the body. He was half-Apache, but he'd been baptized and raised in his mother's faith. "You have the students to look after. I'll go." But he didn't move.

"I'll take photos and notes," I said, looking at the ground around the body. "There's something odd here."

"You mean *besides* the rock under his head and the way he's laid out?" Joaquin stepped back carefully, using the footprints he'd made before.

I moved to stand beside him at the edge of the clearing. From that vantage point I could see bird tracks around the body. Some had been obliterated when the killer picked up the corpse's legs and swung his body to a new position. "Whoever moved him didn't leave any footprints."

Joaquin pointed to where he'd crouched before. The underlying tuff layer broke the surface only at that spot. "Stood there to swing the body, and knelt there," his index finger aimed at two indentations in the dirt, "to position the arms. Pretty smart."

"Or just lucky. It must have been dark up here last night."

"But the moon was almost full."

We turned toward the van. We'd nearly reached the others when I said, "Take one of the students with you."

"Why?"

"Humor me."

"What is it? What did you find?" said Harriet, the elder stateswoman of the group. For once, she'd removed the binoculars from her eyes. They dangled from a thin plastic strap draped around her neck.

"A body," I said. "A man's been shot."

"Shot? As in murdered?" Vicente Rodriguez looked over his shoulder. "Are we safe here?"

Wyatt stood on tiptoe and scanned the parking lot. "We're alone."

"It happened hours ago. Whoever did it is long gone," I said. "Joaquin's going down to report it. I'd like one of you to go with him."

"I'll go," said Esmeralda Aquino. She looked uneasy, as if the dead man's ghost had stuck around to keep us company. A Mimbreño Apache from Pinos Altos, New Mexico, Esme was taking horticulture courses at FCC. She wanted to be an ethnobotanist.

Joaquin had noticed Esme when we were loading the van at school. The interaction was subtle—a soft-spoken joke, a dimpled smile in return. She'd taken the seat immediately behind him. They made eye contact every time he glanced in the rearview mirror.

Esme, intelligent and quietly determined, had skin the color of dark cedar, hair the luster of coal turned to jet. She wore it long, no bangs, held back with a beaded-leather clasp she'd made herself, she'd told me, when I admired the intricate pattern. She sold them at Indian gatherings to help pay for school. Except for her Apache cheekbones and slim, fine-boned build, she reminded me of Joaquin's mother, Rosa.

Esme and Joaquin looked at each other for a long moment. Joaquin hadn't yet found a girl who wanted to live in the Chiricahuas. But he preferred to help run the ranch rather than find a city job. His heartland was here. His Apache ancestors had lost it once. He didn't want it to happen a second time.

"Why can't we all go?" said Vicente.

"Because we have to stay with the body, guard the site," Wyatt said.

Something unspoken passed between Joaquin and Esme, questions asked and answered. Without another word they climbed into the van, leaving me with three students and one tough decision to make. I postponed it. "Wait here," I said. "I won't be long."

Throwing my daypack over one shoulder, I headed back to the victim. I took close-up shots of the body and a couple of wide-angle shots of the scene. Putting the camera away, I pulled out my compass and noted the orientation of the body. The axis aligned with 105 degrees, or 15 degrees south of due east. It might not be important, but I entered it in my field notebook.

A choking sound came from behind me. I turned. Vicente was bent over, just outside the clearing, retching onto the blood red bark of a manzanita. Harriet and Wyatt stood beside him. Harriet put a comforting hand on Vicente's shoulder. "Sorry," he said, wiping his mouth on his sleeve.

"Your first dead body, Vince?" Wyatt said, as if he'd seen a hundred in his twenty-three years.

Vicente nodded and brought up the rest of his breakfast.

"Don't come any closer." I handed Vicente a stick of gum from my pocket. "We don't want to muck up the crime scene."

"Anymore than Vince already has," Wyatt said. He was holding his nose, as if the smell of vomit were more offensive than a corpse.

"Since you're here," I said, "we've a decision to make. Once the police are through with us, do you want to go home to Tucson or continue the field trip? If you're too shaken to go on, I'll understand and give you credit for the exercise. But if you choose to stay, there's just one caveat— it has to be unanimous."

"I don't want to go home," said Wyatt. He looked at the others. "Anyone disagree?"

Harriet shook her head. "What's a caveat?" asked Vicente.

"In this case, it means a stipulation, a requirement," Wyatt said, before I could answer. "Though one common usage is caveat emptor, or 'let the buyer beware.'"

"No shit?" Vicente asked me.

"'Fraid so," I said.

"Man, what'd you get on your SAT?" Vicente looked at Wyatt as if he'd turned into an alien.

"Only 780 on the verbal." Wyatt's admission was greeted with groans. He flushed and adjusted his wire-framed glasses. "I couldn't help it," he said. "I'm a nerd."

Vicente shrugged. "Okay, I'm in," he said to me. "Don't have anything else to do this weekend."

"Then I want you to go back to the table by the van. Write down what you saw, and when. Make sure you include your name, address, and phone numbers."

They didn't argue. They'd all seen crime shows. As soon as they left, I stood with my back to the victim's feet and snapped a couple of frames of the distant scene. Sugarloaf Mountain, capped by gray dacite, another volcanic rock, filled the middle distance. Below, Rhyolite Creek carved its way through Heart of Rocks toward Sulphur Springs Valley.

To avoid thinking about the body, I turned my mind to planning. The two-mile-loop hike I'd scheduled dipped into the edge of the wilderness area. It would have taken no more than two hours, even with frequent stops to examine rock textures, structures, and weathering phenomena. Two hours. Easy. That was the plan. Now I had to come up with a new plan—or go home.

The students, silent for once, handed me their statements. "What now?" Harriet asked.

"We wait."

"I know we can't take the hike," she said, "but could we at least do the nature trail? It's short. We'll be within shouting distance if you need us."

I glanced at Vicente, who still looked peaked. He shrugged. "We came all this way. Might as well do something."

"Besides," Wyatt said, "it'll help to focus on something else."

They were resilient, these three. So I sent them up to the exhibit building on the knoll. They were to take notes on the displays, then do the same at all the stations on the nature trail. I told them I expected a report and photos of all the geological phenomena they saw along the way—hoodoos and balanced rocks, jointing, differential erosion, physical and chemical weathering, volcanic textures. It was an easy assignment. The display stations did the work for them. I gave them ninety minutes to complete the loop.

Just as the exhibition building door closed behind them, the minivan turned into the parking lot, followed closely by a weather-beaten Jeep. My heart and lungs constricted.

3

I took a step before my intellect reasserted control. The Jeep wasn't mine. This one had a dark green stripe on the side. And I'd had to replace my white Cherokee seventeen months before.

The Toyota pickup I now drove didn't carry the memories associated with my old field vehicle. I told myself attachments needed time to develop. Just like my attachment to Philo Dain. Although we'd known each other since childhood, we'd been a couple for only six weeks before he was called up. That had coincided with the loss of my Jeep. Somehow, in my mind, they were linked.

Joaquin parked the minivan in its former slot. He and Esme got out and walked to where I waited. The vultures hadn't given up, so I'd stayed close enough to the murder site to prevent the birds from landing, far enough away that I didn't have to look at the body.

The Jeep continued slowly around the center island and parked on the other side, a stone's throw away. The morning seemed strangely quiet when the engine died. A Mexican jay flew up to perch on a dead limb of the alligator juniper behind me, squawking. Two men, wearing uniforms and holstered sidearms, stepped out of the Jeep. I didn't move.

"*Two* rangers?" I said to Joaquin.

"Rasmussen's the chief ranger. The other one lives onsite. He was responsible for doing random checks of the parking areas and campgrounds after hours."

"Apparently he didn't see the body during his random checks."

"Manzanita's a pretty good screen. And he'd have been looking for cars, not bodies."

"Or maybe he skipped a check or two."

"Cynic."

The older ranger was forty-something, round-faced, husky, and blond, with large square hands. His nametag said *H. Rasmussen.* The other was shorter and dark, with long arms and heavy brow ridges. Both men wore sunglasses, as I did. The glare reflecting off pastel rock was intense.

"Over there," I said, pointing.

With a simple "Wait here," the men headed for the clearing. But I didn't wait. The body didn't need protecting anymore.

I sent Esme off to join the other students. Joaquin watched her till the exhibition building's doors closed behind her. "She moves gracefully," I said.

Joaquin's black eyes danced. "You think?"

Behind us, the dark-haired ranger began stringing crime-scene tape. Rasmussen was talking on a two-way radio.

"Any luck while we were gone?" Joaquin pitched his voice low enough that it wouldn't carry to the rangers.

"You might say that." I pulled out the camera and scrolled back through the shots. "There's definitely something odd there. Not just the way the body's arranged, but—" I pointed to a wide-angle shot of the body and the dirt next to it. The bird tracks and drag marks showed clearly.

"Ah, yes," he said, holding the camera close to his eyes. "It's nice to be right."

I started to ask him what the hell he'd seen, but he stopped me with a finger to the lips. Turning, he took a mug and a thermos of coffee from the van and set them on the picnic table.

The vultures continued their hopeful circling on wind currents blowing down from the north. A rainless winter had been followed by a mild early spring and the typical dry heat of May. We'd be baking in another hour, even at nearly seven thousand feet. I hoped the sheriff and forensics team showed up soon. I didn't want to be here with the body when the west face of the Chiricahuas caught the brunt of the afternoon sun.

I collected topographic and geologic maps from the van and sat next to Joaquin at the table, our backs to the dead man. Joaquin filled the mug, then poured coffee into the thermos lid and set it in front of me. I drank it in three gulps, craving the caffeine jolt.

"More?" he said.

"Yes, please." I handed him the cup and a yellow tablet of paper. "I asked the others to do summaries of what they saw and did." I waggled my thin sheaf of student statements. "Maybe these'll get us out of here faster."

"You are an optimist." He took the pad and pulled a pen from his pocket.

"I thought I was a cynic."

"Depends how the wind blows."

I wrinkled my nose at him. "Don't forget your contact information."

"What about Esme's statement?"

I grinned. "Maybe you can jog over and ask her for it."

"I can do that." His eyes were innocent.

I downed the second cup of coffee and stood. "I'll use the rest room, then hold the fort while you're gone."

Joaquin grunted, his head bent over the tablet. When I returned a few minutes later, he was adding his statement to the pile held down by my rock hammer. The rangers had finished securing the scene and were headed in our direction.

"I'd best skedaddle," said Joaquin, and was off toward the nature trail before I could reply.

I looked around the parking area. No other cars on this weekday morning. The smart hikers would have taken the shuttle van up to the trailheads, leaving their cars below.

The rangers joined me, but faced the opposite direction, keeping an eye on the scene.

"You found him?" said Rasmussen.

"I saw the birds. Joaquin checked it out first, then I went over." I handed the statements to him. "There's one missing," I said. "The student who drove down with Joaquin. He's gone to get it from her. I sent the students to walk the nature trail. They'll be back in an hour or so if you have any questions."

Rasmussen leafed through the pages, three in ink, two in pencil. "You're Francisca MacFarlane?"

"Yes."

He looked over my statement, sized me up. "Geology of Arizona class?"

"Yes."

"You arrived this morning?"

"Yes."

"Did you know the victim?"

"No."

He studied another page. "Joaquin Black's an instructor?"

"A friend. I asked him to drive. He knows the area."

"He's a local?"

I pointed. "The family has a ranch over on the east side. I'm surprised you haven't met."

"I arrived last month," Rasmussen said. "I'm still settling in. How long have you known Black?"

"All my life. His parents, Charley and Rosa, are my godparents."

"Does Black know the victim?"

"Not that he said."

"He drove with you from Tucson?"

"Yes. We left at dawn." Anticipating his next question, I said, "He spent last night with his grandparents, his mother's folks."

"In Tucson?"

"Yes."

Rasmussen made a few notes. "Any cars in the lot when you arrived?"

"No."

He closed his notebook. The other ranger put the statements in a plastic bag pulled from his pocket. His nametag said *L. Bascom*. Either he hadn't been wearing it before, or I'd missed it. Unsettling thought. I needed to focus. I didn't usually miss details.

"Will we be able to leave when the students finish their assignment?" I asked.

"Sorry. You'll have to wait till the sheriff's team arrives," Rasmussen said. "Detective Cruz will want to interview each of you."

He and Bascom turned as a unit and walked back to the crime scene.

I sighed. After our morning hike among the hoodoos, I'd planned to check out the Mesozoic sedimentary and volcanic rocks visible from the road into Rucker Canyon. Our last stop would be at the Black family ranch in Coues Canyon, where we'd pitch our tents for the night. From there, tomorrow morning, we'd visit the Paleozoic section on the northeast side of the range before heading home.

But now, we wouldn't have time to visit Rucker Canyon today. I'd have to fit it in tomorrow. Picking up the topographic map, I plotted a route over Onion Saddle to Cave Creek Canyon. The route was shorter than going around the south end of the range, but the road might not be open. Joaquin would know.

Joaquin climbed up from the nature trail to the parking lot, Esme's statement in hand. He took it directly to Rasmussen. Twenty minutes later he rejoined me at the table.

"Anything interesting?" I asked him.

"The usual. You?"

"They asked if you knew the victim. I said no."

"Good."

"What are you not telling me?"

"Nothing that'll change anything." He took a small twisted piece of manzanita root from his backpack. "Borrow your knife?"

"What happened to yours?"

He lifted the cuff of his boot-cut jeans, revealing a hand-tooled leather holder attached to his calf. His sister, Teresa, wore a hunting knife just like it. So did Charley.

"Too unwieldy," Joaquin said, and sat down beside me at the table. He was good at waiting. I'd always liked that about him.

I pulled the stiletto-thin blade from the leather sheath that hung around my neck, under my field shirt, and handed it to him. A neighbor, a Rom healer, had given me the tinker-made knife eighteen months ago. It had seen a fair bit of use since then.

Joaquin ran his fingers over the haft and edge, saying, "Think of the stories this blade could tell."

"If it's all the same to you, I'd rather not."

"Wise choice."

He made a series of parallel grooves in the manzanita root. The carmine color reminded me too much of the body. I went back to revising my afternoon route.

All was not lost, I decided. The dirt road up Pinery Canyon and over Onion Saddle would provide a good cross section of the various rock units in the range.

"Is the road to Portal open?" I asked Joaquin.

"They graded it last week," he said. "The van can make it, no problem, long as we take it slow."

"That's what I have in mind." I went back to perusing the map. "Paradise," I said aloud, focusing on one of the communities we'd pass on the other side of the range. The name reminded me of adventures I'd had in Pair-a-Dice, Nevada.

"What?"

"I was just thinking how names repeat themselves in the West."

"Yeah," he said. "How many Turkey Creeks and Red Rocks you think we got just in Arizona?" He checked the knife for a moment, then returned to shaping the wood. It looked like an ear of red corn. "Not as good as the Indian way of naming things."

"Such as, Place-where-two-rivers-come-together-and-the-grass-grows-belly-high-to-a-rutting-elk?"

Joaquin's lips twitched, but he finished outlining a row of corn kernels before saying, "More like, Place-where-Lieutenant-Bascom-promised-a-parley-then-accused-Cochise-of-kidnapping-a-white-child-and-murdered-Cochise's-relatives."

"Or, as the White Eyes say, Apache Pass." The historic meeting place, northeast of where we sat, marked the boundary between the Dos Cabezas Mountains and the Chiricahua Mountains. "English names aren't as descriptive, but they have the benefit of brevity."

"Granted."

"And didn't Cochise murder a few hostages as well?" I prodded him.

It was Joaquin's turn to laugh. "You bet." But then his expression turned grim. "That war gained us a reservation—for four short years. And then we lost everything."

His right arm swung out to encompass the Chiricahua Mountains, the Sulphur Springs Valley, the Dragoon Mountains on the western horizon, and the Peloncillos off to the east.

"Everything," he repeated, and bent to his whittling

again. Under his quick, sure strokes the highest corn kernels on the carving were metamorphosing into a red-skinned woman with flowing hair. "But at least, before that happened, Cochise was able to retire peaceably into his mountain stronghold. A better resting place than Fort Sill, at least for an Apache."

Geronimo, who'd continued the hostilities, had died at Fort Sill, Oklahoma. The government never allowed him to return to southeastern Arizona or southwestern New Mexico, the lands he'd fought over. That was one reason Charley Black had bought property here in the Chiricahuas. Though Charley'd been born on the Mescalero Apache Reservation in New Mexico, I knew he considered this place his homeland. So it was here he'd come to raise a family and put down new roots.

"Did you see the second ranger's nametag?" I said.

"Bascom? Yeah. Let's hope history isn't going to repeat itself."

Joaquin took a piece of fine sandpaper from his shirt pocket and began rubbing it over the carving. Two minutes later he held it up for me to see.

"White Painted Woman?" I said.

"There's hope for you yet, Sis."

He was referring obliquely to my lack of knowledge of my Apache heritage. And to our blood-joining ritual when we were seven. But at most I'm only one-sixteenth Lipan Apache. My great-grandmother was raised from birth by the MacFarlanes, then married into the family. We know who her mother was, but not her father. My great-great-grandmother died before she could reveal whether he was Apache, white, or Mexican.

"One day I'll look into it," I said.

"Don't wait too long." Joaquin pressed the carving into my hand, closing my fingers around the warm smooth wood.

"I can't—" I started to protest.

"Take it. She'll protect you."

"From what?"

He handed back my blade, haft first. "You name it. Tell me who else in the family's gotten into scrapes in half the western states."

"You exaggerate. It's more like a third."

"And Mexico."

"Point taken." I ran my fingers over the warm red wood. The fetish glowed in the light. "She's lovely. Thank you," I said, zipping it into my breast pocket for safekeeping.

Joaquin nodded, took an unfiltered Camel from his hat brim, struck a wooden match against a chunk of welded tuff, and lit the bent and flattened cigarette. He carried one cigarette with him at all times, in his sun-bleached plaid shirt or tucked inside the ribbon of his battered straw Stetson. I'd seen him carry the same cigarette around for days, transferring it from shirt to shirt. It was "for emergency use only," whether as tinder for a fire or for smoking. I guess finding a dead man qualified.

Joaquin was named for my father, Carson Joaquin Mac-Farlane. Dad, back before he was of voting age, had rescued Charley Black from a bunch of redneck hunters who'd treed him down on West Turkey Creek. That was forty years ago. Anti-Indian sentiment was a lot stronger back then—or at least more openly expressed. Dad and Charley had become close friends. Charley and his wife, Rosa, were my godparents, though Charley, being a non-Catholic Apache, had to have a proxy at the baptismal ceremony. Rosa was from a large Mexican-American family in Tucson. My brothers and I had been raised playing with their children, Raul, Joaquin, and Teresa. In two weeks, when my younger brother Jamie finished his residency in pediatrics, he and Teresa would tie the knot, and the families would be officially joined.

Wind blew the cigarette smoke toward Mexico. I looked at Joaquin's fingers. He smoked with attentiveness, drawing slowly on the white cylinder, savoring the taste and the moment. *I bet that's the way he makes love,* I thought—*with attentiveness, savoring all of the sensations, smell and taste, touch and sight and sound.*

The corner of Joaquin's lips lifted, the ghost of a smile. "Philo's been gone a while," he said.

Joaquin didn't miss much.

A couple of A-10s on a training mission from Davis-Monthan Air Force Base made a broad sweeping turn over the valley. War planes. War—or, more specifically, the hunt for Osama bin Laden—had taken Philo Dain to Afghanistan. But I hadn't talked to him in over a year.

He'd sent me a present for my thirtieth birthday—a sky blue burqa, something I'd never wear. The gift confirmed where he was, and that his sense of humor remained intact. From its folds had fallen a massive carnelian-and-silver ring—a man's ring, the stone carved with an intaglio, what appeared to be a pair of waterbirds rising from a pond. I wore it now. The color reminded me of the blood-coated stone under the victim's head.

I'd mailed a letter to the return address on the package, but Philo hadn't replied. I didn't know why.

Worry hovered on the edges of my psyche like a fog just offshore. Seeing the dead body had allowed tendrils to drift in. *You'd know if Philo were dead,* said the little voice inside my head. But I wasn't convinced. Once, long ago, I'd been told he was dead. I'd lived with that certainty for years. *You'd know, Frankie.* Maybe. Maybe not.

"Seems like he's been gone forever," I said.

Joaquin blew one smoke ring, sent another ring through the first. "Celibacy's not all it's cracked up to be."

"You should know."

"Yup." He stubbed out the cigarette on a piece of dacite float and put the butt in his pocket.

We sat together in comfortable silence. Around us the hoodoos, clothed in vibrant green lichen, danced in the heat waves. A veneer of tragedy and mystery now overlay this place of magic.

"What did you see in the photos?" I asked him. "Why did you say it was nice to be right?"

"Bird tracks."

"What about them? The vultures had been there."

"The vultures came later. Underneath their tracks were others, maybe roadrunner tracks. Pop'll know."

It took me a minute to get it. "I thought roadrunners lived down in the scrub desert, among the mesquites."

"Or out in the grasslands. Not in the chaparral. But these tracks make a nice circle around the body—at least where they weren't rubbed out when the body was shifted."

I pondered that, waiting for meaning to suggest itself. Nothing clicked.

"There was a white man, long time ago," Joaquin said. "I don't remember his name. He lived at one of the pueblos in New Mexico. Wrote that the Puebloans made roadrunner tracks around their dead."

"Why?"

"To confuse the ghosts long enough for the dead man's spirit to reach its home."

"You're saying the tracks are a magical sign?"

"Or somebody's idea of Indian ritual. That's why I didn't mention it to Rasmussen or Bascom."

"Southwestern hoodoo?"

Joaquin smiled grimly. "That's the question, isn't it? Who'd *do* something that bizarre?"

4

It turned out that the choice—to leave or not to leave—was moot. Rasmussen received a call on his radio. Within seconds, he and Bascom were stringing yellow tape across the entrance to the parking lot on Massai Point. We and the van were within it, now part of the crime scene.

Joaquin took another piece of wood from his backpack. Assuming he'd want my knife again, I took off the leather thong and sheath I wore around my neck. I didn't have a license to carry a concealed weapon, or something that could be construed as a weapon. I stuffed the holder in my back pocket and handed Joaquin the blade. "It might be prudent to put your knife in the van," I said. I looked pointedly at where his jeans covered the sheath.

"I'm street legal. And it's not as if the guy was stabbed to death."

He had a point, so to speak. I watched the rangers return to the crime scene. Bascom stood with his back to the body. He was keeping an eye on us, the only suspects they had. I hated being confined.

"We could always hike out," Joaquin said, reading my mind.

"I'm not sure Vicente could make it." Vicente was recovering from mononucleosis. He could handle the short hikes I'd planned for the weekend, but not the five-plus miles to the visitors center. "Besides, our van would still be stuck behind the tape. We'd have to have someone pick us up down below."

Joaquin shrugged and went back to his carving. I looked at the fetish taking shape in his hands—a frog or toad, symbol of rebirth, rejuvenation, the power of water. The knife paused. Joaquin was staring east across the ridge, toward Coues Canyon, toward home. At the mouth of the canyon, a new private road blazed a quarter of the way up the limestone face of Gray Mountain. The blight seemed as raw and calculated as the death of the man lying nearby.

The thin air carried the drone of engines, snaking up Bonita Canyon Drive toward Massai Point. Minutes later, a convoy of Cochise County sheriff's detectives, crime-scene unit personnel, and the medical examiner turned into the parking lot.

The ME was a small, slim, quick-stepping brunette in pale blue blouse and navy slacks. Her name was Robyn Royce, Joaquin told me, though he didn't offer where or when they'd met.

Royce said something to the man who climbed out of a dusty Chevy Tahoe—a detective, I guessed. He was wearing a gray western-cut suit, with a dark blue shirt. He could have been actor Lou Diamond Phillips's younger brother—same build, same easy way of moving, same intensity, throttled back.

"Paul Cruz," Joaquin said.

As if they'd heard, Cruz and Royce looked over at us for a long moment. Both nodded at Joaquin, then followed the two rangers to the body.

"How do you happen to know them?" I said.

"Not here."

I didn't push. Joaquin didn't push worth a damn anyway.

Ten minutes later, Rasmussen fetched me. He handed me paper booties to cover my field boots, waited for me to put them on, then lifted the tape for me to duck under.

"I'm Royce," the ME said, from where she knelt next to the body. "You're a geologist?"

"Yes. I teach in Tucson."

She glanced past me to where Joaquin was standing, leaning against the van. "You a friend of Joaquin's?" Her tone suggested more than idle curiosity.

"From way back. Why?"

"Just curious." Royce pointed a penlight at the rock supporting the victim's head and neck.

"What?" I said, bending closer. I tried to block out the man's face, focusing instead on the blood-stained rock. I wasn't successful. That single gunshot had done a lot of damage to the soft tissue. My body started to feel cold again. I swallowed, breathed, detached.

"Best guess," Royce said. "Is this rock local, or was it brought here?"

"Local, I'd say." My voice sounded normal, professional.

"What kind of rock is it?" The voice came from behind me. I turned my head to find Detective Cruz, dark against the sunlight, looking over my shoulder. He squatted down beside me. He had a narrow face with high cheekbones, a long nose with a bump at the bridge, and a mouth that turned up at the corners. I couldn't see the color of his eyes behind the reflective glasses, but his brown-black hair had a natural wave only partly controlled by the short cut. He was holding the sheaf of statements I'd handed Rasmussen. He said, "Francisca MacFarlane?"

"Frankie."

"Geologist," said Royce.

"I gathered that. I'm Paul Cruz."

He didn't offer to shake hands. Instead, he tucked the notes under his arm and used his pen to point to the rock. "Well?"

The texture was obscured by the dried blood. "Without a fresh surface I can only speculate."

"That's better than 'Rock, indeterminate.'"

"Okay. We're in the middle of volcanic terrain. Old tuffs and flows," I said, with a sweeping gesture that included the hoodoos of the monument and the ridges in the distance. "I'd guess that this is a rhyolitic ash-flow tuff."

"Spell that," Royce said.

I did. "Not much welding. The pumice fragments aren't deformed, compacted. And it's still pretty friable—the blood soaked into the rock." I pointed to the place Joaquin had crouched earlier to look at the body. "It's consistent with what's cropping out at the surface here, but . . ." I paused. Cruz waited politely. "But the rock was placed under his head. He didn't fall on it."

"You're positive?" Royce said.

"No. But I'm willing to bet that you'll find blood on the bottom of the rock and the ground underneath."

A look passed between Royce and Cruz, but all he said to her was, "Time of death?"

"Rough estimate? He was killed between eight and midnight. I'll know more after the autopsy. But I can tell you he was killed here, not just dumped. And there are no apparent defensive wounds."

"You'll do a tox screen?"

Royce closed her bag and collected her gear. "Of course. The victim's muscular, athletic, and was in apparently good health. There had to be some reason he didn't defend himself."

"Did you find a wallet, business cards, anything to ID the body?"

"No. And there's no wear outline indicating he carried a wallet in his pants pockets."

Cruz looked at me. "Did you or your students see a sport coat or jacket anywhere around when you arrived?"

"I didn't. And if the students have found anything on their hike, they'll let me know."

"Okay." Cruz made a few notes, closed his notebook, and slipped it into his pocket. "That's all I need from you right now, Dr. MacFarlane. I'll talk to your students when they return."

I got to my feet and backed away from the victim. A body repositioned, a stone pillow under the head, *and* what looked like roadrunner tracks? Someone was playing games.

A loud voice came from the direction of the nature trail. I turned. Wyatt bounded onto the parking lot, shouting my name. He crossed at a lope and slid to a halt, breathing hard, outside the tape.

"What did you find?" I said, expecting, at the very least, a mountain lion sighting.

Wyatt took a deep breath, letting it out slowly. His grin was like sunshine on a gloomy day. "A gun."

"A gun?" I said.

"Did you touch it?" Cruz said at the same time.

"How stupid do you think I am?" Wyatt looked affronted. "The others are guarding it."

"Show me," Cruz said.

When Wyatt hesitated, I introduced Cruz.

"Alrighty then." Wyatt sounded like Jim Carrey. "Let's go."

He galloped back down the path to the nature trail, long legs eating up the ground. In seconds he disappeared around a bend. Cruz and I, joined by Joaquin, followed a bit more sedately. Rounding a corner we saw the students, murmuring excitedly.

"There," Wyatt pointed up to a cleft in a Jabba-the-Hut hoodoo.

"Where?" said Cruz. Harriet handed him her binoculars. "Still can't see it," he said a minute later.

Wyatt climbed partway up the hoodoo, pausing about eight feet above our heads. The wind shifted a branch on a nearby juniper. Light glanced off metal.

"How the hell did you find it, Wyatt?" I said.

"I was climbing the hoodoo—" He stopped, confused. "That's all right, isn't it, Dr. MacFarlane?"

"Going off-trail damages the ecosystem."

"But—"

"But we'll overlook it this time."

Wyatt's face cleared. His grin returned. "Great. Anyway, I saw the gun, just sitting there." He looked at Paul Cruz. "Somebody threw it, right?"

Cruz smiled. Wyatt had that effect on people. "Looks like it, Mr. Cochran. Good job. You can come down now. We'll take it from here."

One of the crime-scene techs had followed us down to the nature trail. She stood next to Wyatt's feet, peering up at the hoodoo.

"Okey-dokey," Wyatt said and launched himself off the hoodoo, landing heavily. His feet skidded on the gravel trail. He fell on his butt.

I gave him a hand up. "Are you okay?"

"Everything but my pride." He dusted off his khaki shorts. "No great loss."

"Did you finish the assignment?" I said to the students.

They had. But they asked to stay and watch from a nearby bench as the crime-scene tech did her thing. "We could eat our lunches here." Harriet patted her backpack. "We were just about to do that when Wyatt found the gun."

The others nodded. Apparently they'd found the detachment they needed, too.

Cruz had no objections, as long as they didn't intrude. Joaquin walked back to the van to get our lunches, and I found a seat on a boulder. We munched as we watched Cruz and the tech take pictures, measurements, and notes. When they were finished, the tech climbed up to snag the gun from the cleft. She handed the revolver to Cruz, who'd donned clean gloves.

"Smith and Wesson .45," he said, turning the gun over in his hand. He checked the cylinder. "One shot fired." He handed the revolver back to the tech, who bagged and tagged it. "Check for prints as soon as you get back, will you?"

"You betcha." She and the evidence bag disappeared up the trail.

"Can we go now?" Wyatt asked Cruz.

Everyone stopped talking, waiting for the detective's answer. He studied the students' faces, then mine. He saved Joaquin for last. Joaquin didn't blink.

"You have our statements," I said. "If you need more, we'll be at Joaquin's ranch tonight."

Cruz nodded. "Okay. You can go as soon as they take the body." Turning on his heel, he headed back toward the crime scene.

Wyatt, still beaming, fell into step with the other students. Joaquin and I brought up the rear. He hadn't said a word since we'd gone down to retrieve the gun.

"What's up?" I asked him as we approached the picnic table. The students were lining up to use the rest room. They were out of earshot, but I kept my voice low and turned my back to the crime scene.

"Nothing special. Tired, I guess."

I suspected there was more, but it wasn't the time or place to press him. "Want me to drive the next leg?"

He laughed, the sound incongruent in that place of death. "You forget, I've ridden with you on narrow, twisty roads with good outcrops. No, Frankie, you do your geologist thing. I'll keep the van on the road."

Cruz and Royce were debating something. They looked at Joaquin. Royce waved him over.

"Uh-oh," I said. "What'd you do this time?"

"I'm sure they'll tell me."

Joaquin sauntered over to where Royce was zipping the anonymous body into a bag. A pissing contest, Apache-style, wouldn't score him any points, I thought. But he didn't seem worried.

Ten minutes later Joaquin split from Royce. Cruz watched the body being loaded into the ME's van, then sent Rasmussen to release us. It was just after one.

With a final glance at the hoodoos, shimmering in the white heat of afternoon, we drove down the winding road to the monument entrance. There, we turned south on Pinery Canyon Road, aiming for the heart of the Chiricahuas.

5

The grasslands of Sulphur Springs Valley, which should have been green and laced with wildflowers, glowed yellow and brown. Fall and winter rains had skipped Arizona this past year. Drought seared the Southwest again, as it had in the time of the Anasazi. But this time, no one was escaping to wetter climes. Instead, the local population continued to swell.

Each day, it seemed, subdivisions were being cleared and graded for new homes. As the parcel size decreased, the house height increased. I could almost hear the sucking sound as the water table sank beneath the valley floors.

The van sailed in and out of washes like a yacht on gentle swells. A roadrunner paced us for a hundred feet before darting into the undergrowth. On one low ridge, I saw black spots on the asphalt—moving spots, like tarantulas, crossing the road toward the mountains. Joaquin tried to miss them, but the van was sluggish. I winced at each crunch.

"Cicadas," Joaquin said.

"In spring? I thought they hatched in summer."

"Drought drives everything a little crazy." He looked in his rearview mirror toward where we'd found the body on Massai Point. "And everyone."

"You think drought had something to do with the murder?"

"Directly or indirectly. In this country it's all about water . . . or the lack of it. Always has been."

We lapsed into silence until I decided it was time to ask the questions he'd avoided earlier. "I gathered that you and Cruz and the medical examiner know each other?"

"Paul and Robyn? Yeah, we went to school together. She was in my class. Paul was a year ahead of Raul."

"Nothing more than that—with Royce, that is?"

"Not since sixth grade." He smiled at the memory, but didn't add anything.

"So what did they want to talk to you about? And what did those long looks mean?"

Joaquin glanced in the mirror again. The movement of the van had lulled the students to sleep. Everyone except Esme. She was looking out the window.

"There was a trailer fire in the canyon Wednesday night." Joaquin meant Coues Canyon, where his family lived. "A man was trapped inside. I didn't reach him in time. Robyn was the ME that night." He hesitated. "And Paul's working that case, too."

"Arson?"

"Murder," Joaquin said. "Robyn told me back there. According to her autopsy, he was hit on the head with a cast-iron skillet before the fire started."

Dear Lord, this put a different slant on things. "And when they find you at two murder scenes in less than two days, they begin to wonder if you're just an unlucky witness . . ." My voice petered out.

"Or the killer," he finished for me.

"Shit."

"Hip deep."

"But you have an alibi for last night. You were in Tucson, with your grandparents."

His hands tightened on the steering wheel. He looked down, surprised, then forcibly relaxed.

"Don't tell me you lied to the police," I said so softly only he could hear.

Joaquin's tone matched mine. "Nope. You told them I was at *abuelito*'s house. I just didn't correct that impression."

"They'll find out."

"Maybe, maybe not. I'll deal with that when it happens."

"But why not tell the truth?"

"I have my reasons." He glanced in the mirror again. The movement of the van had lulled the students to sleep. Everyone except Esme. She was looking out the window.

"What weren't you telling me back at the scene?" Again, my voice was soft.

"I saw the victim—on TV. He's the mining company rep who led the meeting in Dragoon Wednesday night." He motioned with his head toward the mountains west of us. "It made the evening news."

"Excuse me?"

"You heard me."

"You told them you didn't know him."

"No, you told them that."

"Splitting hairs, Joaquin."

"I don't even know his name. Besides, why should I do their work for them?"

"I'll remind you of that when I have to bail you out of jail."

He laughed softly. "I'm not too worried. Now it's your turn. Why did Royce call you over?"

"Tuff."

"Like the rock?"

"Yes. Royce and Cruz wanted me to confirm that the stone pillow wasn't brought to the site from somewhere else."

Joaquin took his eyes off the road to look at me. "No shit?"

"No shit."

"And was it—local?"

"I think so . . . Joaquin?"

But he'd stopped listening. He was deep in thought, staring at the road unfurling under the tires.

Leaving the grassland behind, we entered Pinery Canyon. The blacktop petered out. The dirt was rutted but passable.

"We'll make it," Joaquin said. "The van's no longer than Raul's truck. He took that over the top last week."

Raul drove a one-ton Dodge Ram, a serious truck. I said, "Then we're good, as long as we don't meet a rig coming the other direction."

"Long as," he agreed.

In the lower reaches of the canyon, mourning doves called, Mexican jays chattered, and cardinals flitted across the road with food in their beaks. Apparently the birds weren't confused about the season. I found that reassuring.

In the nineteenth century, this was the homeland of the

Chiricahuas—of Cochise, leader of the Central Band, and of Juh, chief of the Southern, or Pinery, Band. It was a land as rich in beauty as in history. It was of this place, and the mountains farther north, that Geronimo dreamed. It was to this homeland that the displaced Chiricahua had been forbidden to return, the cruelest punishment of all.

We climbed, gradually at first, passing summer camps and cabins tucked in among the trees. Then the canyon walls closed in and the road narrowed, with switchbacks that reminded me of suture marks on an ammonite shell. We hugged one wall, close enough to reach out and touch the Tertiary volcanic flows and tuffs.

"We're going back in time," I said to Esme. Wyatt was snoring. I'd wake him, Harriet, and Vicente when we could pull over and look at the rocks. "These are the same volcanic units you saw at the monument."

She nodded, and rolled down her window. So did I. The air was soft and sweet enough to drink. We were driving so slowly we could hear the breeze soughing through the pines.

A little farther on we stopped where the volcanic rocks had been eroded away. There, in the dense shade of the narrow canyon, I opened my door and plucked a sample from the rock wall. Waking the students, I showed them the lower Cretaceous sedimentary rock, explaining how the fine layers of iron-stained ocher and black siltstone told of deposition in quiet, shallow water.

They struggled to pay attention, but I could tell it was a losing battle. Though they'd been functional back at Massai Point, the emotional effects of this morning were kicking in. They needed time to recover. So did I. "Okay, let's go," I said to Joaquin.

It was cool in the shade. Water seeped from the layers, trickling down the rock faces to be absorbed by the scree and soil at the base of the cliff. Patches of wildflowers— lupine, Indian paintbrush, monkeyflowers, and daisies— grew in the damper places. Higher still, I spotted a lone columbine. At this time of year the water should have been flowing in small streams beside the road. The hillsides should have been carpeted with flowers. The drought had taken its toll here, too.

We encountered no cars. It was as if we were alone in the world. Slowly, the vision of the body at Massai Point receded.

Joaquin pulled to the side of the road at the crest of Onion Saddle. In the distance, glowing apricot and gold, ridges of tuff guarded the reaches of Cave Creek Canyon. I pointed toward the stark cliffs. "Some of those volcanic flows predate the eruptions of the Turkey Creek caldera," I said. "But most of what you see poured as fiery clouds of ash and gas—"

"Ignimbrites," Wyatt interrupted. He seemed to have recharged his energy banks.

I couldn't help smiling. "Ignimbrites," I agreed, "that blanketed the countryside—"

"Twelve hundred square *miles* of countryside," said Wyatt. "At least that's what it says in the monument brochure."

"Kiss-up," muttered Vicente.

"Bite me," said Wyatt.

"We'll drive through Cretaceous rock till we near Cave Creek Canyon," I said. "Then we'll be in the young volcanic rocks again. And when we head north out of Portal, we'll encounter the oldest rocks—a few outcrops of Precambrian granodiorite, and ridges of Paleozoic limestone, dolomite, and sandstone."

"With fossils?" Harriet asked.

"Oh, yes. Some nice ones. Better than those." I pointed to a fine-grained limestone bed in which fossil shells had been replaced with white silica.

"Could we spend a few minutes looking for trogons in Cave Creek Canyon?"

"Sorry, Harriet. I think that'd be pushing it."

Each student had a different reason for coming along. Esme needed extra credit to offset a test she'd bombed. Vicente had missed two field trips, and a couple of weeks of school, when he came down with mono. Wyatt had missed the dawn meeting time of one field trip because he'd overslept. He confessed to being up till three the previous night, playing computer games. Harriet, who already had a perfect grade in the class, had come for the birds. Spring birding was superb in the Chiricahuas—at least, in any other year. The drought had encouraged the migratory birds to hurry through. But Harriet's binoculars still hung from her neck like an oversized pendant. I swore she must sleep with them.

"When will we get to Portal?" said Vicente.

The tiny town of Portal sat in the V where the cliffs intersected. A few miles to the north lay Paradise. I felt as if I'd come full circle. It was good to be back to a place where I'd played as a child.

"Not long now," I said.

For the second time that day, vultures circled, this time due east of us, above the town of Paradise. And as Joaquin started down the long corkscrew grade, the birds began to descend.

6

Cave Creek Canyon, eastern Chiricahuas

2:45 p.m.

Cave-pocked battlements of welded tuff towered above us. Cottonwood, oak, sycamore, and walnut trees, leaves drooping in the still air, lined the banks of Cave Creek. An acorn woodpecker swooped across the road. This deep in the canyon and this late in the day, the place was one of sharp contrasts—sunlight on rock and shifting black shadow. Sycamores, the preferred nesting spot of the elegant trogon, stood like white ghosts in the half-light.

The Chiricahua Mountains are an ecological crossroads of flora and fauna from four separate ecosystems, I told the students—the Rocky Mountains to the east, Sierra Madre to the south, Chihuahuan Desert to the southeast, and Sonoran Desert to the west and north. Eleven thousand years ago, toward the end of the last ice age, when mastodons, camels, horses, and giant sloths shared the territory with prehistoric hunters, large standing bodies of water, such as glacial Lake Cochise, filled the valleys. Rivers flowed freely. The land was greener and the ecosystems more connected.

When the weather patterns changed, the valleys became drier, the lakes turned into playas, and the big game died out, helped along by humans. The hunters left clues to their presence, projectile points embedded with the fossil bones of mammoths at kill sites along the San Pedro River and the margins of Lake Cochise. Over time, plants and small mammals that once flourished widely in the region became restricted to ranges separated from each other by broad desert valleys. Now, the largest resident predators in the Chiricahuas were the black bear, mountain lion, and coyote. And man, of course. Some things haven't changed.

"I'm starving," Wyatt said. "I need junk food."

Vicente blinked. "I need Red Bull." His first words since the Onion Saddle stop.

"Five minutes," I said.

It took six. While the students explored the Portal Store, I took bottled tea from the ice chest and commandeered a table under the cottonwoods.

Nearby, two men sat on the tailgate of a diesel pickup. A late afternoon wind sprang up, gusting downcanyon, carrying their conversation in waves . . . A ranger had sighted a jaguar, one said, near old Camp Rucker, farther south in the range. My ears perked up. I remembered Charley Black telling me about a jaguar killed by a rancher at Massai Point long ago. But in twenty-first-century Arizona, jaguars were the stuff of legend. Occasionally a hiker or rancher reported seeing one that had strayed north from the Sierra Madre of Mexico. But most sightings turned out to be of mountain lions, the jaguar's less colorful cousins.

The men's conversation moved on to a meeting scheduled for eight that night at the Portal Fire and Rescue building.

"I'll be there. I got the letter, same as you, Rory," said the shorter of the two. "But I don't think I've got anything to worry about. Gramps was savvy enough to buy the mineral rights to most of the spread during the Depression."

"Doesn't matter what rights they *claim* they have," said Rory. "They're not setting foot on our place. Not one little toe." He spit onto the ground and kicked dust over the spot.

His friend gestured with his thumb toward the cab of the truck where two shotguns hung on the gun rack in the rear window. "Loaded with birdshot," he said. His red-checked shirt was weathered to a soft pink that matched his flushed cheeks. "And if that don't do the trick, I got the big guns at home."

Their words resurrected the image of the body at Massai Point. A mining company representative, Joaquin had said. I wondered if Detective Cruz had identified him yet. Was the murder related to the company's mineral exploration? Would tonight's meeting take place or be postponed?

Joaquin emerged from the store, letting the screen door slam after him. He nodded to the two men. "Howdy, Jed. Rory."

The man with the pink shirt must be Jed. Joaquin took off his hat as he walked toward me, scratched his short black hair, and resettled the hat. I stood and stretched. The men checked me out.

"A little tall for you, ain't she, Joaquin?"

"You're barking up the wrong tree, Rory. She's family."

"Can't see the resemblance."

"Her brother's marrying my sister."

"Teresa's getting hitched? When?"

"Memorial Day weekend. In Tucson," I said. I introduced myself and shook hands with the two men.

"I haven't seen Teresa since high school," Jed said to Joaquin. "Give her my regards?" Rory seconded the motion.

"Will do," said Joaquin.

The students trooped out of the store, Harriet at the fore. "Birders?" asked Jed.

"My geology students."

Jed's face stiffened. "Mining geology?"

"General geology." I watched him relax.

"You coming to the meeting tonight, Joaquin?" he said.

Joaquin gave a wry smile. "Wouldn't miss it."

"What about your brother? Is Raul coming? We want to get as many as possible," said Rory.

"If he's not on duty at the fire station. He went to the meeting in Dragoon Wednesday night."

"Saw him on TV," Rory said. "Who-eee, he was madder than a Mojave rattler."

"Yeah." Joaquin smiled. "That's Raul."

"He never did run from a fight," said Rory.

Jed laughed. "That's because he started most of 'em."

The students had gathered around a picnic table. Wyatt and Vicente were devouring bags of chips. Vicente had his Red Bull. Harriet was halfway through a bottle of iced tea. Esme covertly studied Joaquin as he munched a granola bar. I took a geologic map from my vest pocket and spread it out on the table.

Jed and Rory crowded behind me. "What's that?" Jed

said, stabbing at a heavy black line that fell just east of Portal on the map.

"The Apache Pass fault zone." I described how the fault struck northwest from Portal. Like the San Andreas, the zone had more than one strand, each block moving horizontally relative to its neighbor. But the Apache Pass fault was far older than its California cousin. The crust here had broken in the late Mesozoic, when dinosaurs roamed the volcanic hills and valleys. Earlier in the Mesozoic, a tectonic trough and marine embayment had connected this area with the ancient Gulf of Mexico.

Rory looked out at the San Simon Valley stretching east to the Peloncillo Mountains. "You mean this used to be beachfront property?"

"More or less. Back in early Cretaceous time, the shoreline moved back and forth across this area." I turned to the students perched on and around the table. "Remember those fossils I showed you on the road over the mountains?"

"Fossil ghosts, you mean," Wyatt said. "Not very convincing."

"I'll show you clams and oysters tomorrow afternoon, farther south in the range."

"You mean we could have gone clamming here?" said Harriet.

"Roughly a hundred and twenty million years ago."

"Where was Mexico?" asked Vicente.

"Under water," said Wyatt.

"Those were the good old days," said Rory. He and Jed looked at each other and laughed.

"Think of it," Jed said. "Ocean breezes and clean white beaches a stone's throw away."

Vicente bristled at the subtext. So did I. We were in a land at war with its neighbor to the south. Many of the locals would prefer to have an ocean at their doorstep. They felt helpless to stop the waves of migrants who daily crossed the border. Tensions along this section of the border were mounting. It was only a matter of time until the bomb exploded.

Vicente said something in Spanish, his tone low and fierce. Jed and Rory took a step back.

"Like southern California, but only an hour's drive from Tucson," Wyatt said, oblivious of the tension around him. Wyatt lived in a literal world that didn't recognize subtext. "Smokin'!" he said, again in his Jim Carrey voice.

"Time to go," I said. Joaquin nodded and helped me fold my geologic maps.

"Bring Frankie tonight," Rory said. "Might help to have a geologist on our side."

I hesitated, torn between my desire to see how the mining company presented its case and my duties as trip leader. The students were all adults, but I was responsible for their welfare until we returned to Tucson. Not that I'd done such a great job so far. Finding a body hadn't been on the agenda.

Joaquin surprised me by saying, "If you want to come, Mom and Pop will entertain your students for a couple of hours. Mom will love it. She'll organize a card game."

"Texas hold'em?" Harriet said.

"You bet."

"I don't know how to play," Wyatt said.

Joaquin grinned. "You will by the end of the night."

I looked from one face to another. Despite the long, emotionally exhausting day, they seemed to have bounced back—though that might just be the energizing effects of Red Bull, tea, and junk food. Perhaps an evening of cards would take their minds off the day's events and save them from nightmares.

"Okay," I said. I pulled a twenty from my pocket and handed it to Harriet. "For Necco Wafers. If you're going to play poker, you'll need chips."

Wyatt's eyes lit up. "Candy chips? I'm in."

"And if they don't have Neccos?" Harriet said.

"Anything you think will work."

"I'll go with you," Wyatt said.

A black Ford F-250 with a dented fender pulled in next to Jed's truck. A sandy-haired woman of medium height, dressed in red shirt, worn blue jeans, roping boots, and cowboy hat climbed stiffly out of the Ford cab. She was thirty-something and slender as a boy. Her face looked pinched, exhausted. After glancing at the students and me, she turned her attention to Jed and Rory. "Let's talk inside," she said. "I'm parched."

Taking their assent for granted, she headed for the café door. But as she passed us, she stopped. "Joaquin. I didn't see you there."

He'd been sitting at the picnic table, screened by Esme and Vicente. He stood and tipped his hat. "Afternoon, Jody. You're a ways from home."

She bent to straighten a pant leg. Her shoulder blades were sharp against the cotton blouse. "I'm here for the meeting. Thought I'd grab a bite and visit a bit beforehand. You coming tonight?"

"He'll be there," Rory said.

A man came out of the Portal Café. His worn and weathered khaki shirt, pants, daypack, and field vest gave the impression he'd sprouted from the desert floor itself. He was in his mid-sixties, I guessed. My height, rangy, his long gray ponytail held back by a leather shoelace. Face as angular as quartz just chipped from the outcrop. Intelligent, compassionate, lupine blue eyes, heavy with sadness.

Those eyes swept the group, paused on the minivan with the state license plate, the cluster of people, and the two trucks, lingered on Jody just long enough that I wondered if they had a history. He took a step, paused again, smiled at Joaquin. That brief movement of the lips changed the angles of his face, lightened the sadness. He lifted a hand to the group and strode quickly past us in the direction of the library and post office. He never said a word.

"Who *was* that man?" Esme said. "And why do I feel like he knows everything about me?"

Rory laughed. "Ron Talmadge. Walks a lot. Doesn't say much."

"Doesn't say anything at all, you mean. Hasn't for years," Jed said. "Kind of eerie, if you ask me."

"He's harmless enough," Jody said. "Just a scientist. This place is full of scientists." She made it sound like a disease.

I'd known a man like that in Pair-a-Dice, Nevada. They called him Walker. Most towns have a Walker, a man or woman who sets out each morning to cover a prescribed circuit of city blocks or dusty backroads. They speak to no one in passing. Some focus on the ground, watching the dust kicked up on the verge as they stride by. Others look at the trees or weeds or cacti. Some mumble or hum. Some stopped talking so long ago that no one remembers the sound of their voice. But they listen. They know all that goes on in their neck of the woods, though they may not know what it means. They know us; we don't know them.

To Joaquin, Jody said, "See you later, then?"

"Later."

Jody nodded and walked quickly away, Jed and Rory at her heels. At the café, Jed jumped ahead of her to open the door. It slammed behind them.

"Jody who?" I asked Joaquin, wondering why he hadn't introduced us.

Joaquin was still watching the door they'd entered. Now he turned to look at me. "Jody Lufkin. She and her father own Hoodoo Ranch, over on the northwest side. Family's been in these parts since Geronimo left. She's the last of them, though."

"How sad," Esme said.

"More than you know. Old Nate Lufkin's a piece of work. Can't be easy to live with."

Harriet and Wyatt trotted back. Harriet carried a bulging brown paper sack. Wyatt looked like he'd struck pay dirt. When they reached us, I said, "Anybody gives Rosa and Charley any trouble tonight, I'll flunk them. Understood?"

Wyatt clicked his heels and saluted. "We shall resist," he said. French accent.

"*Finding Nemo?*" said Vicente. When Wyatt nodded, Vicente added. "You're good."

"Thanks. Any chance you can teach me the basics of Texas hold'em before we get to the ranch?"

"What'd you score on the math portion of the SATs?"

"Eight hundred."

Vicente shook his head. "Then it shouldn't be a problem."

This was one reason I loved field trips. Students out of their comfort zone form friendships where they might not otherwise.

Joaquin and Esme had moved closer together and were talking in soft voices. He looked at the sun. "We better get moving," he said to me.

I tossed my empty iced tea bottle into a recycling bag in the back of the van. Joaquin nodded toward his friends and followed me.

"I'll drive the last leg," I said. "Harriet, you want to ride shotgun?"

"Love to."

As the students disposed of their trash, I told Joaquin what Jed and Rory had said about a jaguar sighting down in Rucker Canyon.

"Really? Peaches sighted a jaguar last week."

I searched my memory banks. "Peaches, the man who used to help with your roundup?"

Joaquin nodded. "An old friend of Pop's. He's foreman at the Lufkin ranch."

I hadn't been to a roundup in fifteen years, but I remembered Peaches as a quiet man, a patient teacher with a warm sense of humor, who more than once let me help rope and brand a calf. He would play practical jokes on us children, then stand back and watch our reactions. Like the time he announced that Rosa's cat, Tawny, had delivered kittens in the barn. He took us out to see them. But when we peered into the delivery room, an unused stall, there was Tawny surrounded by a half-dozen baby rabbits. I was seven, and about to make my First Holy Communion. Steeped in religious training, I was sure I was witnessing a miracle—until Peaches started laughing. Gently, he'd extricated Tawny from the long-eared brood and replaced her with momma rabbit.

"I don't remember a Mrs. Peaches," I said.

Joaquin was staring at the café door again. "No. I've always thought he was sweet on Jody." Joaquin gave himself a little shake. "But that couldn't work."

"Why not?"

"Nate's a bigot. But Peaches stayed anyway. And he's always treated Raul and Teresa and me as if we were his own. He took us hunting if Pop was too busy, things like that. And when Raul and Pop got crosswise, Raul would take his horse and run away to Peaches' cabin at Hoodoo Ranch. We all had a standing invitation."

"Where'd he see the jaguar?"

"Over on the northwest side, near a spring," Joaquin

said. "Peaches was hunting strays. The cat was just—"
Joaquin paused.

"Hunting?"

He nodded. "It had brought down a deer."

"Pretty far north for a jaguar. And pretty low."

"The drought again," Joaquin said. "There's still water and game up north."

"Did the cat attack?"

"No, just perched on a ledge above its kill, watching."

"Did Peaches report it?"

"And have everybody and his brother show up to hunt it with a camera or a gun?"

"You're right. Bad idea. So what'd he do?"

"Just took it as a sign, a warning, and left."

The students were all in their places with tired, sweaty faces. "Anytime, Teach," Wyatt called from the rear seat.

I pulled a deck of cards, one of the necessities of life, from my backpack and tossed it to Wyatt. Closing the sliding door behind Joaquin, I hopped in the driver's seat. I love to drive, even a clunky van.

Wyatt and Vicente were talking poker in the back. Joaquin sat in the middle seat next to Esme. Harriet glanced at them and smiled.

"What?" I said.

"It's spring."

"'Twas brillig, and the slithy toves/Did gyre and gimble in the wabe"?

"Ah, a Carroll fan," she said. "Who'd have thunk it?"

"My mother teaches lit at U of A."

"That explains it, then." She looked west toward the monument and the saddle we'd crossed. "I've always viewed 'Jabberwocky' as more of a cautionary tale than a nonsense poem."

"Beware the biting jaws and 'frumious Bandersnatch'?"

"Precisely. You don't know how long I've been searching for the Jubjub bird."

"Is that why you came today?"

"We all have our quests. Hoodoo Country seemed the logical place for mine." Her brows knit, and her face grew serious. "But I should have considered that if you go looking for a Jubjub, you just might find a body."

7

Charley Black's ranch house sat on a knoll above Coues Creek. I parked the van in the space occupied by a trailer during the seasonal cattle roundup. The aromas of *posole* and chicken wafted from the house. Rosa had been cooking up a storm.

Marty, their brindle border collie–Australian shepherd mix, danced a welcome outside Joaquin's door. As we exited, he sniffed each of us in turn, then led us around the house and onto a broad patio rimmed by a rock wall. Charley and Rosa were there, unstacking plastic chairs and dusting them.

My godfather, a doctor of psychology by training, was a counselor and healer. He and Joaquin were built alike—all lean muscle and sinew. Joaquin, at five nine, was perhaps two inches taller than his father. But where Joaquin kept his black hair short, Charley's blunt-cut silver mane hung smoothly from a center part to brush the middle of his neck.

Charley offered to help Joaquin and the students set up camp, near the pump house. Rosa pointed them toward a cooler full of soft drinks. They grabbed cans and followed Charley, Joaquin, and Marty back to the van. I heard the engine growl as it climbed the hill behind the house. Quiet descended. I could put aside my teacher persona and relax, at least for a little while.

"Beer?" asked Rosa, as I trailed her into the kitchen. Rosa was shorter than her husband and softer around the edges. Round face, round body, round deep-brown eyes.

Thick salt-and-pepper hair, cut short, framed her face with natural waves.

"Something with caffeine, I think. I said I'd go with Joaquin to the meeting tonight." I lifted the lid of a large kettle. "*Arroz con pollo?*"

"One of your favorites."

I kissed my godmother's cheek. She barely came up to my clavicle. "Everything you cook is my favorite, Rosa. Thank you for hosting us." I felt my throat tighten. "What can I do to help?"

"Nothing." Rosa poured me a glass of iced tea and pointed me toward the big mission-style dining room table. "Sit, *m'hija*. Tell me what happened today."

I didn't ask how Rosa knew the day had been difficult. She was my godmother, my "other mother." It was a given that she knew me as well as she did her own daughter. But telling her about the body on the mountain meant retrieving that scene from its holding cell. I wasn't sure I was ready.

I bought my psyche some time by picking up the place-mats and napkins stacked beside the utensils and plates on the counter. As I set the table, Rosa scooped homemade guacamole into the center of a ceramic platter, surrounding the dip with tortilla chips. When she saw I was finished, she carried the platter to the table. "What is it, Frankie?"

I couldn't avoid the subject forever. "Joaquin and I found a body."

Rosa hugged me to her. She was one of the few people who saw the emotional and physical scars that marked me—scars left by other traumatic incidents over the past two years. She'd watched me struggle to cope with pain and loss, to fit the shards of my life back together each time they'd blown apart. The pieces never fit, of course. This was the real world. One or two shards were always lost or turned to powder. So each time I had to make a new mosaic me.

A hug can change the world. When she let me go, I plopped down in one of the chairs and dipped a chip into the guacamole. Suddenly I was ravenous. Between bites, the day's story tumbled out. I told her about the body on the mountain, Detective Cruz, and Dr. Royce, knowing Joaquin would be doing the same with Charley. Rosa was a good listener, prodding me with the occasional question to keep me on track. It seemed like no time had passed before the troops were back, dragging chairs into a circle on the porch.

Through the screen door I could see Marty flop down midway between us and the six people on the deck. He took his herding duties seriously. When he wasn't working the cattle, he'd keep track of all of us, day and night.

"How long till dinner?" I asked my other mother.

"Thirty minutes."

"How would you feel about entertaining the students tonight while I go with Joaquin?"

"I'd love nothing more. We can play cards."

"Joaquin figured you'd say that. We brought Neccos. I don't want the students losing their allowance."

"Would I do that?"

"You've done it to me often enough."

"But you're family, Frankie." She patted my arm. "Now, go see to your students while I finish supper."

I took what was left of the guacamole and chips onto the deck and gave the students a lab assignment. They were to find examples of limestone, sandstone, granite, rhyolite, and altered tuff in the rock wall that surrounded the ranch house patio.

The sun had slipped behind the Chiricahuas. Though light still filled the western sky, I turned on the porch lights. They worked in pairs—Wyatt with Vicente, Esme with Harriet—scurrying from one rounded cobble to another. Their laughter echoed in the dry air. Innocent laughter, untainted by what they'd seen today. Through the kitchen window came the pat-patting of Rosa making tortillas and slapping them on a griddle. Marty crept over and nudged my hand with his nose until I stroked his head. All was right with the world, at least in Coues Canyon.

Charley rested his hand on my shoulder for a moment, then sat next to me. He knew what had happened today. I knew he knew. He was there if I needed him. Enough said, or not said.

The porch door slammed. Joaquin came out carrying a couple of books from Charley's extensive library. Sitting cross-legged in front of us on the concrete, Joaquin thumbed through an ancient copy of Charles Lummis's *Some Strange Corners of Our Country*. My father had the book in his library at home. The essays concerned Lummis's years spent with a Pueblo tribe in the late nineteenth century. I couldn't remember which tribe, nor any references to Apache traditions. And the Chiricahuas had been Apache homeland, not Puebloan. So why were there roadrunner tracks around the body?

Joaquin found what he was looking for. I knelt beside him and looked at the paragraph he pointed to:

When a person dies here, the medicine-men, who come to insure the safety of the departed on his four days' journey to the other world, perform very intricate and mysterious rites, very largely designed to hide his trail from the evil spirits, who would otherwise be sure to follow and harass him, and would very likely succeed in switching him off altogether from the happy land and into "the place where devils are." Among other things the body is surrounded during these four days with the tracks of the road-runner to lead witches on a false trail, and the sacred smoke is continuously blown about that they may not see which way the departed went.

Charley was at the edge of his chair, trying to read the print upside down. Joaquin handed him the book. I retrieved the digital camera from my backpack and found the images of Massai Point. Marty, feeling abandoned, went to guard the kitchen door.

While Charley studied the digital images, Joaquin looked up roadrunners in the *Sibley Guide to Birds*. Not finding what he was after, he took that into the house and returned with Peterson's *Field Guide to Western Birds*. A minute or so later, he shook his head. Neither book discussed the elevation limits of a roadrunner's habitat.

"We can work the problem a different way," I said. "We know roadrunners prefer mesquite groves and desert scrub. How high do mesquites grow?"

"Maybe thirty feet," Charley said.

"Very funny," I said. "Let me rephrase. What's their elevation range?"

Joaquin went in a third time and came back with a smile on his face and an Arizona plant guide in his hand. "Depends on the species of mesquite," he said. "But the limit's about five thousand feet."

That confirmed what we'd suspected. I looked out at the hillside, a blaze of yellow. We were at fifty-two hundred feet, and mesquites here grew up the hillside another two hundred feet. Apparently the limits weren't hard and fast. There was local variability, depending on soil and which direction the slope faced.

Joaquin saw where I was looking. "Cattle forage on mesquite beans. They spread the seeds all over these hills. Where the climate and soil are okay, they grow among the piñon and juniper. But up where I'm building my house, they don't grow more than waist-high. Stunted. That's at 5,450, or thereabouts."

"Still well below where we were today," I said.

"Right. Here, we don't find roadrunners much higher than the pump house."

"The roadrunner that left these prints wasn't alive." Charley handed the camera back to me. "Spacing's wrong. And it's just one foot—the right one."

"Show me," I said.

I leaned over his shoulder to get a better look at the digital image. Joaquin leaned over the other shoulder. The tracks looked random. Only a few were isolated and clear.

Charley took a mechanical pencil from his breast pocket and used it as a pointer. "Roadrunners have two toes forward, two behind, shaped like an X—or maybe a K. Turkey vulture tracks are very different." He pointed to a second print. "Three toes forward, one back, like the Gambel's quail. Only quail tracks are a lot smaller." The pencil tip moved to a third print. "Here, the vulture tracks are right on top of the roadrunner's."

"I still don't see it," I said. "And I don't understand how you can say the roadrunner prints are of just one foot. They all look the same."

He smiled. "Elementary, my dear MacFarlane. Tracking 1A." He pointed first at one roadrunner print, then at the one right behind it. "Each footprint should be canted a little to the right or to the left, just like in humans."

"But these are canted exactly the same way," I said.

Joaquin closed the plant book with a snap. "A one-legged roadrunner?"

Charley nodded. "Pretty strange."

"The roadrunner was supposed to protect the spirit of the dead person during his journey to a happier place," I said. "Why would someone murder a man and then protect his spirit from evil?"

"You're assuming the symbolism is legitimate," Charley said, "or used in its original context."

"Did Lummis know what he was talking about?" I asked him.

Charley shrugged. "He saw and wrote about what the Tigua allowed him to see. But I can tell you that leaving roadrunner tracks was never *our* custom." By *our* he meant the Chiricahua Apache. "And it doesn't matter anyway. That ceremony's only for a Puebloan. Your victim's white."

"So either the murderer wanted the police to believe that the murder was somehow related to magic or witchcraft . . ." My voice trailed off as my mind tried several paths at once.

"Or he wanted them to believe that an Indian's responsible," Charley said.

"Or he sees the police as evil spirits that need to be confused?" said Joaquin. "Problem is, I don't think Cruz noticed it. The rangers and medical examiner smudged most of the tracks."

"You didn't mention it to them?" Charley asked.

"And point them toward looking for an Indian?"

Charley shook his head. "If that's what the murderer wants, he'll find another way of doing it."

"Are there any Puebloans living in these parts?" I asked.

"Maybe," Charley said. "But the only one I know is Peaches. I'll give him a call while you're at the meeting."

Joaquin seemed about to say something, but he stopped and looked off to where a split peak caught the last of the sun's rays.

"Well, if we're going to that meeting," I said, "we'd better help Rosa serve dinner."

8

Joaquin and I wanted to reach Portal early to scope out the situation and gauge the mood of the locals as they arrived. So, leaving the dishes for my crew, I hotfooted it up to my sleeping quarters in the pump house. Joaquin and Charley had left my gear on the loft bed. I quickly changed into clean field shirt and jeans, traded my boots for running shoes, ran a brush through my hair. Just as I finished braiding it, Joaquin arrived in Rosa's red Honda CR-V.

"Think I should bring my rock hammer?" I closed the door to the pump house, pulling until it latched tightly. I didn't want to spend the night with packrats.

"In case things turn nasty?" He laughed. "A rock hammer won't be much good against a gun."

"The Old West is alive and well in Portal?"

"It will be tonight."

We drove down the dirt road at a leisurely pace, both of us immersed in thought. The west face of Gray Mountain, scarred by the lightning bolt of the freshly cut road, reflected the alpenglow of a dying day. When we reached the turnoff to the new road, I saw, maybe fifty yards in, a pile of charred metal.

I pointed to the remains. "This is where it happened?"

"This is it." Joaquin stopped the truck.

"Who was he?"

"Byron Locke. An activist lawyer. I didn't know him, except to say 'howdy.' He represented several of the regional tree-hugging organizations—endangered species, wild lands initiatives, wilderness area and roadless designations, reintroducing the Mexican gray wolf—"

"I get the picture."

"He tried to get the courts to block further road construction on Gray Mountain. Lost the first round, but the court granted a stay during the appeal process."

"Which made him pretty unpopular around here."

"Yes and no. A lot of locals were against the road."

"Including you?"

He nodded. "And everyone else in the canyon. It's an eyesore, a desecration . . . Anyway, just to make sure the Haydons—Mark and Ginny Haydon, the owners of Gray Mountain—abided by the stay, Locke pulled his trailer across the road. He knew that if they went ahead and bull-dozed the road, they'd just be fined."

"A slap on the wrist for a fait accompli."

"Act now, apologize later. That's how it's been done in these parts for over a century."

"How long had Locke been here before he was killed?"

"Not long. He brought the trailer in in the wee hours of Monday night. He was killed two nights later."

Joaquin put the truck in gear, and we picked up speed. We were near the entrance to Coues Canyon now, and the grade had flattened out. At the intersection with the Portal Road, we turned south.

"Cruz interviewed you after the fire?" I said.

"And Ron Talmadge."

"The scientist we saw in Portal?"

Joaquin nodded. "He didn't talk, of course."

"Is he mute?"

"He stopped talking a couple of years ago, when his wife died."

"Just like that?"

"Pretty much. At the end of her memorial service he announced he'd be mute until further notice. Said it was out of respect for Nadine—that was his wife, Nadine Der-oucher."

"Doesn't he have to speak at work?"

"He retired about then. Was an ethnobotanist. Worked all over the world before he ended up at the Southwest Research Station down in Cave Creek Canyon. He met Nadine in Africa. She was a Belgian doctor, and a lot younger than Ron. A May-December thing."

"What happened to her?"

"Cancer. It was late stage by the time they discovered it."

She was a doctor, I thought. Why didn't she recognize the signs? Why didn't one of her colleagues?

As if he'd read my mind, Joaquin said, "Nadine didn't practice here. She stayed home to raise their boy, Ronnie. He's autistic."

"Is that why Ron retired when Nadine died, to care for their son?"

"They put Ronnie in a care facility in Tucson when Nadine got sick. Ron couldn't care for both of them. I think Ronnie's still there."

Which explained how Ron could choose to lead a silent life. He had no one at home to speak to.

"So how did Ron deal with the interview after the fire?"

"Same way any other mute person would, I guess—answered their questions in writing."

"Now that the autopsy's confirmed Locke was murdered, are you and Ron considered suspects?"

"Yup. We arrived at the same time, so we give each other alibis. But there's nothing to prove that one of us didn't leave the scene and then come back. We came from opposite directions."

"Damn."

We were silent for a mile or so, then Joaquin said, "I saw the way you looked at that Gray Mountain road. 'Fess up—you were itching to climb it."

"Guilty."

Geologists love road cuts. They expose what lies beneath the surface. And they're prime locations for taking directional attitudes and collecting rock, mineral, and fossil samples.

"Why did you choose geology?" Joaquin said.

It wasn't an idle question. Joaquin never made pointless conversation. In good time I'd find out what he was after.

"I like detective work," I said, "the mysteries in the rocks, the stories they tell."

"Detective work—is that why you and Philo got together?"

Philo was a private investigator, when he wasn't off chasing terrorists. "Maybe," I said. "But the link, the attraction, was there from the first time I met him."

"You were what—nine? Ten?"

"Nearly eight. Don't laugh, Joaquin. I'm not saying I understood the feeling, only that the awareness was there."

"And Philo?"

"He's male. It took him a while."

I remembered the scene very clearly. My mind wandered down the overgrown path to that night, more than fourteen years ago. "My sixteenth birthday. I was helping Kit and Philo on their UA homecoming float their senior year. Philo jokingly asked me to marry him. And suddenly it wasn't a joke . . . But I was too young, and his life was mapped out. He was going to graduate, play pro baseball, marry Sally . . . But then he blew out his knee. By the time he was out of rehab, he'd lost his edge. He was fit, but not as fast as he'd been. He threw his hat in the ring the next year, but he wasn't drafted."

"Is that why Sally broke it off?"

"Apparently."

"So he joined the army, and you went your separate ways."

It sounded melodramatic when he said it aloud, but Philo's life had, indeed, been dramatic. When his helicopter went down in Colombia, I'd thought he was dead. I hadn't found out differently till twenty months ago.

"I came close to doing the same thing my senior year," Joaquin said. "Almost joined the marines in a fit of pique."

"Over a girl?" I asked.

"Yeah."

"But you didn't."

"No. I was lucky. Unlike Philo, I had parents and a home to come back to. It makes a difference."

"All the difference in the world." I turned to him. "You know, Joaquin, I've missed this."

"Talking?" When I nodded, he said, "You only had to call."

"I know. But . . . I needed time away, time to figure things—myself—out. In California, nobody knew my name, my family."

"And nobody vetted your dates?"

"That too. Though, as it turned out, my dates could have used more vetting." I was thinking of my disastrous relationship with Geoff Travers. I thought of him less frequently now. But he still haunted dreams in which I was running, always running, with him just a step or two behind.

"Well," Joaquin said, "it's good to have you home again."

I knew he meant not just Tucson, but the Chiricahuas, my second home as a child.

"This morning," he said, "at Massai Point, you told Paul and Robyn the rock pillow was local." He paused.

"Yes." This is it, I thought. This is what he was aiming for all along.

"Can you always tell if a rock doesn't belong where you found it?"

"Well, I have to have a pretty good knowledge of the local geology, or the difference has to be obvious—for instance, a fossiliferous limestone cobble on a trail crossing a basalt flow."

"Your eyes just naturally pick out what shouldn't be there?"

"If I'm paying attention . . . and often when I'm not. The subconscious mind can be trained to watch for subtle incongruities."

" 'What's wrong with this picture?' "

"Exactly. When I'm prospecting for fossils, for instance, walking miles of terrain, I can be thinking of other things, but my mind is programmed to look for certain shapes, forms, even color contrasts—much as you'd notice a cow's brand from a mile away."

He smiled. "While you'd just see the cow?"

"Uh-huh. Though I'd probably note what breed it was—if I recognized it. I'm not up on my breeds."

Joaquin didn't answer. Gravel crunched under the tires. A jackrabbit darted into the road and then out again. The western sky still held a faint glow. On the eastern horizon, bright Jupiter seemed to pull a fat moon into the sky. It would be full a couple hours after midnight. A splendid night, a night for lovers.

I thought of Philo, half a world away. Worry hummed in the background of my mind like bees in the honey mesquites. No news was just that—no news, I told myself. It didn't mean something had happened to Philo. I tried to shove worry back into its box.

"We call that the Corn Planting Moon," Joaquin said, nodding toward the orange orb just clearing the Peloncillos. "Not that the Chiricahuas were great farmers."

I was grateful for the distraction. "My grandmother called it the Flower Moon. I remember her gardenias bloomed on Mother's Day every year." My mother's mother had willed me her house when she died ten months ago. I'd be able to watch the blossoms open magically this next week.

"Mother's Day—that's tomorrow, right?" Joaquin said.

"Rosa will be glad you remembered."

Joaquin grinned. "I wouldn't have if you hadn't mentioned it."

"I'll never tell."

"How's your grandmother's house working out?"

It had been like inheriting a time capsule. So I'd left my stuff in storage, moved into the guest house, and begun major renovations to the main house. "I'm still in the guest house."

"Ouch."

"But it's kept me busy." My teaching job plus dealing with the day-to-day problems of renovation gave me little time to brood about Philo.

We lapsed into silence. Along the road, signs announced land for sale. The road itself was pretty good, except for the last two or three miles. The combination of barely concealed alluvial cobbles and washboard ridges made for a teeth-rattling ride until we turned west on the paved Rodeo/Portal road. Streets branched off with names such as Stargazer and Poorwill. A white-on-blue Peace banner, a holdover from the sixties, flapped from a metal gate. The symbol resembled a turkey vulture track and reminded me of the birds that had circled over Massai Point and Paradise today. Not auspicious portents.

A great horned owl swooped across the road in front of our headlights. Joaquin didn't seem to notice. Something was wrong.

"What is it, Joaquin?"

"I don't know. I've just got a bad feeling, like something's gonna happen. Soon." He looked at the black maw of Cave Creek Canyon. "Maybe tonight."

I knew those feelings. I trusted them. They mirrored my own. "You think something's going to happen to you?"

"I don't know. But keep your eyes open. Look for anything that doesn't seem to fit."

9

Portal, Arizona
7:30 p.m.

Joaquin parked near the store, and we walked to the Portal Fire and Rescue building, a nondescript green metal structure on a rise across the road. Two sheriff's deputies were setting up a table at the door.

I could feel Joaquin tense up beside me, but his voice sounded normal when he said, "You expecting trouble, Curt?"

The taller of the two officers stiffened. His hair was so short it looked as if he'd just arrived at boot camp. "Oh, it's you, Joaquin." He nodded to me. "Miss."

"Doubt if we'll have to arrest anyone," said the second officer. "Either of you carryin'?"

"A gun? No." Joaquin patted his pockets.

"Knife?" said Curt.

"The usual." Joaquin lifted his pant leg.

"I'll have to hold that for you." Curt opened a plastic bag and waited.

Joaquin took the hunting knife from its sheath and dropped it in the bag. The second officer gave him a yellow claim ticket and put the matching half in the bag.

"Miss?" Curt said.

"A penknife," I said, glad I'd left my long blade back at the ranch. I surrendered my field bag to be checked. The black bag—a new one, or nearly so—served as my purse. The last one burned up in the Mojave Desert.

Curt examined every zippered compartment but couldn't find anything more lethal than the knife with a three-inch blade. He bagged that and returned my purse along with a claim ticket. "You can go on in," he said.

"Let us know in advance if word comes down to round up 'the usual suspects,' " Joaquin said, his voiced laced with humor. "A five-minute head start will do."

Curt smiled. "I'll give you ten, if you promise to save me some of your ma's venison sausage this fall."

"Sounds fair," Joaquin agreed, and stepped aside to allow me to enter first.

The door was at one end of a long rectangular room. At the other end, a deputy fiddled with a video camera mounted on a tripod. She looked up for a moment, then returned to adjusting the lens. If it were a wide-angle lens, it would capture most of the room.

Only one other person was there. Ron Talmadge. At a table along the rear wall, below a bulletin board, he was collating photocopies of a wordsearch puzzle with a solution page. He must have felt my attention. He looked up.

"Evening," I said.

He nodded, smiled, and returned to his sorting. Roughly twenty copies. He took the first set, folded it in thirds, put it in an envelope, and sealed the flap. The envelope was addressed to an environmental magazine. He tucked the envelope in his pocket, took a second set from the pile, and pinned it to the center of the bulletin board. Without a word, he picked up the other copies and went out the door.

I stepped closer to take a look. All the clues dealt with plants and animals that inhabited the Chiricahua Mountains. His initials, RT, were at the bottom of the page. I started to mentally circle words. Joaquin interrupted, handing me a sheet of paper he'd taken from the trashcan. It was an announcement about tonight's meeting. He held a duplicate in his hand.

"I'll copy the puzzle if you copy the word list at the bottom," he said.

"Okay."

It didn't take long. I folded the papers and tucked them in a pocket of my field bag, thinking that Ron Talmadge, himself, was a puzzle.

The room was filling up. Joaquin and I studied the crowd. No happy faces here tonight. They grumbled to each other, with one notable exception—Jody Lufkin. She was talking animatedly to two men—mining company reps, I guessed—who'd come in a back door. The three moved to stand behind the video camera.

"Where, exactly, is Hoodoo Ranch?" I asked Joaquin.

He tracked my gaze. "Other side of the range, north of the monument. Nate's father did some prospecting, way back when. So did Nate. All the old families dabbled in mining."

"Including the MacFarlanes," I said. "Ranching couldn't always pay the bills."

I knew that the mines on the eastern side of the Chiricahuas had boomed for only a few years before playing out. Ranching, fruit orchards, and farming became the mainstay of the local economy. Unfortunately there wasn't enough water in the Chiricahuas to support numerous large farms or ranches. And rustling, long tolerated in the rough country of the Chiricahuas and Pinalenos, had been the final nail in the coffin of big operations. In the last decade or two, new owners—midwesterners and easterners, mostly—who hadn't thought about mineral rights, moved in to try their luck with smaller operations. They were here tonight, along with retirees who wanted better year-round weather than they had at home.

Portal, which had begun as a ranching and farming community, was now heavily populated with retired scientists. Herpetologists, botanists, geologists, and astronomers had found a new mother lode in the Chiricahuas—a wilderness on their doorstep, land that couldn't be developed. They didn't need a lot of water, just enough for household use. Some had their own astronomical observatories so they could ponder the stars in night skies undimmed by light pollution. The off-grid types erected straw-bale or rammed-earth houses, installed solar power systems, and harvested rainwater. Small-scale experimental stuff.

Whereas Portal had been grounded in farming and ranching, Paradise had begun as a mining community. When the mines closed, so did the town. A hippie commune had moved there for a few months in the sixties, but Paradise was an illusion. Making a town required work and dedication. And lots of paperwork. The hippies moved out. The community languished. It now was home to artists and craftspeople, and a few bed-and-breakfast operations that catered to birders and hikers. The community was as different from Portal in the twenty-first century as it had been in the nineteenth. The only thing that could unite them was a threat to their way of life—a threat to their water supply.

Ron returned, nodded to Joaquin, and took up his earlier position by the table. Joaquin introduced us. I held out my hand. "Nice to meet you, Ron." His grip was warm and firm and dry.

"Frankie's a geologist," said Joaquin.

Ron smiled, thought for a moment, and then pulled a small piece of rock from an inside pocket of his field vest. He handed it to me.

"Azurite and malachite." I looked at the beautiful intermingling of indigo blue and green copper minerals, Arizona's famous treasure. "I love them. They always remind me of sky and earth." They were also appropriate to the occasion. Copper exploration had brought us here tonight.

I offered it back to him, but he wrapped my fingers around the rock. "A gift?" Ron nodded. "Thank you," I said, zipping the present into my shirt pocket. "Thank you very much."

Ron nodded again. Taking a small black notebook and mechanical pencil from another vest pocket, he began sketching someone on the far side of the room. Jody Lufkin. With a few sure strokes, Ron captured the arrogant tilt of her head, the expressive brows, the animated gestures. And her age. Looking from the drawing to the unaware model, I realized she was older than I'd thought. Early forties. She wore it well.

With a couple of strokes, Ron completed Jody's picture. Nodding, as if satisfied, he turned the page. This time he chose a man in new Levis, crisp green Oxford-cloth shirt, running shoes, and Yankees baseball cap. He stood off by himself in a front corner of the room, the only place that wouldn't be caught by the camera lens. I looked at Joaquin and raised an eyebrow.

"Mark Haydon," he said softly.

The Haydon who owned Gray Mountain with his wife, Ginny. Byron Locke died in a trailer fire at the entrance to their new road. No wonder Haydon looked uncomfortable. He must feel like an outcast. Or maybe he felt guilty.

"Is Ginny here?" I asked Joaquin.

"Haven't seen her. Look for a redhead."

I looked. Not a redhead in the room. But a gray-haired Latino, dressed in a charcoal Dickies jumpsuit, came in and stood next to us.

"*Hola, amigo. ¿Que pasa?*" Joaquin said. He shook hands and introduced me to Enrique Mendoza. "Enrique used to work for the phone company. Now he sells guns."

"At shows, mostly," Enrique said. "I repair them, too. And speaking of guns, Joaquin, I got something pretty to show you." From a holster at his hip Enrique took an ancient, but still lethal-looking, Colt .45.

"How'd you get that past Curt?" Joaquin said.

Enrique chuckled. "He took the ammo. They don't want to be responsible for the weapons themselves. And a revolver's not much of a threat without ammo."

I looked around. Half the people in the room packed handguns—most, I was sure, with permits. This was Arizona, and a percentage of the locals in the room also volunteered with the Minutemen Project, patrolling the border to stop and detain border crossers. Others just liked guns.

"Jed and Rory, now," Enrique went on, "they had them a couple of SIG-Sauers. Semi-autos, you know? They took offense when Curt asked them to empty their weapons and hand over the extra clips. He told them to lock them in their vehicles, or skip the meeting. They were pretty pissed off, you know, but they emptied their pockets. Enough ammunition to start a war." He laughed again. "Pretty funny. Kept talking about a citizen's right to bear arms. But Curt, he didn't budge none. He told them to think of it like an old-time western trial, where you checked your weapons at the door."

Enrique handed the revolver to Joaquin, who passed it to me. I liked the balance and heft of the gun. "It has a story?" I asked, returning the revolver.

"Every gun I own has a story," he said. "Or a legend. Take this one." He rubbed his fingers over the revolver. "My wife's great-great-uncle Manny received this Colt from Pancho Villa himself. Of course Tío Manny was only a boy at the time. But he'd crossed into Columbus with Villa—or so the old man claimed."

The event Enrique mentioned was legendary in this corner of the country. In the wee hours of March 9, 1916, Pancho Villa crossed the border in a retaliatory raid, attacked and set fire to the sleeping town of Columbus, New Mexico, and killed eighteen people.

"Your wife's uncle was a Villista?" I said.

"So Tío Manny said." Enrique popped open the loading gate with his thumb and showed us the cylinder. "See how smooth the action works? It's for sale," he said, slipping the revolver back in its holster.

"But doesn't your wife want to keep it?" I asked. "Whether legend or fact, it's part of her family history."

Enrique looked down at the vinyl floor for a long moment. When he looked up, his eyes were moist. "My Lupe died two winters ago. We were not blessed with children . . . And guns weren't created to sit in bedside drawers or vaults."

No, I thought, *guns were created to kill.* But I said, "I'm so sorry about your wife, Enrique. You must be lonely without her."

"God willing, it won't be for long," he said. "Is your father here, Joaquin?"

"He's riding herd on Frankie's geology students," Joaquin said. "But I'll tell him you asked after him."

"And your mother, too."

"Of course." To me, Joaquin said in a stage whisper, "Enrique had a crush on Mom way back in the Pleistocene."

Enrique snorted. "Everybody did. Rosa was the prettiest gal in Tucson." He sighed theatrically and put his hand over his heart.

Joaquin grinned. "It's amazing you and Pop have stayed friends, then."

"I've never been one to hold a grudge."

"And it helped that Lupe was there to pick up the pieces of your broken heart."

"She did bring me comfort, *chico. Sí,* she did bring me comfort."

Something or someone over my shoulder caught Enrique's attention. A quizzical expression crossed his face. I turned. The mining company representatives shook hands with Jody Lufkin, then took their seats. The lean tanned man on the right looked like an exploration geologist or mining engineer, someone who spent a lot of time working in the sun. The other looked like a public relations guy whose tan had come out of a bottle. His hair was blow-dried and held in place with spray. He was sweating in his brown-plaid sport coat.

The first man wasn't sweating, though he didn't want to be here. He sat in his denim shirt and pants, leg crossed at the knee, eyes glancing from his watch to the clock on the wall and back again. Time, I surmised, was standing still for him in "the land of standing up rocks," the Apache name for the Chiricahua Mountains.

"Excuse me, Joaquin," Enrique said. "I must say hello to another old friend."

Perhaps eighty people, now, maybe more, stood in small groups at the edges of the room or were seated in folding chairs in the middle. Just as the PR guy began the introductions, someone flung open the door. Raul Black strode in, fit and healthy, black eyes shining. I hadn't seen him since Teresa and Jamie's engagement party. Tonight he looked ready to battle a firestorm.

"Okay," he said. "Let's dance."

10

Raul had a big voice to go with his barrel chest and stocky build. He was the same height as Joaquin, but outweighed him by thirty pounds. He pumped iron and biked the foothills of the Sulphur Springs Valley to stay in shape for fighting fires. Tonight he wore a black T-shirt with white letters that said FIREFIGHTERS MAKE BETTER LOVERS. It was probably an extra large, but it looked a size too small.

People surrounded Raul as soon as he walked through the door. He was as gregarious and expansive as his brother was introspective and quiet. Raul had inherited Rosa's flashing smile, dimples, and curly black hair. But the hairline, I noticed, was receding at the temples, a reminder that we were all growing older.

The Down Under Copper rep with the blow-dried hair tried to call the meeting to order. He couldn't be heard. Finally Jody Lufkin walked over to the back wall and flicked the lights. The crowd quieted. The man introduced himself as Peter Prebble. The other rep was mining geologist Linc Chapin. He'd moved to the rear door. He stood, cell phone to one ear, left hand covering the other to keep out the noise. If his cell phone worked here in Portal, it was a better model than mine.

"Our colleague has been delayed," Prebble said. American accent, not Australian. "We'd like to hold our presentation and discussion until he arrives."

So he and Chapin hadn't heard about Massai Point. Had Cruz identified the body yet?

"Whoa—are you sayin' I drove two hours to get here, and now I have to wait?" Raul hollered above the grumbling throng. "Let's get on with it."

A veritable chorus seconded the motion. Prebble looked at his watch, then at the deputy taping the meeting. Her hand rested on her sidearm. His trembled. He cleared his throat. "Should only be a few more minutes."

Prebble looked over his shoulder at Chapin. I could read nothing from Chapin's posture or face. Prebble picked up a pile of handouts. He passed them to Jody, who began circulating through the crowd. Apparently Prebble wanted to keep his distance. I didn't blame him.

The handouts were copies of the Mining Law of 1872, the Enlarged Homestead Act of 1909, and the Stock-Raising Homestead Act of 1920. The Mining Law authorized prospectors to stake claims for certain metallic minerals, mine them, and ultimately obtain patents giving them title to the land and all its surface and subsurface resources. The homestead acts were designed to help farmers and ranchers settle the West. In order to support the mining industry, however, the acts withheld timber and mineral lands—and later, mines and coal deposits—from homesteading. And within those exceptions lay the rub.

Any homesteader who couldn't prove they owned the mineral rights to their property as of February 18, 1909, or who had homesteaded public land after that date, didn't own the mineral rights. The government did. The land could be bought and sold, but the mineral rights weren't attached. A mining company or prospector could still file a claim on certain minerals, such as gold, silver, and copper. One might own the surface of a homesteaded piece of land, but a mining company could extract ore from under your feet. And they could cross your land to explore for minerals, too. Or drill. Or open a processing plant on land next door to which they owned the mineral and surface rights.

That was what was happening here. DUC had purchased previously owned mineral rights to many small separate tracts of land over the years, when the price of copper was down. Now copper was up. It was time for them to explore, to see what cards they actually held.

This scenario had been played out across the West for nearly a century and a half. Mineral exploration had helped settle the West, and mining continued to play a major role in most western states. Copper, the mainstay of Arizona, was used in everything from pennies to pipes and semiconductors. Profit was a delicate balancing act between extraction and processing costs, and the going price.

New landowners in the Southwest—retirees and young buyers who'd never thought about mineral rights—were ignorant of western mining laws. The real estate agents either didn't know or didn't bother to inform them. And in Arizona, most realtors represent the seller, not the buyer. Caveat emptor, as Wyatt had said this morning.

When DUC had sent out their initial letter advising local landowners of the forthcoming mineral exploration on their lands, the landowners saw red. It wasn't just what they perceived to be trespassing on private property, though that rankled. More profoundly disturbing was that the future processing of minerals would require water, always in short supply.

This southeastern corner of Arizona didn't have healthy aquifers. The water supply came in the form of runoff from the mountains, iffy in the best of years. Worse, seepage from potential mineral-processing holding ponds could harm the limited water supply and pose a danger to landowners' health and the health of their children. The mines, they acknowledged, would offer employment, but at a cost to the beauty of the environment, the reason many of these people had chosen to live here. Just the threat of mining would affect the value of their little pieces of paradise. Land values would plummet.

The conflict was, and would continue to be, a hydra-headed beast.

Time dragged on. The grumbling grew louder. Prebble's body language shouted tension. Chapin closed his cell phone and put it in his breast pocket. He shook his head at Prebble and went back to his seat.

Deputy Curt came in, his face a mask. *This is it,* I thought. *This is the reason I came tonight.* I wished I could watch everyone at once. There was a high probability I was sharing the room with a murderer. Joaquin's joke about rounding up "the usual suspects" took on a whole new meaning.

Curt went directly to the front of the room to confer with Chapin and Prebble. Jody Lufkin joined them. Chapin turned his back to the audience. Prebble's posture was stiff, but whether from shock or tension, I couldn't tell. I wondered if, like me, Deputy Curt was taking mental notes.

Chapin pulled out his cell phone again and, without turning, stepped to the back wall. Prebble swallowed, took a long drink from a bottle of water Jody handed him. He moved to the front of the group and faced us. I stood on tiptoe. The room grew quiet as the eye of a category 5 hurricane.

Beside me, Ron Talmadge stopped drawing. His pencil hovered above the notebook. He frowned, gaze darting from person to person. No doubt, as an artist, he could read more into a person's posture and tilt of the head than I could. I've never been great at reading people. Rocks and fossils, on the other hand, speak to me.

Ron's eyes seemed to focus on one area of the room, but there were at least ten people in the vicinity. I recognized Rory and Jed, deep in conversation. Jody Lufkin's shoulders were rigid. Mark Haydon seemed to be trying to merge with the metal wall.

A thud and simultaneous gunshot brought screams and curses. People backed away from the area so fast they stepped on each other's toes. Enrique and Raul stood in the center of a circle. As Enrique bent down to retrieve the Colt, I heard Raul say, "Jesus, Mary, and Joseph, Enrique. You scared the shit out of me. You're lucky no one got killed. Didn't Curt check the chamber?"

Enrique, face suffused with blood, mumbled apologies. Curt took the revolver, none too gently, from Enrique's hand and carried it out the door. Enrique followed, hat pulled down to hide his face.

"Ladies and gentlemen," Prebble said. And louder, "Ladies and gentlemen. Thank you. We've just received some . . . terrible news. Our colleague, Sam Bruder, was found murdered this morning. I'm afraid we'll have to cancel tonight's meeting."

Prebble let the announcement hang in the air like a tethered balloon. The video camera continued taping. Feet shuffled. Whispers broke out. Raul, standing near the front, turned his head to look back at Joaquin. They exchanged a silent message.

The body at Massai Point now had a name. Sam Bruder. Names make things personal. In one sentence, Peter Prebble destroyed the victim's anonymity, and with it, the objectivity that had allowed me to distance myself from the murder. I lost my emotional chain mail. For some reason, that made me angry. I wasn't the only one.

"You're canceling?" Raul shouted. "But I've got questions." His right arm swung out to include the entire group. "We've all got questions."

"I have no answers to give you. Mr. Bruder didn't just represent DUC, he *owned* the company. Until we talk to our lawyer, we can't discuss anything. We don't know where we stand."

So Bruder's murder effectively hamstrung the company. I wondered if the killer had known that would happen. I was willing to bet that if Prebble or Chapin had been the victim, the mining exploration would have proceeded with hardly a hiccup. Public relations reps were a dime a dozen. And there always were competent mining geologists searching for work.

I looked at the faces around me. The people who would benefit the most were right here in the room. But how many of them, besides Prebble and Chapin, possessed inside information about Bruder's ownership of the company?

Mark Haydon's voice interrupted my train of thought. "How long?" he was saying. "How long before you know what'll happen next?"

"I can't tell you that. Give us time. We only just found out about this ourselves."

Linc Chapin closed his cell phone and joined Prebble at the microphone. "We meet with the legal team on Monday. Once we know where we stand, we'll send letters, as before, to apprise you of the plan."

"So your illegal drilling operations might be canceled?" Raul said.

"Our *legal* exploration is on hold for the moment. I can't say more than that."

I could feel the frustration and confusion of the audience. They'd anticipated a fight. They weren't going to get it.

Jed and Rory shouldered their way through the crowd and left the building. Mark Haydon inched his way around the perimeter and followed them. Joaquin watched them go with a thoughtful expression on his face. Ron gestured to the pen clipped to my shirt pocket. I handed it to him, thinking he'd use it on his sketches. But he switched from drawing people to tracing letters on a wordsearch puzzle. It looked like a draft copy of the one on the bulletin board. He *was* an odd duck, I decided.

Joaquin whistled, a curve-billed thrasher's call. Raul's head turned. Joaquin pointed toward the exit. Raul nodded. A few seconds later, he was beside me. He gave me a quick buss on the cheek and said, "Let's get out of here."

He didn't need to say it twice. I'd learned what I came here to learn.

Outside, we retrieved our knives. Prebble, Chapin, and Jody Lufkin huddled with deputy Curt near the corner of the building. He was on his radio. I had the feeling Detective Cruz wouldn't get much sleep tonight.

I took a deep breath of scented air and expelled it slowly from my lungs. "Well," I said, "I've had enough excitement for one day."

The brothers exchanged a look I couldn't interpret. "Raul and I want to talk to the DUC reps, Frankie," Joaquin said. "Could you drive the Honda home? Raul will bring me later."

"No problem," I said, accepting the key he held out. "Take your time."

I started down the hill toward the store. The road was lined with pickups. More were parked by the store and café. The entire area looked like a used-truck lot, with here and there an SUV sandwiched between the workhorses.

Footsteps crunched behind me. Ron Talmadge. His strides were even longer than mine. I remembered that he'd been afoot when I'd first seen him this afternoon. He was Portal's Walker.

"Would you like a ride back to Paradise, Ron?" I asked as he drew abreast. "Joaquin's riding with Raul."

He paused for a moment and considered the offer. Then nodded. I found it relaxing to walk in silence after the hubbub of the meeting hall. The moon leached all color from the landscape, leaving only black and white. Scorpio was rising. Jupiter glowed.

"A beautiful night for a drive," I said, opening the passenger door for Ron. His teeth gleamed as he climbed aboard. I smiled back. "Next stop, Paradise."

Chiricahua Mountains, southeastern Arizona
Saturday, May 13

I paid special attention to a large writing-table, near which he sat, and upon which lay confusedly, some miscellaneous letters and other papers, with one or two musical instruments and a few books. Here, however, after a long and very deliberate scrutiny, I saw nothing to excite particular suspicion.

—Edgar Allan Poe, "The Purloined Letter" (1845)

11

Black Ranch, Coues Canyon
5:25 a.m.

Thunderstorms, unusual for May, mostly skirted us that night. But the pattering of rain on the pitched tin roof of the pump house had awakened me several times. The accompanying breeze was laden with the pungent scents of piñon pine and juniper mixed with creosote from the desert below. The storm cell let loose just enough water to settle the dust, raise the humidity, and lay a golden coverlet of mesquite blossoms on the ground.

Clouds still hovered, veiling the rising sun, turning the tuff of the split peak to russet and coral. Sunset colors in the morning. Today, I suspected, wouldn't go according to plan.

As I rolled up my sleeping bag, a cool wind from the west rustled the junipers. A branch scraped the roof. A mist of yellow pollen drifted by the window. The air was filled with the hum of bees in the mesquites, the calls of cardinals, jays, and house finches. The thermometer on the pump-house wall read sixty-four degrees.

Perhaps it was the thunderstorm, perhaps the full moon shining through the skylight, but I hadn't slept well. My dreams were fretful. At one point I was discussing *Lolita* with Nabokov while drinking Scotch on a porch in Paradise. That, at least, made some kind of sense. Nabokov had spent time in the Chiricahuas fifty years ago. I doubt there was any more secluded spot in America back then.

The odd thing about my dream wasn't Nabokov. The odd thing was that I'm not, as a rule, a Scotch drinker. Yet I was swilling it down while Nabokov put the moves on me. I don't know where his wife was, but all of a sudden Philo Dain appeared in dusty fatigues. I was sketchy about the next part. I don't know whether I decided to leave with Philo or hop in the sack with Nabokov. What I did know, in the cool light of dawn, was that my worry about not hearing from Philo was triggering real fear for his safety. And Fear's handmaidens, Anger and Resentment, provoked me to lash out at the defenseless Philo in my dream. Not my finest hour.

I collected my gear and opened the door, nearly tripping over Marty. The pump-house stoop was as close as he could come to a middle ground where he could watch everyone at once. His ears came up. He gave a low *whuff,* ducked out from under the pat I'd aimed for his head, and took off down the road.

I stowed my gear in the van and headed for the composting outhouse twenty yards away. Spindly cane chollas by the path sported new magenta blossoms. A covey of quail scattered, squeaking and crying as they scurried between clumps of golden rabbitbrush. Leaving the outhouse a few minutes later I saw, beside the step, a broken projectile point. It seemed to shout, *Massai was here!* Or Geronimo. The point had been fashioned from maroon welded tuff. It lay on a desert pavement of angular rock fragments, all roughly the same size. I was almost sure it hadn't been there when I'd entered the outhouse.

"Very funny, Joaquin," I called out, though I couldn't see him. I hadn't heard him, either, which bothered me. We were back to playing cowboys—or cowgirl—and Indians. In our version of the game, the Indians always won.

Smiling, Joaquin stepped out from behind the pump house, Marty at his heels. I threw the point at Joaquin, but he ducked at the last second. It would have hit him squarely between the eyes. It barely missed the dog.

"I forgot you played softball. Your aim's still pretty good," he said, picking up the point and tucking it in his pocket.

"Was that some kind of test?" I ambled over to the water spigot, washed my hands, and dried them on my pants.

"A pop quiz. You passed. And first thing in the morning, too. I'm impressed."

Together we walked to the tents to wake up the students. Harriet and Esme were already rolling up their sleeping bags. Vicente, on the other hand, was snoring so loudly I wondered how Wyatt could sleep. But it took a lot of face-licking from Marty to finally rouse them both. And then they weren't coherent.

"The van leaves for breakfast in five minutes," I announced. That got the boys moving. "We'll finish packing up after we eat."

"I'll see you later," Joaquin said, and started up the road. He was camping farther up the hill, where he was building a straw-bale house. Marty ran ahead, foraging for rabbits and quail.

"You're not eating with us?" I called after Joaquin.

He stopped and turned around. Sunlight caught his face. He looked tired, as if he'd slept as poorly as I. "I've eaten." He smiled. "But I left a little for the rest of you." With a wave of his hand and an exchange of glances with Esme, he whistled for Marty.

A mule brayed in the canyon. A dog barked. A pair of ravens soared in the morning breeze, cawing to each other before swooping down to the trees by the creek. A cacophony of birdcalls filled the morning air, then swearing from the boys' tent. Wyatt stepped out, rubbing his head. The pop-up tent was several inches too short.

Vicente stumbled out after Wyatt. "Coffee?" he said, with a huge yawn.

I drove the students down to the main house where Rosa and Charley had scrambled eggs and bacon cooking. And coffee, freshly ground. Thank God. I needed it as much as Vicente did.

Coffee in hand, I looked at the bacon. Charley grinned. "Wilbur," he said. I'd fed that pig the last time I was here. "It was his time."

"You mean we're eating a pig named Wilbur?" Wyatt said. "Like in *Charlotte's Web*?"

"He tastes mighty fine, too," Rosa said, laying crisp bacon on a paper towel.

Wyatt reached around her, snagged a strip. "I always thought Wilbur was a little sanctimonious."

And with that he went back out on the deck where Charley had set chairs around a plank table. Esme and Vicente were already seated. Vicente, eyes closed, had both hands wrapped around a mug of steaming coffee. Harriet, binoculars glued to her eyes, was focused on the feeder hanging from a mesquite limb not ten feet away. "A black-headed grosbeak. Did you see that?" she said to no one in particular or everyone in general. "And look, acorn woodpeckers."

"Harriet," I said, "Charley's reserved a spot just for you. You can watch birds while you eat."

"At the table?" exclaimed the retired headmistress.

"Just this once," Charley said, offering Harriet a chair.

"Thank you, sir." She sat and pulled herself up to the table. A small cloud of tiny butterflies danced over a flower bed nearby, pausing momentarily to take the moisture from the soil. Two separated from the crowd and chased each other, landing on her plate. Harriet lowered her head until she could view the insects at eye level. "What are they?"

"Nabokov's blues," I said, coming over to the table. "Aren't they lovely?"

"Particularly the 'eyes' on the lower edge of their wings." Harriet stretched to work out the kinks. "Did you say Nabokov? As in Vladimir Nabokov?"

I nodded. "Butterflies were his passion, especially the blues."

"Why does his name sound familiar?" Wyatt said.

Harriet grinned. "Nabokov wrote *Lolita,* among other things."

"And he studied *butterflies—these* butterflies?" Wyatt watched the two small insects beat an erratic retreat toward the flower bed. "It doesn't compute."

"After *Lolita* was published, he spent the summer in Paradise, working on butterflies," I said.

"Cool," said Vicente. He'd opened his eyes when I mentioned *Lolita.*

"I thought you didn't read," Wyatt said to him.

"Saw the movie."

With the butterflies gone, Harriet returned to watching birds. "I could have sworn I saw an eagle as we were setting up camp last evening."

"Could have been," Charley said, coming out with a carafe. "We get them here. Coffee?" When she said yes, he poured a cup and put it next to her right hand.

She picked it up without looking at it and took a sip. "Thank you," she said again.

I moved to stand near the kitchen door so I could carry food to the table. "You don't have to wait on us, Charley."

"I know. But we ate early."

"Early? It's not yet six o'clock."

"Yeah, but Raul didn't drop off Joaquin till four thirty."

"Four thirty? But they said—" I stopped, thought back. "Joaquin said they'd be along shortly. Did they have a flat tire?" Flat tires were common on these unimproved dirt roads.

Rosa nudged open the kitchen door. I set my cup on a nearby ledge and took the bacon platter and bowl of eggs. "There are biscuits and honey coming, too," Rosa said. "Tell her," she threw over her shoulder as she went back inside.

"Tell me what?" I plunked the eggs and bacon on the table and went back for the biscuits and honey. When I'd handed those to Esme, I turned to look at Charley. He was searching for words, which meant it was something serious. "Just spit it out," I said, retrieving my coffee and taking the remaining seat at the table. Esme passed me the eggs.

"The boys found Ron Talmadge's body at the Turkey Creek bridge."

12

Charley pulled the bowl of eggs and spoon from my frozen fingers, finished serving me, and handed the bowl to Wyatt. Harriet, oblivious of Charley's bombshell, broke the silence. "A Wilson's warbler. I didn't think they made it this far west."

"Who's Ron Talmadge?" said Wyatt, piling eggs on his plate.

Vicente, mouth full of biscuit, looked from Charley to me.

"A friend," said Charley.

Esme said, "The old man we saw in Portal yesterday."

I found my voice. "The Turkey Creek bridge? At Paradise? That's where Ron asked me to drop him off. Not in so many words, of course. He just tapped me on the arm and pointed . . . But he was fine when I left him."

The students murmured among themselves about this new development. They'd been brushed again by violence. But this was a stranger, just as yesterday's victim had been a stranger. It wasn't personal. They were objective, not emotionally involved. For me, it was different. I couldn't get my mind around the image of Ron, lying dead on the bridge. He'd smiled as I drove off. He'd been happy.

Charley touched my shoulder. "Did you see anyone behind you on the road?"

I elbowed emotion aside. "A pair of headlights. I thought it was Raul and Joaquin."

"They were maybe thirty minutes behind you. Ron was dead by the time they reached him. But it took the medical examiner and sheriff's deputies quite a while to get there."

"Who in the world would hurt Ron?"

"That's what the detective wants to know."

I caught the present tense. "Paul Cruz wants to talk to me?"

Charley nodded. "He'll be here shortly."

"You're on the hot seat again?" Wyatt said to me.

"Looks like it."

"Does this mean you'll cancel the field trip?" Vicente said.

The worry in his tone got through to Harriet. "Cancel the field trip? Have I missed something?"

"You've missed another murder," I said. "The others will fill you in. As for the field trip—since I have to spend time with Detective Cruz this morning, we won't be able to do the Rucker Canyon Mesozoic rocks today." They all looked disappointed. "But as soon as I'm free, we'll do the Paleozoic section."

"That's all right, then," Vicente said, smiling as he grabbed another biscuit and slathered it with honey.

While Wyatt and Esme brought Harriet up to speed, Charley and I spoke softly together. "Three murders in as many days," I said. "And Joaquin—" I stopped.

"And Joaquin was at all three. Unfortunately, Cruz can count, too."

We both knew what that meant. Joaquin was a "person of interest." And, as of last night, so was Raul.

"How are they taking it?" I said.

Charley read my look. "Raul was only at one scene, but you—" This time he stopped, as if not wanting to say the words aloud.

I did it for him. "But I was at two."

"Yes. You'll want to watch what you say to Cruz."

An understatement. "I'll be careful. Have you called a lawyer?"

"Your brother. Joaquin, Rosa, and I are meeting Kit in Bowie. He's bringing one of his partners."

My eldest brother, Kit, specialized in international law, but a couple of the partners in his firm handled criminal cases. "You're meeting at Baskin-Robbins?" I said. Kit had a weakness for malts and shakes.

"Where else?" Charley smiled. "Kit's driving Joaquin's truck to save us a trip into Tucson."

Marty barked a warning from the hill behind the house. I heard the sound of an engine pause on the road below.

The big metal gate whined open. The vehicle turned onto the dirt driveway, paused again while the gate closed. Paul Cruz was here. He must have come directly from Paradise.

Rosa, a determined smile pinned to her face, set a second basket of biscuits and a thermos of coffee on the table. "Do you think we should postpone the wedding?" she said to Charley.

I'd forgotten all about my brother Jamie's wedding, now only two weeks away. Rosa's eyes met mine. I saw the anxiety and questions lurking there. Would Joaquin and Raul be allowed to attend the wedding? Would they be in jail?

I returned the hug she'd given me last night. "It'll be fine, Rosa. Everything will be fine." But even I didn't believe the words.

A white Tahoe pulled up beside the house. Paul Cruz got out and stretched. His face was etched with lines of exhaustion, but his clothes were neat, unrumpled. I wondered how he managed it.

"Will you take the students up to finish packing once the dishes are done?" I asked Charley.

"Of course," he said. Picking up the empty platters from the table, he followed Rosa inside.

"My stuff's already in the van," said Esme. "If it's okay with you, I'll stay and help Rosa clean up while the others break camp."

I smiled at her. She smiled back. Staying would give her a chance to overhear the questioning. She'd also be able to distract Rosa—and maybe pump her for information about Joaquin—while I faced the detective. "Fine with me," I said.

Cruz stepped onto the deck, notebook in hand. He greeted Charley and Rosa. The students, even Harriet, pushed back their chairs and carried their plates inside, leaving us alone for the moment. I offered him Wyatt's chair. "Coffee?" I said. Wyatt wasn't a coffee drinker. His cup was still on the table.

"I could use some, thanks."

He sat down, brushed crumbs from Wyatt's breakfast into his hand, and tossed them over the rock wall. Mourning doves slipped from the undergrowth and snatched them up. I poured coffee from the thermos and handed Cruz the cup. He set his sunglasses on the table and looked at me. His eyes were green hazel, flecked with gold, the iris rimmed with charcoal.

"You heard about Ronald Talmadge?"

So much for preliminaries. "Just now," I said.

"You drove him home from the meeting in Portal last night?"

"Yes."

"Did you stop along the way?"

"No."

"What time did you reach Paradise?"

"About ten. I didn't look at the clock."

"And where, precisely, did you leave Dr. Talmadge?"

"At the bridge."

"Why didn't you take him up to his house?"

"Because he indicated he wanted to be let off at the bridge."

"Did he say he was meeting someone?"

"Ron didn't speak, either then or at the meeting earlier. Joaquin told me he's been silent since his wife died."

Cruz nodded. "Was that the first time you met Talmadge?"

"Yes, though I saw him walking in Portal around four."

"What kind of interaction did you have last night?"

"I did all the talking."

"I understand that. But did he communicate with you in any other way?"

"He was drawing pictures in his sketchbook for most of the meeting."

"Sketchbook? We didn't find one with the body. Can you describe it?"

"One of those little black Moleskine books—accordion-pleated, heavy-grade paper. He kept it in a vest pocket."

"What did he sketch?"

"Various people at the meeting—Peter Prebble, the mining company PR man . . ." I stopped, thinking how odd it was for a PR person to be named Peter Prebble. So many *P*'s and *R*'s . . .

"You were saying?"

"Sorry. I'm not local, so I don't know everyone's name. But besides Prebble and Lincoln Chapin, the mining geologist, I recognized Jody Lufkin. She was in Portal earlier, too. Joaquin told me her name. And Jed and Rory—I don't know their last names. And Enrique Mendoza."

"Anybody else?"

"Not that I recall."

Cruz reached for the thermos, poured himself another cup of coffee, and took a biscuit from the basket. Breaking it in half, he squirted honey on each side. Downing those in four bites, he proceeded to do the same with a second, then a third. From the kitchen came the sound of running water and the clatter of dishes being washed. The water pump turned on. Behind the house, I heard the van doors close and the engine start—Charley, driving the students up to finish packing.

Esme came out and, without speaking, collected the honey bottle and the empty biscuit basket. Pouring a little water from the pitcher onto a clean paper napkin, Cruz wiped his fingers. "Can you think of any reason someone would harm Ronald Talmadge?" he said, picking up his pen again.

"No. But it couldn't have been Joaquin and Raul. Besides lacking a motive, would they have stuck around and called for help?"

Cruz didn't answer. Instead, he changed tack. "Do you own a firearm?"

"No."

"What time did you reach the ranch last night?"

"Around ten thirty. I was in bed at the pump house by eleven."

"Any witnesses?"

"Charley, Rosa, and my students. I picked up the students here and drove them to their campsite."

"By the pump house?"

"That's right."

He closed his notebook. "Do you have a business card?"

I pulled one from my pants pocket. It was crinkled but luckily hadn't gone through the wash.

He handed me his. I expected him to leave then, but he didn't. He got a toolbox out of the Tahoe and brought it back to the table.

"I used to work Crime Scene," he said, when I looked puzzled. "I still double up when they're overloaded."

"Such as three deaths in three days?"

"Yeah." He pulled on rubber gloves—blue, instead of the usual off-white. "Are you wearing the same shirt you wore last night?"

"Yes."

"I need to do a couple of tests."

"You're joking."

"I don't find it humorous that you were the last person to see Ronald Talmadge alive."

"Except for his killer." When he didn't respond, I rolled down my right sleeve and held out my arm. "Gunshot residue test?"

"And trace metal." He sprayed and swabbed the sleeve and my skin. "Could you take it off, please?"

I unbuttoned the aqua shirt and handed it to him. I was wearing a cotton camisole printed with swirls of black and gray on white. I wondered what he would have done if I'd been wearing nothing underneath.

He laid the shirt atop the wide rock wall and tested the front and sleeves again. After bagging the samples and labeling them, he picked up the shirt. His fingers touched the pocket that held Ron's gift.

Cruz frowned. "Do you mind?"

"Go ahead." I watched him unzip the pocket and extract the ore sample. It was even lovelier in the morning light. "Last night, when Ron learned I was a geologist, he gave me that. It's azurite and malachite," I said. "Copper minerals."

He was standing very still. His mouth hardly moved when he said, "I know. Why didn't you mention this before?"

"I'd forgotten all about it."

"You *forgot* that Dr. Talmadge gave you something shortly before he was killed?"

"It was a sweet gesture on Ron's part, but it's not a rare specimen." I pointed to the rocks Charley and Rosa had built into the wall enclosing the patio. "Copper minerals are in altered zones throughout this range. They're under our feet."

"Exactly."

I was missing something. "What possible significance can it have? I didn't take it off his body, for God's sake."

"Any witnesses to Dr. Talmadge giving it to you?"

"Joaquin was there."

"He was also with you up on the point yesterday morning." Cruz paused, looking at me, waiting.

"And he and Raul discovered Ron's body."

"So they say. Just as *you* say he was alive when you left him."

"He was. But you still haven't told me why my mineral sample is important."

Paul Cruz dropped the specimen in a bag and made notes while he weighed his answer. He hadn't asked for permission to keep Ron's gift. I guessed we were beyond that. Cruz might be standing on terra firma, but I was stepping lightly, looking for solid ground in a bog. Not a comfortable feeling.

Beyond his shoulder, a Scott's oriole landed upside down on the hummingbird feeder, setting the branch bobbing. Cruz packed away the specimen and handed back my shirt. "Yesterday afternoon, during the autopsy," he said, watching me struggle to fit the buttons into their proper holes, "Dr. Royce found a sample of copper ore tucked under Mr. Bruder's tongue."

"Azurite and malachite?"

"With minor chrysocolla, Royce said."

"You think Ron killed Bruder and put it there?"

"That's one possibility. We haven't begun tracing Talmadge's movements on Thursday and Friday."

Belatedly, the light went on. Cruz sat down. So did I, saying, "You think *I* killed Bruder and Ron?"

"What were you doing Thursday night?"

"I was in Tucson, at home, preparing for a field trip that left at dawn."

"Any witnesses? Boyfriend or relative who saw you there?"

"I live alone. My *boy*friend—if you can use that term for a thirty-six-year-old man—is in Afghanistan." Or was, the last I heard, I thought.

"Any phone calls?"

"No. My last conversation of any kind was at school, late Thursday afternoon."

"So you have no one to vouch for your alibi? Pity."

Pity, indeed. "What now?"

"How long were you planning to stay here?"

"We're leaving this afternoon."

"Can someone else take the students back to Tucson?"

"Joaquin's authorized to drive the van."

"Anybody else?"

So both Joaquin and I were restricted. "Not here."

"I'd prefer you stay until at least tomorrow."

"Tomorrow?" I stood up. "Not an option."

But he was making a note. "Tomorrow. Can you arrange that?"

"I don't know."

"The question was rhetorical."

"Then, yes. I'll make it work."

"Good."

We pushed back our chairs at the same time. He tucked his sunglasses atop his brown-black hair and we faced each other, unmoving. His eyes glittered in the sunlight. He'd be a dangerous adversary, I decided.

"Detective Cruz, do you think that if I'd killed Sam Bruder and Ron Talmadge, and put a piece of copper ore in Bruder's mouth, that I'd be walking around with a matching piece in my pocket?"

He smiled, a real smile that showed straight white teeth. "In my line of work, Dr. MacFarlane, I've seen far stranger things than that."

Round two to Paul Cruz. It was time to call in reinforcements. "Well, if you find you're on the fence about me, call Detective Toni Navarro, Pima County Sheriff's Office." I hadn't talked to Toni in months. I hoped she wasn't on vacation or assignment in Timbuktu.

Cruz dropped his eyes to his notebook. "I know her. We trained together."

The way he said it suggested they were more than colleagues. Or had been. He wasn't wearing a wedding ring. I'd ask Toni about it the next time we spoke.

A faint smile touched his lips when he caught me looking at his hand. He tucked the samples in a compartment and closed the toolbox. "If I reach her *and* she'll vouch for you, then you might be able to return to Tucson tomorrow morning. No promises."

"Good." Given my involvement in one of her cases not long ago, I didn't think she'd be surprised by the call.

Cruz picked up his kit. I said, "If you tested Joaquin and Raul for trace last night, don't you already know they're not suspects?"

"Raul tested positive. He says that on the way to the meeting he stopped to test fire a couple of pistols a friend was selling. We're checking it out."

Somebody dropped a pan in the kitchen. The clang reverberated in the morning air. Had Raul neglected to tell his parents this little detail?

"What vehicle were you driving last night?"

"Rosa's Honda CR-V."

"Show me."

I led him around the far side of the house. The Honda was parked in the shade of a big old one-seed juniper. Dried berries littered the ground. The vehicle was unlocked. Cruz set down his case and opened the passenger-side front door. He looked disappointed. I guess he'd hoped to find some signs of a struggle—*Pulp Fiction*-esque blown-out window, blood on the seat and floor and ceiling.

From where I stood, there was no evidence Ron Talmadge had been in the vehicle. But Cruz ran tape over the seats, then took a small vacuum cleaner from the back of his Tahoe. After vacuuming everything in sight, he sprayed a few stains to check for human blood and semen. Nothing glowed under ultraviolet light. So I hadn't killed Ron in the vehicle, nor had I had sex with him in the passenger seat of the car before knocking him off.

Cruz shined his light under the seat and ran his hand down between the cushions. He came up with maybe thirty cents in change, a Butterfinger wrapper, and the discarded top and straw from a fast-food soft drink. No little black sketchbook.

He took photos of the tire-tread patterns, then dusted the vehicle for fingerprints. He found a plentiful supply. I was sure at least some of them were mine and Ron's. They'd confirm we were in the car, but not much else.

Charley and the students came back while Cruz was stowing the samples and equipment away. Ninety minutes had passed since they'd left. Charley parked the minivan next to his own shiny truck and camper. When the students piled out, Cruz headed them off at the pass.

"If you don't mind, I need to ask a few questions," he said.

Wyatt grinned, set his artist's tablet on the ground, and raised his hands. Vicente and Harriet crossed their arms. "And if we do mind?" Harriet said, her tone frosty.

"Then we'll be here a while."

Wyatt lowered his arms and eyed Cruz warily. "Okay, shoot."

"What vehicle did Dr. MacFarlane drive to the meeting last night?"

"Well, it wasn't the van," Wyatt said, pushing his glasses farther up on his nose. "I know because, after she left, I had to go out and get my tablet—you know, so I could draw." He picked up the tablet and held it out. "I'm not much for card games. Want to see what I drew?"

Wyatt opened the tablet and started flipping through the pages. They were extraordinarily detailed drawings of mechanical armor, the kind warriors might wear in, say, the twenty-fourth century. Wyatt accompanied his page turning with a blizzard of specifications for every model.

Cruz started to back away, but Wyatt followed him, now firmly launched into his own passionate monologue. Harriet finally took pity on Cruz.

"They took that car," she said, pointing to the Honda. "I was outside, looking at the sunset, when they left. Joaquin was driving."

"Okay." Cruz's single word held a world of relief. He made a note. Turning to Charley, who'd watched the previous exchanges with a smile, Cruz said, "Raul's fire chief said he'll keep an eye on Raul for the next few days, so he can keep working while we wait for the lab tests to come back."

"What about Joaquin?" Charley said.

"I've asked him to stick close to home since this is where he works."

Charley looked at the sky, alive with scudding clouds. A common nighthawk swooped and circled erratically, chasing a to-go breakfast of insects-on-the-wing. "Okay," he said. His eyes met Cruz's squarely. "I'll make sure he stays on our land."

Did I imagine the slight emphasis on the last two words?

Cruz evidently saw nothing amiss. He nodded. "Good enough for me. I've also asked Dr. MacFarlane to stick around, at least till tomorrow."

"She's always welcome. Her students, too." Charley put a hand on my shoulder and gave it a gentle squeeze. "Paul, I'd like to collect Ron's cat, if it's okay with you. She'll be missing him by now."

"And hungry, too, no doubt." Cruz silently considered the pros and cons of allowing Charley into Ron's home. It wasn't a crime scene, but might contain clues to why Ron was killed. At the same time, a hungry, lonely cat, cooped up in an empty house, might destroy evidence. "We haven't searched the house yet. We're still waiting on the warrant. So don't disturb anything."

Charley promised, then turned and led the students toward the house. I took a step. Cruz stopped me. "A few final questions, Dr. MacFarlane. Did you know the lawyer who was killed Wednesday night?"

"No."

"At one time or another he did work for various wilderness and wild-land coalitions—most of the biggies."

"Never heard of him," I said.

"You're a geologist. Mr. Bruder owned a mining company. Had you ever met him?"

"No. I first heard his name in Portal last night."

"You didn't go to the meeting in Dragoon? Raul did."

"I was giving a final that night. You can check with the school."

"I'll do that. Are your fingerprints on file?"

"I worked for the federal government for three years, and now I teach for the state. So, yes, my fingerprints are on file. They're in lots of files."

"Good. I'll call you if I need anything else, Dr. MacFarlane." I was dismissed.

Paul Cruz accompanied me in silence to the entrance of the house. Joaquin and the students were outside in the shady alcove off the kitchen. They'd dismantled the plank table and moved the chairs into a little circle. Two hours sleep and a shower seemed to have done Joaquin a world of good. Or maybe he was cheered by my company in the prime suspect lifeboat.

Cruz nodded to Joaquin, poked his head in the door and thanked Rosa for the coffee and biscuits, then climbed back into the Tahoe. We all watched it roll quietly down the driveway.

"Looks like you'll be staying another night," Joaquin said to me. But he was looking at Esme.

"You heard?" I said.

"Enough. Welcome to the persons-of-interest club."

"Not a list I wanted to join. By tomorrow he'll have talked with Toni Navarro. She'll set him straight."

I turned to my students, a subdued group. "Anybody have a commitment today or tomorrow, something they can't miss?" A chorus of No's accompanied by head shakings. "What about Mother's Day? Anybody have to shop for a present?"

"Tomorrow's Mother's Day?" Vicente said.

"You can get flowers and a card on Sunday," Wyatt said. "And maybe offer to do some yard work for her. That's what I always do."

"What about you?" I said to Esme.

"My mother died last year." She looked at the horizon and blinked a few times.

"Oh, Esme, I'm so sorry," I said.

Vicente put an arm around her shoulder. "That's rough, *amiga.*"

Wyatt said, "You can borrow mine, Esme," as if mothers were toys or computer games.

Esme took a deep, calming breath and said, "Thanks,

Wyatt." To me, she said, "I'm not in any hurry to go home."

"Then since we're here, let's do some geology. You can call home and alert your families from there. Your cell phones will work at the bottom of the canyon. Ten minutes, everyone."

"I just love your field trips, Dr. MacFarlane," Harriet said, opening the kitchen door. Her tone held no trace of sarcasm.

"You might as well call me Frankie."

13

"I'm good to go," Wyatt said as the screen door closed behind his classmates. He stretched and yawned. "This is a nice place to relax."

He began picking up objects, one at a time, from the stucco shelves that jutted from the alcove walls. My siblings had brought back many of the knickknacks—minerals, deer antlers, a javelina skull and lower jaw—from hikes over the years. For me they captured the magic of the Chiricahuas.

Wyatt lifted the javelina skull and turned it over to examine the teeth. He needed to touch things, I'd noticed over the past semester. Setting the skull back on the rock ledge, he rotated it this way and that until he was satisfied. Taking his sketchbook from his backpack, he proceeded to draw the ventral view, his pencil slipping over the paper.

A roadrunner zipped by on the other side of the wall and stopped under the feeder. He made a hollow whirring and clacking sound with his beak before trotting over to an alligator juniper. Flying awkwardly to a low branch, he scrabbled noisily up the tree. A mournful series of coos filled the air—six pulsing notes, unresolved, followed by eight or nine notes, dying away. When I moved nearer, he flew off to the east and continued hunting on the ground. His nest would be somewhere close. I wished I could wander off and find it.

"Just making his rounds," Charley said.

I went down the deck steps to look at the fresh tracks the roadrunner had left in the dust under the bird feeder. Charley hunkered down beside me. "They look like a pair of chromosomes to me," I said.

He tilted his head, considering. "You know, you're right. I hadn't thought of that."

"What time do you meet Kit?" I said.

"Nine," Charley said, getting to his feet. "We have to leave soon."

Rosa was at the deck wall, her smile a shadow of her normal effervescence. "Shouldn't you come with us now that you're, you know, a suspect?"

She was right, of course. But I had a hard time believing Cruz considered me a serious suspect. Besides, I couldn't ride two horses at the same time. At the moment, I had students to look after, a field trip to lead. My potential legal difficulties would have to wait.

"Would you tell Kit I'll call him as soon as I get back?" I said.

"Of course."

A thought hit me. "And you might discuss whether we're going to try to keep what's happened from Jamie and Teresa. You know they'll both be out here like a shot if they find out. And they need to focus on the wedding."

"I think Elvis has already left the building," Rosa said. "Teresita called while Paul was here. She wanted to talk to you, and when I tried to . . . well, she knows me too well, that girl." Rosa came down the steps, wrapped her arms around Charley's waist and gave him a hug. "Just like her father."

"She's on her way?" Charley said.

"She and Jamie will leave after work. They'll be here for dinner." She slipped out from under Charley's arm, trotted up the steps, and disappeared into the house.

"Looks like the powwow's coming to Coues Canyon," I said. "Why don't you invite Kit, as well?" I said, thinking I could pick my brother's brains over dinner.

"He can't. He's prepping for a court case on Monday," Charley said.

In the shade of the alcove, Wyatt was nearly finished with his drawing. He hadn't sketched the entire ventral aspect. Instead, he'd chosen a back-centered view. From this oblique angle, the large empty area within the zygomatic arches resembled empty eye sockets in a gaunt, spectral face. This Caspar, however, was not a friendly ghost. His "mouth" was the bottomless, roughly triangular opening at the base of the skull. He seemed to be screaming in pain. And from the "forehead," the rear of the javelina's palate, grew two small "horns," the last two molars on each side.

"A denizen of Dante's Hell," I said. "Or John's Apocalypse."

"Dali-esque," said Charley, studying Wyatt more than the drawing.

"Excellent." Wyatt's cheerful tone contrasted oddly with his subject matter. "That's what I thought."

"You see the world differently than I do." I watched Wyatt pencil *Hoodoo* at the bottom of the page, followed by his name and the date. He was left-handed, his writing cramped and awkward.

"I'm an Aspie," he said. "You're a Normal."

I looked at Charley, knowing the psychologist would be able to translate. "Help me out here."

"Asperger's syndrome," he said, "the highest-functioning end of the autism spectrum. Sometimes called the 'genius syndrome.'"

"Right on." Wyatt beamed.

For me it was one of those ah-hah moments. It explained so much—Wyatt's intellectual brilliance and social awkwardness, his inability to modulate voice tones, his seeming lack of empathy, his objective and literal view of events. "I bet you're looking forward to a quiet afternoon in the house, Wyatt?"

He grinned at me, though he maintained eye contact for less than a second. "Quiet and computer work. Typing's easier for me than writing. And I'm not much of a hiker."

"I think you'll enjoy this hike," I said, watching him tuck away his sketchbook.

Joaquin, face somber, opened the door. "Raul's meeting us in Bowie," he said. "Cruz found out he was off-duty Thursday night. And Cindy said he came home late."

Charley's eyes narrowed. "Where was he?"

"He won't say."

I'd rarely seen Charley taken aback. As a counselor to abuse survivors, inmates, and addicts, he'd heard so many horror stories that nothing surprised him anymore. Except this. He walked to the edge of the deck and looked down the valley. "Does your mother know?"

Joaquin moved to stand next to him. "She's upset. She thought Raul had stopped playing around."

"Didn't we all."

The door slammed behind Esme, Harriet, and Vicente.

"Maybe we should cancel this morning's field trip," I said to Charley. "Maybe our time would be better spent on background research on the victims."

"But we're ready to go," Harriet said.

"You *promised*," said Vicente.

"I know, but—"

Joaquin stopped me. "It'd be a waste of time and energy at this point, Frankie. The situation's changed. Give us a couple of hours to figure out how much trouble we're in, then we'll know where to start digging."

"Fair enough," I said.

"Meet you at the van," Harriet said, before I could change my mind. She looped her binoculars strap around her neck, and set off toward the van at a fast walk. The other students followed like ducklings in her wake.

I kissed Charley and Joaquin on the cheek as I passed. "I'll expect the backstory later."

"The backstory is simple," Joaquin said. I stopped. "My brother's an idiot."

"Joaquin." Charley's voice was sharper than I'd ever heard it.

"A lovable idiot," Joaquin amended. "But an idiot all the same. I wonder who she is this time?"

14

I parked the van near an unnamed mountain of carbonate rock at the mouth of Coues Canyon. "The rancher has given us permission to cross his land and collect at the old mine," I said. I led the students through a maze of corrals and holding pens, some with cattle and horses staring at us wild-eyed, and entered the dry wash.

As we trudged through coarse sand, I pointed out sedimentary textures and structures in the arroyo walls. Vicente, livelier than I'd seen him all semester, hummed as he snapped digital photographs of graded bedding, imbricated cobbles, cross-bedding, and channel cuts.

After a quarter mile we climbed the bank and hiked three hundred feet up a rutted road toward a mine dump. I explained that millions of years ago, while volcanic eruptions deposited the tuff layers of the Chiricahua National Monument, subsurface water migrated along the fracture zones. The geothermally heated water carried elements from deep within the earth, as well as elements leached from the older crustal rocks through which it traveled. Metals such as copper, gold, silver, iron, and zinc, carried in solution, interacted with each other and with the country rock to form suites of ore minerals. The search for these minerals had triggered waves of prospecting and mining ventures, and led to the settlement of the Southwest.

I'd chosen this site specifically for the fresh exposures. The entire mountain consisted of marine sedimentary rocks, some of them altered. The mine had been carved into Mississippian Escabrosa Limestone, a unit replete with fossils. The students should be able to find horn corals, brachiopods, bryozoans, and abundant crinoid debris.

The limestone beds of the hillside, originally deposited on a flat seafloor, now dipped steeply to the southwest. The mine entrance resembled a dented trumpet, the upper edge slashed, the sides flaring out toward the canyon. A short way in, where the shaft took a downturn, the owners had installed a locked gate of metal bars. But we didn't need to go deeper into the mine. The first twenty feet, unroofed and open to the sky, provided a textbook three-dimensional view of dark gray crystalline rock studded with nodules and lenses of black chert. Those relatively unaltered rocks contained all the evidence the students needed to accomplish their task.

The students prospected in the mine dump for a few minutes, finding small perfect prisms of quartz and samples of copper and iron ores. Calling the group to the mine entrance, I gave each a clipboard and a lesson handout. The goal was straightforward: to determine, based on the lessons and labs they'd had all semester, the composition of the country rock, its rock name, and approximate age.

"This is your chance to prove you can solve a mystery," I said. "Go to it."

I was confident they'd discover enough clues to work out the puzzle. Although I'd dropped hints that we'd be visiting the Paleozoic section this morning, I knew students rarely listened. Harriet was an exception. I wanted them to work together, and, even if Harriet remembered what I'd said and shared it with the others, they'd still have to substantiate their conclusions.

"May we collect samples?" Harriet asked.

"As long as you're careful and don't trash the site."

I gave them cold chisels, rock hammers, safety glasses, sample bags, and felt pens. While they investigated, I sat on a nearby rock in the sun and pondered that last exchange between Joaquin and Charley. I thought I knew Raul as well as I knew my own brothers, but apparently I was wrong. He and I had both spent many years away from southern Arizona. We'd both changed in the interim. Did I really know him anymore?

Raul, firstborn son and Joaquin's elder by two years, had always been fire to his brother's water. Raul needed to be around people, needed to physically embrace the world. In high school he'd run track and played football. He'd been the class cutup. College held no appeal. Instead, he'd wanted to try his wings far from southeastern Arizona. The summer after graduation he'd found a job on a ranch in Montana. In Missoula, the closest town, he'd run into a couple of smoke jumpers. Always an adrenaline junkie, he'd applied, survived training and his rookie year, and spent the next eight fire seasons working all over the West. The money was good, and the life suited him. In the off-season, he'd go down to Las Vegas and work as a bartender. There were a lot of available women in Vegas.

I remembered the effect he'd had on my schoolmates when they'd met him at a family party. I was thirteen. Raul and Joaquin were bunking with my brothers during La Fiesta de los Vaqueros, a uniquely Tucson celebration held each February. Teresa Black, my soon-to-be sister-in-law, and another friend were sharing my room. I remember the friend saying that when Raul walked into the family room, the atmosphere crackled. Everything else seemed to fade away.

Teresa just shook her head. I seemed to be immune, having already fixated on Philo Dain. When I asked Teresa if this happened whenever she had a girlfriend over, she said Raul was such a distraction that her Girl Scout meetings had to be held in a schoolroom that didn't overlook the playing field.

But that was a long time ago. I tried to remember snippets of gossip I'd heard at recent weddings and Christmas gatherings . . . Raul had been stalked by a lovesick dancer in Vegas . . . A woman in Missoula swore he was the father of her child. He was on the verge of marrying her when a paternity test proved otherwise. Those two events must have scared him, because when that fire season ended, he'd returned to Arizona.

He'd met Cindy the first week he was back. They were married six months later. And seven months after that the first of their two girls was born.

The clear air carried the sound of a door closing. Across the canyon dust rose in a line along the base of Gray Mountain. I pulled binoculars from my daypack. Paul Cruz's white Tahoe drove slowly along a road tucked behind a low ridge of old stream gravel. The road wasn't on the topo map, but seemed to connect the Portal/San Simon road with the one being built on Gray Mountain. Mark Haydon had been busy.

Parked in a hollow at the origin of the dust cloud was a motor home. I hadn't noticed it before because the ridge screened it from the main Coues Canyon road. But from where I sat, three hundred feet above, I could see a couple of chairs and a picnic table under the shade of a striped canvas awning. A red-and-white checked cloth covered the table. Mark Haydon stood next to it, watching Paul Cruz drive away. So that's where Cruz had gone when he'd finished with me.

A woman stepped out of the motor home, closing the screen door behind her. She had a cascade of bright red hair held off her face by a lime green bandeau. The bandeau matched the color of the sleeveless camp shirt she wore with blue jeans and running shoes. Ginny Haydon, I presumed. She was tall and athletically built. She put her hand on Mark's forearm. He shook it off, picked up a phone that was lying on the table, and punched in some numbers. Nodding curtly, he tossed the phone to Ginny. She caught it, climbed into the motor home, and slammed the door behind her.

Paul Cruz had turned south toward Portal. Mark was staring north toward San Simon. He looked at his watch. Expecting company, I wondered?

I trained the glasses on the San Simon road. Two miles out I saw another dust cloud, this time rising behind a convoy of vehicles. It hadn't been there five minutes ago, I was sure. Had Mark asked them to hold up while Cruz was with him?

The convoy included five flatbed trucks loaded with cinder block and cement, a crane, a dump truck, and a bulldozer. Mark Haydon was taking delivery of his building material and equipment. He was going to finish the road up Gray Mountain.

Paul Cruz knew, though I hadn't, that the Haydons lived only a half-mile from where Byron Locke was murdered. Either Mark or Ginny could have run or driven that distance in nothing flat. So where were they while Byron Locke was being conked and toasted?

I turned the glasses back on Mark. He was sitting on

the metal step of the Winnebago, changing from running shoes into work boots. He finished tying his boots, stood up, and strode toward the table. Behind me, the students yelled my name. Four hammers attacked four chisels in a syncopated rhythm. Mark stopped abruptly and searched the hillside till he found movement. He reached for a binoculars case that hung from the light fixture beside the door. I quickly lowered my own glasses, tucking them inside my shirt as I turned to intercept the students.

"Eureka," Harriet said, as if she'd just discovered the mother lode. She, Wyatt, and Vicente held out samples of gray crystalline rock. Solitary horn corals, crinoid plates shaped like tiny white washers, curved fragments of brachiopod shells, and netlike encrusting bryozoa showed stark white against the dark groundmass.

"This is limestone, right? With fossils, right? Like in an ocean?" Vicente said.

"Right," I echoed, feeling Mark Haydon's eyes boring into my back. "What types of fossils?"

"That man's looking at us with binoculars," Esme said, pointing at Haydon.

I turned around. Mark was in shadow. Without binoculars, I had a hard time picking him out.

"Where?" said Harriet, lifting her own glasses. Esme guided the glasses to the spot. "Got him. Can't believe you picked him out. You must have amazing eyesight."

"I guess," Esme said. She seemed embarrassed by the compliment.

I made a show of taking out my own binoculars. Mark was still watching us, trying to figure out what we were doing. I raised my hand and waved. After a pregnant pause, he waved back. I lowered the glasses and turned my back on him again. He couldn't know I'd been watching him earlier.

From the corner of my eye, I saw the convoy reach the turnoff to the Haydon property. I smiled. Mark would have other things to occupy him for the next few hours.

"He stopped," Harriet said. "Who is he, do you know?"

"Mark Haydon," I said. "A man named Byron Locke, a protestor, died in a fire on his land a few days ago."

"Protesting what?"

"The road he's building up the mountain."

Harriet's glasses were still trained on Haydon. "Nice Winnebago," she said. "Expensive . . . Was this protestor murdered?"

"Yes."

Vicente bobbled the rock sample, almost dropping it. "So he's one of the suspects?"

"Along with Joaquin. He and Ron Talmadge came to fight the fire."

"Ron Talmadge, the man who was killed last night?" Esme said. When I nodded, she frowned, looking at the activity below. "I liked him. He seemed . . . special. Is Mark Haydon a suspect in his murder, too?"

"I imagine so. Haydon was at the meeting—and Detective Cruz just left his place."

Wyatt was only half listening. "What're all those machines for?" He pointed to the convoy, parked like toy trucks at the base of Gray Mountain.

"With Byron Locke dead, there's no one to stop the Haydons from finishing what they'd started."

Wyatt shivered. "That's cold."

"Motive, means, and opportunity," Harriet said.

"I wonder if he owns a gun?" said Esme.

"Since we can't go home today," Wyatt said, "maybe we can help by doing some online sleuthing? You know, see if Vince and I can find anything that connects Locke and Bruder and Talmadge."

"I'm not sure—"

"Sounds like fun," said Vicente. He held out the rock sample again. "Did we pass?"

I returned to teacher mode. "What kinds of fossils did you find?" I asked again.

They talked among themselves and came up with corals and clams. I explained that the clams were actually brachiopods, then pointed out the sea lily plates and bryozoan fragments. They compared them to the pictures I'd included in the handout. "In what kind of environment would you find these life forms?" I asked them.

"Corals grow on reefs in warm ocean water," Wyatt said.

"The tropics," Harriet said. "They need lots of light."

"So there used to be reefs near where we're standing?" Vicente said.

I nodded. "How old do you think this rock formation is?"

Everyone except Harriet flipped pages in their handouts. "Paleozoic," Harriet said. "Most of the brachiopods died out at the end of the Paleozoic."

So she *had* been listening. I smiled at her.

"Yes, Paleozoic," said Vicente and Wyatt together, jumping on the bandwagon.

"Good detective work, great teamwork. You pass with flying colors," I said.

They clapped each other on the back. Wyatt's enthusiastic thumping made Harriet stumble.

"I'd like to pay the Haydons a visit," Esme said, watching the trucks below unload their cargo. "Just to see their reactions."

I sensed Esme wanted to do anything she could to get Joaquin off the suspect list. I put a hand on her shoulder. "Computer searches are one thing, impromptu visits are another," I said. "Promise me you won't, Esme."

"No women have been killed," she said, with the naïveté of the young.

"And you're not going to be the first." My hand dropped from her shoulder, and I turned to the other three. "Lesson's over. Bag your samples. We're heading back to Charley's."

15

Although Esme seemed to acquiesce, I decided I'd keep her busy as far away from the Haydons as possible until we left the Chiricahuas.

Marty, tail wagging, met us at the gate. Charley, Rosa, and Joaquin returned to the ranch a few minutes after we did. It was only eleven, but Joaquin started gathering lunch ingredients on the butcher-block island in the middle of the kitchen. Rosa headed for the garden to take out her frustration on the weeds. Marty kept her company.

"What did Kit say?" I asked Charley.

"About what you'd expect a lawyer to say. That we need to proceed as if the police will be looking for a scapegoat. All other things aside, a murder spree plays hell with the tourist business."

The phone rang. Joaquin picked up the kitchen extension. His expression said it wasn't good news. "Okay, thanks," he said, and hung up. He looked at Charley. "That was Hank. Our cattle are loose at the turnoff to Mackey Canyon. The fence is down."

Mackey was farther south in the range, but the access road led off of the Coues Canyon road.

"Cut?" said Charley.

Joaquin started making a chicken sandwich on whole grain bread. "Hank didn't say. I'll take Marty, round them up, and fix the wire. Shouldn't take too long."

"Keep your eyes open," Charley said.

"I've got Marty and Sidestep." Sidestep was his horse. "What more do I need?" He looked at me. "Since I'm going to be out on the range and Raul's stuck in the fire station, it's up to you to find something to keep us all out of the pokey. I don't suppose you came up with a plan while you were knocking on rocks this morning?"

We hadn't come up with anything as formal as a plan, but we'd discussed options on the way home from the mine—activities that wouldn't put them in danger, but would help pass the time. While we were still within cell phone range, I'd cleared the extra night's stay with their families—except Harriet's, of course. She'd retired last fall after forty years of teaching. For the first time in her life, she'd told me, she was responsible to no one. The other students had given me written permission as well. They were all over twenty-one, but it covered me with the school.

"We need information most of all, so we can figure out who had more motive than you did to kill those men," I said. "Harriet, Esme, and I will start with Portal. Ron might have dropped his sketchbook there last night. I'll search the parking lot and the road up to the meeting-house, then have lunch at the café."

The café was the local clearing house for information and gossip. Half the population wandered through during any given day. "If you don't mind, I'll come with you," Charley said. "We can take the Honda. It won't be as conspicuous as the van."

"And it gets better gas mileage. Where was I? Oh yes, the plan. Miss Marple," I nodded toward Harriet, "will add to her birding life list at the hummingbird sanctuary."

"Birders like to talk," Harriet said. "Quietly, of course."

"If you're Miss Marple, who am I?" said Esme.

"Lozen," said Joaquin. "Scout, warrior, medicine woman—"

"And born to the Chihenne, the Warm Springs Band, from my neck of the woods," Esme said, looking pleased.

Joaquin had scored points there. The legendary Lozen had guided and fought alongside Geronimo, another Chihenne, in these very mountains.

Joaquin took from his pocket the maroon arrowhead we'd played with at dawn. He handed it to Esme, explaining that he'd found it on the hillside near her tent. "Keep it," he said. "Who knows, it might even have been Lozen's."

When Esme seemed lost for words, I said, "Lozen will be scouting the library and post office. Her cover is that she's researching the town's history, seeing who she can interview."

"But I'll be asking questions, too," Esme said, tucking the arrowhead in the pocket of her jeans. "Someone must have heard something about the murders."

Wyatt and Vicente had joined Joaquin at the island. "We'll be Ahab and Ishmael, hunting the white whale on the Internet," Wyatt said.

"Come again?" said Vicente.

"*Moby Dick*. I'll tell you the story while we work." Wyatt added butter and honey to one of the biscuits left over from breakfast. "We have everything we need—our two computers and your Ethernet," he said to Charley. "If we can hijack your Web connection?"

"No problem," said Charley.

"You're aware that Ahab came to an untimely end," Harriet said to Wyatt.

"But he found what he went looking for." Wyatt grinned. "And hey, at least Ishmael lived to tell a whale of a tale."

"We'll be gone a couple of hours," Charley said to Joaquin. "We'll pick up Ron's cat on the way home."

"I was hoping you'd say that," I said, linking my arm through his. "I'd like to have a look inside Ron's house."

Charley laughed. I'd missed hearing that warm, throaty sound. "I guessed as much."

I pulled him toward the door. "You don't really think I'd let you go alone, do you?"

By eleven thirty we were in Portal. People were gathered outside the library and post office—old, converted schoolhouses—shooting the breeze as they would in any small town. We drove past the post office, dropped Esme off at the Myrtle Kraft Library, then deposited Harriet at the gate to the sanctuary, a private house with hummingbird feeders. A sign asked for donations to help feed the birds. I saw Harriet slip a five into the box before she went in.

Turning around, Charley parked the CR-V near the store. We searched the parking area and the road to the Portal Rescue building for Ron's sketchbook. Nothing. If Ron had dropped it, someone else had picked it up. "Time for lunch," I said.

The Portal Café catered to a mix of locals and visitors. Ranchers in dusty cowboy boots, straw hats, plaid shirts, jeans and suspenders; day-trippers, from places like Silver City and Tucson, who came for the hiking and birding; local retired scientists; and artists. We chose a battered brown Formica table for two against the interior wall. Before we were seated, the waitress dropped two menus on the table. Inside the back plastic cover of mine was a wordsearch puzzle. It was signed *R. Talmadge,* and dated the day before.

"Charley." I pointed to the back page of his menu. He took one look, stood up, and carried his menu through the doorway into the general store side of the building.

I studied the puzzle while he was gone. The search list included *quail, lizard, jaguar, killer bees, tuff, hoodoo, road-runner, juniper, agave, rattlesnake, Cochise, Geronimo, elegant trogon, raven, coyote, lupine, poppy, hawk, javelina, Apache, pinyon pine,* and *hummingbirds.* It was an exercise designed not only to entertain restive children until the food arrived, but to educate them about the area, as well. Some of the words leaped off the page. Some I'd have to hunt down. But the puzzle seemed simple and straightforward.

```
E D S E I N N O R E N I D A N
A L U P I N E R K W A H N M O
D T A K L E H C A P A O J E D
S H F A I P O P P Y D O S L J
T U F H J L I Z A R D D N T A
L M Q U A I L E I A N O A T V
D M H T G L N E V A R O K A E
U I C U U M A D R U N N E R L
C N O T A O B D E B O R O R I
A G Y S R R T N A G E L E E N
G B O I U N T R O N I E E P A
A I T D O M I N O R E G S I R
V R E N I K F U L Y D O J N O
E D O C O C H I S E Y R O U N
R S C E N I P N O Y N I P J T
```

I picked up one of the erasable pens from the plastic holder on the table and went to work. The words were aligned backward, forward, vertically, horizontally, and diagonally. A few changed directions midword. Although the theme, form, and content seemed the same as the puzzle Ron had tacked up on the board last night, this one was slightly smaller.

The waitress arrived, green pad in hand, just as Charley slid back into his chair. He handed me two copies of the puzzle. I zipped them into one of the many compartments in my bag while Charley ordered the three-enchilada dinner and iced tea. I settled for two chicken enchiladas—half green sauce, half red—a small salad, and a soft drink. I needed sugar as well as caffeine.

We lapsed into silence, studying the puzzle, sipping our drinks, and listening to chatter. Cruz's restrictions and my teaching duties had relegated me to this passive role. It rankled. But for now, I'd have to be content with whatever morsels of information the denizens of Portal dropped on my plate.

I tuned in to a New Zealand film crew gathered around a back table. They'd just finished filming a documentary in Cave Creek Canyon. They talked of lizards ("just birds without feathers"), reintroducing Mexican gray wolves, rattlesnakes ("I'd like to meet one!"), and jaguar sightings. Though the first sighting, down near Old Camp Rucker, might be suspect, there'd been another one last evening. A Forest Service worker had reported seeing a jaguar cross Pinery Canyon Road near Onion Saddle. Peaches' jaguar was getting around.

"Did you talk to Peaches last night?" I asked Charley.

He hesitated. "He wasn't home," he said. His eyes told me there was more, but I'd have to wait till we were someplace private.

The side door opened and Jody Lufkin came in with Mark and Ginny Haydon. They seemed like old friends, though I knew the Haydons were newcomers to the Chiricahuas. They'd made a pile of money in construction back East.

"—as high as we can go," Mark was saying. "It needs a lot of work. I'm assuming all rights are included?"

Jody didn't answer. Conversation in the room had ceased. Heads turned. Ginny elbowed Mark, who'd opened his mouth to add something. He closed his mouth and followed the two women to a table along the inner wall, just behind Charley's chair. Mark and Ginny sat with their backs to Charley and me. Jody faced me. But her gaze was focused on Mark and Ginny. She didn't seem to notice me.

Charley, with his back to the side door, hadn't seen them. I raised my eyebrows to signal something was up, but kept silent. I found it strange that last night Jody hadn't gone near Mark Haydon, while today they were buddies. Apparently, so did the waitress. She almost dropped the menus when she saw them sitting together.

Our food arrived. Charley and I ate quickly, listening to the three weigh in on the topic du jour, the border situation.

"Without a wall, we'll never curb the flow," Jody said, after they'd placed their order. "They'll take back the Southwest without firing a shot."

Mark hesitated, then said, "You'd think it was a conspiracy."

"I think we should let them in," said Ginny. "But only if they agree to be sterilized. Otherwise, they'll completely overwhelm the medical systems."

"They already have," said Jody.

"Then we should electrify the fence."

"And add razor wire," said her husband.

"You'll never get that through Congress," Jody said.

In the awkward lull that followed, Jody picked up her hat and worked the brim with her fingers. Their conversation seemed forced, careful, as if they were hunting for common ground.

Mark switched subjects. "Ginny told me you were on the rodeo circuit."

"Yeah. Barrel racing. I had some great ponies over the years. The last one broke a leg at the Tucson Rodeo. Had to put him down. Damn shame." Jody put her hat aside, picked up her water glass and drained the contents. "Dad got sick about that time. I couldn't travel the circuit. So I started training horses for other riders."

"The sandwich generation, that's us," Mark said. "I'm lucky I have a sister willing to take care of our parents."

"Speaking of sandwiches," Jody said, as the waitress brought their lunch. They were quiet for a minute or two as they tackled their meals. Finally Jody broke the silence. "Sorry about that awkward reception at the library, just now. You came in as Tammi Barnett was telling us about what happened to Ron Talmadge last night."

Mark gave a short, sharp bark of laughter. "It was more than that. We seem to have alienated everyone on the east side of the Chiricahuas."

"People don't like change," Jody said.

"No kidding."

"Tammi said Paul was going to interview everyone who was at the meeting." Jody paused to take a sip of ice water.

"Detective Cruz? He came by this morning," Ginny said. Mark's head snapped toward her. He was frowning. "It's not as if it's a secret, Mark. Everyone knows we're on the list." She turned back to Jody. "Because of the fire."

"But that was an accident," Jody said.

"You haven't heard?" Mark said, and gave that bark again. "The grapevine must not be as efficient as I thought."

"But who—"

"Cruz's short list includes Ginny, me, Talmadge, that half-breed—"

"Excuse me?" Jody bristled.

Charley quietly and deliberately set down his fork. I reached across the table and squeezed his hand. Behind him, Ginny said, "Joaquin Black."

Mark nodded. "That's the one. And of course now that Talmadge is dead, the list just got shorter."

"And there's the new list for who killed Ron Talmadge and Sam Bruder," Ginny said. "We're on that one, too."

"Paul Cruz actually accused you?" Jody picked up a green chile and popped it in her mouth.

"We're persons of interest."

"Because of Byron Locke? Because of the fire?"

"And the brouhaha over the road," Mark said. "Talmadge helped Locke with the environmental report."

Ginny laughed. "Cruz wanted to look at our guns. How stupid does he think we are? If we'd shot Talmadge or Bruder, we wouldn't have held on to the weapon."

"And you have alibis for Locke's murder, I'm sure," Jody said.

"We were driving home from Willcox when the fire started."

"Unfortunately, we didn't stop for gas or a meal along the way," Mark said. "My fault, as Ginny will tell you. She wanted to stop for ice cream in Bowie. I wanted to get home."

"But you must have passed someone on the San Simon road."

Mark shook his head. "Not that I remember. We were arguing."

Ginny's fork paused halfway to her mouth. She flashed Mark a glance I couldn't read, then said, "About ice cream."

Charley and I had finished. He raised his eyebrows and nodded toward the door. I tucked four dollars under the edge of my plate and picked up the bill. "My treat," I said, when Charley reached for it.

"I won't argue," Charley said, and pushed back his chair. It bumped Ginny Haydon's and she turned around, noticing us for the first time. A blush stained her neck and cheeks.

"Sorry," Charley said.

Jody's mouth snapped shut on whatever she was planning to say next.

"No problem," Ginny said. Her smile was forced. "Not enough room to swing a cat in here."

"You got that right." Charley settled his hat on his silver hair. "Afternoon, Jody."

"I didn't see you at the meeting last night, Charley." Jody's tone held an implied question.

"Raul and Joaquin were there. Figured two of us were enough."

Jody looked at me then. I could see the curiosity turn to recognition. "You were there, too," she said. "With Joaquin . . . and Ron."

It was like an electric shock passed through Mark and Ginny. Their heads turned as one. Mental gears clicked and whirred.

Jody held out her hand. "I'm Jody Lufkin. I own the Hoodoo Ranch." Her handshake was limp, contrasting oddly with her manner and voice.

"Frankie MacFarlane."

"Weren't you part of a group on the mountain this morning?" Mark said.

I smiled in what I hoped was a disarming manner. "We were looking at rocks. I teach geology in Tucson." I paused to let that sink in. "Is that your Winnebago parked over by Gray Mountain?"

"Yes," he said, not knowing how much Charley'd told me of the situation.

"Looks like you've made some nice road cuts."

"You like road cuts?" said Ginny.

"I like fresh rock exposures."

"Oh, well, you're welcome to check them out any time," Ginny said, as if trying to make up for her earlier faux pas. "Just stop by."

"Maybe I'll do that," I said, "if you don't mind my bringing the students. Your rocks are a little higher in the section than the ones they saw this morning."

"I don't mind at all—if you'll let me tag along," she said. "I don't know anything about rocks."

"Later this afternoon, then? After it cools off? We head home tomorrow."

"We'll be expecting you." Mark didn't sound pleased at the prospect.

Charley looked at Jody, who'd been quietly finishing a fruit cup. "Sorry to hear about Peaches," he said.

I was all ears. Maybe I wouldn't have to wait to learn what he'd had been holding back.

Jody set down her spoon, pushed the cup away, and said, "Who told you?"

"Carolina. When I called last night."

Jody studied her hands and said nothing. I hadn't a clue who Carolina was.

"He'd been on the wagon a long time," Charley said.

She sighed, looked up. "Fifteen years."

"What derailed him?"

Long pause. "He met Sam Bruder when he came out to talk to Dad about mineral rights. Even with his mind half gone, Dad knows more about mining in these parts than most anyone else."

"Mining talk set Peaches off?" Charley clearly wasn't buying it.

"Sam was a mean drinker. He and Dad had a few—well, more than a few—last week, after we lost the Strong Ranch appeal."

"One of your New Mexico properties?" said Charley.

"Yeah. It'll be surrounded by wilderness area and wild land. We won't be able to drive to the ranch, so it's useless—for cattle or for mining."

"I hadn't heard. I'm sorry."

"Thanks, Charley. Anyway, Sam came by to commiserate with Dad. I was out, but Peaches was there. Sam was a bigoted SOB, the kind of guy who sensed people's weaknesses and then worked them. He called Peaches an 'abo.' Rode him about, oh, every stereotypical thing that's ever been written about Indians. Said that if he'd been conquering America, Australia, or Africa, he would have eliminated all abos, wiped them clean off the face of the earth. Except for a few of the women. They were useful."

"Peaches has dealt with bigots before. Why didn't he just walk out?"

"He did. But Sam was too drunk to drive back to town. Peaches had to drive his vehicle while I drove the truck. Sam sent Peaches a case of Jack Daniels as an apology. I thought Peaches had dumped the bottles out or given them away . . ."

"You couldn't give him another chance?"

"He broke trust. He was watching Dad while I was at the meeting in Dragoon Wednesday night. When I got home, Dad was wandering outside, lost and confused. Took me an hour to find him. Meanwhile, Peaches was passed out on the sofa."

"I see."

"I'm sorry, Charley. I know how close you were."

"When did he leave?" Charley's tone was casual, but I sensed something urgent underlying the question.

"Thursday morning," Jody said. "He lined up a couple of job interviews closer to Ysleta. Sam Bruder came to the ranch for breakfast with Dad. Peaches caught a ride with him to the bus station."

"Peaches accepted a ride into town from Bruder, even after what happened?"

"It was better than walking. You know cowboys. If it

can't be done from the back of a horse or the seat of a pickup, it ain't worth bothering with."

A puzzled look crossed Charley's face, but all he said was, "I wish he'd called me."

"I figured he had, you being so close and all. But maybe he was feeling too ashamed to admit he'd fallen off the wagon."

"Maybe. Shame's a powerful thing."

"And maybe he'll call once he finds a new job. He's got to come back and collect his things. He only took enough for a few days away."

"Ysleta?" Charley said. "He took the bus to El Paso?"

She nodded. "He wants to be closer to home. I think he misses his family."

"It must have been hard for you to let him go after all this time," Charley said.

Jody looked down at the hat brim she was working with her hands. She blinked a couple of times. "Twenty-five years." Her voice was gravelly. "I was seventeen when you suggested Dad hire him. He's a top hand. Having Peaches here freed me to compete." She looked up. "I'll always be grateful to you, Charley." She took a deep breath and released it slowly. "You still interested in that quarter-horse mare?"

"The one Joaquin took a shine to? I thought you were going to train her for barrel racing."

Her fingers sought the hat brim again, smoothing and shaping the felt. "I changed my mind. Don't seem to have the time to train her properly. You sure you're looking for a mare? I've got a gelding for sale, too."

"I'm not going to race her. I'm just looking for a good quick all-around ranch horse. And I can breed her with Tulapai when the time's right."

Tulapai was Charley's quarter-horse stallion. He was named after an Apache drink of fermented corn. The name suited him. Only Charley, Joaquin, and Teresa could ride him. And maybe Raul.

"I see. Well, she's quick all right. But she's got a mind of her own . . ." Jody's sentence kind of petered off at the end, as if she were ambivalent about selling the mare.

"That isn't a drawback," Charley said. "Why don't I come by next week? Things are a little . . . busy, right now."

After her earlier hesitation, Jody surprised him with, "Next week's not good. How about this afternoon?" There was a note of urgency in her voice.

"I don't really—"

"I'm going to check on a water hole on the way home, but I'll be back at the ranch by two thirty." Urgency had morphed into desperation.

"All right. I'll see you then." Charley tipped his hat to Jody and the silent Haydons, and followed me into the store to settle the bill.

At the register, Harriet was paying for a bag lunch and a couple of Snapple iced teas. She smiled at us as she left, but didn't speak.

"Jody must need the money," I said when Charley and I were outside.

"I hadn't realized things were that bad at Hoodoo Ranch."

"Could that be the real reason she let Peaches go?"

"Maybe." He stopped abruptly.

"What's up, Charley?"

"When we talked to Kit this morning, Joaquin told us he'd recognized the gun you found up at Massai Point yesterday . . . I gave that gun to Peaches years ago."

"Why didn't Joaquin tell me?"

"Because he didn't want you any more involved than you were."

"That ship had already sailed, Charley."

"I know."

"Do you think *Peaches* killed Sam Bruder?" It didn't sound like the man I remembered.

"Doesn't matter what I think. Once he finds out, Paul Cruz will have to go after him."

"But if Peaches left the ranch Thursday morning to catch a bus for El Paso, how did his gun end up at a crime scene Thursday night?" I said.

"He could have waited, killed Bruder, then caught the later bus." Charley looked at the rocky ridges guarding Cave Creek Canyon. "Or he's still out there, in these mountains."

Charley's mention of the mountains triggered a memory. "Yesterday afternoon," I said, "Joaquin said Peaches saw a jaguar last week. He took it as a sign."

"Sounds reasonable," Charley said.

"But a sign of what? Danger?"

"More like a message telling him to take a look at his life, maybe see if there were areas where he wasn't being honest with himself—or others . . . He called me a few days ago. Tuesday, I think. Asked if he could use the sweathouse this weekend."

The sweathouse was a rough stone enclosure up the hill from the main house. Years ago, Charley, Peaches, and the boys had walled in an adit, a horizontal mining cut, leaving an opening that faced east. Below it, in a natural depression dammed by a rock wall, a spring welled up to create an artificial pool. They'd added rock benches to it over the years. They'd sweat for a while, then cool off in the pool, which was big enough to accommodate fourteen people. The males of my family had used the sweathouse whenever we came to visit. Teresa and I had been excluded, but we'd jump in the pool on hot summer days.

"Jody said she fired Peaches because he was drunk," I said. "When you talked to him on Tuesday did he give you any indication he was worried enough about something to fall off the wagon?"

"He was sober when he called. But he was out of harmony. He'd done something that didn't sit right, or he'd allowed something bad to happen without saying or doing anything to stop it. Maybe he started drinking again. I just don't know. But seeing the jaguar might have been enough to push him to get right with himself," Charley looked at the mountains again. "He wanted to talk with me. To sweat it out."

"But if he'd arranged to use your sweathouse this weekend, why would he change his mind and go to El Paso without telling you?"

"I don't know. I wish I did. Maybe I'll find some answers at Hoodoo Ranch."

So that was why Charley'd given in to Jody's pleading. He had another reason for wanting to visit the ranch.

"Jody mentioned Ysleta—that's the Tigua Pueblo near El Paso?" When Charley nodded, I said, "So Peaches was Tigua?" I was thinking of the roadrunner tracks.

"Tigua/Apache. He was born near Ysleta Pueblo. His sisters still live in El Paso. Once the police link the gun to Peaches, it'll be the first place they look."

"I'd start where he was last seen. Will we have time to drop off Esme and Harriet at home before heading over to Hoodoo?"

Charley grinned. "If we don't spend too much time at Ron's place."

"Then let's round 'em up and head 'em out."

16

Harriet and Esme were waiting on the far side of the CR-V, away from the café windows.

"Neither of us wanted a full lunch, not after that breakfast. So we're sharing." Harriet held up the brown bag. But when Esme offered four bills, Harriet said, "No, this one's on me. You can get the next one. You eat like a bird anyway."

"Time well spent?" I asked as Charley unlocked the doors.

Harriet and Esme grinned at each other but climbed inside before answering. "Oh, yes," Harriet said, closing the door. She handed Esme half a turkey sandwich. "I saw a magnificent, a lucifer, a couple of broad-bills, a plain-capped starthroat, and a bunch of females I couldn't identify."

"Harriet," I said. Charley cranked the engine as punctuation.

She laughed. "Okay. A couple was there, talking in whispers. Locals. A retired ornithologist and a gynecologist."

I touched Charley on the shoulder. "Bill and Mary Ochs," he said.

"That's right," Harriet said. "Mary and Bill. Anyway, when I asked them about the female hummingbirds, that kind of opened up the conversation. Then another birder came in, another local, though he's only been here a couple of years. I didn't catch his name. He started talking about what happened to Ron Talmadge last night—wanted to know more about him. I just listened."

Harriet paused to take a couple of bites of sandwich followed by swigs of tea. We were on the Paradise road, driving through a narrowing canyon between ridges of Paleozoic rock. The rocks on the east were a dip slope of limestone and fine sandstone. Here and there the surface of a bed showed old mud cracks or fossils. I wanted to stop and explore, but there wasn't time if we were going to check out Ron's place and make it to the Lufkin ranch by two thirty.

Harriet's information reiterated what I'd learned from Joaquin last night, with only a minor addition. Mary Ochs said Nadine died of pneumonia.

"That's odd," I said. "Joaquin heard it was cancer."

Harriet shook her head. "Pneumonia."

"Maybe it was both," Charley said. "Sometimes cancer patients are too weak to fight off massive infections."

Charley was right. That was what had happened to my grandmother the year before.

"But there was another odd thing about Nadine," Harriet said. "She believed she'd been cursed in Africa, that that's why their son was autistic."

"Nadine was a doctor," I said. "Surely she wouldn't believe something as irrational as that?"

"Bill said the same thing. But Mary insisted that whatever Nadine had experienced in Africa haunted her."

This was interesting background information, but I didn't see how Nadine or her death could have had anything to do with Ron's murder. She'd been gone two years. Whatever ghosts she carried died with her.

"What about you, Esme?" I said.

Esme wiped her lips with her napkin, crumpled it up, and tucked it into the brown bag. "Most of my time was spent in the library, though I bought a few stamps at the post office, too. Everyone was talking about the two murders."

"Which two?" Harriet asked.

Esme looked down at her notes, neatly printed in a tiny red notebook. "Dr. Talmadge's and the man we found on the mountain."

"Sam Bruder," I said.

Esme nodded. "They never referred to him by name, only as 'that DUC guy.'"

"They hadn't heard that the police are trying to connect Byron Locke's murder with the other two?" I said.

"I don't think they'd heard that it was murder," she said. "His name never came up."

"Did Joaquin's or Raul's?" I had to ask it sooner or later, might as well be sooner. "Do people know they found Ron's body?"

"Yes. And they know you and Joaquin found Mr. Bruder's body."

"They know my name?"

"Jed told a woman named Tammi. And he told her you're a geologist."

"Did you recognize anyone?"

"Not at first. I asked the librarian if she could recommend a book on local history. She pointed me to a book called," Esme looked at her notes again, "*A Portal to Paradise,* by Alden Hayes. I asked her if she had any information on when Nabokov was in Paradise, and she said to look for his wife's memoir in the UA library. She couldn't remember the wife's name. Anyway, I sat and flipped pages and took notes on what the people were saying. Want to hear them?"

"Yes," we all said together.

Esme said there were five people in the library—a librarian, one using a computer, two browsing the shelves, and one reading the paper. What they'd heard about us finding Mr. Bruder was pretty close to the mark, though they thought Joaquin was somehow leading the field trip, and they didn't seem to know that we were staying at Charley's ranch.

They thought Ron had walked home from the meeting and met his killer on the road. They'd heard he was still alive when Joaquin and Raul found him, that Raul did CPR while Joaquin went to a nearby house to use a landline. Their cell phones didn't work in the canyon. Tammi, the woman whose phone he used, was one of the women browsing the stacks. She said she didn't hear a shot or a car, but the wind was blowing pretty hard and her dogs were barking.

Esme paused. "This Tammi said Joaquin and Raul could have killed Ron and made up the part about CPR. She wouldn't have known the difference."

There was silence until Charley said, "And what did the others say to that?"

"The woman at the computer was the one we met in Portal yesterday. She wasn't wearing a hat in the library. I didn't recognize her till she started talking."

"Jody Lufkin," I said.

"Yeah, Jody. She asked if anyone had heard anything more about the fire that killed the lawyer. Nobody had. She said she thought it was pretty odd that Joaquin had found two bodies *and* been at Locke's trailer that night."

"Nice of her to add fuel to the fire," I said. Charley grunted assent. "Did Mark Haydon come into the library?"

"The man we saw with the binoculars this morning? Yeah. How'd you know?"

"Lucky guess."

"He came in with the red-haired woman we saw at the Winnebago."

"Ginny Haydon," I said. "His wife."

"Well, it was interesting. Everyone stopped talking when they came in, that's why I looked up."

"What did the Haydons do?"

"Jody Lufkin said she wanted to talk to them about something. She asked if they'd had lunch yet. They hesitated, but then said no. She left with them."

"They had lunch at the café. Charley got us invited over to her ranch after we leave Paradise."

Charley looked at me. "I wonder what Jody wanted to discuss with the Haydons?"

"It was something involving money and mineral rights." I repeated what I'd heard Mark say when he came into the café.

"Sounds like Jody's selling one of their properties— maybe East Ranch. With Peaches gone, she'll be hard pressed to keep several properties going."

"Maybe we should have stuck around and asked her," I said.

"If we'd stuck around," Charley said, "I might have put a knife into Ginny Haydon."

17

We stopped at the concrete bridge spanning the dry bed of East Turkey Creek. A blacktail rattler, awakened by the engine noise, flicked his tail in the shade of an Apache plume. A marine blue butterfly settled on a cluster of ground daisies. Nothing else moved.

Along the banks, cottonwood, juniper, and sycamore trees stood as silent witnesses, their noonday shadows as dark as those thrown by the full moon last night. But last night they might have hidden a killer.

At the far side of the bridge, a sagging polygon of yellow tape had been strung from a sapling and looped around three orange cones. Two of the cones had toppled over, casting the tape in the dirt. The polygon enclosed a dark stain. A tall votive candle flickered beside wildflowers, probably offerings from Ron's neighbors. The candle couldn't have been here long. A gust of wind would have put it out.

Sunlight slanted down. Heat waves shimmered, distorting the stain. It seemed as if Ron's death should have left more of a mark. But I felt nothing lingering in the atmosphere. The shadows today were just shadows, the stain just a stain.

"What *didn't* you tell Cruz about last night?" Charley said.

A slight breeze set the cottonwood and sycamore leaves dancing. The candle flame sputtered. I thought back. "When I stopped the car, Ron didn't get out right away," I said. "He sat very still with his eyes closed and his hands clasped in his lap. His breathing was even, as if he were meditating. He stayed like that, not moving, for a couple of minutes. Then a wind gust came downstream and rocked the car. He opened his eyes and smiled at me. He looked . . . I don't know how to describe it . . . joyful. But somehow I wanted to cry. He put his hand on my shoulder, then on my head for a moment. It felt like a blessing, a benediction."

Charley digested this. "Why didn't you tell Paul?"

"It didn't have anything to do with Ron's death . . . and it was personal."

"Fair enough. What happened next?"

"Ron opened the door and stepped out. But then he reached in, picked up my bag from the floor and set it on the seat. He smiled again and gently closed the door. As I drove away, he was standing there," I pointed to the stain, "at the Paradise side of the bridge, staring at the moon, still smiling . . ."

Silence followed my statement. Could Ron have known what was coming, I wondered? Was he preparing for it? Did he want that glorious full moon to be the last thing he saw?

Charley turned off the engine and left the vehicle parked in the middle of the road. I walked across the bridge. Below, East Turkey Creek was a jumble of bleached boulders awaiting the monsoon rains of summer. An acorn woodpecker glided by, followed by the rat-a-tat-tat of his beak on a cottonwood. A twig snapped on the opposite bank. I halted as if I'd been slapped.

A deer stepped from the shadows of a sycamore. A whitetail. The four-point buck paused, nose lifted, testing the air. His head swiveled sharply, staring down toward the bridge. Then he turned and trotted upstream. He stopped once, in a patch of shade, before bounding from sight into the thicker brush of the canyon. The wind sighed, sending up puffs of dust.

Charley, Harriet, and Esme joined me at the yellow tape. Ants were busy on the bloodstain and the flowers. A wind gust swirled, lifting the short hair on my nape, stirring dust into a small pillar that billowed up, then was gone. I felt an overwhelming sense of loss.

I knelt down. Ironically, the stain's shape resembled Africa. A branch of cane cholla with a magenta blossom lay where the Great Rift Valley would be. A bouquet of purple daisies marked Cape Horn. The pale white candle sat in the middle of the Sahara. I reached across the tape and touched the blood—I don't know why. The residue was warm, heated by the sun. Esme handed me a posy of white paper-flowers she'd collected from the bank. I placed them in the center of the stain. Charley knelt beside me, breathing a prayer in Apache.

"What did you say?" Harriet asked him.

"He wished Ron a safe journey," Esme answered.

"Look," Harriet said. A roadrunner had paused beside the Honda. Head cocked, he looked at us, then flicked his tail and disappeared silently into the brush.

"Wow," said Harriet, as Charley and I stood up. "I've never been so close to one. That was splendid."

"Thank you for the flowers," I said to Esme.

"You're welcome." Her voice was husky. She turned her face away. "While you check out the house, I'd like to look around the town, maybe talk to a few people. Would that be okay?"

Though Ron's killer might live in Paradise, I thought the town would be safe in the revealing light of day. All three murders had taken place under cover of darkness. But I wanted to err on the side of caution. "Not alone," I said.

"I'll go with you," said Harriet.

"As long as you're careful and keep track of each other."

"The buddy system," Harriet said. "I know it well."

Esme nodded and said, "Deal."

I looked at my watch. If we were going to drop off Harriet and Esme before heading to Hoodoo Ranch, we needed to get moving. "We'll meet you over there in thirty minutes." I pointed to a collection of mailboxes on the far side of the bridge.

They were out of sight before Charley and I reached the Honda. Ron Talmadge's property was on a hill at the edge of town. It was a secluded place, screened from the main road by a brushy slope dotted with cottonwoods, Emory oaks, juniper, piñon pine, and spruce. The dirt driveway led steeply up through a cut to a grassy clearing. At the back, a small hip-roofed home nestled against the ridge. Above the house I could see the black hole of an old adit burrowed into the Paleozoic limestone. The only sounds were the gabbling cries and whirring wings of a covey of Gambel's quail.

Charley and I sat in the SUV for a moment, absorbing the scene. A dusty, weather-beaten brown-and-tan Bronco occupied the carport. The house seemed suspended in a peaceful bubble, as if nothing violent had ever touched the place.

"What do you suppose he did all day, once Nadine was gone?" I said.

"He had his routine. Like clockwork. Each day he left home, followed Graveyard Canyon south to Portal. He'd stop by the post office, then the library, have a meal at the store, and buy a bit of fresh fruit for the trip home. If it was raining, he wore a yellow poncho. The library's only open for a few hours a day, so Ron had to time it just right to return one book and take out another. Never more than one. He had a long walk home."

"And once he got home?"

"Tended his garden and bird feeders."

"Do you know why he didn't bring Ronnie home after Nadine died?"

Charley looked at the silent house with its neat border of marigolds. "Guess he thought uprooting him would be too much for the kid. Plus, he took a lot of looking after. Ronnie'd just up and follow a butterfly or bird, anything that caught his attention, and then he'd be so turned around he wouldn't be able to find his way home. I helped out on a couple of searches. Found him eight miles away one time. Then he kept running away from us until Nadine and Ron got there. Nadine could work with him. Ron, not so much, especially as Ronnie got older.

"But earlier—" Charley paused, remembering. "I used to watch them together, looking at bird books and plants. Ronnie carried a field guide to insects with him every-where. Ron had to replace it every couple of years, it got so dog-eared."

"How old is Ronnie now?"

Charley thought for a minute. "Twelve, thirteen. About that."

"He's severely autistic?"

"Yeah. Pretty classic. Nadine had him tested when he was two, and again at three. He wasn't speaking. Lived on another planet. She took him to Tucson to work with specialists, but it didn't help. And it stressed him out so much she brought him home to Paradise. He never went to school. She and Ron taught him what they could. Ronnie liked art. They had it up all over the house."

"I'd like to see it," I said, getting out of the CR-V.

Charley and I walked up the steps and across a wood porch. Charley tried the handle. Locked. He found the spare key under a clay pot of jojoba.

"What's the cat's name?" I said.

"Spica. Nadine named her after one of the brightest stars in the sky. She's pretty reclusive—we may have to hunt for her."

"Suits me," I said.

We entered, calling her name. She didn't come running. That meant I'd have an excuse to explore—not that I'd ever needed one.

The rectangular family room was the oldest part of the structure. It dated back to the early twentieth century, the mining heyday of Paradise. The kitchen and privy would have been outside then. But the present kitchen, next to the family room, looked down on Paradise. Spica's food bowl was empty, her water bowl half full.

We made a silent circuit of the house, checking under beds and in closets. It didn't take long. Over the years owners had added indoor plumbing and electricity. They'd tacked on rooms as necessity demanded. The rooms were variably wood-framed, adobe, and straw bale, the last being the most recent.

Two cramped bathrooms, three bedrooms, and an office opened off a dark hallway. Spica's cat box was in the second bathroom. The office and family room walls contained floor-to-ceiling built-in bookcases with orderly journals and science books. It took all of two minutes for me to determine that Ron's relationship with Nadine had been unconventional. For one thing, they'd had separate bedrooms of long standing. All three bedrooms had twin-size beds.

Ron's simple, austere bedroom had white walls, off-white woven curtains and bedspread, simple brass standing lamps, and a brown wool blanket draped over a beige lounge chair. A small desk caught the light from one window. The extra-long bed fit under the second. A crucifix, the only wall decoration, hung crookedly at the head of the bed. I straightened it.

Charley opened the closet door. A narrow chest of drawers fit snugly on the left side. I yanked the chain to the overhead light. In the top drawer of Ron's bureau, I found a narrow stole and a breviary. The name inside the prayer book was Ian Ronald Talmadge, SJ. The date was 1968.

Ron was—or had been—a Jesuit priest.

"Did you know?" I said, handing the breviary to Charley.

Charley read the inscription, closed the book, and ran his hand over the black cover. "No. But it explains a lot."

The picture of Ron I'd assembled disintegrated, leaving me with more questions than answers. When had he left the order? Did anyone else know of Ron's past? Had he and Nadine ever married?

Perhaps Nadine's room held the key. I put the breviary away, turned out the light, and followed Charley into the hall.

Nadine's space was more feminine, with handmade quilts and pillow shams, soft shades on the bedside lamps, a sewing machine on the desk. No medical journals. But here, too, a crucifix adorned the wall. Nadine had been Catholic.

"We have a Jesuit priest, living as a silent monk, arriving at Byron Locke's trailer at the time of a deadly fire," I said, half to myself. "He gave me a sample of copper ore seemingly identical to one placed under Sam Bruder's tongue after he was killed at Massai Point."

"Ron Talmadge was not a killer," said Charley.

"Maybe not, but why was he shot and killed in Paradise? Because he knew too much, or saw too much?"

18

"I'll call Wyatt and Vicente," Charley said. Turning, he headed for the phone we'd seen in the family room. I followed more slowly. I'd wondered, at first, why a man who didn't speak still had a phone line, until I saw the computer beside it.

I tuned out Charley's voice and studied the family room. Here were the answers to my earlier question about what Ron Talmadge did with his days. All puzzles, all types, all the time.

Ron downloaded the *New York Times* crossword puzzle and did it in ink. There was a number at the top. 28:52. He'd timed himself. Sudoku puzzle books were stacked on one end table, crossword puzzle books on the other. He'd dated the pages as he'd finished them. All within the last year. I looked more closely at the dates. Nothing older than March 21. He'd done his spring cleaning less than two months ago, I presumed, tossing out old puzzle books, reducing the clutter. That would make it easier to discover what Ron felt was important—besides puzzles.

A swiveling Scrabble board sat on the coffee table. Four wooden tile holders, each with letters, faced the couch. Apparently Ron had been playing himself. But it wasn't a real game. All of the words were biological, some of them proper names. He'd been using the Scrabble board to construct a wordsearch puzzle like the one I'd seen at the library meeting Friday night . . . the last night of his life.

Ron had worked on his puzzles all over the house—at the kitchen table, in the family room, in his office. The kitchen table was a heavy old door, stripped and sealed, with four wrought-iron legs. At one end, facing the window over the sink, was a sky blue placemat, matching napkin, silverware, and midnight blue plate. The loneliness of that single place setting, waiting for Ron to come home, spoke volumes.

I shook off my black thoughts and turned back to deciphering Ron's life. Photographs leaned against books in the bookcases. Ron with colleagues, mostly, out in the field. The vegetation varied from lush, dense jungle and rain forest to grassland and desert. In none of them was he wearing Jesuit garb. In all of them he was smiling. He'd aged gracefully, his hair sliding from brown to gray. But where, I wondered, were the photos of his wife? His son?

"The boys are on it," Charley said, putting down the phone. "They've already compiled a list of cases Byron Locke was involved in, organizations he was affiliated with. They'd gone about as far as they could with him, and were about to start on Bruder when I called." He looked out the window. "Fifteen minutes, then we have to leave. I'll see if Spica's in Nadine's studio."

"I'll check the house again." I wanted to revisit the bedrooms. Something was missing.

The screen door giving access to the small backyard slammed shut behind him. I jumped. Loud noises in a dead man's house always give me the willies.

I went back to the bedrooms to confirm I hadn't seen photos. *Nada*, at least on display. In Ronnie's room I opened an old cedar chest at the foot of the bed. On top, a shoebox held small black sketchbooks—Ron's pen-and-ink drawings of plants, mountain scenes, and birds. And one tree, done over and over, as if he couldn't quite get it right.

Under the shoebox was a photo of a small woman, in profile, her light brown hair twisted into a knot at the back of her head. She wore a white lab coat. Behind her was a one-story white-washed building. The background looked like an African village. Children and mothers, so thin their bones showed in bas-relief, sat or lay in the dirt forecourt. In this photo, no one was smiling. A second photo showed the interior of a clinic or hospital. The same woman stood by the bedside of an emaciated man. Sores marked his dark face and hands above the white sheet. An AIDS clinic? On the back of the photo, in pencil, I found: *Nadine Deroucher and patient, Goma, 1994.* At least now I had a time frame for when she'd been in Africa—and a place-name.

There was a picture of Ron and Nadine, at a ship's rail, the sea in the background. Though it wasn't dated, I suspected it was taken not long after the first two photos, perhaps on their voyage home to America. Their shoulders touched, but the pose wasn't intimate. Her hair, loose and blowing in the breeze, framed eyes that were huge, haunted. Her mouth looked as though it would never laugh again.

At the bottom of the chest, wrapped in a sunny yellow baby blanket, was a photo album featuring a child—a beautiful child with red gold hair and bright blue eyes. In the baby and toddler photos, he was smiling and looking at the camera. I flipped through the rest, occasional pictures taken at Christmas and birthdays. In these he looked down or off to the side. In others he was painting, holding the brush at an awkward angle. Next to these were kiddie art projects, including a handprint cast in plaster of Paris, Ronnie's name scratched on the back. A faded blue satin ribbon ran through two holes punched while the sculpture was damp. Around the bottom someone had written *Happy Mother's Day*.

I rewrapped Ronnie's photos in the worn baby blanket, placed them on top of the other photos, and closed the lid. The room's bookshelf held children's picture books heavily weighted toward those with animals. And one tattered field guide to insects. Over the bookcase were two pencil drawings, no signatures. But I thought I recognized Ron's style. The first captured his son in profile, sitting on a beach, facing the ocean. Sand trickled through the fingers of his left hand. He was staring off into the distance.

The second drawing was of Ronnie sitting under a tree, his back against the trunk. He was looking at a butterfly that had landed on his hand. The sketch captured the wonder of the moment, and made me want to cry. What would happen to Ronnie now? Would anyone care?

Ronnie's bureau top held a collection of treasures—a 1930 penny, plastic lizards, a bug box with a 10× magnifying lid, and an assortment of dusty rocks and minerals, most of them copper-bearing. Three, I saw by the empty dust rings, were missing.

Had Ron given one sample to me, and one to Sam Bruder's corpse? Why? What meaning did they have for Ron? Had he used them to send messages? If so, the mes-

sages hadn't gotten through—at least to me. They'd certainly carried a message to Paul Cruz, linking me to crimes I hadn't committed . . . And where was the third piece? Still in Ron's pocket?

Ron's yellow field notebooks were on built-in bookshelves in his office. I opened the first one, dated 1963 on the spine. The name inside the cover was Ian R. Talmadge. The notes and drawings were from botany and field ecology courses at Fordham University. His drawings were exquisite. Opening the notebooks one by one, I was able to track his doctoral research in ethnobotany in the Southwest, and his teaching, research, and conference field trips during his years at George Washington University. His research led him to a sabbatical in the Congo Basin in 1993–94. All the later notebooks were from the research station in Cave Creek Canyon. I wondered why he'd left GW, and if he'd ever published the Congo material.

I pulled the Congo notebooks, three of them, from the shelf. He'd been using Jesuit schools in Kigali, Rwanda, and Goma and Bukavu, Zaire, as bases, but he'd spent months out collecting in the field. The plant drawings and descriptions in the first two were tied to photographs that weren't included. Latitude and longitude coordinates were given. The third notebook, beginning March 20, 1994, ended after thirty pages. Except for a short note indicating he was in Kinshasa, Zaire, on July 25, the last dated field entry was April 6. I couldn't remember why that date was important, but it rang some kind of bell.

As I was closing the notebook, something caught my eye. The edges of the last few pages were smudged. I opened the back cover. Nothing. But the page before the end had what looked like a wordsearch puzzle, shaped like the continent of Africa. No date. No list of words to find. It couldn't have anything directly to do with his murder, but it might help me understand Ron. I needed to study it when I had more time. Thumbing my nose at Cruz's strictures, I tore out the page, folded it in quarters, and zipped it into a side pocket of my field bag.

The back door closed softly. Footsteps sounded on the old plank floor. "You have to see Nadine's studio," Charley said from the doorway.

19

In the mud room, beside the back door, stood plastic bins of birdseed and cat food. A cat carrier sat on the washing machine. Charley filled a scoop with birdseed and carried it out to the feeder. I refilled Spica's food and water bowls in the kitchen and closed the door behind me. If Spica was inside, I didn't want her to escape.

The scent of star jasmine filled the air. Birds were calling from an oak tree in the center of the yard. It was the tree Ron had sketched, over and over. A tire swing dangled from a frayed rope. A ring of flowers, hemmed in by rough limestone blocks veined with azurite, malachite, and chrysocolla, encircled the base of the tree.

Ron had planted the flower bed some time after he'd drawn his son leaning against the tree, looking at a book. The altered limestone probably came from the adit dump above the house. The coarse texture of the rock contrasted with the lovingly tended garden. No weeds poked through the bark mulch that helped the soil retain moisture in this dry climate. And I could see where Ron had trenched the yard to lay an irrigation line.

"He mixed Nadine's ashes with the soil he brought in to make the garden," Charley said. "That was the last thing she asked for, this garden. She loved flowers."

Ron had chosen different flowering plants for each segment of the circle. Tiny white roses rubbed shoulders with dwarf pink oleander, African daisies with lemon-colored lilies. An iridescent green hummingbird sipped from aloe vera. "Roses for love," I said. "Lilies for remembrance. What's that purple flower with the furry leaves?"

"*Nama,*" Charley said. "Purple mat."

"A wildflower?"

Charley nodded. "He probably grew it from seeds he

collected. *Nama* doesn't transplant well."

"What will happen to Ron's remains?"

"Depends on whether he has kin," he said, leading me up a red-brick path toward the studio. Star jasmine clung to two trellises on either side of a turquoise-painted door. In the Southwest, Native Americans and Hispanics believe turquoise wards off witches.

"He never mentioned family?" I said.

"We talked about plants and birds and the weather," Charley said. "Come to think of it, we always talked more about my family than his, though he'd bring me up to date on how Ronnie was doing. But when he stopped talking, I stopped asking anything that couldn't be answered with a nod or a head shake."

"And pretty soon people forgot he could hear, I bet."

"Yeah. They'd just talk around him. He didn't seem to mind."

Charley had left the door ajar, but an edge like a fault scarp showed where leaves and dirt had piled up against the blistered paint. I pushed. The door opened with a scraping noise that seemed to echo off the cliffs above. I paused just over the threshold, overwhelmed by the chaos of the place.

The room had no windows. Light flooded through two rectangular skylights set in the pitched ceiling. After a short entryway, broad steps led down to a twenty-by-twenty-foot slate floor ringed by built-in cabinets of unfinished wood. Perhaps three hundred paintings were stacked on the cabinets or leaning against them. Easels supported half-finished canvases of varying sizes. But each painting had the same background, a volcano spewing black ash and streams of glowing lava that looked like rivers of blood.

"Nadine had issues," I said.

I flicked through a cluster of paintings leaning against the wall at the bottom of the steps. The artist's view was that of a balloonist gliding silently over the earth. In the left middle ground a few whitewashed buildings. Each painting focused on the hillsides and fields in the foreground. The dark-rust-colored soil was dotted with white, like a pointillistic rendering of a cotton field. But the dots weren't in rows, and the scale was wrong.

Weaving my way to a group of large canvases leaning against the east wall, I discovered different views of the same landscape, all untitled. Dots covered the roads, the spaces around the buildings. They resembled primitive studies in black, red, and white.

A paint-spattered rolltop desk sat in the corner. Clean brushes and tubes of acrylics filled the pigeonholes. A faint odor of mildew hung in the stale air. Taking a stack of small canvases from under the desk, I set them on the square of particle board that straddled two bar stools in the center of the room. These paintings were close-ups of black children missing limbs, of black women emaciated to the point of death. Their eyes were huge, devoid of emotion, as if their souls had been stolen, leaving behind empty husks.

I opened the drawers of the desk. More paint, more brushes, a crusty old palette. A cloud passed over the sun, changing the light on the large, incomplete painting nearest me. It stood on an easel next to Nadine's stool—the only chair in the place. Her coffee can full of brushes seemed ready for her day's work. The unfinished part of the painting had pencil sketches. She'd lost a lot of detail when she covered them with paint.

I looked more closely. I went back to the first stack I'd flipped through. "Charley," I said.

He was studying a painting of a child. "Hmm?"

"The white dots are humans."

"What?"

"They're rivers of humans, fields of humans. In places there are so many you can't see the ground."

I picked up a painting I'd thought was just an abstract study in red, black and white. "These are bodies, covered in blood, piled in mass graves. They have no face, no sex, no age, no identity."

I couldn't look at the paintings anymore. I went back to the desk. In the bottom drawer I found a journal. Opening the cover, I saw strong, bold, well-formed handwriting. The words were in French. Though my reading proficiency was good enough to get me through scientific articles, I'd never mastered idioms. But her entry was limited to one paragraph. Roughly translated, it said:

Ian believes it would help me to write down what hap-
pened, but I cannot. I have had this book for a year, but
each time I open the cover I am so overcome with fear
that I vomit. Maybe when my son is older, I will try again
to lift the stone and face what lies beneath. In the mean-
time, I will try to exorcise the demons with paint and
canvas.

The passage drew my attention to what wasn't in the room. "Charley?" He turned from thumbing through a pile of drawing pads. "Have you found any paintings of Ronnie?"

"Not yet."

"So Ron drew him, but his mother didn't. How very odd."

"But Ronnie was here with her."

Charley held up a sketchbook so I could see the artwork. The tarantula, rendered in perfect detail, seemed ready to crawl across the room. Charley flipped the page. The tarantula again, but this time a *Pepsis* wasp was stinging and immobilizing its prey. The art was unsympathetic, dispassionate . . . scientific. "Jesus," I said. "They're beautiful . . . But very different from his mother's work. Closer to Ron's plant drawings. Are you sure they're not his?"

Charley pointed to a crudely printed name in the bottom corner of the page. *RONNIE.* The *N*'s were backward.

"Do I have time to take some photographs?" I asked.

Charley looked at the angle of the light coming through the skylights. Charley didn't wear a watch. "Barely."

My digital camera was in my pocket. I clicked images of five of Nadine's large canvases and five of Ronnie's drawings of invertebrates. Sometimes photos emphasize details you miss the first time around.

I left Charley to close up the studio and went back to the house. I found the photographs of Nadine and Ronnie and snapped a couple of Ron's plant studies. Opening the back door again, I took a couple of views of the oak tree, just for good measure. Charley paused on the brick path to serve as scale.

"I'll give Jody a call and let her know we'll be a little late," Charley said. Our cell phones, of course, didn't work in Paradise. When we went back inside to use Ron's old rotary model, the kitchen clock said 1:30. A black cat with white paws was calmly munching her dried food. She didn't even look up. I went to pack up her food and litter and ready the carrier.

Charley's call was answered immediately. From eight feet away I could hear the sharp, high-pitched voice at the other end of the line. There was no greeting.

"Ron? *Ron?* No, wait—" Anger replaced fright. "Who *is* this?" Without pausing for breath she tumbled on. "If this is a joke, it's not funny. Whoever you are, you shouldn't be in Ron's house. I'm calling the police." The line went dead.

"Didn't figure on Caller ID," Charley said. Taking a red paisley handkerchief from his pocket, he wiped his fingerprints from the phone. "You touch anything?" He offered the cloth.

I took it, handed him the cat carrier, pointed to the containers of litter and food I'd set on the table, and ran to the bedroom to wipe down the top of the chest. I thought I'd been careful not to leave fingerprints on the items inside, but I couldn't be sure. There wasn't time to wipe them all down. Ditto with the edges of the paintings in the studio. I doubted they'd dust those for fingerprints, but I'd cross that bridge when I came to it.

"Why didn't you ease Jody's mind?" I said, as, cat carrier and litter box in hand, we reached the car.

"She didn't give me much of a chance."

I just looked at him as he stowed the carrier and box in the rear of the Honda. He'd already loaded Spica's water bowl and food.

"I don't know," he said. "Her reaction was odd. I wouldn't have thought she'd believe in ghosts. And I was caught off-guard. I was expecting the answering machine to pick up. She said she wouldn't be home for another hour."

I'd forgotten. Jody was going to check a water hole on the way home. She must have changed her mind. "Will you tell her you were the one who called?"

He shrugged. "Maybe. I'll see how it goes."

"Should be interesting."

Harriet and Esme were waiting at the bottom of the driveway. We were running late enough that we couldn't take them back to Charley's place first. They'd have to come with us.

"Have cat, will travel," Harriet said. Esme just smiled.

20

The fastest way to Jody Lufkin's Hoodoo Ranch was to go west through Paradise. The road up East Turkey Creek connected with Pinery Canyon Road near Onion Saddle. Charley turned right, aiming for the high country.

Paradise, a canyon community overshadowed by limestone ridges, had been settled in the late nineteenth century. A few houses flanking the track up East Turkey Creek were all that remained of the old town. The George Walker House, built by one of the town's founders, had become a bed-and-breakfast inn. The nearest restaurant was the Portal Café, where we'd eaten lunch. Paradise had no pizza parlor, no Starbucks, no general store. No tourist-grabbing sign announcing "Nabokov slept here." The closest gas station was a truck stop in San Simon, up north on Interstate 10. With the price of gas skyrocketing, I wondered how the residents could afford to live here.

Private driveways branched off the main track, leading to properties screened by low ridges of old stream gravel. Having just come from Ron's home, a place laden with secrets, I wondered if secrets lay hidden up these tributary roads, as well.

Harriet broke the silence. "We checked the creekbed near the bridge. Didn't find Ron's sketchbook. When we hit town, I took one side of the road, Esme the other."

"You split up?"

"And suffer the MacFarlane wrath? We stayed within hailing distance. I ran into a woman who was collecting rocks to build a fountain." Harriet paused to look at her notes. "Tammi—with an *i*—Barnett."

"The woman I saw at the library," added Esme. "She didn't hear any gunshots last night, but her dogs were upset."

"That's the one. I met her dogs. Three rescued grey-hounds." Harriet smiled. "Tammi's also the local psychic. She offered to read my palm."

"Did you let her?" I asked.

"No time."

"Did she say anything about last night?"

"That she'd just gotten home from walking the dogs when they made a beeline for the side door. Greyhounds don't bark much, but last night they were whimpering. She opened the door, but the wind was pretty strong, blowing downcanyon. The only thing she heard was a truck going by in front of the house a few minutes later. But there had been several trucks—returning from the meeting, she fig-ured—so she didn't think anything of it."

"No distinctive motor sounds?" I said.

"I asked her that. She said she's not a truck person. Can't tell one from another. Her husband could, but he wasn't home. And then, maybe twenty, thirty minutes later, Joaquin was pounding on her door and asking to use the phone."

"Did she say which way the truck was going?" Charley asked. "Towards the valley or towards the mountains?"

"I didn't think to ask her." Harriet considered for a moment. "But Tammi talks with her hands." Harriet ges-ticulated as if she were a traffic cop at a crowded intersec-tion. "When she mentioned the truck, her hand waved toward the mountains."

I looked at Charley. "So Ron's killer might live in Par-adise."

"Ron's killer could be Tammi," he said. "Or her hus-band, Norm. Did she say where he was?" he asked Harriet.

"No. But I doubt Tammi's the killer. I'm a pretty good judge of people, and she seemed to be telling the truth."

"Maybe, maybe not," said Esme. "I made it as far as the Walker House." She pointed out the side window at a forest green-painted dwelling. "The sign says the house isn't open, but you can look around the grounds. An artist had set up his easel at the corner of the lot. Sells his stuff on the Internet and to galleries all over the country." She looked at her notes. "I asked him about the local history and whether he knew of any property that was coming up for sale. That brought him around to what would happen to Ron's place. He said Tammi and Norm had had their eye on Ron and Nadine's property. They'd told the previous owner that if it ever came on the market, they wanted first crack at it. But suddenly Ron and Nadine were moving in. Stole it right out from under their noses."

"Interesting. Ron never mentioned that." Charley searched Esme's eyes in the rearview mirror. "How did Tammi and Norm take it?"

"According to the artist, Norm and Ron almost came to blows—at least Norm did. He has quite a temper. Ron tried to pacify him. When that didn't work, Ron took out a restraining order on him. Norm threatened a lawsuit. The former owner sold Norm the piece they're on right now, but that didn't help much. Norm still wanted Ron's lot. Something about the old mine above it on the hill. He thought Ron's lot carried the mineral rights with it."

Harriet clapped her hands. "Ladies and gentleman, we have motive."

"And opportunity," Esme said, "if Tammi or her husband was at the meeting last night."

"Even if they weren't," I said, "Norm could have waited for Ron to walk home."

"But why last night?" Charley said. "Ron and Nadine bought that property eight years ago."

"Because eight years ago, DUC—if it even existed back then—wasn't interested in buying up mineral rights in southeastern Arizona," I said.

I looked back at the houses clustered in the narrow canyon. Time might stand still here, but passion and greed didn't. Was the desire for land and mineral rights enough to push someone to murder a neighbor?

Yes. It always had been here in this corner of the Southwest.

Esme took a plastic sack from her daypack and began carefully sorting small glass beads in a channeled bead tray. Though the road was rough, and the Honda bounced from rut to rut, Esme's body swayed to absorb the jolts. She didn't lose a single bead. Her notebook, on the seat beside her, lay open to a rough pencil sketch. The pattern looked like letters on a white background.

"WWMMD?" I said, squinting at the sketch.

"What Would Miss Marple Do? It's a bracelet for Harriet." She smiled, her fingers deft and quick as she picked up beads with the tip of the fine, clear filament.

"I think that's the nicest thing anyone's ever done for me," Harriet said. "Thank you, Esme."

"Happy Mother's Day," said Esme.

21

Charley called Jody Lufkin on his cell when we reached the floor of Sulphur Springs Valley, warning her he was bringing a couple of guests along. He turned up the volume on his phone so I could hear her response.

"Fine." Her voice was matter-of-fact, not shrill or excited like her earlier tone. Charley shrugged, disconnected, and handed me the phone. But a frown creased his forehead as he put the CR-V in gear.

We hugged the east side of the valley and the mountain flank as the road curved past the turnoff to the Chiricahua National Monument. In the distance, at Apache Pass, the Chiricahuas met the Dos Cabezas Mountains. Locally, dirt tracks splayed off into the northernmost Chiricahuas. Charley chose a track entrenched by generations of traffic, from horse-drawn wagons to heavy trucks. About a mile in we passed under an arch of old logs from which hung a carved sign announcing "Hoodoo Ranch. Registered Herefords."

But we saw no cattle. On either side of the dirt road, the fenced pastures were brown from the drought. Up ahead, the road disappeared around a ridge of welded tuff that was fractured and eroded into a cluster of hoodoos. One pillar towered over the rest. Behind the ridge, at the mouth of a deep canyon, a golden dust cloud muted an oasis of green trees.

We parked in front of the house in the shade of a dusty cottonwood. The kitchen and flower gardens had been ploughed under at the end of last season and not replanted. The weeds between the pistachio and apple trees in the orchard were a brittle tangle, the trees themselves in desperate need of pruning. Everything seemed to be holding its breath, praying for thunderstorms that were at least a month away.

In contrast, the old two-story pitched-roof ranch house sported fresh white paint with green trim. The screens on the front veranda looked new. Bright orange and yellow lantana stood in huge earthen pots beside the steps, as if spots of color could counteract the effects of drought.

Jody opened the screen door of the veranda. Her smile was set. "Welcome to Hoodoo Ranch," she said, after Charley introduced Esme and Harriet. "I've made iced tea and lemonade. It's so hot I thought we could take it with us to the corral. Come on in."

She was right about the temperature. Ridges of pale volcanic rocks trapped the afternoon heat, reflecting it down onto the ranch.

"Mind if we bring the cat?" I said.

"Cat?"

"Ron Talmadge's cat," Charley said. "We picked her up on the way over."

Jody looked startled, as if she were making the connection between the phone call from Ron's house and our collecting the cat. But all she said was, "Well, you certainly can't leave her in the car."

The darkness within the house offered a welcome respite. Stepping into the parlor was like entering a time warp. Heavy Victorian mahogany furniture crowded the room. Though the louvered shutters were closed, light seeped through cracks and poured through the north-facing French doors. Elk, desert bighorn sheep, deer, and bear heads stared down from the walls. The trophy heads contrasted sharply with a collection of porcelain shepherdesses on the mantle above the stone fireplace. Black-and-white photos in tarnished silver frames decorated a Steinway upright piano that probably hadn't been played in twenty years. A moth-eaten jaguar rug, mouth snarling, lay before the hearth. I set the carrier by the door. Spica was curled up in a ball, asleep.

Harriet hunkered down to examine the rug. Esme turned away. Charley put a hand on her shoulder. She smiled at him.

"Where's Fritz?" Charley asked Jody.

"We had to put him down. He was deaf and blind—couldn't even find his food anymore." She brushed the corners of her eyes with her fingertip. "It about killed Peaches. He'd had him since he was a pup."

"When was this?"

"Tuesday. We took Fritz with us to Tucson. One last car ride. He loved car rides."

"Could that have triggered Peaches', uh," Charley searched for the right word, "setback?"

Jody looked surprised. "I didn't connect the two, but maybe that had something to do with it."

Charley waited, but Jody didn't take the bait and suggest that perhaps she could give Peaches another chance.

I looked away. At the far end of the room, an arched opening in the right-hand wall led to a small den. Though the lights were off, I could see more louvered shutters. A glass case full of trophies and ribbons occupied the corner next to the doorway. The trophies were for barrel racing. They bore Jody's name. All were more than ten years old.

"Fascinating place." Harriet stood up. "Who took the jaguar?"

"My great-grandfather, up near Massai Point," Jody said.

"Is Nate home?" Charley asked.

She gave a wry little smile. "Sometimes. He has more bad days than good, lately."

"I'm sorry," Charley said. "Does he welcome visitors?"

"When he's feeling well. But don't be surprised if he doesn't remember you. Most of the time he doesn't know who *I* am." Looking around the room, she said, "I left him here, dozing on the couch, not five minutes ago."

Voices cursed somewhere behind the house. "Shit," Jody said, and ran from the room. Her boots pounded on the hardwood floors of the hall, then softened to a muffled clip-clop. A door slammed. She shouted, "Jed? Rory?" from somewhere outside, in the back.

"I'd better see if I can help," Charley said. His booted footsteps were almost silent as they followed Jody.

I turned back to the trophy case. A hand snaked out of the darkened den and grabbed my right wrist. I jumped. The fingers tightened like a vise. "Jenny?" The raspy voice was urgent. "Is he hidden?"

An old man's head poked from the dark den into the relative light of the parlor. He was bald, except for a fringe of white hair just above his ears. His right hand held a double-barreled shotgun.

Harriet and Esme stepped to the side, against the wall. No screams, no hysterics.

"I'm not Jenny," I said. Under the circumstances, that might not have been the wisest thing to say.

"Don't play games." The man's grip tightened. "Did you do what I said? Is he safe?" It was little more than a whisper.

Outside the cursing stopped. The shotgun barrel lowered a mite. "Who?" I said.

"Keep your voice down," he hissed. "Cal, of course. I told you to stay with him in the hidey-hole till the posse left. Sounds like they got him cornered."

"No, he's safe," I whispered. "They won't find him." With my left hand I signaled to Harriet and Esme behind my back. I heard the rustle of cloth as they moved toward the hall, out of harm's way.

"Carolina?"

The movements halted. The old man glared at the women. I turned my head to track his gaze. Esme turned and stared calmly back at him.

"What'd I tell you would happen if you ever showed your face here again?" he said. He let go of my wrist and fumbled with his belt buckle. But he held onto the shotgun.

A whisper of sound behind me. Esme and Harriet were off to get Jody. A door slammed again as I backed away, bumping into Charley. He said, "Howdy, Nate."

The old man looked up, confused, glancing from Charley to me. "Let me help you with that," Charley said.

Nate looked down. "I may be getting on, but I can still buckle my own damn belt," he said. His hand shook as he pushed the tooled leather tongue through the buckle and found the hole with its metal bit. "See?" he said, as if he'd just roped and tied a steer, one-handed. "Slick as goose grease on a skidder. Who're you?" he said to me.

"Frankie," I said. "A friend of Jody's."

Another door slam. "Dad?" Jody's voice, in the hall, out of breath.

"Who's that?" Nate's face was pinched, as if he were trying to match the voice with a name.

"Jody, Dad." She stepped into the parlor entrance. Esme and Harriet were right behind her. "Your daughter."

"That's not funny. I don't have a daughter." He sounded angry. "Nettie couldn't—" he looked confused for a minute. "I don't have any children." A long pause. He looked at me. "Do I?"

"I'm Kendra's daughter, Dad."

"I don't know any Kendra."

"You married Kendra after Nettie died. Now put the shotgun down. You wouldn't want to shoot somebody by mistake, would you?"

"No mistake. I heard them," Nate said. "They're coming for Cal. I can't let them take Cal."

"Cal's safe in the hidey-hole," I said. "And the sheriff's gone."

"You're sure?"

"I'm sure. Didn't you hear them drive off?"

"Maybe." Nate lowered the shotgun.

"Why don't I lean that by the door?" I said. "Just in case they come back."

"Good idea, Jenny."

Nate handed me the shotgun. I passed it to Charley. He broke open the breach, ejected the shells, and held it out to Jody, who stood white-faced in the doorway. When she didn't take it, he gave it to Harriet. She and Esme carried it off down the hall.

"I'm tired." Nate turned back into the den, shuffling to a worn recliner by the window. "I think I'll sit down."

"Here, let me help you," I said, putting a hand under his elbow.

He shook me off. "I can do it myself, Jenny. Go tend to Cal. He has to leave tonight."

Once I saw Nate was safely seated, I turned to go. "Who're you?" he said.

My wrist throbbed, the bruises appearing as red marks that would soon be purple. "Frankie," I said to eyes that no longer looked confused.

"Hell of a name for a girl," he said.

I took a deep breath. "Yes, well, I'm a friend of Charley Black's. He's here to look at a mare."

"Charley's here?" Nate leaned to the side. "Hey, Charley. Long time no see. How're Rosa and the boys?"

22

Hoodoo Ranch
2:45 p.m.

The ringing of the phone brought Jody out of her trance. "Excuse me," she said. "I have to take that." She darted across the hall and into the dining room. I heard door hinges creak.

I left the two men visiting and made my way down a hall hung with photos and newspaper clippings of Jody's rodeo days. Esme and Harriet were seated at a long table. Pitchers of cold tea and lemonade sat on a wood-topped island in the middle of the huge country kitchen. I filled a glass with a mixture of lemonade and iced tea, my standard drink after a day in the field. I figured this qualified.

"I'll try that." Harriet stood up and set the shotgun on the table. "We were guarding it."

"Good idea," I said.

I heard Jody's voice coming from a smaller room connecting the kitchen with the dining room. I moved closer. The swinging door was open. The space seemed to be an old pantry, converted into an office. White-painted cabinets and counters lined the walls. A computer, printer, and phone sat on one countertop, portable file bins on the opposite one. Jody perched on the edge of a drafting stool, her back to me.

"Maybe later," Jody said. "I've got work to do." Pause. Sigh. "All right, if it can't wait. Come whenever. I'll be here. But you'll have to wait to question Jed and Rory till after the cattle are loaded."

I was leaning against the kitchen table when Jody came in. The sight of the shotgun centerpiece brought her up short. Using a chair as a stepstool she plunked the shotgun on top of the cupboard over the dishwasher, then replaced the chair. Dusting off her hands, she said, "Thought I'd sold all his guns. He must have squirreled some away. It's a never-ending battle."

Tense situations make me thirsty. "Who's Jenny?" I asked, refilling my glass.

"My aunt. Dad's older sister. Died years ago. You do favor her." She looked at the purpling bruises on my wrist. "Dad?"

"Yes."

"Sorry about that."

"Is Cal your uncle?"

She nodded. "Dad's younger brother. The proverbial black sheep."

"Nate was worried a posse would find him."

"That was back in 'thirty-eight."

"During the Great Depression," Harriet said.

"Right. The rancher who used to own Charley's place accused Cal of rustling. I don't know if it was true, but Cal dabbled in a lot of things. There's a still upcanyon where he used to make moonshine. Made him popular during Prohibition, but brought the law down on him. Dad and Aunt Jenny sent Cal away. He died on Omaha Beach."

Harriet nodded. "My dad died at Midway."

"That must have been rough." Jody took a plastic tumbler from a cupboard and filled it with ice. Using the chair as a stool again she pulled a dusty bottle of Jack Daniels from atop another cupboard, poured a generous slug into her cup, and held up the bottle. "Ladies?"

"No, thanks," we all said, though I noticed Harriet hesitated.

By the time Jody had replaced the bottle and the chair, Charley was standing in the doorway. "He's sleeping," he said.

"Thank God. We should have half an hour's grace." Jody waved at the iced tea and lemonade and said, "Pick your poison—unless you'd like something stronger."

Charley shook his head.

She shrugged. "Shall we have a look at the mare?"

Glasses in hand, we followed Jody through the mudroom, across the rear screened porch, and down the steps into the yard. This was the real heart of the ranch. A metal-roofed wooden barn, stable, various outbuildings, and corrals spread out toward the mountains. An old arroyo curved around the southern perimeter, but its bed was dry. The place smelled of horse and cattle; dust, urine, and hay.

At the back of the property, cattle were confined in two large holding pens. They were on their feet, milling and bawling. That explained the haze enveloping the ranch house and why we hadn't seen any cattle on the drive in. Jody made a beeline for an empty corral, stopping at a section of fence shaded by a cottonwood. But even here the heat enveloped us. Dust coated my skin. The noise and the golden glare were giving me a headache.

"Not enough grass on the lower range to feed them," Jody said, following my gaze.

"What about East Ranch?" Charley said. The question seemed innocent, but I knew he was fishing for information about Mark Haydon's comments at lunch.

Jody climbed the bars of the wooden fence, pausing at the top. "One of the wells at East Ranch is dry. And the grazing—" She winced as she swung her leg over the top bar.

"You okay?" Charley asked.

"Pulled a groin muscle." Lips compressed into a thin line, she settled her rear on the fence. The tightness about her mouth smoothed out, but her voice was bitter. "The grazing's no better there than it is here." She tipped her head toward the cattle pens. "So we're selling this lot."

"You're downsizing?" Charley said.

Her smile held no warmth. "That's one word for it."

"The rains will come," he said.

"I know. But it's not just the drought. You saw Dad. It's hard to take care of him and run a place the size of Hoodoo. Carolina's been here during the week, but now that she's quit . . . I've got to increase cash flow so I can pay a caregiver."

"You could—"

"No, Charley. I won't borrow money and I won't accept charity." Jody turned toward the stables. "Anytime you're ready, Rory," she called.

"When did you hire Jed and Rory?"

Jody kept her eyes on the stables. "I called them as soon as I fired Peaches."

"How'd he feel about selling the cattle?"

"He wanted to ride it out."

Rory and Jed came out of the darkness of the stable leading a mousy gray quarter horse with black mane, tail, stockings, and dorsal stripe. Charley's eyes lit up. "A grulla." He pronounced it *grew-ya*. "Pretty rare. Is she registered?"

Jody shook her head. "Grulla dam and dun sire—but the dun's dam was Morgan."

"Did they compete?"

"Barrel racing and calf roping. Both of them had good dispositions, agility, speed, and conformation. That's why I wanted her. But she'd make a good broodmare, too—or an all-purpose ranch horse."

A look of longing crossed her face as Jed opened the corral gate and Rory brought the mare inside. When she stood broadside to us, I could see a hint of olive in the gray.

"I raised her from the time she was weaned," Jody said. "She turned five last month."

Rory led the mare to the fence. Jody reached down, brushed the forelock off her face, and rubbed her delicate ears. The mare nuzzled her pocket. Jody pulled out a carrot and handed it to Charley. The mare's eyes and muzzle tracked the treat. Charley broke it into segments and held them out in his palm, talking quietly. She shied away at first, tossing her head and butting Jody's leg. Charley didn't move. I waited to see whether the bond with Jody or the desire for food would be stronger. Food won.

"Any training?" Charley said, stroking her cheek with his free hand.

"Ninety days. Pretty basic, but she started well. Peaches broke her to saddle, but I've ridden her, too. She's not a one-person horse. She loved Peaches—" She stopped. "Jed, would you grab her saddle?"

Charley said, "I don't really have time—"

"Please, Charley." Jody's voice held an insistent note I hadn't heard before. "I need to see you together . . . see if you fit."

Charley threw me a look and gave a little shrug. "Okay, let's do it."

Jed disappeared into the stable and came back with a worn western saddle. The grulla skittered to the side when she saw it. Jody climbed down off the fence and stroked her neck. Charley joined her, talking quietly in the mare's ear.

"She can be feisty," Jody said, "especially when she hasn't been ridden for a while. With the roundup, Peaches and I didn't have time to exercise her . . . But she doesn't spook easily on the trail." She looked at Jed who stood off to the side, holding the saddle. He ignored her. "Though I can't vouch for how she'll react with all the chaos out here."

She must have meant whatever had brought on the spate of cursing earlier, because Rory's face turned red. But he silently held the lead rope.

"What's her name?" Charley asked, smoothing over the moment. He ran his hands over the mare's legs and back, checked her teeth and hooves as she stood quietly.

"I call her Shoefly Jo." She spelled it for him. "She threw a couple of shoes the first week I had her. Overall, she's got a good temperament—loads easy, and stands for the farrier and vet."

"How's her mouth?" Charley took the bridle draped over Jed's shoulder.

"Peaches was gentle with her."

Charley took a couple of leftover horse treats from his pocket. The mare nuzzled his hand before accepting the treats. Charley nodded at Rory, and he slipped the halter off. Shoefly accepted the bit after a couple of tries. Once the bridle was in place, Charley handed the reins to Jody and took the saddle from Jed.

Charley didn't give Shoefly a chance to think. Within seconds the blanket and saddle were in place, and he was tightening the girth. Shoefly stood, tail swishing at flies. But as soon as Charley swung aboard, the mare started bucking. Charley stayed with her, even when she crowded the fence, trying to rub him off.

It'd been years since I'd seen Charley ride, but it was still a thing of beauty, an art form. Charley circled the pen until Shoefly quieted down. At Charley's signal, Rory opened the gate. Horse and rider trotted calmly around the house and out of sight as the dust settled in the corral.

"I have to check on my father," Jody said. "Care for some more tea while you wait?"

"I'll have some," Jed said.

"She wasn't talking to us, stupid," Rory said.

"I just moved here from Massachusetts," Harriet said. "I've never been on a ranch before—other than Charley's. Would you mind if I looked around?"

Jody hesitated. Her face looked so pale and drawn that the age spots and freckles stood out. "Of course not," she said. "The boys'll show you around."

Esme threw me a glance. I nodded. "I'll tag along and keep you company," she said.

They hopped down and headed toward the barn. Rory and Jed had to trot to catch up. I closed the corral gate. Jody held on to the fence for a moment, eyes closed, a hand pressed to her abdomen. Blotches of color stained her arms. Her head brushed the top bar. The hair looked coarse and dry.

"You okay?" I asked.

"Just cramps," she said, opening her eyes. "They'll pass in a minute."

"Let's get out of the sun." I offered my arm, but she ignored it.

Straightening, she turned and strode purposefully toward the back stairs. At the top, in the shade of the back veranda, she sank into a wooden rocking chair. It was as if she couldn't take another step.

"I'll get you a refill and check on your father," I said, taking the glass from her hand. Her breathing was shallow. "Can I bring you something?"

She nodded. Beads of sweat dotted her forehead and trickled down in front of her ears. "Vicodin. Upstairs, back bathroom. In the cabinet. Use the stairs off the kitchen."

The staircase was just to the right inside the kitchen door. I set our glasses on the island and took the stairs two at a time.

The bathroom hadn't been redone in at least eighty years. A large clawfoot tub sat to one side on a floor of hexagonal white tiles. The towels and walls were white. So was the ancient toilet, which had a water tank affixed high on the wall. A pull chain with cracked porcelain handle hung down. There wasn't a vanity, only a white pedestal sink with a medicine cabinet over it. The porcelain had broken off the metal fixtures. Scattered hand-braided rag rugs provided the only splashes of color.

The mirror on the cabinet door was smoky and spotted with age. On the second shelf were two prescription bottles—Vicodin, and a generic medicine, trazodone hydrochloride. The Vicodin was to be taken for pain, every six hours, as needed. The prescription was dated a week ago. The trazodone hydrochloride, prescribed a month ago, was for Nate. The bottle was half full.

I went down the front stairs. Nate was still asleep in his chair. I filled Jody's glass with water, mine with the Arnold Palmer mix of tea and lemonade, and took the glasses outside. She was leaning back, eyes closed again. "Jody?"

She opened her eyes. I held out the Vicodin bottle. "Oh. Thanks . . . Frankie, is it?"

"Um-hmm."

Jody shook out two pills and put the bottle in the breast pocket of her shirt. I handed her the water and then sat down in a plastic armchair. "You're father's still sleeping."

"Just means he'll be up half the night." She looked at my wrist. "Wicked bruises. There's ice in the kitchen."

"I'll be fine. Your father called Esme 'Carolina.'" I didn't mention the context.

"Carolina Cruz, Paul's mother. You've met Paul?"

"Yes."

She nodded. "Carolina came to us as a teenager. She helped my mother look after me during the summer. I was eight when mother died. Carolina became our housekeeper. Off and on."

"I'm sorry about your mother. What happened?" I don't know what I was expecting, maybe cancer or pneumonia or a fall from a horse.

"She killed herself." Before I could respond, Jody switched subjects. "Charley said you were visiting for the weekend. Where are you from?"

"Tucson. Harriet and Esme are my students. We're looking at rocks."

"You teach geology?" Her face, which had relaxed, became guarded.

"Yes."

"You must be the woman Jed and Rory were going on about yesterday."

"We met in Portal. They suggested I go to the meeting last night. It was . . . interesting."

"Peter does enjoy dropping the odd bombshell."

I took advantage of her opening. "You know him then?"

"Peter grew up in Bisbee. He and Linc Chapin used to work for Phelps Dodge. They're old friends of Dad's."

I remembered the DUC men at the meeting last night. I now understood why they'd seemed so friendly with Jody. I said, "Nate worked in the industry?"

"He dabbled, buying up old claims and mineral rights and such." Jody brushed gray horse hair off her pants. "Peter's an odd choice for a public relations rep. He's not much of a public speaker."

She'd used "odd" in the same sentence with Peter's name twice in the space of a minute. I wondered if that meant anything. "He did okay last night."

"I guess. Is that what you do—mining geology?"

"No. I teach introductory courses." I realized we were each trying to direct the conversation down a different path. I decided to steer it back to my topic. "If Chapin and Prebble are both local, I'm surprised they didn't take a more tactful approach to DUC's exploration plan."

The lines around Jody's eyes tightened. "That was Sam Bruder's idea. He even wrote the letter."

"Oh?"

"Linc and Peter wanted to go in softly, see if they could build up some support before they lowered the boom."

"Sounds like a good plan. Had Chapin known Sam Bruder long?"

"Five years—maybe longer. Sam started DUC and later recruited Linc to head up the exploration arm of the company. Local copper had taken a nosedive. He was looking for a new job."

"What was Bruder like?"

Jody hesitated so long I thought she wouldn't answer. "A man who always got what he wanted," she said at last.

"I know the type."

"Except this time—" She looked down at her empty glass, as if it held the answers to all the questions in the universe. Or at least to Bruder's death.

I waited. Hoofbeats sounded on the dusty road. Abruptly Jody stood, setting the empty rocking chair in motion. I stood, too. She was easily eight inches shorter. She took a step back. "Except this time?" I prompted.

"This time Sam pushed somebody too far."

23

The hoofbeats slowed to a walk as they approached the ranch house. Charley came around the corner riding a lathered Shoefly Jo.

"Got company," Charley said, tilting his head toward the road.

"Paul?" Jody looked at her watch.

"Yup." Charley swung his leg over the saddle and dropped lightly to the ground.

"Shit." Jody skipped down the steps. The painkillers, or adrenaline, must be working. She ran a hand down Shoefly's nose. "Well?"

"I'll take her—if the price is right."

"We'll work something out."

When Jody took the reins from him, Charley said, "Peter Prebble and another man ran into trouble out on the road."

"What kind of trouble?"

"Two flat tires. And their cell phone's not receiving. I offered to go back and pick them up in the Honda so they could use your landline—if that's okay with you."

"Paul couldn't help them?" Jody sounded cranky.

"Doubt if he saw them," Charley said. "He's coming from the south. They're in a dip, just north of your cutoff."

I heard an SUV pull up out front. A door closed.

"Of course it's okay." Jody handed the reins back to Charley. "I'd better go meet Paul. Would you ask Rory to brush down Shoefly?"

Jody took the steps two at a time and flung open the screen door to the veranda. I wasn't sure whether to follow her into the house or stick with Charley. He sensed my indecision. "Be interesting to know what Cruz asks her," he said.

I smiled. "I'll go offer him some tea."

It was Charley's turn to smile. "While I'm gone would you call Rosa and see if we've got thirty-five hundred bucks in the business account?"

"How do you know that's what Jody'll ask?"

"That's as much as I'm willing to pay."

We parted as the afternoon breeze rustled the cottonwood trees. In the kitchen, I filled a clean glass with iced tea and picked up the plate of cookies. I wondered if Paul Cruz had eaten anything other than biscuits and honey all day. Adding cookies might just overload his system.

Outside, I heard the sound of Charley's Honda turning around in the front drive. Voices came from the dining room, so I headed in that direction, making no effort to be quiet. Conversation ceased when I entered. Paul Cruz, seated with Jody at the dining room table, seemed unsurprised to see me here. I set the tea and cookies in front of him.

Cruz picked one up. "These look like my mother's peanut butter–chocolate chip cookies."

Jody nodded. "She made them yesterday. You know how Dad likes his sweets."

She sent me a look that said it was time for me to skedaddle. I held my ground, and said, "May I use your phone?"

"In there," she said, pointing to a swinging door standing open at the end of the wall. "Close the door, will you?"

As the door swung shut behind me, Cruz said, "If I remember correctly, Nate used to like the raw dough as much as the cookies."

"Still does," Jody said, voice muted but clear. "He can demolish an entire batch before they get to the oven. Carolina always puts half the dough in the freezer so he won't find it when he's wandering around in the middle of the night."

"That never stopped me," said Cruz.

"I know . . . We had some good times on this ranch, didn't we, Paul?" Her tone was wistful. "Pity things had to change."

"Nate thinks in black and white, Jody. To him, I'll always be the son of a wetback. He only tolerates my mother because . . . well, you know."

"Carolina quit yesterday. Again. I don't know what I'm going to do without her. Dad's pissed off every other caregiver I've brought in. Word's gotten around. He's toxic."

"Maybe there's somebody new in town. I'll ask. Barring that—"

Jody interrupted with a hard, dry laugh. "Dad insists he'll die at ninety-five in some young woman's bed—not in a nursing home, surrounded by strangers."

"How old is he now?"

"Eighty-eight last month."

"He won't last that long . . . He can't." Cruz's voice was soft. "Question is, can you take seven more years of this?"

In the silence that followed, I surveyed the small room. A feedstore calendar hung crookedly on one upper cabinet door. A small corkboard was screwed to another. A letter from DUC, announcing their exploration plans and the meetings in Dragoon and Portal, was pinned to the board. It was dated February 15. A large question mark had been scrawled across the letter with a red felt pen.

Beside the computer sat a phone with several extensions. Extension number 2 was blinking. I pressed the red button and lifted the receiver. Jed's voice said, "I don't think so. I've just started—"

A woman's voice cut him off. "Norm's got a delivery in Silver City tomorrow. He'll stay over to install it. He always does." I could hear a dog making soft, swallowed baying sounds in the background. Her voice turned away from the phone as she said, "All right, Pepper. I'm coming." She turned back to the phone. "Gotta walk the dogs. If you can't make it tomorrow, then forget it."

"But—"

The line went dead. I heard Jed slam down the phone.

Curiouser and curiouser. Jed and the Tammi from Paradise? Or is there another Norm in the area? Charley will know.

I dialed Rosa's number. She answered on the second ring. The funds were in the ranch account if Charley wanted to write a check. And Jamie and Teresa had been delayed in Tucson. But they were on the road.

I disconnected, but kept talking as if I were still on the

phone. And while I talked and pretended to listen, I searched.

The only item in the wastebasket was a newspaper ad for a gun show at the Tucson Convention Center during the last weekend in April. Had Jody gone to Tucson last month to sell Nate's guns?

I turned the calendar back to April. The Friday of that weekend was circled, *TCC* written in black ink. I quietly rifled through the drawers below the phone and computer. There was a receipt from Enrique Mendoza, dated April 30, for one gun. Underneath the receipt was a bill of sale, also signed by Enrique. He'd paid Jody one thousand dollars for five guns—two rifles, a shotgun, and two pistols.

I flipped the calendar back to May. The meetings with DUC on Wednesday and Friday nights this past week had been entered in red. Tuesday's square noted an appointment: *Reynolds—3 p.* On Tuesday Jody and Peaches had driven to Tucson to put down the dog, Fritz. Was this the vet appointment?

I hadn't a clue. But on Thursday, at seven, Jody—or someone from the Hoodoo Ranch—had another appointment, either with someone named *R* or at a place beginning with *R*. Was that seven a.m. or p.m.? Did the initial stand for the Reynolds noted on Tuesday, or was it a different person or place?

Thursday bore a second note: *Call Jed and Rory.* So Peaches must have left on Thursday, at the latest. Why hadn't he called Charley to cancel their weekend sweat bath?

I'd forgotten I was supposed to be listening to the conversation in the dining room. The interview had been going on for a few minutes, but they'd kept their voices low. I stepped closer to the door.

"You still own firearms?" Cruz was asking.

"I sold them all to Enrique a couple of weeks ago. I've got a receipt somewhere."

"Could you find it?"

"In the office."

I heard a chair creak. I said a loud good-bye to Rosa and hung up as Jody entered the office. I think she'd forgotten I was there.

"Everything okay?" Jody asked.

Paul Cruz stood behind her, leaning against the door jamb. A faint smile touched the corners of his lips. Or maybe I imagined it.

"I called Rosa," I said. "Looks like Charley can write you a check for the mare, once you come to an agreement."

Relief crossed Jody's face. She looked younger. "Excellent. Excuse me, will you?" She pointed toward the drawer I'd just checked.

"I'll go tell him," I said, moving out of her way. I stepped through the kitchen door and stopped around the corner.

"Have you talked to Enrique yet?" Jody said to Cruz as she rifled through the contents of the drawer.

"He's next on the list." A pause. "But it's getting late. It'll have to wait till tomorrow."

I moved to the island, picked up my glass. I was refilling it when gunfire erupted outside.

"God damn it. Those boys—" Jody blew by me on her way out the back door.

I saw Paul Cruz slide his gun back into the holster. From the front of the house came the sound of something—or someone—falling. I ran toward the sound. Cruz took the route through the office.

The cat was kicking up a fuss in the parlor, but otherwise the room was empty. "What the hell?" I said, bending down to shush the cat. She stopped crying, yawned, licked her face, and curled back into a ball.

"They're coming, Jenny."

Nate's hoarse whisper came from the shadows of the den, just beyond the doorway. A stray beam of light glanced off a gun in his right hand. *Shit.* It looked like a brother to Enrique's old Colt .45. Nate might be unsteady on his feet, but the muzzle of the gun didn't waver. It was pointed at the front door. I stepped to the right, out of the line of fire.

Cruz had stopped in the dining room. He couldn't see Nate from that vantage point, and Nate couldn't see him. Just as well. I didn't want to be caught in a cross fire. But I did want to warn Cruz that all wasn't well.

Since Nate's mind had again retreated to the past, I opted to play along. "No, Nate. They've left. You can put the gun down."

My peripheral vision caught the movement as Cruz slid his sidearm back out of its holster. He took one silent step toward the hall, then another.

"I heard gunfire," Nate said, but he seemed uncertain. The rear yard was silent now, except for the bawling of the cattle.

"Just Cal, practicing out back."

"Stupid boy." Nate shook his head and lowered his revolver. "The sooner he leaves, the better. I'm tired of the law nosing around."

I was curious. "What could they find, Nate?"

Nate laughed. "Cal said he hadn't finished branding the last bunch."

Ever since I'd entered this house, I'd felt as if I were in an alternate reality. Time and place converged in a tension-laden *Now*. The living and the dead coexisted on a plane as convoluted as a Möbius strip. A different kind of normal. A different kind of intrigue. Had Hoodoo Ranch been built on rustling? There was only one way to find out.

"People are talking about how big the herd's getting," I said.

"So? I'll sell off a few head. We could use the cash." Nate was looking at the gun in his hand, as if wondering where it had come from.

Paul Cruz was standing motionless behind me. I hadn't been aware of him moving into position. He put a hand on my shoulder, pointed to the back of the house. His other hand held his pistol.

I stepped to the side and said to Nate, "I'll go tell him."

"Tell who?" said Nate. "Who're you? And who's that with you?"

"I'm Frankie," I said. "A friend of Jody's."

Paul Cruz stepped in front of me, saying, "How're you doing, Nate?"

"Paul? Tell Carolina I'm hungry."

"Mom's not here."

"Not here? When's she coming back?"

"She's not coming back."

"She can't quit." The gun waved around. "Call her. Tell her she can't quit."

"I can't do that." Cruz stepped closer to Nate. His voice was level, easy. "But why don't you put that gun down and ask her yourself."

"I will." Nate looked around his den. "Where's the damn phone?" When we didn't answer, he said, "Guess I'll have to use the one in the office."

Nate set the gun on the recliner, grabbed a four-footed cane that had been standing beside it, and shuffled toward the dining room. Cruz picked up Nate's revolver and quickly slid it under the chair. His own gun was back in its holster.

"Peaches?" Nate yelled.

"Peaches left," Cruz said. "He's looking for another job."

Nate turned confused eyes on us. "Yeah. That's right. Guess I'm just used to having him around." At the office door, he stood for ten seconds, unmoving. He turned his head and looked at Cruz. "What was it I was going to do?"

Cruz seemed at a loss for a moment. "You were heading to the kitchen for a snack," he said.

Nate's eyes cleared. "So I was. You eating with me, Cal?"

Cruz flashed me a look. "Sure," he said. "Just a quick bite."

"Roast beef sandwich, that's what I want." Nate laughed as if it was the funniest thing in the world. "Our neighbors have been generous this spring." Wiping tears from his eyes, he led the way into the kitchen. Plunking himself down in the chair at the end of the table, he said to me, "Two roast beef sandwiches, Jenny."

Cruz sat down, a little smile on his face. "Sounds good to me, Jenny."

I was the serving wench at the Mad Hatter's tea party. But I couldn't see a graceful exit. I shrugged, found roast beef and condiments in the refrigerator and white bread in a box on the counter. Three minutes later I plunked the sandwiches in front of the two men. "Who're you?" Nate asked.

"A friend of Cal's."

"My little brother does have a way with the ladies." Nate's faded gray eyes twinkled as he took a bite of the sandwich, chewed twice, and swallowed. He took another bite. "You make a mean sandwich, Cal's friend."

"Thanks."

Jody stomped through the back door. Esme wasn't far behind. I wasn't sure what had happened to Harriet.

"Sorry about the ruckus," Jody said to the room. "The boys were just giving your students a bit of target practice." Her face was flushed, her voice shook. She got a glass of water from the tap at the sink, keeping her back to the room, shoulders rigid.

I didn't blame her for being angry. Caretaking a loved one with Alzheimer's and dealing with hired hands who took potshots around a cattle pen would strain anyone's reserves.

Jed and Rory wisely stayed with the cattle. Through the kitchen window I saw them opening gates between connecting pens, herding the cattle into two corrals closer to the house. Bellowing marked their progress. Dust hung thick in the air beyond the veranda.

"Everyone okay?" I asked Esme in a low voice.

"Oh, yes. We both managed to hit the target. Rory and Jed are great teachers."

Nate snorted. "Waste of good ammunition, if you ask me."

"Harriet?" I said to Esme.

"She'll be along in a minute. She had to retie her boots."

Harriet came up the back steps just as the front door opened.

24

Boots scraped on the sisal welcome mat outside the front door. "We're in the kitchen," Jody called.

Footsteps in the hallway. Peter Prebble and geologist Linc Chapin followed Charley into the room.

"Howdy, Linc. Peter. Sorry about your car troubles," Jody said. Her tone had a forced brightness, as if she weren't used to having her home invaded by so many people at once. But she smiled as she added, "You know where the phone is."

"Thanks, Jody." Chapin nodded a hello toward Nate on his way into the office off the kitchen.

"Sorry to intrude," Prebble said.

I expected Jody to reassure him that they weren't. She didn't, which struck me as odd after their friendly exchange at the meeting last night. She made no move to introduce Prebble to her other guests. An awkward silence descended, broken only by Chapin's muted, one-sided conversation.

"They'll send someone," he said, coming back into the room. "Should be here within the hour." He went over to the island and poured himself a glass of tea. He didn't ask permission.

"We can wait at the car," Prebble said. The fluorescent ceiling lights exposed gray roots in his ash brown hair. His wrinkled tropic-print shirt, khaki pants, and face were damp with sweat, his brown eyes bloodshot.

"Don't be silly, Peter. It's hotter than hell out there." Jody moved to the island. "Tea or lemonade?"

"Tea," he said.

Paul Cruz had been watching the exchange with interest. Now he stepped forward. "I'm Detective Cruz," he said to the men. "I spoke with you on the phone yesterday, when you reported Mr. Bruder missing. I was just about to call you both."

"Oh . . . yes." Prebble seemed taken aback, but recovered quickly. "Found his killer yet?"

"Not yet," Cruz said. "And I need to ask you a few questions. How about right now, since we're all here?"

Put on the spot, Prebble said, "I'm not comfortable answering questions without counsel present."

The tension in the room ratcheted up a notch.

"That's your right, of course," Cruz said, making a note in his little black book. "We'll conduct the interview at headquarters then." He looked at the calendar in his cell phone. "Tomorrow morning, nine o'clock." He handed Prebble a business card with the address. "You know where that is?"

Prebble tucked the card in his shirt pocket without looking at it. "Of course. Bisbee's not very big."

"And you, Mr. Chapin?"

"It's Dr. Chapin," Prebble said.

Nate Lufkin had finished his sandwich and moved on to a bunch of seedless red grapes. But at this he paused with his mouth open. His eyes narrowed. Watching him was like watching a lightbulb flick on and off at the whim of a hyperactive three-year-old. At the moment, the filaments glowed.

"Hey Linc, hey Pete," Nate said. "You here to talk business?"

"Nope. We're good, Nate." Chapin's shoulder had been holding up the doorjamb. Now he pushed away from the wall and said to Cruz, "I've got nothing to hide. I'll answer your questions."

"Fine," Cruz said. "May we use the dining room again?" He directed the question at Jody, but her father answered.

"Only if you'll tell me what the hell's going on."

Chapin looked from Nate to Jody, eyebrow raised. He had a lean build, all muscle, no fat. A triathlete's body. Buzz-cut gray hair, almost like a soldier's. His aqua knit shirt enhanced his large, piercing eyes.

"I haven't told him," Jody said.

"Haven't told me what?" Nate's eyes narrowed.

"About Bruder," Chapin said.

"Get to the point, man. I haven't got all day."

Prebble hid a smile behind a cough.

Chapin sent Prebble a warning look and said, "Sam was murdered Thursday night. Up at the monument."

"Don't look at me," Nate said. "I was here all night." The light flickered behind his eyes. He looked at Jody. "Wasn't I?"

Jody picked up his plate and carried it to the sink, turning her back on the group. "Where else would you be, Dad?"

"I don't know," Nate said. "Any more of those cookies?"

I retrieved the cookies from the dining room, offering them to Cruz and Chapin as they passed me in the office. Chapin took two. Cruz closed the door behind them

The top of one of the file bins was open slightly. Had Chapin taken a leaf from my book and rummaged through the files as he spoke on the phone?

Harriet stepped into the doorway. "Diversion," I whispered and handed her the plate. She nodded. The door swished shut. I heard her say, "Well, Charley, what did you think of Shoefly Jo?"

I smiled. That should occupy them for a minute or two. I lifted the top of the file bin. One file stood a little askew. The label said *Down Under Copper*. The folder was empty. I closed the bin softly and slipped into the kitchen just as Charley said, "—feisty. But she seemed to enjoy the workout."

A wistful look crossed Jody's face. The mare was her baby.

Charley noticed. "I don't think she's fickle, like Jezebel was." He'd raised Jezebel from a filly. She'd died last winter at the ripe age of thirty-five. "She's just curious. It'll take a while, but I think we'll come to an understanding."

"She would have made a great barrel racer," Jody said.

"Want to reconsider?"

Jody shook her head. "It's now or never. Let me print out a bill of sale, and we'll dicker on the back veranda." She went into the office. I heard the printer humming. She must have boilerplate forms on the computer.

As the screen door closed behind Jody and Charley, Nate said, "I need to take a piss."

Esme, Harriet, and I looked at Peter Prebble. He sighed, looked resigned. "Need a hand up the stairs, Nate?"

"Just this once."

Prebble walked around the table, gave Nate his cane, and helped him to his feet. I slipped back into the pantry office, leaving Harriet and Esme holding the fort in the kitchen. As before, the voices in the dining room carried clearly through the cracks around the swinging door. A part of me felt guilty for eavesdropping, but it was shouted down by common sense. Joaquin and Raul were suspects. Any information could be important.

"—last see Mr. Bruder?" Cruz was saying.

"I already told you that. It hasn't changed."

"Remind me."

Linc Chapin had last seen Bruder on Wednesday night. The meeting in Dragoon broke up about nine. Bruder drove the Escalade to his motel in Willcox. Peter's sister picked him up and took him to Tombstone for the night. Chapin drove the Lexus back to Tucson. He had meetings scheduled for Thursday. He wasn't due to return to Willcox till Friday afternoon. They'd planned to drive together to the Portal meeting that night.

"When was Mr. Prebble scheduled to return to Willcox?" Cruz said.

"Thursday afternoon or evening, in time for dinner with Bruder. They were going to visit a few properties on Friday."

"Do you know if Mr. Prebble returned on time?"

"Peter called me Thursday night. Said they'd had a shitty dinner at the café next door."

"Riva's Café?"

"Right. It had changed cooks since the last time we were here." Chapin paused. I could hear the amusement in his voice as he added, "Peter couldn't wait to get back to Tucson."

"Did he say anything else?"

"That Bruder'd gone off to find a liquor store."

"Bruder was a heavy drinker?"

"About average, from what I've seen of Australians. He could put it away. But it didn't seem to affect him much."

The silence lasted a full minute. "Did Bruder ever—" Cruz paused again, searching for the right words. "Did

Mr. Prebble say anything that would indicate that Bruder was after more than liquor last night?"

I heard the swish of the kitchen door opening behind me. Prebble paused when he saw me standing there. But he slipped into the room and let the door swing shut. I wondered where he'd left Nate.

Nervous energy emanated from Prebble in waves, filling the small office. Should I stay, or go? To hell with him. I was there first. I turned my back to him and focused on the voices in the dining room.

Chapin laughed, a robust sound that came from deep in his chest. "Cigarettes, you mean?"

"Companionship."

"That's a nice way to put it."

"Well?"

"Bruder was always after more than liquor . . . But yes, Prebble said Bruder had a lead on a date."

"Meaning a woman?"

"The more the merrier."

"Where'd he find them?"

"Bars, grocery stores, fast-food places, upscale restaurants. He read people like you read a book. He could zero in and cut a woman out of the pack, or . . ."

"Or just bring home the whole pack?"

"A time or two."

"Ever pick one up on a corner?"

"If he were that desperate, he'd call an escort service or visit a massage parlor."

Cruz paused again. "To your knowledge, had one of Mr. Bruder's liaisons ever led to his being arrested?"

Someone was tapping on a hard surface—Prebble, flicking his finger against the desk. I looked pointedly at the finger. He stopped.

Now it was Chapin's turn to pause. "As far as I know, this was Bruder's first trip to the U.S."

"Interesting. Then where did you meet?"

"At a conference in Canada, five years ago."

"Where in Canada?"

"Toronto."

"Was that where he met Mr. Prebble as well?"

"No. Prebble was working for an Australian mining

company at the time. The same company Bruder was working for. Prebble introduced us."

"Bruder found the capital to break away and start his own firm?"

"With a little help from me."

I shot a quick glance at Prebble. His face was taut with shock.

"You were willing to invest after one meeting?" said Cruz.

"I'm a gambling man."

Cruz must have sensed that this line of questioning was going no place. He changed tack. "Tell me about the meeting Wednesday night. Did anything happen?"

"The usual. A lot of angry people, some of them vocal."

"Byron Locke?"

"He was there. Played to the cameras. Made an impassioned plea about the watershed. Said the days of mining exploitation of sensitive areas in the Southwest were over, that it was his life's work to halt the degradation of the environment due to mining and big cattle ventures . . . That he'd stopped them in New Mexico, stopped the road up Gray Mountain, and he'd find a way to stop this venture, too. As I said, the usual. It's all on tape."

"Had you met Byron Locke before the Dragoon meeting?"

"Not personally. But he and DUC had locked horns." Chapin's pun fell flat. After a long pause, he said, "We were on opposite sides of several lawsuits in the past couple of years."

"What about?"

"Same old, same old. His client wanted wilderness designation for various tracts of land. We wanted to keep them open for multiple use, including mineral exploration."

"So he was a thorn in DUC's side."

"You could say that."

"Who won?"

"They did." Chapin sounded matter-of-fact. "We appealed. The results came in last week. We lost on appeal."

"How did Bruder take the news?"

"He was pissed."

"I'd like you to furnish me with the case histories."

"Sure," Chapin said. "I'll have my office fax them to you."

"Had Prebble or Bruder ever met with Locke personally?"

"We were all in the courtroom last week."

"Prebble and Bruder were there?"

"Yes. Bruder had words with Locke outside the courthouse. Prebble can tell you what was said."

"You son of a bitch," Prebble muttered. He seemed to slump a little in his shoes. He lifted and flexed his shoulders and twisted his neck like a batter working the kinks out before taking his stance. He needed a massage.

"Did you know Locke had been killed in a fire Wednesday night?"

"Heard it on the news. Can't say I was sorry."

"Do you have an alibi for Wednesday night, after the meeting in Dragoon?"

"Like I said, I drove back to Tucson. I was at my motel by ten, ten thirty."

"Any witnesses?"

"No."

I could hear a clicking sound, as if Linc Chapin's thumb were repeatedly depressing the switch on a ballpoint pen. Prebble did that thing with his shoulders and neck again. Cruz had struck a nerve in both men.

"Anybody else stick out at the Dragoon meeting?"

"One of the locals. I didn't get his name that night, but he approached us after Friday night's meeting. Name's Black."

I thought Cruz would follow that up, but he left it alone. "What about earlier in the day on Wednesday?"

Prebble was now standing very close behind me, straining to hear every word. The three DUC men had left Tucson early Wednesday morning, Prebble and Bruder in the Escalade, Chapin in the Lexus sedan. They'd stopped at the Johnson mining area to visit a couple of properties, then driven to Willcox to check Bruder into his motel and park the Lexus. After an early lunch, they'd visited a ranch on the east side of the Chiricahuas, then stopped at Hoodoo Ranch to talk business with Nate and Jody. They'd returned to Willcox, cleaned up in Bruder's room, had dinner and driven to Dragoon. They'd taken both cars so Chapin could head back to Tucson after the meeting. They'd split up around nine fifteen.

"How'd the discussion with Nate and Jody go?" Cruz asked.

"Nate was lucid most of the time. He and Sam had met the week before. They seemed to hit it off. They're a lot alike."

"Really?"

"Really." When Cruz waited for clarification, Chapin added, "Overbearing, aggressive, egocentric, wily."

"You didn't like Mr. Bruder?"

Chapin laughed. "I detested Sam Bruder. But he paid top dollar, and he didn't stint on field expenses like transportation, equipment, field assistants, per diem. You get what you pay for in this business."

"Did you kill him?"

Chapin didn't miss a beat. "You've got to be kidding. Kill the goose that laid the golden eggs?"

His answer wasn't a denial. But Cruz didn't pounce.

"Who'll be top man at DUC now?"

"You're looking at him."

25

Behind me, Prebble was tapping again. I was afraid Cruz would hear it. I reached out and pressed my hand over his. It was slippery with sweat.

"Bruder didn't have a family?" Cruz said to Chapin. "None at all?"

"That's what he claimed. His will leaves the bulk of his company shares to me. I'm a silent partner."

Prebble's exhaled breath sounded like a volleyball deflating.

"Were there other partners, silent or otherwise?" Cruz asked. I could almost see him scribbling *Motive* after Chapin's name.

"Not that I know of. Ask Prebble."

"Let's talk about Thursday. You were in Tucson all day?"

Chapin said he'd spent both the day and night in Tucson. He'd copied documents at the FedEx Kinko's at Craycroft and Broadway, met with a couple of property owners, and gone for a run at Reid Park. He'd eaten dinner, alone, at a Thai restaurant on Speedway, then gone back to his room. He hadn't talked to anyone after he left the restaurant—except Prebble. He'd called around ten.

Cruz asked for a list of the people Chapin had seen in Tucson, then said, "Prebble always calls you on your cell, not your office or motel room phone?"

"Right."

"So you could have answered his call from anywhere, including Willcox."

"I suppose so. But the cell records will show I was in Tucson."

"But you could have driven to Willcox, killed Bruder, and returned to Tucson in time to get Prebble's call."

"Just as Prebble could have killed Bruder and lied about his going out for liquor."

"I'll get to Prebble tomorrow." Cruz switched subjects at light speed. "Do you know a Francisca MacFarlane?"

"No. Should I?"

"She was standing in the kitchen when you arrived."

"Tall, black hair, gray eyes?"

"That's the one."

"Never seen her before."

"You sure? She's a geologist."

Chapin laughed. "It's a pretty big field. Is she involved in this? Was *she* the hot date Bruder had Thursday night?"

"She discovered his body."

Prebble took a step to the side, putting distance between us. He probably figured I was tight with Cruz. He couldn't know I was on the suspect list.

"Small world," Chapin said.

"Isn't it." Statement, not question. "Getting back to Mr. Bruder . . . He was from Australia, you met in Canada, he died in the U.S. I take it he traveled a lot?"

"Goes with the job."

"To many different countries?"

"Wherever the minerals are."

"To your knowledge, Dr. Chapin, had Mr. Bruder ever been arrested in another country?"

Lincoln Chapin was clicking his ballpoint pen again. "No," he said at last.

Prebble leaned toward the door. *Ask the question a different way,* I silently prompted Cruz.

"You don't *know* of any arrests or detentions?" Cruz's voice was patient.

"That's right."

"Do you suspect that such detentions or arrests occurred?"

"It's possible."

"Did Mr. Bruder avoid traveling to certain places?"

I smiled. *Nice move.*

"Peru, Mexico, and Africa."

"Were there reasons he avoided them?"

"Such as fear of being kidnapped in Peru or Mexico? No, Bruder didn't fear anything or anyone on earth."

Chapin was stonewalling Cruz. I wondered why.

"Had Mr. Bruder ever visited those countries?"

"I was with Sam at meetings in Lima two years ago. He left abruptly, ahead of schedule. And the Peruvians broke off negotiations."

"Do you know why?"

"A young woman claimed he'd raped her. Bruder told me it was consensual sex, that she'd claimed rape because her fiancé caught them together."

"Did you believe him?"

"At the time. Bruder was a convincing man."

"And now?"

"I'm not sure. Prebble later told me the same thing had happened in Mexico City the year before."

"Do you know why Bruder wouldn't travel to Africa?"

"No."

"Was it the whole continent he avoided?"

Chapin didn't answer.

"Kenya?" Cruz prodded. "South Africa? Namibia?"

"The whole shebang."

"Interesting. What do you know about Bruder's past?"

"Not much. I do remember Sam saying once that his family had owned a copper mine when he was young. He certainly knew the ins and outs of copper production and marketing . . . But Prebble said Bruder was working for a coltan-mining company when they met."

It was my turn to lean forward. I knew little about coltan except that the smuggling of coltan and conflict diamonds helped finance wars in Africa.

"C-O-L-T-A-N?"

"That's right. Short for minerals in the columbite-tantalite series."

After a pause, Cruz prompted, "Which are important because . . . ?"

"They're primary ores of niobium and tantalum. Coltan's used in everything from cell phones to semiconductors. The big producers are in central Africa and Australia."

Cruz pondered this. "So Mr. Bruder might have traveled to Africa when he was involved in Australian coltan mining?"

"Likely."

"You know nothing else about him or his family background?"

"No. But I have a good ear for languages and accents. I'd guess Bruder wasn't from Australia or New Zealand."

"South Africa?"

"Possibly."

I heard pages flipping, a chair scooting back.

"Am I finished?"

"Almost." Paul Cruz ruffled pages again. I knew from our earlier conversation that he tended to save the big questions for last. "It was Mr. Prebble who reported Bruder missing, at—" More page shuffling. "At nine thirty a.m. Friday. What time did Mr. Prebble call you that morning?"

I listened to Chapin's version of what unfolded in Willcox while Joaquin, the students, and I were driving to Massai Point and discovering the body. Bruder was supposed to meet Prebble for breakfast at six thirty. When he hadn't shown by seven and wasn't answering his cell, Prebble convinced the manager to let him into Bruder's room. The bed hadn't been slept in. The Escalade was parked by the door. Prebble called the hospital, then Chapin. Chapin made it to Willcox by nine. Still no Bruder. They decided to call the police.

"Where were the keys to the vehicle?" Cruz asked.

"Under the driver's seat. That was standard operating procedure, so we'd all have access to the vehicle."

"You didn't lock it?"

"It was leased. We didn't worry about anyone stealing it."

"Did you find Mr. Bruder's jacket in his room or the car?"

"It wasn't on him?"

"No," Cruz said. "Where did he keep his wallet?"

"In his jacket pocket."

"Do you know a Dr. Ronald Talmadge?" Cruz changed direction so quickly it caught me flat-footed.

"Doesn't ring a bell."

"From Paradise?"

"I think I met a Talmadge at the Research Station maybe eight, nine years ago. But I don't know if it's the same one. Botanist, I think. Why?"

"He was murdered last night after the meeting in Portal."

"No shit?" said Linc Chapin. I could almost hear the wheels in his mind cranking, struggling to assimilate the ramifications of Ron's death . . . or scrambling to come up with an alibi.

"What time did you leave the Portal meeting?"

"Around nine thirty. As I said earlier, we stayed to talk to Black—and his brother. They wanted to see if we could find some common ground."

"And did you? Find common ground?"

"No. Black wanted guarantees that the water supply wouldn't be affected by any exploration or mining activities. I told him we'd do our best."

"He wasn't satisfied?"

"You kidding? He was pissed. He told us to go back to Australia. That there was no earthly way the project would be approved after an environmental impact assessment was done."

"That's all?"

Prebble put his hand out as if to push open the door, then caught himself.

"He threatened to sabotage our drilling activities if we stayed," Chapin said. "He said to think about what happened to Sam Bruder."

I had no way of knowing if Chapin were telling the truth. He might be lying to throw suspicion on Raul, but it sounded like something Raul would say.

"Did he physically threaten you?" Cruz asked. "Did he have a weapon?"

"No weapon that I saw. And he didn't raise his fist or anything like that. But his tone was serious—deadly serious. So I pointed him out to the deputies that were on duty. They noted my concerns and spoke to Black."

Damn Raul for being such a hothead.

I jumped when the office phone rang beside me. Prebble stumbled backward, hitting the door frame with his shoulder. He half fell into the kitchen. I couldn't help it. I laughed as I picked up the phone. Cruz and Chapin opened the door to the dining room as I said, "Hoodoo Ranch."

"Dr. MacFarlane?"

"Wyatt? How'd you track me down?"

"I pressed redial on Rosa's phone."

That was quick thinking, and I told him so.

"Wait'll you hear—"

"Hold on a sec, Wyatt." Conscious of Chapin and Cruz standing just behind my shoulder, I covered the mouthpiece. "One of my students," I said. They didn't move. "A private matter. You understand."

"Why don't you wait for me on the back veranda, Dr. Chapin," Cruz said. Two could play at the eavesdropping game.

Chapin shrugged but crossed behind me into the kitchen. I heard the screen door open and close. Cruz then did an about-face, leaving the dining room door open. I heard his footsteps enter the hall and go up the front stairs.

"Wyatt?"

"Haven't changed my name."

I heard a click on the line. "Detective Cruz is on the extension, Wyatt."

"I'm cool with that. Hi, Detective Cruz."

"You found something, Wyatt?" Cruz said.

"Damn straight."

I winced. Wyatt had trouble modulating his voice tones in the best of circumstances. When he was excited or enthusiastic, like now, you could hear him in Mexico. "Tone it down, Wyatt."

"I copy." His voice was decibels lower.

"That's perfect."

"Okey-dokey. As I was about to say, Vince and I went as far as we could on Byron Locke, then switched to the guy we found on the mountain yesterday."

"Sam Bruder."

"That's the one. Most of the hits were related to his Australian mining work. The trail pretty much ended there. But there was one link to a history book—wait, let me read you the title . . . *Shredded Empire: The History of Zimbabwe.* There's a site with the book's introduction and table of contents. The name "Samuel Bruder" is mentioned in a footnote. Let's see . . . He was a rich guy, had a big spread and a few mines in Rhodesia. Where's Rhodesia?"

"A former country in central Africa, governed by the white minority. When they were overthrown in the sixties, the country split up into Zimbabwe and Zambia."

"You're old enough to remember the sixties?"

"No, Wyatt. But I studied geography and history."

"I got most of my geography from *Where in the World Is Carmen San Diego?*"

Figured. "Can you and Vicente find out anything more about that family? Our Sam Bruder isn't old enough to be the man mentioned in the footnote, but they might be related. The accent fits."

"That's the best part. Vince posted questions on a couple of bulletin boards. He's already got a hit from a guy in—" Wyatt rustled a paper. "Angola. Where's Angola?"

"West coast of Africa. Next to Namibia, Zambia, and the Democratic Republic of Congo. We really need to do something about your geographic illiteracy."

"You think I'm bad, you should listen to Vince."

I could hear thumping, followed by "Ouch." I tried to get Wyatt back on track with, "What was the message?"

"Vince is IM-ing with him right now. He was a soldier in Angola during some border war—"

"The South African Border War," I said. "Began back in the sixties when Namibia was part of South Africa."

"Right. And this guy fought later in the Angolan civil war."

"Began in the midseventies, after Angola got its independence from Portugal. There were several factions, plus mercenaries from countries like the U.S., Cuba, and South Africa fighting in Angola."

"Mercenaries. How cool is that?" Wyatt was on familiar ground. "And it jives with what this guy says. A white mercenary named Sammy Bruda—B-R-U-D-A—was brought in from South Africa to advise and train the UNITA troops. Haven't a clue what UNITA means."

"It was one of the factions."

"Vince just asked him for a description of Bruda—age, weight, hair color, the years he served there. He's waiting for the reply."

"Ask the Angolan if he remembers any stories about him." It hit me suddenly. "Wyatt? Wait. There's a more important question. Did Bruda survive the civil war?"

"I'll check," Vicente said, bypassing Wyatt. Apparently I needed to work on my modulation, too.

I heard the clicking of computer keys. "Holy shit!" said Wyatt.

"What?" said Cruz. I'd forgotten he was on the line.

"Vince got a message from a Dutch journalist named Van de Ven, who says Bruder—spelled the way we spell it—disappeared one day in 1979 or 1980. Went out on a mission and didn't return. The rest of his unit was slaughtered—to the last man. This guy figured Bruder was killed, too—or captured."

"But they never found a body?"

"Nope. And, wait for it—here's Bruder's description. I'll read it to you: 'About one and three-quarters meters tall—'"

"Roughly five eight, five nine."

"Thanks," Wyatt said. "I was never great at metrics. There's more—'perhaps seventy-six kilograms—'"

"Roughly one sixty eight," I said. "A kilogram's about 2.2 pounds."

"Okay. Van de Ven says Bruder had 'light hair, blue eyes, stocky build, square face. Heavy drinker. Smoker. Liked his ladies young—very young. Wasn't particular about race.'"

"Ask if he knows anything about Bruder's background, his education. Did he have a temper? Was he quiet or social, coarse or well-spoken?"

"Damn, the IM quit. Vince has to reconnect. If he does, I'll save the answers and print them out for you—compliments of Charley and Rosa."

"Would you and Vicente forward those e-mails to me, Wyatt?" Cruz gave Wyatt his e-mail address. "He may not be our victim, but it's a start. Good job, guys."

"Thanks, Detective Cruz. Oh, I almost forgot, Dr. MacFarlane. Rosa wants to know when you'll be home for dinner."

I heard the click as Cruz disconnected. I said, "Tell her by seven, at the latest."

"Got it."

The phone rang as I settled it into its cradle. Instinctively my hand jumped back, as if I'd triggered the noise. "You going to get that?" Chapin said from the doorway as the second ring came. Prebble stood next to him.

I picked it up. "Hoodoo Ranch."

The man on the other end of the line informed me that the tow truck would be there in thirty minutes. "Let me get your party," I said.

I handed the phone to Chapin, who said they'd be waiting at the car. He turned to Cruz, who'd pushed open the dining room door. "We done?"

"Almost."

"You said that before." Chapin sighed. "Well, let's hurry it up."

Cruz threw me an enigmatic glance and sat back down at the table. Chapin followed. The door swung shut behind him.

I stayed to listen to the final questions. I no longer cared if Cruz knew I was there.

"Do you own any firearms?" Cruz asked.

"I used to. I gave them to my ex-wife when I moved to Australia. They have stricter gun laws than we do."

"Did you kill Byron Locke?"

"Whoa, there's a switch. No, I did not. And I didn't kill Talmadge, either." This time his answers were clear and emphatic denials.

A truck engine approached up the drive. I heard footsteps cross from the back veranda through the kitchen and down the hallway.

"I told them I'd meet them at the Escalade." Chapin's tone was sharp. He'd run out of patience—or was anxious to leave.

"That's not the tow truck." Jody's voice came from the foyer. I heard the rumble of two semis driving slowly past the house to the rear yard. They were followed by a pickup truck. "They're here for the cattle." Her footsteps headed back through the house to meet the trucks.

"Still, we'd better get going," Chapin said. His chair scraped back for the second time.

"I'll need your fingerprints, Dr. Chapin. And Mr. Prebble's. Just for comparison purposes," Cruz said. "Wait here, please."

The front door closed. Cruz was retrieving his kit from the Tahoe.

Prebble stepped around me and pushed open the dining

room door. It stayed open. "You heard?" Chapin said.

"Most of it. You could have kept me out of it—especially the Locke part," Prebble replied in a low voice.

"They'd have found out once they started digging. It's better to volunteer it at the beginning."

"My pappy taught me never to volunteer for anything."

Paul Cruz came in with his kit and placed it on the oiled surface of the old oak table. "Dr. Chapin?"

Chapin stepped forward and was fingerprinted. Prebble reluctantly followed. "I'm not sure this is legal," he said.

"It's standard procedure. But I'd be happy to wait while you call your lawyer to check."

"That won't be necessary." Prebble held out his right hand. "But I don't see what good my prints will do you."

"We'll need them after we process your vehicle."

"Excuse me?" Prebble said.

"I'm going to follow you to Willcox, impound your vehicle temporarily, and have the crime scene unit process it. From what Dr. Chapin told me, it was the last place Bruder was seen alive. We'll need your prints so we can discover if someone else was in the vehicle—if they perhaps drove it down from Massai Point."

Prebble and Chapin exchanged looks. Neither had expected this. "But we need that vehicle," Prebble said. "We can't use the Lexus for fieldwork."

"We'll process it as quickly as we can."

"May I at least take out my field gear?" Chapin said.

"Sorry. Not till we've examined, photographed, and logged it."

"But my gear was in the Lexus from Wednesday evening till Friday noon."

"We have only your word for that, Dr. Chapin. And even if your gear wasn't in the vehicle at the time Bruder left, it might have picked up or contributed trace material."

"Peter?" A note of anger, and something else, colored Chapin's tone. He'd lost his self-assurance.

"Sorry, Linc. I'm waiting for my lawyer."

"Why the hell didn't you process the Escalade last night?" Chapin demanded.

"Because the vehicle wasn't at the crime scene . . . and because we'd only just ID'd the body. Since last night we've been investigating three murders simultaneously. It was only after speaking with you that I found out how important the vehicle evidence might be."

"You and your big mouth," Prebble said to Chapin.

"Stuff it, Peter."

But their words held no heat. They exchanged a look. I could have sworn they were feeling satisfied, even smug.

"I need a few minutes with Dr. MacFarlane. I'll meet you out back," Cruz said.

Ten seconds later I was alone with Cruz. What crucial question, I wondered, had he failed to ask Chapin?

26

"Well," Paul Cruz said, packing the fingerprint samples into his kit, "how much of my conversation with Chapin did you catch, Dr. MacFarlane?"

"Most of it."

"I see." His gaze pinned me, tried to read answers to questions he hadn't asked. "What about Prebble?"

"He missed the beginning and the end, but caught the rest."

Cruz locked the case and picked it up. "And what was his reaction?"

"Tense, agitated—particularly when you started questioning Chapin about Byron Locke."

"Really." Half question, half comment.

"When the phone rang, I thought he was going to have a heart attack."

Cruz considered this. A half smile flickered across his mouth. "Interesting."

"I thought so."

I waited for his comments on my conversation with Wyatt. From the rear yard came the clank and whir of a metal ramp being lowered and locked into place. Rory and Jed yelled. Hooves clattered on metal.

"This isn't a game, Dr. MacFarlane."

"Don't patronize me, Detective Cruz. And don't insult my intelligence by implying I don't know what's at stake here. I damn well know three men are dead, and you haven't a clue who did it. I'm up there on your list because I found Sam Bruder's body and was the last friendly face Ron Talmadge saw in this world. My freedom and reputation are on the line. So are Joaquin and Raul's. But if you think I'm going to leave the resolution in the hands of an overworked, underpaid police force, then think again."

"I didn't mean—"

"Yes, you did."

Cruz stood there for a moment. His face was etched with lines of exhaustion. Shrugging, he picked up his kit, tucked his notebook in his pocket.

I didn't understand why Cruz had backed down. All day he'd flip-flopped from bad cop to good cop, sometimes tugging on my leash, sometimes sharing information. I couldn't read him, and it bothered me. It was like trying to get a clear reflection from a wind-ruffled pond.

I said, "You're wrong, you know."

His hand paused. "How so?"

"To the killer or killers, this *is* a game—or at least a puzzle."

He set the kit down with a thump. I had his attention. He waited, motionless.

"Someone, or maybe more than one person, threw the gun and repositioned Bruder's body, put a rock under his head and copper minerals under his tongue. Someone left the tracks of a one-legged roadrunner around the body—"

"What?"

"You didn't see them? Probably because Royce and the rangers scuffed up the site."

"I saw buzzard tracks."

"They came later, according to Charley."

"Charley was there?" His voice was sharp.

"Charley saw my photos."

"You took photos before the rangers arrived? Digital photos?"

"Yes."

"I want your camera. Now."

"The camera won't do you any good. I uploaded the images into my computer last night and cleared the memory card."

He frowned, trying to solve the problem another way. "Where's the computer?"

"Back at Charley's. But this is your lucky day. I saved the pics on my flash drive." I fished in a pocket for my keys, pulled them out. The flash drive dangled from the key chain.

Cruz was already moving toward the back door. "I'll

ask Jody if we can borrow her computer," he said over his shoulder.

He was out the door before I could say anything. In the silence that followed, I heard soft snores coming from the parlor. I tiptoed across the dining room and hall. Nate was stretched out, mouth open, on the parlor sofa.

I might never have another opportunity to find Nate's stash of guns. I tiptoed past him, opened the curtains covering the window behind his recliner. Light flooded the room, falling on an old Navajo rug with a red diamond design on a cream background. The corner nearest Nate's chair was flipped up.

"What are you doing," Cruz whispered behind me.

I jumped. I'd been so intent on the rug, I hadn't been listening. I put a finger to my lips. When he nodded, I bent and folded back the rug, revealing the worn plank floor beneath. Cuts crossed two of the planks at right angles. I lifted up the neatly fitted boards to expose a rectangular hole maybe two feet by four feet by two feet deep. Nestled inside were shotguns, rifles, a couple of handguns, and enough ammunition to start a revolution.

"Jesus," breathed Cruz.

"We took a shotgun from Nate when we first arrived. Jody put it on top of the kitchen cabinets."

Kneeling, Cruz took the guns from their hiding place and carried them to the kitchen. I heard soft *thunks* as they joined the other guns atop the cupboards. I stacked the ammunition behind Nate's recliner. Quietly replacing the boards, I pulled the rug back to its original position.

"Jody grew up in this house," I said, when Cruz rejoined me. "Wouldn't she have to know this stash was here?"

Cruz shook his head. "I lived here for fourteen years, and *I* didn't know about it. Besides, Jody was more interested in horses than housework. After her mother died, Nate always had a housekeeper."

Like Carolina Cruz. "If there's one stash, do you suppose there are others?"

"More than likely," Cruz said. "But what bothers me is that both those revolvers are Ruger .38s."

I didn't know one gun from another. "That's unusual?"

"No. But we found a .38 shell casing next to Talmadge's body. Still, neither of Nate's Rugers has been fired recently."

Cruz the good cop was back again. Was he bipolar? Why was he sharing information with a suspect? What did he want from me?

Whatever his reasons, I decided to take what I could before he reverted to bad cop. "What kind of pistol did Raul buy yesterday?"

"He test fired a Smith and Wesson Military and Police pistol—a .40 semi-auto—but didn't buy it, he said. That checked out, too. And his other registered guns are nine mils."

"What about Joaquin?"

"He owns a Glock. Nine mil."

"So they're in the clear for Talmadge's murder. And you already have the gun that killed Bruder, right?"

"Ballistics aren't back yet for either case. And we don't know if either Raul or Joaquin has any unregistered guns." Cruz looked at his watch. "Chapin and Prebble will be getting antsy."

"Did Jody give you permission to use her computer?"

"Reluctantly."

"Then let's do it."

In the office, the computer hummed softly. Like Charley's, it had an Ethernet connection. The screen saver was a mandala pattern, hypnotic in its color-on-black permutations. When I plugged my flash drive into the only free port, the desktop popped up. The background was a photo of a tropical beach, aquamarine water, palm trees, white coral sand. A long way from Hoodoo Ranch.

Cruz took a chair from the dining room and sat next to me as I scrolled through the photos.

"It'll take too long to send the whole batch," I said. "Do you have a flash drive with you?" Cruz shook his head. "Okay, pick the ones you want most, and I'll send you the rest when I get back to Charley's."

"I've a better idea. I'll just take your flash drive." He held out his hand.

"You have a warrant?"

"No."

"Then we'll do it my way."

Cruz didn't like it, but what choice did he have? He examined the photos carefully. I pointed out the two sets of bird tracks and explained what Charley had shown me about their different characteristics.

"A crazy one-legged roadrunner?" he said, as the six photos he'd selected were being uploaded.

"Hopping around above seven thousand feet."

"Could Charley explain it?" When I hesitated, he said, "You want me to ask him?"

"It would be better."

"What if I promise to follow up with him?"

"Okay." I told Cruz about Lummis's description of the Tigua ritual designed to confuse harmful spirits.

"Tigua?"

"Yes."

"Someone wants us to think a Puebloan did this?"

"That's our guess. But, as Charley pointed out, a Tigua would only have done this for another Tigua. Bruder was white."

"What about the other changes to the murder scene? Were any of them in Lummis's book?"

"Not that Joaquin found."

"So several different messages were being sent at the same time." Cruz was thinking aloud. "The copper connection might be a warning for DUC personnel if they continue the exploration . . . But I don't get the shift of the body and the rock pillow."

While he mused I looked at the folders on Jody's desktop. The cursor hovered over *HR-Business*. Cruz leaned back, arms crossed. His posture said he'd watch, but not participate. Was he so desperate for information that he'd allow me to compromise evidence? Only one way to find out.

I opened the *HR-Business* folder. Cruz leaned forward but didn't stop me. Scrolling through the files I saw *C. Black—Shoefly Jo*. The other file with today's date was *Collins Transfer*. That would be the stock trucks loading outside. Going back by date, I saw that the next two most recent files were labeled *DU Copper* and *Strong Ranch Appeal*.

Cruz leaned forward as I opened the DUC file. It contained archived e-mail correspondence between Jody, Chapin, and Bruder about mineral rights to East Ranch and the Strong Ranch in New Mexico. DUC was interested in purchasing the rights, but no deal had been struck.

Cruz looked pointedly at the print button. He didn't seem concerned that these files were illegally obtained and couldn't be used in court. Maybe he had some other use for them. I, on the other hand, was beyond questioning the legalities of my search. Jody would know the next time she opened Word that someone had visited her files. But she'd given us permission to use her computer, and these files were in plain sight on the desktop. I hit the print button.

"Aren't you looking for someone who's anti-mining?" I said.

"Anti-Bruder will do," said Cruz, folding the printed pages and tucking them into his pocket.

"But the Lufkins were negotiating with DUC. Jody and her father wouldn't have any reason to kill Bruder."

I closed the file and copied it and the other three to my flash drive. What was good for the gander . . . The server told me the photos had been sent. I ejected the flash drive and stood up.

"Peaches Tarango is Tigua/Apache," Cruz said. He waited, watching my reaction.

This was shaky ground. Peaches was Charley's oldest friend and Raul's godfather, just as Charley was godfather to me. A special connection. If Charley hadn't told Cruz he'd given Peaches the gun that almost certainly killed Bruder, then I wouldn't—at least, not till I had to.

"I can't help you there," I said. "I only met Peaches a few times. But you must know him well."

"He's been like a father to me . . . and an uncle to Charley's kids." He smiled. "Raul showed up here a time or two, when he got crossways of his family. Peaches has always been a safe haven. I can't imagine someone else as foreman at Hoodoo." He looked at his watch again. "I'd better get Chapin and Prebble to their car."

Picking up his kit from the table, he moved to the front door. I opened it for him. Light spilled into the foyer. Cruz's shadow stretched all the way down the hall toward the kitchen. "Were you able to reach Toni Navarro?" I said.

I'd tried to phone my friend in the Pima County Sheriff's Office, but hadn't succeeded. I was hoping Cruz had had more luck.

Cruz looked out at the dry land beyond the ranch yard. "We've been playing telephone tag. I'll try again tonight."

"So I'm in the Chiricahuas till tomorrow morning?"

"At least." He looked at me for a long moment. "Why did you take pictures of the site?"

"There was something out of kilter there. I didn't have time to figure out what, not with the police coming."

He started down the steps, stopped, turned. "You've been helpful, Dr. MacFarlane. Or maybe just clever." Cruz the bad cop had returned. "But I keep going back to the fact that you discovered Bruder's body and drove Talmadge home last night."

"One coincidence too many."

"Yes. How do you feel about the mining company's exploration plan?"

"Without mining we wouldn't have the products we use every day. But DUC came in with guns blazing—so to speak. From what I hear, that was Bruder's style. I suspect it made him lots of enemies."

There was no good-bye. He just nodded once, continued down the steps, tucked his kit in the Tahoe, and walked around the house to the noise and dust of the cattle loading. A minute later he was back, Chapin and Prebble beside him. Prebble had a pinched expression on his face. Chapin's had no expression at all.

"Lawman rides off into the sunset," I said to myself, watching the SUV disappear down the dusty road.

"For today," Charley said behind me. As usual, I hadn't heard him come in.

I collected Spica, still sleeping, then followed Charley out to say good-bye to Jody. A pickup with a state license plate was parked off to the side. Jody was signing papers on the hood. She handed the clipboard to the lanky man next to her.

"Brand inspector," Charley said. "He checked Shoefly Jo for me while he was here."

The inspector waved to Charley, climbed into the pickup, and took off. The stock trucks, packed with lowing cattle, followed him around the house and down the road. Jody handed envelopes to Jed and Rory. With identical motions, they tucked them in their breast pockets, nodded to Jody, and waved to Esme, Harriet, and me. Without a word, they climbed into Jed's truck and followed the cattle. Dust glittered in the air as silence descended on Hoodoo Ranch.

Charley looked at the hoodoos that stood sentry duty on the ridge above. The sun's rays struck the center hoodoo. The tuff was the color of Jody's hair.

"We'd better get moving," Charley said.

Jody accompanied us to the front parking area. Purple half-moons lay under her eyes. Her cheekbones stood out in sharp relief. "You'll pick up Shoefly Jo in the morning?"

Charley smiled. "Before my check clears?"

"I've known you all my life. If you're not good for it . . ." She sighed as she turned toward the front steps. "I'd better check on Dad."

I could have said something, then, about Nate's gun cache, relocated to the top of the kitchen cabinets. I didn't. There was something about the set of her face and shoulders that said she'd withdrawn into her own little family hell. I'd ask Charley to tell her tomorrow.

I tucked the carrier back into the space Charley had made. Spica woke again for a moment, hissed at me, and then curled up again. I climbed into the front passenger seat of the CR-V. Esme looked uneasy as she joined Harriet in the back.

"What?" I said. Beside me, Charley put the car in gear and drove slowly down the rutted road.

"There's something disturbing about that ranch," Esme said. "A dark energy. But I don't know where, or what, it comes from."

"Or from whom?" I said, looking back. A cloud moved in front of the sun, casting a shadow over the house. Around it, light bathed the empty orchard and ranch yard. A bend in the road put the ranch out of sight. Above, on the ridge, the hoodoo glowed.

Harriet, beaming, pulled two small cloth sample bags from her pockets. The first was labeled *From Rory's gun;* the second, *From Jed's gun.* "Maybe these will help."

27

"What'd you find?" I said.

Harriet smiled as she related her adventures with Esme. Jed and Rory had jumped at the chance to give them target lessons. They didn't know that both women had handled guns from an early age. The women had purposefully aimed for the posts below the targets. When the stock trucks arrived, they'd slipped back and dug the bullets from the posts so that Cruz could compare them with the weapon that killed Talmadge.

"Why didn't you give them to Cruz?" I said.

"We're not the ones under suspicion," said Harriet. "We thought it would be better coming from you or Charley."

Esme nodded. "And we didn't want to do it while Jed and Rory were there. Unfortunately Detective Cruz left first."

"So you have one more reason to come back in the morning, Charley." I tucked the samples in my field bag. "Did you get them to talk about the murders, Harriet?"

"Oh, yes. Esme and I started speculating about the victims and who might have wanted to kill them," Harriet said. "Pretty soon the boys were tripping over each other to set us straight. You tell them, Esme."

"Jed said all the ranchers hated Byron Locke. He got what was coming to him for working with the tree huggers." She unclasped the beaded barrette and combed her long black hair with her fingers. "They went off on a long harangue about wildlife corridors and reintroducing wolves. It took a while to get them back on track." Without glancing in the rearview mirror, she twisted her hair up in back and replaced the barrette. "But Rory said the ranchers wouldn't have killed Locke. The Haydons had to have done it—probably an argument over the road."

Harriet nodded. "So I told them I'd heard that the Haydons were driving back from Willcox at the time of the fire, and that's why they didn't respond. Jed and Rory looked at each other and laughed. Rory said they'd passed them on the San Simon road an hour before the fire."

One more piece of the puzzle for Paul Cruz. I'd have to mention it to him when I sent the other digital images tonight. "Did they say anything about Bruder?"

Harriet laughed. "Rory got all red in the face and called him a son of a bitch. Jed said Bruder had hit on Rory's girlfriend. She waits tables at the café next door to the motel where the DUC guys are staying. Must have been early Wednesday evening, before the meeting in Dragoon. Anyway, she turned him down. Bruder wasn't used to being turned down, Jed figured, because he kept after her until she said she'd meet him at the motel Thursday night, after her shift ended."

"The boys thought that was pretty funny." Esme smiled. "She had no intention of meeting Bruder, Rory said. She was just putting him off. I said, if I were Rory, I'd have been tempted to go in her place and teach him a lesson."

"And that's when they changed the subject and offered to let us shoot their pistols," Harriet said.

"Did they mention Ron Talmadge?"

"I brought him up later, after Jody interrupted our target practice," Harriet said. "I let slip that we'd stopped by the place where he was killed. How sad it was, and how I couldn't understand who would want to kill such a quiet, innocent man."

"Jody was still there. She said Talmadge had enemies. Same ones Locke had. She said in this neck of the woods you had the ranchers and farmers on one side, the environmentalists on another, and the mining companies on a third side. Like a pyramid. The ranchers just want to be left alone to do what they've been doing for generations—raising free-range cattle, not beef that has been fattened on some feedlot. The tree huggers want to put a fence around the prime land, limit it to people on foot. No cattle. They want to reintroduce predators the ranchers worked hard to get rid of. And mining wants to poison what little water they have left."

"Jody said that, about the mining companies?"

"Vehemently."

"That's interesting. She seemed pretty friendly to Chapin and Prebble."

In a singsong tone, Harriet said, " 'If it was so, it might be; and if it were so, it would be; but as it isn't, it ain't. That's logic.' "

"Say what?" Esme said.

"Tweedledee," I said. *"Alice in Wonderland."*

"I must have missed that part," Esme said. "Anyway, while Harriet was digging bullets from the fence post, I checked out the bunkhouses. I didn't find anything in the main bunkhouse. Guess Jed and Rory aren't living on the ranch. But there's a separate little cabin, the old house, I think. Someone else's stuff—boots, blanket, and a saddle— was stacked in the back room. That's when I came looking for Charley."

"You've been holding out on me?" I said to Charley. He'd been silent the entire time, concentrating on driving and listening.

"Only temporarily."

Esme took a life-size delicately painted and rendered metal sculpture of a roadrunner from her backpack and passed it to me. The bird was missing its right leg and foot. No wonder Charley had been silent since we left the house. "I found it in the trash," she said. "Along with this." Esme handed me a piece of an envelope. It was addressed to Carlos Tarango.

"Who's Carlos Tarango?" I said, handing back the envelope and sculpture. "A relative of Peaches?"

Charley shifted down to negotiate a pothole. "It's Peaches' legal name."

"I also found a copy of the book Joaquin was using last night," Esme said, almost reluctantly.

I said, "Lummis's book?"

"I gave it to him," Charley said. "Thought he'd get a laugh out of a white man's description of his people."

"And did he?"

"What do you think?"

"The passage about the roadrunner tracks was highlighted in yellow," Esme said.

Charley's grip tightened on the steering wheel. "He wouldn't have needed to mark it. He'd know the old stories."

"Then who did?" Esme asked. "And his holster was there. His gun wasn't."

"I don't know," Charley said. "But he has some explaining to do. When we get home I'm going to see if I can track him down through his family, get him to turn himself in before the police come knocking."

"Did Peaches have more than one gun?" I said.

"Not that I ever saw. Why?"

"Well, we're pretty sure Peaches' gun killed Sam Bruder. But Cruz found a .38 shell casing next to Ron's body."

"If he had another gun he would have bought it from Enrique."

"Or been given it by Nate Lufkin?" I said.

"It's possible."

"What's the bus schedule from Willcox to El Paso?"

"Two a day. One leaves just before noon. The other leaves around nine thirty at night. Peaches would have taken the earlier bus."

"Let's say, just for argument's sake, that Peaches *didn't* catch that bus, but left Willcox later," I said. "Let's say he waited in town, killed Bruder at Massai Point around eight or eight thirty, then drove the Escalade back to town in time to catch the nine-thirty bus. If that's true, then someone else shot Ron Talmadge Friday night—with a different gun."

"The time frame's pretty tight," Charley said. "But we can check with the Willcox station on the way home and see if anyone remembers seeing him Thursday morning or late that night."

"Or any time at all," I said.

Charley answered with what sounded like a grunt, but maybe it was Apache.

"Now, the picture changes if Peaches had two guns. Maybe he stayed in the vicinity, tracked down Ron, and killed him," I said. "But why? Was there bad blood between them?"

"There weren't any magical signs left around his body," Charley said. "It was a different type of killing. Joaquin said he was shot in the back of the head."

"And how did Peaches get from Willcox to the other side of the mountains?" Harriet said. "Hitchhike?"

"He wouldn't have wanted to be seen. He'd have had to go by foot or horse." Charley stopped the car. We'd reached the juncture with the main road. There was no sign of a tow truck or Cruz's Tahoe. The Escalade must already be en route to Willcox.

"Were any horses missing from the Lufkins'?" I said.

"Peaches' horse was in the barn," Charley said. "I checked. And he wouldn't have stolen one."

"Even if he were on the run?" Harriet said.

"Even then. He might have borrowed one, but he would have asked first, or left a note."

Impasse. "Which takes us back to why Ron was killed. He must have seen something—"

"Maybe who killed Bruder?" said Harriet.

"I wonder if the ranger saw anyone else at Massai Point earlier on Thursday evening?" I said.

"Someone like Ron Talmadge?" Harriet had the bit between her teeth. "He could have witnessed the killing, then left?"

"Exactly." I looked at Charley. "The monument's still open. Why don't we ask?"

"I'd better call Rosa."

While he dialed, I dug around in my field bag for some lip balm. My lips were cracked and dry. When I pushed aside the sample bags of spent shells, my fingernails scraped something hard, pushed flat against the bottom. I pulled it out.

Ron's Moleskine sketchbook.

He must have tucked it into my bag before he got out of the car last night.

28

Mutely, I stared at the small black book, aware on some level that Charley had ended his call to Rosa, that the car was silent. Charley gently took the book from my hand.

I turned my head away, brushing tears from my cheeks. I remembered Ron, waiting on the bridge under the full moon, waiting with a smile on his face. He'd known he would be murdered. But he hadn't wanted his killer to find whatever was in that sketchbook. Why? And what would happen if and when someone found out we had it?

Charley grunted as he opened the accordion-pleated length of heavy card stock. As Charley unfolded the pages, I saw they resembled a storyboard, with scenes leading from one page to the next. He handed it to me.

The first drawings were of Wednesday night's meeting in Dragoon. I tried to focus on one small segment at a time. "Who's this?" I pointed to a pencil sketch of a man leaning against the back wall of the room.

"Byron Locke," he said.

A smug little smile played about Locke's mouth. He was staring at a trio off to the side—Jody Lufkin and the Haydons. The Haydons were glaring at Locke. Jody had her back to him, facing Linc Chapin, Peter Prebble, and a third man, sitting on the stage. The third man must be Sam Bruder. At the edge of the meeting tableau, Ron had drawn a close-up of Bruder's head and shoulders. His eyes lacked light. He looked younger than he did in the group drawing—hairline less receding, cheeks less fleshy, nose thinner, neck heavier, almost bullish.

"I wouldn't want to meet *him* in a dark alley," Harriet said, leaning over the seat. Then, haltingly, "Is that . . . ?"

"Yes." I didn't want to think of Sam Bruder's eyes,

plucked out by vultures yesterday morning. I folded the sheet so I could concentrate on the next scene. This central tableau captured a trailer on fire. Locke's trailer. Late Wednesday night. Flames shot into the dark sky. Joaquin, with gloved hands, struggled to open the trailer door. Ron shoveled dirt on the fire, trying to smother it. There was no hose, no water barrel.

"Ron must have drawn this from memory, after the fire," I said.

"That's his Bronco." Charley pointed to the far left edge of the scene. Set apart, as if it were at a distance, a vehicle, headlights on, drove toward the fire. I recognized the beat-up old Bronco I'd seen at Ron's house a few hours ago. A windmill, lower half illuminated by the headlights, showed pale against the night black sky. Dimly seen, behind the windmill, were the outlines of an SUV.

I collapsed the storyboard and opened the notebook from the back. As I turned the pleated pages we went back in time. There were the drawings of Friday night's meeting. One page had the original of the wordsearch I'd copied from the board in the hall. I remembered he'd borrowed my pen for a moment to go over certain letters.

I took out the copy Joaquin and I had made of the puzzle posted on the rear wall. Using a felt marker, I quickly darkened the letters Ron had emphasized. They didn't immediately tell me anything, but they might later.

Ron had followed the wordsearch puzzle with the drawing of Jody, and then, spread over three pages, a tableau capturing the moment Prebble delivered the news about Bruder. Chapin, focused on Prebble, looked . . . satisfied, sardonic, as if he'd known all along. Prebble looked self-important—and relieved.

Most of the figures in the audience were anonymous, just roughly sketched in. But Raul was looking at Enrique, who'd just dropped the gun. Enrique, as he bent to retrieve his revolver, was looking at Jody. Her body was angled so that her shoulders faced the stage, but her eyes were focused on Ron. She didn't look surprised. She looked . . . scared, angry, wary. And Mark Haydon, standing at the edge of the crowd, was watching . . . me, I realized with shock.

Oddly enough, Ron had drawn me as I'd been before the meeting started. I was holding the mineral sample, smiling. It was an uncomplicated smile, full of wonder and delight. I was the only figure in the entire sketchbook who was smiling.

"That's how you look when you're talking about geology," said Harriet. "Now, would you open up the whole thing? The suspense is killing me."

I stretched it out. In the center, Ron had sketched Bruder's murder scene, illuminated by Thursday night's nearly full moon. He couldn't have shown the scene so perfectly if he hadn't been there—the body angled toward the bottom right, hands crossed like a corpse in a coffin, head supported by a stone pillow, face looking toward a tiny word written near the bottom margin. I used my hand lens to magnify the fine letters: *Goma*.

Charley took one look at the drawing, passed me his cell, put the car in gear, and drove as fast as he could toward the monument. I handed the sketchbook to Harriet and speed dialed Charley's home number. Wyatt picked up. "Black Ranch. We never close. How may I direct your call?"

I asked him to get the flat plastic geologist's protractor from his backpack and draw a line on Charley's wall map of the world. "Fifteen degrees south of due east, beginning at the monument—or the northern Chiricahuas," I said. "Can you do that?"

"Slicker'n snot," he said. "Hold on." A minute later he was back. "This map is sadly out of date, Dr. MacFarlane. It still shows the USSR and a bunch of obsolete countries in Africa."

"What about my line, Wyatt?"

"I'm getting to that. Your line crosses Texas and the tip of Florida, heads into the Atlantic, crosses central Africa, then the Indian Ocean and Australia."

Australia, where DUC headquarters were located. Coincidence?

I dragged my focus back to the main question. Ron's field notebooks said he'd been in the field in Rwanda when the genocide broke out. Nadine had been at Goma. "Where in central Africa? Does it go through Rwanda?"

"You got it. Crosses right through the border region of Rwanda and, well, Zaire—though you told me there isn't a Zaire anymore."

"Does it intersect any towns in that region?"

"It runs between Bukavu, on the south shore of Lake Kivu, and Kigali."

"What about Goma?" I spelled it.

"Yup. It's on or near the north shore of Lake Kivu, close to your line. I'll check out all three names, if you want."

"I want."

"Excellent. Vince and I already finished our field report. We worked together. Vince played around with the photos. I did the line drawings. We collaborated on the text. It's awesome, if I do say so myself. Since then we've been helping Rosa make wedding favors—Jordan almonds in turquoise netting, tied with ribbons. I've never been great at tying bows."

I could hear him typing as he spoke. He must have propped the phone on his shoulder.

"Is she feeding you?" I asked.

"Oh, yes. She's wonderful. I'm ready to move in."

"Then after you do the Web search, get back to tying those bows."

"Roger dodger, Glorious Leader."

I turned off the phone and handed it back to Charley. "Well?" he said.

"I took a compass direction on Bruder's body. He'd been shifted until he faced southeast. I wanted to know why. At Ron's I found a picture of Nadine at a clinic in a place called Goma. It was in Zaire, then. Ron wrote the name at the bottom of his sketch of Bruder's murder scene."

"So Ron repositioned Bruder's body to face Goma?"

Charley's question brought me back to Bruder's sightless eyes. I suspected they'd haunt me for years. "And put the copper minerals under his tongue," I said. "*And* tossed Peaches' gun, damned if I know why."

"Where's this?" Esme said. There was something in her voice—dismay or alarm, as if the world had turned ugly. She was pointing to a series of scenes at the far right of the back storyboard.

"Haven't a clue," said Harriet.

I reached for the sketchbook. Four small scenes took up the last five pages. The first panel held the drawing of a white building I recognized as the exterior of the Goma clinic. The second panel showed a sparsely furnished bedroom lit by a naked bulb, dangling from the ceiling. No curtains at the window. Cross hanging above the bed. Two black men in sweat-stained uniforms, one on each side of the bed, held down a dark-haired white woman, her mouth stretched open in a scream. A white man was raping her.

The man was Bruder. I don't know how I knew it—something about the receding hairline, the bull-like neck, the set of the head—but I was positive. Ron had captured the horror in a few pencil lines. The scene was smudged, as if time had blurred, but not erased, the memory.

"It's awful," Esme whispered.

"It's Nadine," I said. "And Sam Bruder."

"If somebody hadn't beaten me to it," Harriet said, "I'd have shot him myself."

The next scene showed the same bed, same room. Two bodies sprawled on the floor—the men in uniform, I presumed. Nadine sat on the side of the bed, bandaging Bruder's right shoulder. Another bandage wrapped his left thigh. His face grimaced in pain. Hers, in profile, was set. The artist didn't inject himself into the picture, though he must have been standing in the doorway. Instead, he drew just the tip of an automatic rifle. In the lower right-hand corner, that word again: *Goma*.

An empty page followed. The next-to-last frame held a drawing of a woman, back to the artist, dark hair twisted into a knot. She held a young boy with curly hair, a broad forehead, and eyes looking toward the left. His chin rested on her shoulder, but his face showed no emotion. He wasn't there.

The storyboard captured the traumatic events in Ron's life. Nadine's rape. Ronnie's autism. Locke's fire. Bruder's murder scene. Everything was there. But the last frame held only a tree—the tree I'd photographed in Ron's backyard. A rope swing hung from a bough. Flowers ringed the base, just as I remembered—oleanders, purple mat, miniature roses . . .

"We need to get that sketchbook to Cruz as soon as possible," Charley said. We were almost to the entrance of the monument. He'd made record time. "It lets you off the hook."

"How so?" said Esme.

Harriet chuckled. "If Ron Talmadge thought Frankie murdered Bruder or Locke, would he have given her that sketchbook for safekeeping?"

"That's one interpretation," I said. "But Cruz might just believe I plucked it from Ron's cold, dead hand."

29

We reached the monument visitors center five minutes before it closed. The ranger behind the desk called Bascom for me. I reintroduced myself. He remembered me.

Yes, Bascom said, he'd seen Talmadge's Bronco at Massai Point around sunset. He'd parked at the far end of the ellipse. Talmadge came often to meditate in a small clearing near the exhibit building. Three-hundred-sixty-degree view. He'd watch the sunset over the Dragoons, then turn and meditate as the moon rose over the Peloncillos and Gray Mountain. Sometimes he'd stay like that all night. But not that night. Ron's Bronco was gone by eleven.

"Want me to show you the clearing?" Bascom asked.

Charley, standing close enough to hear both sides of the conversation, shook his head.

"We'll find it," I said.

Coming back to Massai Point was oddly disconcerting. As before, we had the place all to ourselves. We parked as close as we could to the exhibit building, then walked back to the murder site. The yellow tape was gone, the evidence gathering finished. Someone had washed down the island, removing the blood, the roadrunner and vulture tracks, the last traces of a man's death.

I tried to see it as Ron had seen it Thursday night. Hot air rose off the desert and ruffled my hair. No visions came. Turning, I followed Charley, Esme, and Harriet to the exhibit building.

It took Charley less than a minute to find Ron's meditation place among the waist-high manzanita. Bascom was right: the view was lovely. On the southern horizon, beyond the ascending ranks of hoodoos, were the vestiges of Turkey

Creek Caldera. To the west, across more legions of shadow-dappled sculptured stone and the Sulphur Springs Valley, lay Cochise's Stronghold in the Dragoon Mountains. To the east, Gray Mountain, scarred by the Haydons' new road, guarded the mouth of Coues Canyon and directed the eye to the Peloncillos. And to the north, Cochise Head reclined as if in sleep.

But I knew Cochise Head was made up of two mountains, the angle of observation aligning them. We cannot trust our sight. Viewpoint obscures or reveals, presents truth or merely the appearance of truth. Angle is everything. I needed to remember that.

A lightning-struck piñon pine had toppled at the edge of Ron's clearing. Its smooth, twisted gray bark would be eerie in the moonlight. But now, in the full heat of late afternoon, it made a warm bench for Harriet and Esme as they watched Charley work.

"He put a rug or pillow down here," Charley said, squatting near the center of the clearing.

"And he left us a present," said Esme. She plucked something from a cleft in the upturned roots of the old pine. Standing, she held it out to us on her palm.

"Azurite and malachite," I said. "Just like the piece he gave me Friday night." *And the piece tucked under Bruder's tongue.* "Why, Ron?" I asked aloud.

"Perhaps because he and Ronnie collected them together," Charley said.

Harriet was examining the mineral sample. "Copper minerals, right?" When I nodded, she said, "And Sam Bruder was the head of a copper-mining company. So the simplest explanation is—"

"That Ron was leaving a clue—Bruder was killed because of the exploration plan," I said. "Which doesn't, unfortunately, eliminate any suspects."

Esme put the azurite-malachite into a sample bag and handed it to me.

"Yes it does," Harriet said. "Dr. Chapin, Prebble, and the Lufkins weren't protesting the plan. Neither were you, Frankie."

"True. But that doesn't clear me of Ron's murder. I drove him home. Detective Cruz doesn't like coincidences."

"Then we've got to give him a better suspect," Charley said.

In a perfect world, we'd find the evidence that would clear Raul, Joaquin, and me. In the meantime, I'd settle for reasonable doubt.

"Ron was here, meditating, when Bruder was killed," I said, tucking the sample bag into a pocket. "Ron might not have seen the killer in the dark, but he would have heard the shot and seen the vehicle leave . . . And the killer would have seen Ron's Bronco parked at the end of the lot. You have to circle the ellipse to leave the parking area."

"If the killer recognized it," Charley said, "that would be reason enough to kill Ron. He's the only witness."

"And that would seem to count out Prebble and Chapin," I said. "They didn't know Ron, or at least not well enough to know what car he drove. And it narrows down the list to people who did."

Unfortunately, that list included Raul and Joaquin. But who else? The Haydons. Rory and Jed. Jody Lufkin . . . And Peaches. I'd forgotten about him. "You last talked with Peaches on Tuesday night?" I said to Charley as we walked back to the car. "And he wanted to use your sweathouse because he was feeling out of balance, out of harmony?"

"Yes. That was *before* Jody fired him."

"But after she put down Fritz," I said. "And she said he'd caught a ride into town with Bruder on Thursday morning, in time to catch the bus to El Paso." We were back to square one.

Charley opened the car door and looked at me over the roof. "Willcox?"

"You bet. Next stop, the Greyhound bus station."

Only then did I hear the echo of the last words I'd spoken to Ron Talmadge. *Next stop, Paradise.*

30

The next stop turned out to be a gas station in Willcox. The price of gas seemed to have gone up since I left Tucson.

I cleaned the bugs off the windshield while Charley filled the tank. But both of us were paying more attention to a black vehicle parked off to the side, beyond the service bays. The Escalade's doors were open. Two forensics technicians leaned inside. Evidence bags sat on the ground nearby. I heard the sound of a vacuum cleaner, but I didn't see Detective Cruz.

Peter Prebble strode out of the station to stand by the vehicle, hands on hips, sour expression on his face. When no one paid him any attention, he said, "I'll be at the motel." Turning on his heel he jaywalked across the busy street toward a chain motel with a coffee shop next door. A couple of dusty pickups were parked in front of Riva's Café, which advertised an early-bird dinner special. The only car in the motel lot was Chapin's Lexus.

"Not a good day for the DUC people," Charley said, watching Prebble's retreating back.

"Maybe that's a good thing." I finished cleaning the windshield and dropped the squeegee back into its dirty water. Charley gave me a half-smile as he pocketed the gas receipt.

"Miss Marple needs her afternoon tea while you're at the bus station," Harriet said, pointing to the café across the street. She winked. One of the pickups looked like Jed's.

So that's why he and Rory left Hoodoo Ranch in such a hurry. Rory's girlfriend must be waiting tables at the café tonight.

"Esme offered to go with me," Harriet said. "Could you pick us up after you visit the bus station?"

"No problem," Charley said.

I handed Harriet a five. "Would you mind getting me a large coffee with cream? Maybe you could ask for a fresh pot." Waiting for a pot to brew might give her time to talk to Rory's girlfriend.

"I could do that." Harriet gave me a thumbs-up.

Charley and I watched them trot down to the corner. No jaywalking for Harriet.

The Greyhound station was only a few blocks away. Debbie, the woman on shift behind the counter, knew Charley and Peaches. She'd worked Thursday morning, but hadn't seen Peaches. "I told Raul the same thing when he stopped by a few hours ago," she said.

Charley frowned. That was news to him. And to me.

"Let me check with the guy on the evening shift," Debbie said.

A customer came up behind us. We stepped aside to give him access to the desk. While we waited for Debbie to sell tickets and call her counterpart, I thought about Raul. Joaquin must have told him about Peaches' gun being left at the crime scene. But how had he found out that Jody had fired Peaches and that he was interviewing for jobs closer to Ysleta and El Paso? I whispered the question in Charley's ear.

"We talked about it while we were waiting for Kit this morning. And I told Raul what Carolina said about Peaches being fired. Raul didn't believe Peaches killed anyone."

Had Raul decided to backtrack Peaches in order to prove his friend was innocent? "Why don't you—"

But Charley was already calling Raul. He got the message machine. Same thing with Raul's cell. Charley left messages and called Rosa. "Have you heard from Raul?"

"No." I could hear her as clearly as if she were standing next to me. "Is there a problem?"

"I don't think so," Charley said. "Is Joaquin home yet?"

"No, but he said not to expect him till dinner."

Charley closed his phone just as Debbie the ticket agent said, "He says he sold only a few tickets for El Paso Thursday afternoon or evening."

"Did Peaches buy one of them?" Charley asked.

"I'm not allowed to tell you that." She leaned forward, winked at Charley, and shook her head. Straightening up, she said, "He could have purchased online."

"And gone directly to the bus?"

She nodded. "And I can't access online purchases. Sorry, Charley."

"I understand. You've already been a big help." He looked at me. "What's next?"

"There's nothing more we can do here. Let's pick up Harriet and Esme and head for home."

I spoke too soon. When we reached the coffee shop, Harriet was standing on the curb, clutching two Styrofoam cups, and almost dancing with excitement.

"About time," she said, a grin spreading across her face. "Guess what we found?"

Charley parked the Honda in the shade, opening the windows so the cat would stay cool. Spica stretched, yawned, and blinked a couple of times, then settled back down. I hoped Charley and Rosa were prepared for a cat that was up all night.

Harriet led us around the café to a couple of small commercial dumpsters parked in the rear alley. Esme stood beside the nearest dumpster. She smiled as she lifted the lid. A man's navy jacket lay under a rotting pile of salad greens.

"I heard a cell phone ringing. I wanted to see if there was ID." She pulled a zip-lock bag from her pocket and held it up. "Don't worry—I used this as a glove. Anyway, Sam Bruder's wallet was in the inside breast pocket."

"Worn brown leather, Australian driver's license," said Harriet, handing me my coffee. "Esme put it back, and guarded it till you got here."

"Nice job," Charley said.

Color infused her cheeks. "Thanks, Dr. Black."

"Charley."

The flush deepened. "Charley, then."

We discussed who should contact Paul Cruz. I was under suspicion for Ron's murder—and maybe Bruder's. But Charley's sons were also on the list. Charley handed me his phone.

Cruz answered on the second ring. When I identified myself, he said, "What is it, Dr. MacFarlane?"

"We found—"

"The gun that killed Talmadge?" Irony edged his tone.

I flashed back to Wyatt, finding the gun that presumably killed Bruder. "Sorry, no. It's Bruder's jacket—a navy blazer."

"What color jacket was Mr. Bruder wearing Thursday night?"

"I don't—"

"I'm asking Mr. Prebble, Dr. MacFarlane."

"Navy blue." Prebble's voice in the background. I wondered where they were.

"You sure?"

"He only brought one from Tucson."

"Bruder's cell phone and wallet are in the pockets," I said.

"You touched the evidence?" Cruz sounded pissed.

"My student wore a glove—well, a plastic bag. She didn't know it was Bruder's coat until she checked the license."

"How did she—never mind. Where are you?"

"The dumpsters behind Riva's Café."

Dead silence. I thought I'd lost the connection till he said, "I'm at the motel next door. Stay where you are. The evidence team is across the street, finishing the Escalade."

"I saw them."

"We'll be there in a minute . . . And Dr. MacFarlane?" He waited till I acknowledged the question before he said, "Please don't touch anything else."

Charley left to get a soda at the café. "Have any luck in there?" I asked Harriet as we sipped our drinks and waited for Cruz.

"The place was nearly empty. Rory and Jed were in a booth in the back. Rory's girlfriend waited on me. I could tell they were sweet on each other by the way they interacted. They'll be hitched before the year's out."

"Harriet," I said.

"Hold your horses, I'm getting there. Anyway, while we waited for a fresh pot of coffee, I got her talking about Bruder. Said I'd heard he ate his last meal right there in the café.

'Yeah,' she said, 'He was all hands, that guy. You know the type.'" Harriet grinned. "Well, I agreed, though I haven't had much experience with men of that sort. And then she said he and the other guy had argued over something."

"The other guy being Prebble."

"Had to be. He stormed out of the restaurant. Rory's girlfriend was afraid Bruder would go after him—skip out without paying—so she tallied their bill and headed for the table. Bruder was looking at a piece of paper, a document of some sort. He folded it up and put it in his pocket when she gave him the bill."

I looked at Esme. "Did you—"

"It isn't in his jacket pocket. I checked."

"But Prebble, and presumably Chapin, should know what that document was," I said. "And Chapin didn't mention it during his interview with Cruz."

Right on cue Cruz cut through a breezeway in the motel. Prebble and Chapin were with him. A fourth man brought up the rear. Across the street, a woman detached herself from the evidence team and jaywalked to meet us. She was carrying a sample-collecting kit. I recognized her as the crime scene tech who'd retrieved the gun at Massai Point yesterday.

Bruder's cell phone started ringing again. Harriet raised an eyebrow. I shook my head. This was Cruz's ballgame.

"Would you answer that?" Prebble said.

Cruz stopped short, hands on hips.

"It could be important," said Chapin.

Cruz didn't move. The phone stopped ringing. "I'll give you a copy of the cell log once we download it," Cruz said. Pulling on a pair of pale blue gloves, he opened the dumpster. The smell of rotting food wafted out. Cruz leaned inside. I was standing close enough to see his right hand touch the blazer, followed by a flash of white. Cruz emerged with the navy blazer.

"The cell—that's how you found it?" he said to me, holding up the jacket.

"Yes," said Esme.

Cruz produced a smile. Adrenaline must be kicking in again. "Good ears."

Esme smiled back. "Thank you."

"What brought you here?" An innocent enough question, at least on the surface.

"Harriet and Frankie wanted tea and coffee before we headed back to the ranch," Esme said. "I was just stretching my legs when I heard the phone ringing."

I silently blessed her for her choice of words and for not volunteering information—like the fact that Charley and I had been off at the Greyhound bus station, checking on Peaches' whereabouts. Which triggered an interesting question: If Peaches *had* killed Bruder, why had he parked the SUV back at the motel, dropped the jacket in this dumpster, and left himself a long walk back to the bus station? It didn't make sense.

I thought about that. Why hadn't the killer, whether Peaches or someone else, just left the jacket in the vehicle? Because he didn't want to spend the time going through it for money while in plain sight of the motel room doors and windows? Maybe. This alley was private, well hidden from the street.

The tech set her toolkit down beside the dumpster. "Did you finish the Escalade?" Cruz asked her.

"Just wrapping up. Whatcha got for me?"

Charley rounded the corner of the building, soft drink in hand. A cell phone started ringing. This time it was his. "They're there?" he said to Rosa, after explaining the situation. He listened for a minute, his face impassive. "Put Teresa on, will you?"

"Teresa and Jamie arrived?" I asked.

Charley nodded, then said into the phone, "Do me a favor, Teresa? Your brother's rounding up strays down at Mackey Canyon. Would you and Jamie help him out? Oh, and have your mother call Peaches' sister. See if she's heard from him . . . You, too, Little One. We'll be leaving soon." He ended the call and slipped the phone back into his pocket.

Standing where he could see our faces, Cruz held the blazer while the tech went through the pockets. Slowly, deliberately, each object was taken out, identified, noted, and returned to its respective pocket. Cell phone, billfold with driver's license, credit cards, and cash. Cruz counted the bills. "Six hundred and eighty-two dollars."

That ruled out robbery as the motive for Bruder's killing. But it didn't explain why the killer hadn't left the blazer in the SUV.

The criminalist slipped the billfold back into the jacket pocket. Chapin and Prebble inched forward as she pulled out a passport and a page of typescript, folded into thirds. I reached for Esme's hand, pressed it in warning.

Cruz traded the blazer for the paper, unfolding it carefully, deliberately. The page looked like one of the DUC file pages I'd printed from Jody's computer. Cruz refolded the paper, looking from Prebble's rigid face to Chapin's bland one.

"Is that the—" Prebble stopped, realizing his mistake. Chapin threw him a disgusted look.

"Sales agreement?" Cruz said.

"Yes. I just thought . . ." Prebble's voice petered out.

"You had an argument at dinner with Mr. Bruder Thursday night?"

"I'd advise you against saying anything else," said the fourth man. Prebble's lawyer, I surmised. He must have decided it would be to Prebble's benefit if they got the interview over with today, instead of waiting until tomorrow morning.

Prebble ignored him. "I already told you about that," he said to Cruz. "Bruder was offering less than the mineral rights were worth."

"Sounds like a good business deal to me."

"In ordinary circumstances."

Cruz unfolded the paper again, as if to check that he'd read it correctly. "But these weren't ordinary circumstances, were they? The Lufkins were old friends."

"Nate was, yes."

"You convinced Mr. Bruder to up the ante?"

"No." Prebble looked at Chapin. When he shook his head, Prebble looked confused. "Did Sam get the second signature?" he asked Cruz.

"Shut up, Peter." Chapin looked pissed.

Cruz was silent, waiting.

Prebble frowned at his partner. "What? Jody needed—"

"Damn it, Peter, it's a ruse."

"What?"

"That paper. It's not the Lufkin contract. Detective Cruz is playing a little game with us."

Prebble stepped forward and grabbed the paper from Cruz's hand. "You're right. This is the draft document we sent them. It isn't signed."

"Bruder had a signed contract that night," Cruz said.

"So he claimed," Prebble said. "I didn't see it. But Sam thought he only had to deal with 'the man of the house.' He'd talked Nate into selling the mineral rights to East Ranch, Strong Ranch, *and* Hoodoo for two thousand bucks. Unfortunately he neglected to get Jody's signature. Without it, the contract was worthless."

"Did Mr. Bruder plan to go back?"

"She'd called him to say she'd discuss it, but the price would be higher."

"Then why were you upset? Why did you storm out of the café?"

"Because Bruder was planning to hold firm. He said he had her over a barrel. She could sell now, or he'd wait till the cancer took her."

"Cancer?" Cruz looked stunned. "She was given a clean bill six months ago."

"She found out this week—Tuesday, I think." He looked at Chapin, who nodded. "Tuesday. Jody let it slip when we saw them on Wednesday afternoon. Bruder pounced on it. Came back the next morning with the low-ball offer. She's only got a few weeks, months at the most."

I now understood the pain meds and her quick sale of the cattle and Shoefly Jo. Jody had to turn assets into cash so Nate would be cared for after she was gone. No doubt she'd lined up buyers for the ranches, as well. Maybe that's what she was discussing with the Haydons when they entered the café.

Jody must have told Peaches about the cancer recurrence. She couldn't afford to keep him on any longer. That might have been the trigger, the reason he'd started drinking again. He was losing Jody *and* his job at Hoodoo Ranch. But had he been angry or protective enough that he'd killed Bruder because of his lowball offer? Maybe. It would explain why nothing but the contract was taken from Bruder's jacket.

I caught Charley's eye. He nodded. It was time to tell Cruz about Peaches' gun.

The technician bagged the blazer and stripped off her gloves. Cruz followed suit.

"Paul, we need to talk," Charley said.

Cruz studied him for a moment. "You've been holding something back, Charley?"

"Just till I could check it out."

"That's my job."

"You seem to be stretched pretty thin right now."

"What is it?"

"The gun Wyatt found up at Massai Point."

"You know who it belongs to? You haven't even seen it."

"Joaquin recognized it. I gave it to Peaches a long time ago."

A look of pain crossed Paul Cruz's face, but he didn't waste time chewing Charley out. "I'll order a search. Stay here," he said to all of us. "I'll be back in a minute."

Cruz took off at a lope, cutting through the motel breezeway again. The criminalist took the sealed evidence bag with the blazer inside and headed back toward her buddy at the Escalade.

"Good news?" said Prebble's lawyer.

Prebble smiled. "The best. Peaches Tarango is the foreman at the Lufkin ranch. Local outfit, southeast of town. If his gun killed Bruder, then I'm off the hook."

The man looked at his watch. "And I can make it back to Tucson by dinnertime."

"You can't leave," Prebble said.

"Cruz finished his interview. Just don't make any more statements without me."

"Then I'll walk you to your car," Prebble said, ignoring Cruz's directive. Chapin left with them.

"Can we go, too?" Harriet tossed her cup into the dumpster. I did the same with mine.

"Not quite yet," Charley said. "I think we'd better tell Cruz about Ron's sketchbook."

"I'll wait in the car," said Harriet. "Maybe it'll protect me from the fallout."

31

Charley pulled the Honda into a patch of shade next to the cinder-block wall separating the motel from the restaurant. There we sat, with the doors open, waiting for Cruz to return.

We were a silent bunch. Esme and Harriet worked on their field trip write-up. Charley closed his eyes. Spica, the cat, never opened hers.

I thought about what we'd learned in the hour and a half since we'd left the ranch. Ron's sketchbook suggested that someone driving an SUV had assaulted Byron Locke, then hidden behind the windmill when Talmadge passed by on the way to the fire.

Who could have been driving an SUV Wednesday night? Charley and Rosa, of course. The DUC contingent. Ron Talmadge. There could be others.

Ron's sketchbook confirmed he was at Bruder's death scene. Did Ron kill Bruder? He had good reason, based on what happened in Goma.

Charley yawned, stretched, and glanced at the notes I was making in my field notebook. "Ron couldn't have killed Bruder. How would he have gotten Peaches' gun?"

"Good point."

My mind moved on to the DUC reps, who also drove an SUV. Charley seemed to have some acquaintance with Prebble. I asked him how long he'd known him. Without opening his eyes, Charley said, "Eight years. I know his sister—in a professional capacity."

Which meant Charley couldn't discuss what he knew about Prebble. "But you hadn't met Chapin before today?"

"Never had the pleasure." The last word was said with a trace of irony.

I approached the problem from a different angle. When Cruz dismissed Chapin and Prebble, they'd exchanged a look of relief. I wondered why.

I replayed Chapin's interview, scene by scene, trying to find the weakness in Cruz's questioning. I have a strong visual memory. Unfortunately, this time I had to rely on what I'd heard through a closed door. Prebble was in Tombstone with his sister at the time of Byron Locke's murder. Chapin was in Tucson, or so he claimed. But Sam Bruder had no alibi for Wednesday night. Bruder was a man given to rage and violence, to rape, and perhaps murder.

"Charley, would DUC benefit from Byron Locke's death?"

"I don't see how. The case had already been decided."

"Yet Bruder had words with Locke outside the court-house and again at the Dragoon meeting."

"You think Bruder followed Locke back to his trailer?"

"It would explain a lot. If Prebble and Chapin knew or suspected that Bruder killed Locke, they'd want to cover it up."

Charley shifted in his seat. "The money angle. With Locke dead, DUC might have better luck with future court cases—but only if the company wasn't tied to his murder."

I nodded. "Could Prebble or Chapin have killed Bruder to short-circuit further problems?"

"I have a hard time seeing either of them as mur-derers," Charley said. "And we're back to Peaches' gun. How would Prebble or Chapin have gotten hold of it?"

"They were at the ranch Wednesday, visiting with Nate and Jody."

"But that would mean Prebble and Chapin made the decision to remove Bruder *before* he killed Locke, not after." Charley tapped the steering wheel. "I wonder if they found out about Goma?"

"It wouldn't have to be Goma. According to Chapin, Bruder was persona non grata in more than one country."

"Really?" Charley said. "That puts an entirely different spin on things."

The pieces of the puzzle began to click into place. A pic-ture emerged, an alternative hypothesis for Locke's and

Bruder's murders. Plausible enough, perhaps, to displace the brothers Black and myself as prime suspects.

"It doesn't explain Ron's murder," Charley said, playing devil's advocate. "Prebble and Chapin didn't know him."

"Chapin admitted to Cruz that he'd met Ron years ago."

"But would he or Prebble have recognized Ron's Bronco at Massai Point?"

"Maybe they didn't. Maybe they described it to Jody at the meeting. It's a distinctive vehicle."

Charley nodded. "But does the timing work? They stayed after the meeting to talk with Raul and Joaquin."

"Yes, but if we ask the deputies, I bet we'll find Chapin and Prebble hightailed it out of Portal while the deputies were giving Raul a warning. I would have."

Paul Cruz strode through the motel breezeway and over to the Honda. "Chapin and Prebble took off?" he said, as if he'd heard my last remark.

"And the lawyer," I said. "Time is money."

"That'll make this easier," Cruz said cryptically. "I'm so hungry I could eat a whole steer. We'll talk inside."

Judging by the decor, or lack thereof, Riva's Café had once been part of a major chain. I'd seen the same red vinyl booths, country-kitchen wallpaper, and faux Tiffany fixtures at a hundred highway off-ramps across the West. Without waiting for the hostess to seat us, Cruz made straight for a group of tables in a room at the back. Ignoring the wooden sign at the entrance declaring This Section Not in Use, Cruz pushed two tables together and sat so he faced the door. Charley and I sat across from him. Harriet sat next to Cruz, with Esme on her left.

Rory's girlfriend waited on us. When she'd gone, I took Ron's sketchbook from my bag and handed it to Cruz, explaining where and when I'd found it, and what we'd gleaned from it. When he raised an eyebrow, I said, "I swear I haven't been hiding it all afternoon."

Cruz nodded, then unfolded and studied the various panels. I summarized what we'd found in Portal, Paradise, and Peaches' cabin, at Massai Point and the Greyhound bus terminal.

"You have been busy," he said, making notes.

"We had good reason."

Our food arrived. Folding up the sketchbook, Cruz placed it in the middle of the table. "Why do you think Ron hid the book in your bag?"

"Because he wanted someone to look into Bruder's past, to know who and what Bruder was. And he wanted to document what he saw the night of the fire."

"We already had Talmadge's statement. What does this add?"

"You saw the outline of the SUV behind the windmill? Does anyone other than the DUC reps drive a big dark SUV?"

Cruz swallowed. "Not that I've discovered so far. But Prebble and Chapin have alibis—at least Prebble does."

"Have you checked to see if Chapin's Lexus was parked at his motel in Tucson Wednesday night?"

"It was there."

"What about the Haydons?" I repeated what Jed and Rory had told Harriet and Esme—that they'd passed the Haydons on the San Simon Road an hour before the fire.

"They have a truck, not an SUV."

"Norm and Tammi Barnett?" I told Cruz about the snippet of conversation I'd overheard between Jed and Tammi. Charley confirmed that Norm Barnett did piecework in Silver City.

"Interesting," Cruz said, "but they have a truck, too."

"That leaves Bruder," I said. "He had the Escalade that night . . . and no one was keeping tabs on him after the Dragoon meeting."

Cruz's eyes narrowed. "Locke wasn't shot like the other two. He was struck, and then left to burn. A crime of opportunity—brutal, yet almost casual."

"As if the killer was inured to life and death," I said. "It fits the Sam Bruder Ron and Nadine knew in Africa."

"You're reading a lot into one sketch."

"But you'll check behind the windmill for tire tracks?"

"Yes." He looked at his hands, as if puzzling where the first half of his sandwich had gone. "If it was Bruder, he would have seen Talmadge drive by, but he wouldn't have recognized him . . . or his vehicle."

"And Talmadge might or might not have recognized the Escalade in the dark."

"Depends on whether he saw what Bruder was driving in Dragoon."

I leaped ahead. "We know that the next evening, Thursday, Prebble and Bruder had an argument over dinner. Prebble left. Bruder looked at a document—"

"The bill of sale for the Lufkin mineral rights, signed by Nate Lufkin," said Cruz. "Or so Prebble believes. I'll confirm that with Jody tomorrow." Another note. His list was growing. It couldn't be making him happy.

Harriet excused herself and went out to keep Spica company. "The contract story's plausible," I said. "You and I found the draft document."

Cruz looked up from his notes. "Prebble confirmed that Bruder phoned after he left the restaurant." He was still playing good cop, freely sharing information. "Bruder said he was taking the Escalade. He might have had a date—possibly with Rory's girlfriend. The Escalade wasn't parked outside Bruder's room when Prebble came here for a nightcap at eight." Cruz pointed with his pen toward the batwing doors that led to a bar in the rear of the café. "But the Escalade was back when Prebble returned to the motel at nine thirty."

"Prebble was at the bar all that time?"

Cruz nodded. "Unfortunately I have no way to corroborate what happened earlier in the day—Bruder's visit to Hoodoo Ranch, his giving a ride to Peaches, or his getting Nate to sign the contract. For the moment, we'll assume Jody and Prebble are telling the truth."

"Surely Nate's signature wouldn't be valid on a contract," Charley said.

"If Jody weren't around to fight him, Bruder might have been able to persuade a judge Nate was lucid when he signed." Cruz looked at his notes again. "Moving on to Massai Point—if your information is correct, we know that Talmadge's Bronco was parked there before sundown. His sketches prove he was still there during the murder, though he may not have seen the murderer." Pain touched his eyes as he added, "Presumably Peaches Tarango."

"Maybe, maybe not," I said. "Prebble and Chapin had even more reason to remove Bruder from the picture.

Bruder's actions put the company—and their livelihoods—at risk. And if he were gone, Chapin stood to take over the company."

"But you still have Peaches' gun at the scene."

"You know for sure?"

"Yeah. Ballistics came back positive. Peaches' gun fired the bullet that killed Bruder."

It was a hurdle. "Okay, but if Ron saw Peaches that night, why didn't he put him in the sketch?" When Cruz didn't answer, I said, "And why did Ron rearrange the body and put the minerals under Bruder's tongue?"

On cue, Esme handed Cruz the copper minerals, explaining where she'd found the sample on Massai Point. She then did the same with the broken roadrunner sculpture. I produced Harriet's sample bags with bullets fired from Jed's and Rory's guns.

Cruz made a little pile of the evidence, turned a page in his notebook and continued his numbered points. He swept an upturned hand over the objects. "You realize you've compromised chain of custody."

I shook my head. "Even if we'd waited for your team to process these sites, the articles wouldn't have been allowed into evidence at trial. They were discovered by a person of interest, her students, and the parent of two other suspects. But we couldn't leave these where they were, either. They might have conveniently disappeared. So you'll just have to build your case with other evidence."

Clearly irritated, Cruz scratched his forehead. But he knew I was right. He'd just have to deal with it.

He looked at his notes. "Let's go back," he said. "You said Talmadge repositioned Bruder's body?"

"And raised his head to face Goma, the clinic in Africa where Bruder raped Nadine Deroucher." I opened the sketchbook and pointed to the word *Goma*, written twice, and to the rape scene.

"That's Bruder?"

"I'm sure of it."

Cruz thought about that for a minute. "Then Talmadge had the biggest grudge against Bruder."

"But Ron didn't kill Bruder," I said. "He couldn't have."

"He was there. He had motive and opportunity—and it would let Peaches off the hook."

"But he didn't have Peaches' gun, at least not until after it was used to kill Bruder. Even then he tossed it away. But the gun's not your only problem."

Cruz thought about it. Nodded. "You're right. How could Talmadge have driven two vehicles down off the mountain?"

32

Cruz finished his sandwich while he pondered this new wrinkle. "Talmadge could have towed the Escalade."

"If the Bronco had a tow bar," Charley said. "And in that case, someone here at the motel was bound to have heard him unhooking the Escalade. It makes quite a racket."

"So we're back to Peaches," Cruz said. "He kills Bruder, then sees Talmadge's Bronco in the parking lot. Peaches recognizes the vehicle. Believing Talmadge is a witness, he kills him the next night, after the Portal meeting."

"You have a problem there, too—two, actually," I said. "Where'd Peaches get the second gun? And without a vehicle, how'd he cross the range to Portal?"

"We'll ask him when we find him," Cruz said, staring out the window at the purpling mountains.

My mind drifted to Ron, driving home from Massai Point that night, thinking about what would happen next. The scientist in him was curious, dispassionate. He decided to attend the Portal meeting the next night to see who'd be there and what they'd do.

"Has anyone contacted Ronnie Talmadge's caregivers?" Charley said.

"Toni Navarro called Child Protective Services."

Silence. Little gray cells played tag in my brain. "You talked to Toni?"

Cruz faced me. "Several times. I checked you out with Tucson PD and Pima County yesterday afternoon. Toni's acted as point on the Tucson details. How do you think I found out that Joaquin didn't spend Thursday night at his grandparents' house?"

"Where was he?" said Charley.

"Stopped at a checkpoint in Rodeo. The New Mexico police suspected he'd given a lift to migrants, that he'd let them out on the edge of town. They didn't have proof, so they had to release him. He called Rosa's parents to say he'd arrive in Tucson so late he was just going to sleep in his truck in the college parking lot."

"He didn't want to compound your suspicions by alerting you to the New Mexico stop? What an idiot." When Cruz didn't contradict me, I said, "So why did you keep *me* here?"

"After Ron turns up dead and you're the one who's driven him home?" Both eyebrows went up this time. "Besides, Toni advised me that you might be useful."

I laced my fingers so tightly my knuckles whitened. "You couldn't just tell me this?"

"And get us both into trouble? Your involvement had to be unofficial."

That explained the oscillations I'd observed all day— flip, flop, good cop, bad cop. "You played me, Detective Cruz."

He smiled. "But it's been a balancing act from start to finish."

"We're not finished," I said, intending both meanings. "We still have to find Peaches."

Cruz's phone rang. He took it outside. A minute later he was back. "That was Toni. Child Protective Services hasn't been able to locate Ronnie. And she wants you to turn on your cell phone. She says she had a call from Philo Dain."

I'd already brought my phone to life. There was one message, left last night. Philo's voice, crackling over some kind of background noise. He'd be home soon, in time . . . The message broke off. In time for what? Jamie's wedding?

I stood and walked to the window, keeping my back to the group. The room was warm, but I was shivering. *Philo was alive.*

For more than a year, I'd lived in limbo. I'd gone about my daily routine, thrown myself into my job and into fixing up the house. After the first month, I'd stopped watching the nightly news with its reports on the mounting toll of dead and wounded in Iraq and Afghanistan. Philo had cut off contact for a reason, I told myself. I needed to trust in that. *Trust,* my Achilles' heel.

"Dr. MacFarlane?" Cruz said.

I retraced my steps, picked up my bag. "We're going back to Charley's now. And tomorrow morning, Peaches or no Peaches, Joaquin and Raul are off the leash and I'm heading to Tucson with my students."

"Okay," Cruz said. "I know where to find you." But I swear he was smiling as he pushed back his chair and pocketed Ron's sketchbook. "I do appreciate the help, Dr. MacFarlane."

My anger with Cruz had dissipated. Philo was coming home. Still, I wouldn't ask Cruz to call me Frankie.

We were going to be very late for dinner. While I paid the cashier, Charley went outside to call Rosa. He came back as the cashier handed me my change.

"Raul's gone AWOL," he said.

33

"This isn't one of your jokes, Charley?" said Cruz.

"Not this time."

The story spilled out. Raul's wife, Cindy, had just called Rosa. When Raul didn't come home from work, Cindy had contacted the fire station. Raul had reported back after meeting with the lawyer, but left early. "Raul took personal time, said he had an errand to run for a friend on the way home," Charley said. "An emergency. He's not answering his cell. It keeps rolling to voice mail."

I touched his arm. "Maybe the same friend he was with Thursday night?" I said. I wasn't talking out of school. Raul refused to say where he was Thursday evening. Surely Cruz had already considered the other-woman angle.

"Raul planned to take the girls shopping for Mother's Day. They were going to dinner first," Charley said. "He wouldn't have stood them up. He wouldn't have forgotten."

"An emergency errand, you said? Maybe that friend is Peaches." Cruz tucked his change in his pocket. "If Peaches didn't take the bus, he'll need a vehicle—or a horse. Even if it's just to get him to the border."

"That's what I'm afraid of," Charley said. Pain tightened the skin of his face, emphasizing the high cheekbones. "I have to take Frankie and the students back to the ranch. Would you send someone to stay with Cindy till her parents get there?"

"Of course."

Outside, Cruz climbed into his Tahoe and picked up his radio. Moments later, he turned out of the parking lot and headed south.

Harriet had taken Spica from the carrier so the cat could use the litter box. "She wasn't too happy about the circumstances," Harriet said. "But nature overcame distaste. I gave her some food and water, too."

Spica was sitting on Harriet's lap, cleaning her paws and face. "Time to put her back in the carrier," Charley said.

We closed the windows and turned on the air conditioner. The Honda smelled like a sand box frequented by feral cats. It was going to be a long drive back to the ranch.

As we headed out of town to the interstate, I told Harriet what had transpired after she left the table. She said, "Maybe Peaches is in hiding because he knows someone's trying to frame him."

Charley smiled at her reflection in the mirror. "If so, he'll get a message to us."

"Perhaps he called Raul." Her words encapsulated all our fears. Seeing my expression, she switched topics. "So I guess we won't be stopping at the Haydons' road cut on the way home?"

I shook my head. I'd forgotten all about my request to Ginny Haydon six hours ago. Like our visit to the Rucker Canyon section, the road cut would have to wait for another day.

It was quiet—too quiet—at the Black ranch. They were gathered in the family room. I could see wedding favors, net-wrapped and tied with bows, on the dining room table. Wyatt and Vicente looked no worse for their forced labor. Wyatt was thumbing through the current issue of *Discover*. Vicente, headphones on and eyes closed, was listening to his iPod. But Rosa stood in front of the fireplace, drying her hands, over and over, on a dishtowel.

"Anything from Raul?" Charley wrapped his arms around her.

"*Nada.*" She turned her head against his shoulder and looked at me. "But Killeen called. He couldn't reach you on your cell."

E. J. Killeen, U.S. Army, retired, was an old friend who'd shared several adventures with me. He'd been living in Philo's home and running his private investigation business while he was overseas.

I felt my shoulders tense. "Was it about Philo coming home?"

"You heard?" Rosa's face lightened for a moment.

I relaxed a bit. "In Willcox. Detective Cruz had a call from Toni while we were—Charley will tell you about it. Did Killeen say anything else?"

"Just to make sure you called your home machine."

I went into Charley's office and dialed my answering machine. Five messages, the last from Philo. It began with an apology, full of hesitations, restarts, just like my cell phone message. There was noise in the background. He was sorry, he said, but he'd been unable to communicate till now. He'd explain when he saw me. Couldn't wait to see me. The call ended abruptly.

I replayed it three times, relishing the sound of his voice. In case he'd written, I grabbed my computer and checked my e-mail. Found only the usual department memos and notes from students. I'd answer them at school on Monday.

"Any luck?" Charley said behind me.

"Nothing from Philo." I took my flash drive from my pocket, uploaded the files, and sent them to Cruz. "Do you want copies of the files I got from Jody's computer?"

"What's there?"

I showed Charley the DUC files.

"Why don't you just print me a copy. I'd rather not have to explain why I have them on my machine or how they came into my possession."

"Good thinking." I sent the files to the printer and told the computer to release my flash drive. Tucking my key ring and drive back in my pocket, I followed Charley to the family room. "Can I help with dinner?" I asked Rosa.

"No. It's almost ready. Maybe fifteen minutes."

"I'll wash up then." I headed for the closest bathroom. Teresa had painted hummingbirds on the off-white tiles of the shower and sink. The jewel tones glowed. The birds seemed to be moving . . . or maybe the whole room was spinning. I couldn't tell. I was tired. My reflection in the mirror showed dust-streaked tanned skin, bloodshot gray eyes, windblown black hair. I scrubbed my face and hands, combed and rebraided my hair. "Better," I said to my reflection. "Not great, but better."

Wyatt and Vicente were standing in the hallway outside the bathroom door, waiting. Wyatt was petting Spica, who'd been given the run of the house. I wasn't sure how Marty would take to having his space invaded by a cat. But we'd find out soon enough.

"About time," Wyatt said. "Come see what we discovered."

In the family room, Vicente handed me a sheaf of computer printouts. "Responses to the messages I posted on various boards. They're pretty interesting. I've kinda put them in order for you."

Sitting in Rosa's favorite armchair, I skimmed the pages. Vicente was right. Interesting was an understatement. The clatter of pots in the kitchen and the hum of voices in the room faded away.

I have been researching my mother's family, which is how I came across your post. One branch of the family went to Rhodesia. A great-aunt of mine married a Samuel Bruda (sometimes spelled Brüder or Bruder) in Southern Rhodesia (Zimbabwe, now). Had cotton and tobacco plantations there, and cobalt and copper mines in Northern Rhodesia. My second cousin, once removed, Samuel Bacon Bruda, was born in 1949. I never met him, though I met his father, Jacob Bruda, once in London.

That entire branch, with the exception of Samuel, was slaughtered by guerrillas in 1975. They had refused to leave their property. We heard that Samuel had escaped into the bush and made his way to South Africa. When he contacted us some time later, my father offered to bring him to England, but Samuel chose to enlist in the South African Army. He was sent to the frontier. We were told he was reported missing in action in 1979.

If you think my cousin Samuel might be the man for whom you are searching, or you have news of him, I would very much appreciate you contacting me.

Yours most respectfully, Rupert Bellamy.

The second reply was from a man named Lowe in Angola:

Re: Your post concerning Samuel Bruder, a gentleman associated with mining in [South?] Africa:

I knew a South African soldier, a white man named Sammy Bruda, on the Namibian border during the time of troubles there. He collected maps and knew about mining, too. He made notes in a little book whenever he learned about minerals being mined locally. And he would trade supplies of food, blankets, that type of thing, with refugees for rough minerals and such . . . I met him again during our civil war. Sammy was a mercenary brought in to advise and train UNITA troops. I hope this helps your search.

The Dutch journalist Van de Ven that Vince and Wyatt had exchanged messages with wrote:

I was a young photojournalist covering the Angolan conflict for Reuters. Sam Bruder—a white man—served as a mercenary with various factions in Angola. He was an expert in guerrilla warfare. I came to know him well—or as well as anyone. I did a piece on him and his unit.

Bruder was listed as missing after a raid on a village in 1979 or 1980. The unit was wiped out, but his body was never recovered. I was taken to the site. It would have been a miracle if he'd survived. If I knew why you were looking for him, I might be able to tell you more.

Wyatt tapped a finger on the last line. "So we told him we'd discovered Bruder's body and were seeking any kind of background information."

"Tell me you didn't pass yourselves off as law enforcement." I looked from face to face.

"Give us a little credit, Dr. MacFarlane." Wyatt grinned. "Here's what we got back." He handed me a sheet. The message was terse:

As to Bruder's background and description: He was from Southern Rhodesia originally. Had served in the South African army. Educated. Quick-tempered. Perhaps 76 kg. Hair—blond. Eyes—blue. Stocky build. Square face. Heavy drinker. Smoker. Liked his ladies young—very young. Wasn't particular about race.

The day Bruder went out on that final mission, we heard he'd raped a local girl. There wouldn't have been a trial, of course. The Angolans would have dealt with him informally. Perhaps they did. Or perhaps he just disappeared into the jungle. Either way, I never heard of him again.

"Interesting, huh?" Wyatt said.

"Remarkable." I set that aside and picked up the last printout, unsigned.

Are you sure you have the spelling correct? There was a Sem Bruder, a white man, in eastern Zaire at the time of the genocide. He trafficked in conflict diamonds and gold in the eastern Congo—until world demand made coltan worth more than diamonds. He had his own militia of native guards. Hutu, mostly. Helped him smuggle coltan out of the Congo to sell on the Internet.

A dangerous man, but he always treated me courteously when he brought injured men to the clinic in Kivumu. I did hear that he or his men had killed a Jesuit relief worker and attacked a doctor at the clinic in Goma. I also heard Bruder was injured. He disappeared in 1996, after being accused of trafficking by the new government.

"There were five or six posts that seemed to be from people trying to hook up with us," Vicente said, "and a couple from guys offering to do searches—for a fee."

"What next?" Wyatt said.

"Dinner's ready," Rosa called from the kitchen.

"First we eat," I said to Wyatt. "Over dinner, I'll fill you in on what we found out today. Second, we brainstorm how we can help find Raul."

Joaquin, Teresa, and Jamie came through the back door, my younger brother towering over the other two. Jamie, a pediatrician, was ten months younger and six inches taller than I. He covered the distance in two strides. "Hey, Sis," was followed by a bear hug.

I introduced Harriet and Esme. Wyatt and Vicente had met Jamie and Teresa when they first arrived. Joaquin set his backpack in the corner, quickly filled Marty's food and water dishes outside, and came back in. Marty ignored his food. Ears erect, nose pressed against the screen door, he watched Spica. Her hair stood up. She hissed. He barked. Spica sprang for a safe perch atop one of the cupboards.

"This might not work," Joaquin said. Picking up a plate, he filled it at the stove and sat next to Esme. Outside, Marty continued to *whuff* for a while, then busied himself with his food.

"If it doesn't, I'd be happy to take Spica," Harriet said. "We get along."

Charley smiled. "I'll keep that in mind." Turning to Joaquin, he said, "What happened at Mackey Canyon?"

"Somebody definitely cut the fence."

"Border crossers?"

"Nope. Too far into the mountains. Besides, they had wheels—a truck or SUV."

"Rustlers?"

"No cattle missing. Doubt if it was drugs, either. They'd have used the road. No reason to cut the fence." He took a swig of water. "I took pictures of the tire tracks. I'll figure it out."

"I think it was a prank," Jamie said. "Somebody wanted to cause trouble."

"But why?" said Rosa. "We haven't hurt anyone." The last word was lost in a sob. Rosa shoved back her chair and ran toward their bedroom. Jamie, Teresa, and Joaquin stared after her, openmouthed.

Jamie found his voice first. "Was it something I said?"

"Raul's skipped town," Wyatt said, taking a huge bite of burrito.

"Wyatt," I protested, resolving to get my Asperger student back to Tucson ASAP. "This isn't a computer game where no one really gets hurt. The police are hunting him."

"Oh, sorry." Wyatt looked stricken. "Sorry, Charley. But at least he's not dead."

"Wyatt—"

"No, Wyatt's right," Charley interrupted. Charley never interrupts. "Raul's not where he's supposed to be, but as far as we know he's alive and well. It could be worse."

"I'll just shut up and eat now," said Wyatt.

"Good idea." Harriet put her hand on his shoulder. Wyatt didn't shrug it off.

"So, what happened?" said Teresa.

Charley's summary was short, but complete, ending with, "We've no idea where he's headed. Cindy's waiting by the phone. Her family's with her. We'll go over tomorrow. At the moment, it's in the hands of the authorities." He stood up. "Excuse me, I'm going to see to your mother."

The group fell silent except for the subdued clatter of silverware against plates.

"You said whoever cut the fence had wheels?" I asked Joaquin. When he nodded, I described Ron's sketches of the night of the fire, and offered my hypothesis that Sam Bruder, driving DUC's Escalade, had followed Byron Locke home after the Dragoon meeting. "It would be nice to know if the tracks behind the windmill that night match those left by the vehicle at your fence cutting."

"I'll check it out in the morning."

"You may need to help search for Raul tomorrow," Esme said quietly. "We could make a quick trip to the windmill after dinner. I saw Ron's sketch. I can identify the place."

Jamie looked at Teresa, lifted one eyebrow. The writing was on the wall.

My first responsibility, I knew, was to get my students back to Tucson. "Esme, I'm not sure—"

"I'd like to take a look at those tracks, too," Teresa said. "Jamie and I'll follow in my car." Her eyes twinkled. She was making it possible for Esme and Joaquin to be alone. "It'll be okay, Frankie."

I had to smile. "It's settled then."

Joaquin placed his silverware on his empty plate. His gaze lifted to Esme. "Ready?"

She picked up her plate and accompanied him to the kitchen. Teresa and Jamie followed. They rinsed their dishes, grabbed sweatshirts. The kitchen door slammed behind them.

A murmur of voices came from the patio. I could see hundreds of insects beating their wings against the screen door.

Two engines started up. I looked at my other three students. "Who wants dessert?" Rosa said from the hall doorway. "I made brownies."

I heard the sound of a truck coming up the drive to the house. Had Joaquin forgotten something?

A knock at the screen door. Enrique stood bathed in the yellow floodlight. He took off his Arizona Diamondbacks cap and smoothed his silver hair. Rosa hurried to open the door.

"*Buenas noches*, Rosa. Is Charley in?"

Charley came down the hall from their bedroom. "*Hola, amigo*, what brings you all the way out here?"

"We need to talk, old friend. Face to face."

"What is it?"

"The police questioned me," Enrique said.

"Cruz?"

"No, a woman."

"Please, come in," Rosa urged, gesturing toward the sofa. "Sit."

Enrique perched on the edge of the sofa, put his cap on the table. But he didn't seem to know where to start.

"You told the policewoman something?" Charley prompted.

"She asked if I'd ever sold a gun to Joaquin or Raul. I had to tell her yes. To Raul. It was a couple of weeks ago, at a gun show in Tucson." He tugged his earlobe with blunt fingers.

"What caliber?" I said. They turned to me.

"She asked me if it was a .38. I said, yes, a Smith and Wesson Model 10. I'm sorry, I didn't know what else to do."

"You did the right thing, Enrique," Rosa said. "The truth is always the right thing."

"Ron Talmadge was shot with a .38," I said.

Enrique sighed and shook his head. "That's what I was afraid of."

"Did you sell any other .38s recently?"

"One. Same gun show. A snub-nosed Colt Detective Special—to a woman who was looking for just such a weapon."

"A stranger?" I said.

"Yes. She had black hair. Her clothes fit like—" he paused, glanced at Rosa, "well, you know. And she kept looking over her shoulder. I think she was buying the gun for someone else. It happens all the time."

"Was anyone with her?" I said.

"I saw another woman follow her out. But I couldn't swear they were together." Enrique looked as if he wanted to say something more, but he held back.

"Did you recognize her?" I said. "The other woman?"

"I only saw her from behind."

I'd found two receipts from Enrique in Jody Lufkin's desk drawer—one for the guns he'd bought from her, and a second for a single handgun. But I didn't want to reveal that I'd been snooping in Jody's private papers. "Did you buy guns that day from Jody Lufkin?"

Enrique straightened, tugged harder on the earlobe. "Yeah, out in the parking lot, before the show started. Some of Nate's guns—couple of hunting rifles, a shotgun, and a couple of pistols. Gave her a good price."

"Could it have been Jody who followed the other woman out?"

Enrique nodded. "Doesn't make much sense for her to have someone else buy her a gun. Why didn't she just keep one of Nate's?" He shrugged. "Maybe I'm wrong. Maybe it was just another skinny blonde in a red shirt."

"Maybe," Charley agreed. "When you bought Nate's guns, did you take the whole batch, or just select some?"

"I took everything she had. She said she needed the money."

"Nate has more at the house," I said. "I saw them today. So did Cruz."

"Really? Then that makes it even more strange. I'll check with the other dealers and see if she's dealt with any of them. Might help Raul."

When Rosa started to protest, Enrique said, "It'd make me feel better, Rosa. You don't know how many times Raul stopped by to visit with Lupe when she was sick. He's a good boy. Hot-tempered, but his heart's in the right place." He stood. "You know, don't you, I would never want to make trouble for your sons."

Only then, on the way to the door, did Charley tell him that Raul was missing. Enrique stopped, stunned. "I'm so sorry. I didn't know, old friend." He put his hand on

Charley's shoulder. "Don't worry, *amigo,* God will watch over him."

On the way down the drive, Enrique's truck passed Joaquin's and Teresa's vehicles returning. When they trooped into the house, I could see from their faces that they'd found something.

"No match on the tracks behind the windmill," Joaquin said. "But then we stopped where Byron Locke's trailer burned." He looked at Teresa, who grinned. "You tell them," Joaquin said.

"We found tire tracks on the turnoff to the new road up Gray Mountain," she said. "They match the tracks by the cut fence."

"The Haydons?" Charley said.

Joaquin gave a satisfied smile. "You bet. Mystery solved."

"But why?" I said.

They were all grinning now. Jamie looked at the others. "We asked ourselves the same question. So we paid them a visit."

Rosa touched Jamie's hand. "And?"

"Ginny was pissed that we were against their road," Joaquin said. "She cut the fence as a warning."

"Did you give them a warning of your own?" Charley said.

"I told them we'd press charges if they didn't stop."

"And Jamie told them there were a lot more where he came from, and some of them are lawyers." Teresa put her arm around Jamie's waist. "I think they've had their fill of lawyers."

Was I wrong about Bruder killing Byron Locke, I wondered? Had the Haydons had their fill of lawyers three days ago? And another thought niggled at the back of my mind.

"We've been making an assumption," I said. "We've assumed that the killing's over." I had their attention. "But if Bruder didn't kill Byron Locke, and these murders are random acts of a madman, then he may strike again. And we haven't a clue where he'll strike next."

"Or whom," Harriet said.

I nodded. "I'm not taking any chances with my students tonight. Charley, do you mind if we sleep in the house?"

"It would be best," he said.

"Esme and Harriet can bunk upstairs," Teresa said.

"Vince and I can take the floor in the office," said Wyatt. "We have mats and sleeping bags."

"I'll take the family room couch," I said. "We'll leave first thing in the morning. In the meantime, no one goes anywhere alone."

PART

Northern Chiricahua Mountains, southeastern Arizona
Sunday, May 14

"There is a game of puzzles," he resumed, "which is played upon a map. One party playing requires another to find a given word—the name of town, river, state or empire—any word, in short, upon the motley and perplexed surface of the chart. . . . [T]he adept selects such words as stretch, in large characters, from one end of the chart to the other. These, like the over-largely lettered signs and placards of the street, escape observation by dint of being excessively obvious."

—Edgar Allan Poe, "The Purloined Letter" (1845)

"Here, then," said Dupin to me, "you have precisely what you demand to make the ascendancy complete—the robber's knowledge of the loser's knowledge of the robber. "

" Yes," replied the Prefect; "and the power thus attained has, for some months past, been wielded, for political purposes, to a very dangerous extent. The personage robbed is more thoroughly convinced, every day, of the necessity of reclaiming her letter. But this, of course, cannot be done openly. "

—Edgar Allan Poe, "The Purloined Letter" (1845)

34

Black Ranch, Coues Canyon
Midnight

I couldn't sleep. My mind went over and over the evidence we'd collected, trying to put it into some kind of order. In the morning I'd be heading back to Tucson with the students, but I felt like a failure. I hadn't solved Ron's puzzle. And where was Raul—with Peaches?

Raul and Peaches. Peaches and Raul. Something didn't make sense. Why would Peaches leave his gun behind? To stage what looked like a suicide?

That had a certain kind of logic. He couldn't have anticipated that Ron would come along and change the scene. Nor that Joaquin would discover the body, recognize the gun, and tell Cruz about it. There was no way a killer could plan for those events.

I tossed and turned. The moonlight poured down on the hills. Coyotes yipped and bayed. The pack's cries crescendoed as they ran their prey to ground . . . just as the law was closing in on Raul and Peaches. Where would Cruz find them? Were they together?

My brain protested the mental steeplechase as my mind jumped from Raul's disappearance, to Ron's murder, to the messages Wyatt and Vicente received from their contacts in Africa. I couldn't seem to isolate and focus on any aspect. The excitement of Philo's imminent return hummed like a fluorescent light in the background. My head began to throb.

Giving up on sleep, I turned on the light, found my field bag, and rummaged through it for ibuprofen.

Joaquin's carving of White Painted Woman poked my hand. I pulled her out. She seemed to be smiling. I took it as a good sign and set her on the coffee table, where I could see her as I searched the zippered pockets. I found the African puzzle I'd torn from Ron's field notebook and the puzzles he'd left in the café menu and on the board in the Portal meetingroom. Was it only last night that Ron was murdered? It seemed like an eon had passed in a single day.

The ibuprofen was in the last pocket, of course. I got a glass of water from the kitchen, sat at the dining room table, and spread out the puzzles. It was soothing to work, surrounded by the silence of a household at sleep—except for Spica, of course. She'd slept all afternoon. Now it was playtime.

Spica came over and rubbed against my ankles, then went back to the kitchen. She paced, then paused, sat watching the bottom of the stove. I heard a scrabbling sound. A field mouse, coming in through the stove vent.

Cat and mouse, an age-old story. Today—yesterday, now—I'd been Detective Cruz's mouse. But had he, in turn, been a mouse in someone else's game? Had Raul? If so, who was the cat? I suspected the answers lay in Ron's puzzles, if I could just concentrate long enough to decipher them.

I started with the African puzzle, smoothing it out on the table, looking for clues to that beginning time. In Africa, according to Ron's sketches, the lives of a Jesuit ethnobotanist, a doctor, and a brutal trafficker in conflict minerals had intersected. Ron had been doing fieldwork in the Rwanda-Zaire border country when the genocide erupted. I knew many priests and nuns had been massacred in Kigali. Perhaps the only reason Ron had survived was because he was in the bush.

B
KYRIEAMROGOMA
SBUKWHYAVULGOUMARWANDBRUDER
ALOSTGOMRABUERUDNDIGOMAUBUKAV
SAMUGOMAUGOMZAIREAINFERNOGOMARGOMPAGS
EOMTAGLOMAGOEMLASGORMAGOMAGNOMAAMOAG
CULPARHUTUSWANDAGOOMOAKIGALIRWAINTERHAMWENDA
UBUKAVUTKIGALIRELOIWNAKNDABURUNNDIGAOMAGLOMAGOMAG
OLMCAGDESPAIROMALGMOMAGIBUKRAPINGAVUDBUKAEVUGOMAGOMA
KPIUGAELIKIGWALIOKAPOCALYPSEIGALIRWAINCHRISTEDABUSRUF
NMEADLIBSUSRUNADVOIIRWANDLABUVKAVUGOLOSTMAGSOMVENGEANCEA
ELOSPTLTOSTLONSTGLOSSTLOISTLEOSTLOSTLEOSTLOFOISTGOMMAA
MAXIMALORSTIMLDOSNTLPOSTLNOOSLIFETLOSTFOREINVELIVESRLOR
NSTFGODSORLASCIATEEVERGLOSAFOREVMANSERFOREVERA
GSOMLAYGOMAGOMHABURKSAVUKIGTALICOANGOICGOMAOVALEN
MADNESSGGOUCONEGOLAMACOGNDGINHUMANITYOGOMACONGLO
NKIFGAFORSAKENLIKNIBECOMEGOAOLIMKNOIGODGNALIDEATH
IVERWTANDDARLWATNDAZRAWALNADNALRWANDANOCONGOCONYGEO
LOSTILAMRLOSATCIHDATVSEOFLOSTFARESTITHLOSTA
FAITHINTEVERHYTHCINGIHATEHAVEWLOSTHR
TOPEINHEHVERYDEATHTHAINGIHAVIEMLOSS
TEALLDIAMONDSTRUUSTINTGOBULLETDAAND
RMANNKPIANDTHSEDCOEVENANTIHACKED
GENOCIDESMBROKTHEENFOREPVERMYH
VGOODMYGNODAWHYSHAVHEYATTACKED
EOULFORYESABKENTMWHOEWLHYNHAT
NVETYOUFDORALLSRAKERODENMDEHE
GOMAFORSAKENUSWORLDSWEHYWHYE
ETHNOPEACEEDYKIYLLOEVAERHELL
NOTHQINGHOPEHEATEGRTEEDANL
IDEUNVYKNINLRLTHEEHS
NOBISOUCLTTHECEOLN
GEOBLHEREEPEACE
SAMEDSRTHREACROI
NGOIWBEECPTSS
MISEREREFHOON
RTTUHELOSTNO
EFDORNA
DEINE
RIP

Certain words and letters—*Kigali, Rwanda, Burundi,* and *Bukavu,* for example—were repeated, forming a background rant for other words and phrases. Once I figured out his pattern, I crossed out those background letters and words. The remaining words were a skeletal structure that exposed Ron's long dark night of the soul.

```
                          B
                KYRIE     R
        S     WHY   L     U          BRUDER
      LOST    R     E     D          U
   SAM     U  ZAIRE INFERNO          R      P
     E   T  L   E L  S    R          N      A
  CULPA HUTUS        O O              INTERHAMWE
  U      T      ELOI N  K            N      A      L
  L C  DESPAIR  L       I    RAPING  D      E
  P U  E I   W   O APOCALYPSE      I CHRISTE     S   F
 MEA L  S S   A VOI    L    V      LOST   S  VENGEANCE
  E    P T   N  G  S   I    E         E     OF I    M SAM
 MAXIMA  R    D  N  P  NO LIFE            IN   LIVES   R
   N   GODS  LASCIATE   G    A       MANS        A
   S  L Y       H   R S      T       A      GOMA VALE
 MADNESS G U  E  LAMA  G D INHUMANITY GOMA      L
   N  F  FORSAKEN   N BECOME O O  M NO GOD N   DEATH
 IVE  T    D  L  T   Z A  L A N L       NO       Y E
        LOST L  R   A C  D T S OF      REST       A
            FAITH T    H    C    HATE      W      R
             T    H H    DEATH A      I M    S
             E   DIAMONDS  U     T  BULLET A
              R   N P A    S D   E        HACKED
            GENOCIDE M    THE        P      H
             V  O    N  A    S    H  ATTACKED
             E  L   YE  B  T WHO  L  N    T
             N  T    D  ALL R  RODE  D  HE
            GOMA  R     N  WORLDS E     E
             E  NOPEACE D   Y    E A  HELL
                 Q    HOPE E      T    L
              I  U    N N R   E H
             NOBIS  C  T    E L
                E  HERE PEACE
             SAM   R  R A R  I
                 I B   C T S
             MISERERE H ON
                 T U      NO
                 E D
                   E
                 RIP
```

I silently thanked my parents for insisting on a classical education—my mother, in particular, for her tendency to recite poetry at the drop of a hat. Ron had quoted lines, phrases, and titles from eclectic sources, all concerning violence or death. I listed all the words I could find, then tried to link the ones that traditionally went together.

Ron had taken "I am become Death, the destroyer of worlds" from the Bhagavad Gita, "Man's inhumanity to man" from Robert Burns . . . "Death rode no pale horse" and "No peace on earth" were contradictions of biblical lines. *Paradise Lost* was the title of Milton's epic poem, while "Abandon all hope, ye who enter here" was from Dante's *Inferno*. Ron had even included *Inferno* as one of the words. His African experience must have seemed like the end of the world.

Some phrases, such as *Kyrie eleison, Christe eleison, mea culpa, mea maxima culpa,* and *miserere nobis* hailed from the Catholic Mass in Latin and classical choral music. Others, such as *Apocalypse, Revelations,* and *Eloi, Eloi, lama sabachtani* (My God, my God, why have you forsaken me?), were of biblical origin. Many words and terms (*lost souls, despair, madness, insane, lost faith, forsaken, hopeless, remember, no God, no rest, Rwanda, Zaire, Hutus, Tutsis, rage, vengeance, killing, hacked, bullet, attacked, gore, burning, raping, no life, revenge, destroy, machete,* and *Hell*), spoke to his witnessing the 1994 genocide.

The bottom three letters summed up both Ron's tortured state of mind and his prayer for the victims, including himself and Nadine: *RIP. Requiem in pace.*

The horror of that time and place had changed Ron irrevocably, as it had changed Nadine. The only person who had seemed to thrive on the violence was Sam Bruder—until he came to this isolated corner of the world. Tellingly, Ron had included Sam Bruder's name along with three mining commodities—gold, diamonds, and coltan.

Lost faith and despair had led Ron and Nadine to their refuge in Paradise, Arizona. But tragedy had clung to them like a curse.

I set the African puzzle aside and pulled the wordsearch puzzles to me, placing them side by side. They were almost exactly alike. Almost. The café version was fifteen letters horizontally and vertically. The meetingroom version included one extra column on the left, two on the right. I wondered why he'd tinkered with the original—the version he'd photocopied, put in the café menus, and sent off to the environmental magazine.

Unlike the African puzzle, Ron's recent puzzles came with search lists. I circled all the words, looking for a pattern, or for spaces that didn't contain words.

```
A E D S E I N N O R E N I D A N E N
D A L U P I N E R K W A H N M O G O
E D T A K L E H C A P A O J E D E C
S S H F A I P O P P Y D O S L J R I
I T U F H J L I Z A R D D N T A I D
D L M Q U A I L E I A N O A T V A E
A D M H T G L N E V A R O K A E Z &
R U I C U U M A D R U N N E R L N C
A C N O T A O B D E B O R O R I I O
P A G Y S R R T N A G E L E E N R L
F G B O I U N T R O N I E E P A E T
L A I T D O M I N O R E G S I R D A
O V R E N I K F U L Y D O J N O U N
W E D O C O C H I S E Y R O U N R R
E R S C E N I P N O Y N I P J T B T
```

The top lines of both versions of the puzzle had no words from the search list. Neither did the added columns of the larger version. Why were they added? What purpose did they serve?

Looking at the expanded version, the letters of the top line, taken backward and descending down the left margin, read NENADINERONNIESDEADESIDARAPFLOWE . . . Ignoring the first two letters, I found the words *Nadine, Ronnies Dead*. Then, *Paradise,* spelled backward. And, if I turned the corner on the bottom line, *Flowers*.

I closed my eyes. Took a deep breath. Let it out slowly. Opened my eyes. The puzzles hadn't changed. If I took Ron's words literally, his son was dead.

That was why Toni Navarro and CPS couldn't find

Ronnie in Tucson. He was in Paradise, his grave marked by flowers.

My mind was focused now, and fully engaged. Had Ron left other clues, telling us where Ronnie was buried?

I found my camera, uploaded today's pictures into my computer, and saved them to my flash drive. I scrolled back to the images of Ronnie's tree, the image Ron had drawn over and over, first with the boy under it, later with the empty rope swing.

Ron Talmadge loved word puzzles. I studied the flowers—miniature roses, oleander, purple mat, aloe vera, lily, African daisy . . . Had Ron spelled out his son's name in flowers?

R-O-M-A-L-D. Close. I could hear myself saying to Charley, *Roses for love, lilies for remembrance*. What had he called purple mat? *Nama* . . . R-O-N-A-L-D.

Ronnie was buried under his favorite tree, along with his mother's ashes. She'd asked for that garden, Charley said. Ron had given it to her. But it must have broken his heart.

Ronnie's death also raised more questions. Searching for answers, my mind began to connect the dots . . . Ron had been a Jesuit priest. He and Nadine hadn't shared a bedroom. It was possible Ronnie was the byproduct of Nadine's rape in Africa, that he was Bruder's son, not Ron's. The age was right. And that might explain why they'd hidden away in Paradise—to protect Nadine and Ronnie from Bruder.

Ron wouldn't have killed the child he'd raised as a son. But I could envision Nadine, the traumatized doctor, choosing euthanasia for her autistic son instead of life in a care facility. How guilt-ridden Ron must have felt when he buried his son. It explained the sadness that filled his eyes, and the vow of silence he'd taken after Nadine died. He made sure her secrets didn't escape while he was alive.

Yet he'd left clues to those secrets. He'd wanted the truth revealed after his death. And he'd entrusted the keys to me in Paradise.

I studied the meetingroom puzzle again. The two far-right columns held no words from the list. I followed the same routine I had with the top line and left column, listing the letters, then breaking out groupings; trying them backward and forward to make words. Now that I knew how Ron's mind worked, I had no problem finding words. They led back to Africa, to the root of everything: *Bruder in Zaire, genocide & coltan.* Signed *RT,* for Ron Talmadge.

Within the puzzle, I found other letters that seemed extraneous. TUTSI, in the fifth column, was another reference to Rwanda. NIKFULYDOJ, in the third line from the bottom, was . . . And then it hit me. *Jody Lufkin,* spelled backward.

I grabbed the copy of Ron's café puzzle on which I'd circled the letters he'd highlighted in his sketchbook. At the meeting, he'd decided to leave one final clue—as if he'd just realized he might not make it home alive. He'd borrowed my pen to go over those letters, to emphasize the killer's name.

```
E D S E I N N O R E N I D A N
A L U P I N E R K W A H N M O
D T A K L E H C A P A O J E D
S H F A I P O P P Y D O S L J
T U F H J L I Z A R D D N T A
L M Q U A I L E I A N O A T V
D M H T G L N E V A R O K A E
U I C U M A D R U N N E R L
C N O T A O B D E B O R O R I
A G Y S R R T N A G E L E E N
G B O I U N T R O N I E E P A
A I T D O M I N O R E G S I R
V R E N I K F U L Y D O J N O
E D O C O C H I S E Y R O U N
R S C E N I P N O Y N I P J T
```

There it was—*Jody Lufkin*—listed twice, for good measure. And in the center of the puzzle, diagonaling first to the right, then down to the left, *Killed Bruder.* He'd also highlighted *DUC,* as if hinting at a connection, a motive. Yet if Ron felt compelled to name Jody as Bruder's murderer, he was just as insistent on pointing out Bruder's own accountability—for a past that lay in Africa, in Goma, during the Rwandan genocide and the conflict on the border with neighboring states. He'd highlighted the overlapping words *Hutu* and *Tutsi*.

I went back to the larger version of the puzzle, copied from the meetingroom board. In the upper right-hand corner, again read backward and taking a jog to the top line, was *GOMA*.

But why bury a killer's name in a puzzle? Why leave it to chance? Ron wasn't mad. He was capable of coherent thinking. He'd had no trouble writing answers to Cruz's questions after Locke was murdered. He could have written a straightforward note and given it to me at the meeting, or on the way home.

What would I have done in that situation? I would have taken Ron straight to the deputies for protection. And I'd have called Cruz. For some reason, Ron didn't want that.

What if the puzzle didn't say what Ron *knew*, but what he suspected? Friday night, Ron had planned to walk home. If Jody followed him, he would have known for sure. Perhaps he'd planned to break his silence long enough to tell her about Bruder's past in Africa, about Nadine's rape in Goma. Perhaps Ron wanted to tell Jody he applauded the justice of her killing Bruder . . .

But what if it was simpler than that? What if Ron was tired of living, of the weighty secrets he carried? He couldn't commit suicide, but he could fail to stop his own murder.

Ron was dead. I doubted I'd ever know the answers.

I fixed myself a cup of herb tea and thought about Ron's pointing the finger at Jody Lufkin. On moonlit Massai Point, he hadn't been able to identify Bruder's killer, hadn't even drawn a shadowy form, male or female. But by the afternoon of the Portal meeting, he was positive enough to have accused Jody. What happened Friday afternoon?

I curled up on the sofa, sipping my tea. Spica hopped up on the back of the sofa and looked over my shoulder. I tore a page from my notebook, crumpled it, and tossed it onto the tile floor. She batted it around, content to play by herself for the moment.

I thought back to our stop in Portal on the way to Charley's ranch. Jody arrived. Ron came out of the café.

When Esme asked about him, Jody dismissed him as just a harmless scientist.

That was it. Of course. The silent man listened. He might not have seen the killer at Massai Point, but he'd heard her speak, recognized that dismissive tone perhaps, as she pointed the gun at Bruder's head and pulled the trigger. Somehow, between the time I'd first seen Ron in Portal and the meeting that night, he must have let Jody see that he suspected her. It would have been nonverbal communication—a piercing look, a concentration, a knowing smile.

Sensing that he was at risk, he'd created that word-search puzzle with Jody Lufkin's name spelled backward. He'd put the puzzle in the café, a place where other scientists congregated. He'd posted an expanded version, with more references to Africa, on the wall in the meetingroom. And for all I knew, he'd put them in the library and post office, as well. Jody might manage to destroy the puzzles from the café, but she wouldn't remember the one in the meetingroom.

He'd hedged his bets, just in case his first plan didn't work. He'd watched her that night at the meeting. He'd sketched her. And then I'd offered him a ride home.

On the spur of the moment, he'd entrusted his thoughts, his evidence, to another scientist. If he were wrong about Jody, if he survived the night, he could retrieve his notebook and all the puzzles later. If not, he was counting on my curiosity—that I would decipher his puzzles and eventually piece together all he suspected. Or knew.

Jody had killed Bruder. Why? The obvious answer was that paper Rory's girlfriend, the waitress at Riva's Café, had seen in Bruder's pocket—the contract Prebble and Bruder argued over. It had only one signature. Nate's. Perhaps Jody *wasn't* co-owner of Hoodoo Ranch. Perhaps she'd never legally become her father's guardian. Perhaps Bruder had indeed told her he'd outwait and outwit her. No matter which way you looked at it, Jody'd been betrayed by Bruder and DUC. So she'd killed him. Given the death sentence already hanging over her, she had nothing to lose.

But why had Jody used Peaches' gun and put roadrunner tracks around the body?

Maybe I had it all wrong. Maybe Peaches had helped Jody kill Bruder. Maybe he was on the run. Not wanting to involve his sister, he'd asked Raul for help.

On the other hand, if Peaches *was* innocently interviewing for jobs, where was Raul? Had he lied about where he was going and why? That wasn't Raul's style. He'd tell the truth to your face, whether it hurt you or not—just as he'd told Cindy about his philandering.

I collected the puzzles, folded them, and tucked them back in my field bag. As soon as it was light, I'd wake Charley and tell him what I'd figured out. Then I'd call Cruz and arrange to rendezvous with him on my way back to Tucson.

I was carrying my teacup to the kitchen sink when a question slid to the surface of my brain. *What if Peaches had never left Hoodoo Ranch?*

35

"Bingo," I said to the empty room.

Spica quit stalking the ball of crumpled paper and rubbed against my ankle. "That's it, isn't it?" I whispered as I set the teacup down.

I went back to the table and started doodling in my field notebook, asking questions, drawing arrows. What did I *know*? What were the facts? Where did they lead?

1. Byron Locke was dead (probably killed by Sam Bruder).
2. Sam Bruder was dead. Jody Lufkin shot him with Peaches' gun. The missing foot from Peaches' road-runner sculpture had left tracks at the murder scene. Ron Talmadge had repositioned Bruder's body so that it faced Goma, and placed the copper minerals under his tongue.
3. Ron Talmadge was dead. Shot with a different gun. At Paradise. Because he'd witnessed the murder at Massai Point. Ergo, Jody Lufkin must have killed him.
4. Peaches Tarango was missing. His sister hadn't heard from him. No one outside the Lufkin family (and Carolina Cruz?) had seen or talked to him since Tuesday night. He'd missed a date to meet Charley at the sweathouse. Unless Peaches had bought a bus ticket online and boarded without being seen—or hitched a ride with a friend—he was still in the vicinity. If he wasn't at Charley's, he'd be holed up at Hoodoo Ranch.
5. Raul was missing. He'd checked the bus station, to see if Peaches had left town. He had left work early to run an errand for a friend. If that friend was Peaches, and Peaches was still at Hoodoo Ranch, then that's where

Raul would have headed. If Raul were going to be late getting home, he would have called Cindy and the girls. They'd had a date. Therefore, he must not have had access to his phone. His truck hadn't been sighted on the roads. If he'd gone to Hoodoo Ranch, then he was still there.

The clock on the mantle said twelve fifty. Next to it was a wedding picture of Charley and Rosa. Peaches, the best man, wore a dark suit and bolo tie. His shoulder touched Charley's. Both were smiling.

Okay. I'd strayed far into the Fangorn Forest of supposition. But my little arrows and numbers all seemed to point toward Hoodoo Ranch. None of them pointed away. And Hoodoo Ranch was the home of a woman who'd already killed twice, both with premeditation. The guns and bird prints proved that. Had she killed Peaches and Raul, as well?

Jody'd killed men she didn't care about. But Peaches had been a part of her life forever. And she'd known Raul since he was a baby. So were the two men alive and being held against their will? Why? What would Jody gain?

Time. Jody Lufkin was dying. Time was her most valuable commodity. Time to get her affairs in order. Time to find a place for her father.

She might have panicked when Charley, the students, Cruz, and I started asking questions. If she could divert suspicion from herself and Hoodoo Ranch, and send Cruz hunting for Peaches and Raul, she could buy herself a day or two. Maybe that was all she needed to deposit Charley's check for the horse, the money from the cattle sale, the money from the Haydons for whatever property they were buying. Time.

If Peaches was at Hoodoo Ranch, then Jody had lied to Charley and Cruz about his leaving. Thursday had been Carolina's day off. With Bruder dead and Nate incoherent, there was no one to contradict Jody's story. But if her story was a cat's cradle of lies, how did that change what I took to be true?

Bruder hadn't sent Peaches a case of whiskey. Peaches hadn't fallen off the wagon Wednesday night while Jody was at the meeting in Dragoon. She hadn't fired him. Bruder had come to the ranch Thursday morning, had gotten Nate to sign a contract, but Bruder hadn't given Peaches a ride into town to catch the bus. Peaches wasn't interviewing for a job closer to his family in El Paso, and that's why his sister hadn't heard from him.

It was a circular argument. If Peaches hadn't left Hoodoo, then Jody lied. If Jody had lied, then her house of cards tumbled down—and Peaches had never left Hoodoo. But if Peaches were still quietly working at Hoodoo Ranch, why had Jody hired Jed and Rory to help with the cattle? Why hadn't Peaches shown himself to Charley, his oldest friend? Why were Peaches' things piled in the closet? And why, even if he loved Jody, had he given her his gun to kill Bruder and the foot off his roadrunner sculpture to leave tracks that would implicate a Puebloan?

Answer: He wouldn't. Jody had to have taken them without his permission or knowledge.

The little doodled arrows had coalesced into one large arrow that pointed at Hoodoo Ranch. But it didn't tell me whether or not the men were alive.

I looked back at the numbered list of things I knew, looking again at motive. Sam Bruder was dead, shot by Jody. Why had she resorted to murder? Why not simply take back the contract at gunpoint?

Because the contract was only part of the motive. There must have been something else, a last straw. Sam Bruder must have seen or heard or done something on his visit to Hoodoo Ranch Thursday morning—something that threatened Jody or her plans . . . Had Bruder raped Jody as he had Nadine, as he had women in various cities across the globe? No. Weak as she was, Jody would have fought back. But Bruder's body showed no scratch marks, no defensive wounds at all.

What about murder? The only person who'd gone missing midweek was Peaches. I couldn't picture Jody killing Peaches, even if he'd found out what she was planning to do to Bruder. The bond between them was too great—and she needed him to help with Nate. After all, she'd left Nate in his care Wednesday night, when she went to the Dragoon meeting.

I flashed on my first meeting with Nate. The shotgun. The mental lightbulb blinking off and on, past and present existing in the same instant. But we'd seen no signs yesterday that anything had happened in the house. Had Nate heard something outside Wednesday night? Had Peaches gone to check on the stock and been shot by Nate? Had Jody arrived home to find a disoriented Nate wandering outside near Peaches' body?

The scene was so vivid that I sensed it was true. What would Jody have done? To protect her father, to keep him out of prison or a psych ward, she might have buried Peaches' body and concocted a story . . . But then Bruder showed up early in the morning. How had he figured out what had happened?

Nate must have said something while Jody was outside. Or maybe coyotes had dug around the grave before dawn. Maybe Jody and Nate were digging a deeper grave when Bruder arrived. If Peaches was dead, only Jody could provide answers.

I turned to the puzzle of Raul's disappearance. When he got too nosy about where his "other father" had gone, Jody could have lured Raul out to the ranch simply by telling him that Peaches needed a ride, that *she* had to stay with her father. But was Raul alive, or was he buried in a shallow grave alongside Peaches?

I had to focus on the positive. Jody knew Charley was coming to Hoodoo to pick up a horse this morning. If she was holding Raul at Hoodoo, where would she keep him?

Cal's hidey-hole, the one Nate told me about. But where was it? And how could a small, frail woman overpower a physically fit man?

There were ways. She could have forced Raul into the hidey-hole at gunpoint. She could have drugged him. She could have hit him over the head while he was distracted, looking for Peaches . . . Or she could have shot him.

Was I wrong about her hiding him? Was his body lying by a road somewhere, waiting to be discovered? That's what she'd done with Bruder. And Ron.

I had to know. And the only way to find out was to go to Hoodoo Ranch. Now. If Jody weren't holding him there, I'd force her to tell me where my other brother was.

Outside, the wind had picked up. I smelled smoke. Worried it might be a wildfire, I threw on a jacket, strapped on my Tevas, picked up a flashlight, and went to investigate.

The split mountain above was bathed in moonlight. Smoke huddled in the canyon bottom. It was like walking above the clouds. Somewhere, not far away, cedar and piñon pine burned, but I couldn't see the orange flicker of flames.

I circled the house. Nothing. I crossed the bridge over the arroyo and headed toward the barn. Something ran out of the darkness. A warm, wet nose touched the back of my hand. Startled, I lost my grip on the flashlight. It rolled back down the path a few feet.

"Is everything okay, boy?" In the dark, I couldn't tell if Marty were excited or anxious. I picked up the flashlight. Marty dropped a stick he'd brought me, wagged his tail, and trotted with me toward the barn.

I expected to see it crackling, but all seemed quiet. A single yellow light showed above the barn door. I checked inside. The stalls had been mucked out, the horses fed. Charley and Joaquin must not have been able to sleep, either. In the adjoining corral, Tulapai, Sidestep, and their mates wandered over to the fence to beg for treats I'd neglected to bring. They had to settle for a stroke on the forehead. They didn't move nervously, as they would if they sensed fire, but I knew I wouldn't sleep until I found the source of the smoke.

Wherever Marty was, Charley or Joaquin couldn't be far away. "Marty, find Charley."

He turned and loped up the path to the sweathouse. I trotted after, stumbling once on a half-buried root. The smell of smoke grew stronger. Out of sight, in the darkness, Marty gave a short happy bark.

I topped the rise that hid the sweathouse from the valley. A faint glow defined the outlines of the tanned elk hide that served as a door. I turned my flashlight on the building. An old cow's horn was suspended from one prong of a deer's antler mounted beside the door. The horn would hold corn pollen. Clothes and beach towels dangled from other points. Two pairs of flat-heeled roping boots and a pair of large running shoes were tucked under a log bench. Three pairs of moccasins were in front of the flap. Marty sank down and laid his chin on one of them.

I smelled steam and hot cedar and pine. The fireplace, which had heated the rocks for the sweathouse, still gave off smoke and heat.

"You decent?" I called.

"Depends who's asking." Joaquin poked his head around the edge of the hide door. He looked calm, relaxed, focused.

Charley's disembodied head appeared at the other side of the hide. "What'd you find?"

"Answers."

"Hoodoo Ranch?"

I didn't know how he'd figured it out without studying the puzzles. Maybe he'd read my mind. It had happened before. "Find your moccasins and your bow, old man. We've a raid to plan. Unless you want to wait for Cruz."

"Ten minutes. We need to jump in the pool," came the muffled voice of my brother Jamie. Charley was already reaching for the towels.

I turned and started down, Marty at my heels. Behind me, I heard the soft murmur of Apache—what sounded like a prayer, spoken in unison. I hoped it would help with whatever we faced today. Thirty seconds later, I heard a splash.

Rosa stood in the middle of the kitchen, staring vacantly at the door of the refrigerator. She wore a soft blue dress with a white collar. Her hair was neatly brushed. She looked ready for Sunday Mass. I realized, with a start, that it *was* Sunday. And Mother's Day.

I put my arm around her shoulders. "I think we know where Raul is."

She looked up at me. "Good. You find him, bring him home. I'll be lighting candles and saying rosaries."

Her gaze returned to the refrigerator. On it, magnets held school photos of Raul's two daughters. In another photo, they were playing with Raul and Joaquin in the swimming pool of Teresa's Tucson condo. "They'd planned to paint Pammie's room today."

"Let me guess—yellow?" Pamela, Raul's younger daughter, loved all things yellow. It matched her personality.

"Of course." Her eyes went to the clock on the wall.

"Charley will be here in a minute," I said.

"I've made coffee. Tell him I'm at church."

"In the middle of the night? Is it open?"

"I'm on the Altar Society. I have a key."

Rosa was going to pray, to stand vigil until her son was found. I grabbed my field bag from the floor beside the family room couch and found a few crumpled dollar bills. "Light some candles for me?" I pressed the bills into her hand.

"I plan to light so many the Virgin will melt," she said.

"In that case," I said, handing her a twenty, "you'll need this."

Rosa closed the door softly behind her. I laid out supplies for a quick breakfast. I'd just finished pouring three cups of coffee when Charley, Joaquin, and Jamie trooped in. "Nice of you," Joaquin said, wrapping his hands around a mug.

Teresa came down from the turquoise-painted upstairs bedroom she'd had since childhood. She was dressed for night work—black long-sleeved T-shirt, black pants, moccasins. She carried an assortment of flashlights that she handed around. How she'd known what was planned, I couldn't guess. The Black family communicated on a different wavelength.

In the distance, the engine of Teresa's car started up. Rosa was leaving the Honda for us.

"Mom's off to church?" Teresa said, accepting a mug. I started another pot of coffee.

Joaquin smiled. "I expect she's promising your firstborn son to the Church in exchange for Raul's safe return."

Teresa laughed and looked at Jamie. "We'll cross that bridge when we come to it. Let's find Raul first."

"And Peaches," Charley said.

I looked at the floor. Charley hadn't read my thoughts about Peaches . . . unless he'd meant we'd find Peaches, dead *or* alive.

The smell of coffee brought Harriet and Esme down. I explained the situation. Esme looked past me to Joaquin. "I want to come with you," she said.

He circled the kitchen island to stand before her. "Not this time." He tucked her hair behind her left ear. "But if things go smoothly, I'll drive back to Tucson with you."

"Deal," she said.

"There's no danger to you here," I said to Harriet. "The killer's on the other side of the Chiricahuas. So will you hold the fort till we get back? Keep an eye on Wyatt and Vicente?"

"Esme and I will finish our report," she, then grinned. "And watch birds."

36

We took two vehicles. I went with Charley, Jamie, and Teresa in the Honda. Joaquin followed in his truck, pulling the horse trailer for Shoefly Jo. As we drove north up San Simon Valley, the moon moved to perch on Cochise's forehead. I took it as a good omen.

Lulled by the movement of the Honda, I dozed off. When I woke, the single line of a refrain repeated itself over and over in my brain: *But I just have to know the truth.*

I didn't recognize the tune or the lyrics, but the chorus singing it had been dressed like wannabees at a midnight showing of *The Rocky Horror Picture Show. Ba-da-da-da'-da-da-da-daah* . . . And Philo had been sitting next to me—talking, explaining, reassuring. He was still here, sharing the dark hours of the morning, sharing my fears about Raul and Peaches, sharing my deepest anxiety: *What if I'm wrong? What if I misread the data?*

We passed the chile processing plant on the outskirts of San Simon and joined the stream of west-moving semis. After the quiet of the Chiricahuas, the noise was an alien creature pounding on the fragile shell of the Honda.

I flashed back to where this weekend journey began, wanting Philo to see it as I saw it, wanting him to help me find the path through the maze of events. I was on Massai Point, looking at Sam Bruder's body. Spread out below were the hoodoo sentinels, watching, waiting.

Hoodoos. We're all hoodoos—weathered chemically and physically by every force we encounter. Like sandstone or gneiss, we erode into our peculiar selves.

I loved the hoodoo that was Philo—the boy I'd first met, the man carved from welded tuff by the elements and adversity. What kind of person would he be when he returned? Would he have altered so much that a gulf now separated us that couldn't be crossed?

To focus my thoughts on what lay ahead, I forced myself to concentrate on the layout of the Lufkins' house and grounds, looking for danger points. But when I reached the white-on-white upstairs bathroom, broken only by colors in the braided rug, my mind refused to budge. Some memory struggled to reach the surface . . . I had it.

I turned half around in my seat. Teresa was curled up, her head in Jamie's lap. I reached over the seat and tapped Jamie's knee. He opened one eye. "This better be important."

"What's trazodone hydrochloride?"

"The generic name of an antidepressant. It's sometimes used as a sleeping aid for Alzheimer's patients. Why?"

"It was in Jody Lufkin's medicine cabinet. Nate's got Alzheimer's, I think."

"There can be uncomfortable side effects."

"Such as?"

"Disorientation, confusion, hostility—or a sustained erection."

"Ouch." That explained why there was most of a bottle left. But why didn't Jody toss the remainder if Nate were experiencing side effects?

"Can you die from an overdose?"

"It's happened."

I looked at Charley. "What?" he said.

I told him my thoughts about Nate and Peaches. "You don't suppose . . . ?"

"That if Jody were pushed too hard, her time line shortened, that she'd OD Nate, rather than have him arrested and confined?"

"Only if she couldn't hide what he'd done any longer—or protect him."

No one said anything, but Charley sped up. Behind us, Joaquin followed suit. We were lucky Shoefly Jo wasn't already in the trailer he was pulling.

We didn't call Cruz from Willcox. We waited till we circled the wagons at the base of the hoodoos guarding the Lufkin ranch. He answered on the third ring, his voice brusque. When I launched into an explanation about the clues in the puzzles, Cruz interrupted.

"What puzzles?"

"Ron's. I copied one from the Portal meetingroom bulletin board. The second's on the back of the café menu."

"You didn't mention them before."

"I didn't think they were relevant. I copied the first one down before I even met Ron. And the second's in plain sight, for everyone to see."

"'The Purloined Letter'?"

Cruz was sharp. "Pretty much," I said. "The puzzles say Jody Lufkin killed Sam Bruder. I—we think Raul's at Hoodoo Ranch."

A long pause while Cruz digested this. "And just *when* did you figure this out, Dr. MacFarlane?"

"A few hours ago."

"Did I somehow miss your call?"

It was too late to offer up excuses. "No. Look, Detective Cruz, you have the original puzzle in Ron's sketchbook. I'll show you the others when you get there."

"Where's *there*, exactly?"

"Hoodoo Ranch. We're on our way to pick up a horse."

Before he could reply, I closed my phone and turned it off. I wasn't going to tell him we were a bend in the road away from Jody's home.

"Where would she be keeping him?" Charley said. "She knows I'm coming to pick up Shoefly Jo. The house and barn will be clear."

"The hidey-hole?" I said.

"What?" said Jamie.

"Nate Lufkin thought I was his sister, and that there was a posse outside. He wanted me to make sure their brother Cal was safely hidden in the hidey-hole. I assured Nate he was. But I don't know where it is."

"I do," Joaquin and Teresa said in unison.

"Under the floor of Peaches' cabin," Teresa added. "They built it as a root cellar and a refuge in case of Apache attack. There were still a few of us running around after Geronimo surrendered."

I grinned. "There's a certain irony in hiding an Apache in the Lufkins' place of refuge."

"We can't be positive Raul's there," Charley said. He wasn't smiling.

"No, but it'd be the place Jody'd choose if she were in a hurry," Teresa said. "If Raul came here to help Peaches, and Jody said Peaches was hiding in the cellar, Raul would climb down without suspecting anything. All she'd have to do would be to hit him over the head, tie him up, and remove the ladder. If Frankie's wrong, and Peaches is still alive, she's probably got him there, too."

"What does the cellar look like?" Jamie said.

"It extends under the whole cabin. And there's a tunnel that connects with an old mine adit upcanyon," Joaquin said. "Peaches let us explore. That's where they had their still in the old days. The tunnel was tall enough for a horse and rider. They stored their liquor in the cellar during Prohibition."

"If the tunnel's clear," I said, "wouldn't Jody worry that Raul would free himself and escape that way?"

"Not if he's hogtied—or unconscious," Teresa said. "And for all we know, Jody's installed a locking door on the cellar end."

"If she hasn't, could we enter through the tunnel?" said Jamie.

"It would take too much time to find the entrance," Joaquin said. "It was overgrown the last time we played there—must have been fifteen years ago."

We devised a simple plan. We'd split into two groups, each circling around the main ranch buildings to converge on Peaches' cabin. Pincer movement. Once there, Teresa, Charley, and I would serve as lookouts. Joaquin and Jamie would go in after Raul.

"We want him out by first light," Charley said. "We want to get him back here to the vehicles and wait for Cruz to take care of Jody and Nate."

37

Hoodoo Ranch
3:15 a.m.

I'd dressed for skulking in a pair of earth-toned pants and darker brown camp shirt. Charley had offered me a pair of Raul's old moccasins. They were too short and too wide. My field boots would make too much noise, and my cross-trainers would show glaringly white in the moonlight. I opted for a pair of thick dark socks over the cross-trainers.

Flashlights off to avoid detection, Joaquin, Jamie, and Teresa took the north side of the property. Charley and I circled to the south. Charley led, since he was more familiar with the terrain. I followed, well back. That way, if we stumbled into anyone—or over something that made noise—only one of us would be caught. We were lucky that Jody's dog, Fritz, was no longer on guard. But I hoped the Lufkins were in REM sleep.

I've always liked roaming at night. Unlike my Apache ancestors, I don't fear the dark hours and the ghosts or hoodoos that conduct their business while the world sleeps. The call or appearance of Bû, the owl that carries spirits to the next world, doesn't cause shivers or raise the hair on my neck. Perhaps, being a private person, I welcome the shield of night. In that, I take after my Celtic forebears.

My flashlight stayed in my pocket. The moon, only a night past full, provided plenty of light. I smelled churned earth, hay, and urine from this afternoon's stock sale. Wind whispered down the canyon and stirred the new pistachio and apple leaves as I moved through the orchard. A mockingbird broke into song. But I didn't hear my brother, Joaquin, Teresa, or Charley. They moved silently as specters through the night.

I tripped over a pipe, bit back an exclamation of pain. Ahead, Charley stopped, waited till I recovered, then moved on. He emerged from the trees into a clear space, a road between the orchard and the kitchen garden. We crossed it, one at a time, and navigated the freshly turned garden. Dead ahead I saw an enclosure, fenced with weathered pickets, no longer white. Within, the plot was overgrown with weeds. Headstones leaned drunkenly in the moonlight. But here, too, I thought I smelled freshly turned earth. Perhaps they'd brought Fritz home to bury him with the family.

Everything seemed normal, peaceful as a graveyard. An owl hooted from the top of the house. Charley paused and looked about, scouting for traps and for the easiest route. On the ridge above, coyotes bayed at the moon. The hunters were abroad.

A single light glowed in the front parlor of the house, but there were no exterior lights, not even around the barn. Maybe they were triggered by movement. I'd be sure not to get that close.

As we skirted the far side of the corrals, something snagged my socks. I pitched forward onto gravel, pushed myself up. Charley was there, helping me disentangle my ankles from old wire. I wiped my bloody palms on my socks.

Shadows moved by the barn. I counted three. Good. They'd nearly reached Peaches' cabin. I concentrated on putting one foot silently in front of another.

A gust of wind rattled the screen door of the veranda. I held my breath. The door rattled again—louder, this time. Was it just the wind? Or was Nate awake? He roamed at night, Jody said. But nothing moved in the yard.

And then we were at the cabin. It faced south. Charley took up a position beside the entrance. Jamie and Joaquin, after listening for a moment, eased open the door and disappeared inside. Charley pointed me toward the east wall. Teresa took the west, closest to the main house.

I heard the whisper of footsteps on wooden floorboards, the shuffle of curtains being drawn across windows, a rug being tossed aside. The rusty hinges of the trapdoor squealed. Through the side window I saw the faint glow of a flashlight beam, becoming muted as two shadows descended into the cellar.

"I thought you'd come."

I jumped as Jody's voice emanated from around my ankles. I hunkered down, then eased myself flat on my belly. A wire mesh screen covered a cellar vent. Jody had turned on a utility light hanging from a hook in the ceiling. The room was crowded with old furniture, trunks, trophy heads, and barrels, the flotsam and jetsam of generations. Joaquin and Jamie stood, facing me, at the foot of a hefty wooden ladder on the far side of the room. Jody sat off to the right, profile to me, in a low chair from which the stuffing oozed. Light glinted off her pale hair and the pistol in her hand.

I didn't dare move for fear of betraying my presence. I was surprised she didn't hear the hammering of my heart against my ribs. What were Charley and Teresa doing? Could they hear? Could they see?

"Hey, Jody. We're looking for Raul and Peaches," said Joaquin, as if he had every right to wander Hoodoo Ranch at night.

"Raul's safe. He's my insurance. Who's your friend?"

"Teresa's fiancé," Jamie said.

"You look like that geologist who was here today—you could be twins."

"She's my sister."

"Incestuous little bunch aren't you? Did you come alone?"

"We brought the cavalry," said Joaquin. "Don't you hear them?"

"Funny." She tossed something to Jamie. "Stick your arm through the ladder, then cuff your wrist to Joaquin's. That's right. I'll give the key to Raul when I turn him loose."

I heard a horse blow, then shake, the sounds coming from the cellar. Jody's mode of escape must already be tied in the tunnel. Joaquin and Jamie heard it, too. They looked at each other. Joaquin nodded, the barest hint of movement.

I didn't know what to do. Jody didn't seem to be planning to shoot them. If I barged in, she might change her mind, cut her losses. And we might never know where Raul and Peaches were. They certainly weren't in the cellar.

I stayed frozen in place. Apparently, so did Charley and Teresa. I heard no sounds from the other sides of the cabin.

Jamie moved behind the ladder and poked his arm between the slats, one handcuff dangling from his wrist. I heard a click as Joaquin snapped the other cuff. He lifted their arms to prove the cuffs were locked, and said, "Where's Peaches?"

Jody stood, walked over to check the cuffs, nodded. Now that I knew about the horse, I knew her next move. To her way of thinking, Jamie and Joaquin might rip the ladder loose, but they'd never be able to maneuver themselves and the ladder down the tunnel after her. And they couldn't climb the ladder while they were cuffed to it.

She backed away, still aiming the pistol at Joaquin's body. She knew he and Jamie had free hands. They'd have brought weapons. The only reason they weren't using them was that they didn't know where she was holding Raul. And they wanted to keep him alive. She'd meant what she said about an insurance policy.

"Peaches is dead. Dad shot him Wednesday night, while I was at the meeting—"

"Nate killed Peaches?"

"That's what I said. Dad thought he was the law, come to get Cal." She smiled without mirth. "You've been chasing ghosts for two days. I'd counted on it being longer, but—" She picked up saddlebags with her left hand and slung them over her shoulder.

Joaquin wasn't going to let her go that easily. "Did Nate kill Bruder, too?"

Jody considered, shrugged. "You want the story? I guess you've the right, since I put you and Raul on the hot seat for a couple of days. Someone should know the truth—and I won't be around to tell it."

Wincing, she sank down on the arm of the chair. She put her hand to her head. It came away with a blonde wig. A few wisps of light hair clung to her bald head.

"Jesus, Jody."

"Couldn't have said it better myself, Joaquin." She tucked the wig inside her denim jacket, dropped the saddlebags on the chair. "I killed Sam. Had to. He saw me digging, finishing up in the graveyard, Thursday morning." Jody rested the hand with the pistol on her thigh, as if the gun had grown too heavy to hold. "But I didn't find that out till later, after he left, when I called him about, um, another matter."

"The sale of your mineral rights."

"How'd you figure it out?" When Joaquin didn't answer, Jody shrugged again. "Dad sold Sam the rights for a measly two grand. Even if I challenged the sale, I'd have to prove Dad's incompetent. The court battle would be long. It'd bankrupt me. And I don't have that kind of time. Sam planned to wait till I died. Who'd fight the court battle then?"

"What about the Haydons? I heard they were interested."

Jody emitted a soft snort. "Mark and Ginny offered cash for East Ranch, but only with the mineral rights attached. Sam, the son of a bitch, would have screwed up that sale, too. But that won't happen now."

"Why'd you take Bruder to Massai Point?" Joaquin said.

"I figured it'd be deserted that time of night."

"And he wasn't suspicious?"

"No. We met at the café. I said I wanted to talk somewhere private. Sam hadn't seen the hoodoos under a full moon—hadn't ever seen them, come to think of it. So I suggested we take a drive."

"And you left Peaches' gun to throw us off the track?" he said.

"To buy me some time . . . But there's a certain irony to it, don't you think?" She laughed, a soft, rough sound, like sand trickling over a dry waterfall. "Sam, hoodoos, the odd similarity between Massai Point and the Maasai tribe. You know, the African connection. Ghosts dancing. Roadrunner tracks keeping them at bay. It seemed . . . appropriate to kill him there."

You have no idea how right you are, I thought. Hoodoos and Congo ghosts, Ron and Nadine and Bruder.

Joaquin wrapped his free hand around a ladder bar. "Like it was appropriate to toss his jacket in the dumpster?"

"You found it? Damn. That explains why—" She paused. "No, that was a bit of misdirection."

"Did you know Bruder killed Locke?"

"I figured it out." Jody scratched her bald head. "We all have our tipping points. Sam's was the ruling against us last week. The wilderness designation on the parcels around Strong Ranch made it impossible for DUC to access and mine the property. He and Byron almost came to blows on the courthouse steps. Byron's gloating Wednesday night pushed Sam over the edge." She took a deep breath. "But it didn't take much—Sam Bruder was an amoral man. Rather like Dad. The world was black and white, no love to temper it with shades of gray . . . Sam didn't just walk over anyone who got in his way, he stomped them to death. I did the world a favor by shooting him."

"Like you did when you shot Ron Talmadge?"

"Ron wasn't an innocent, Joaquin. He was helping Byron Locke save the environment for the chosen few. The world was black and white for Ron, too. The West should be reserved for the weekend hiker. Wilderness is good. Vegetables are good. Wolves and spotted owls and desert pupfish are good. Cattle grazing and meat and mining are bad. Black and white, you see? He was just Sam, in different clothes. Brothers under the skin."

"That's no reason to kill a man."

"He'd seen me at Massai Point."

"He didn't, actually."

"Really? His Bronco—" Jody sighed. "My mistake. But in Portal, he looked at me as if—"

"He didn't see you. He *heard* you. It wouldn't have held up in court."

"Oh, well, it doesn't matter now." There was something in her voice that gave me the shivers. "I'm not sorry about any of it, you know. Except Peaches."

"He wasn't drunk?"

"No, I made that up." She stood up. "Make sure you tell Paul that Nate was dead when you got here. It's important."

"Wait—you killed your *father*?" said Joaquin. "Why? Didn't you kill Bruder and Talmadge to protect your plans for Nate?"

"My plans changed when Raul started asking questions, making connections. He was out here Thursday night. I was at Massai Point. The place was deserted. I'd given Dad sleeping pills so he wouldn't wander. Raul kept quiet because he thought Peaches had helped me kill Bruder."

"But then I told him about the tracks around the body," Joaquin said. "Peaches wouldn't have done that. So Raul started digging. He discovered Peaches hadn't caught a bus out of town."

"Your brother's instincts are good," Jody said. "He called me, asking if Peaches was hiding here. I said no. Raul pressed. He wouldn't leave it alone. So I said Peaches was holed up at the old still until things blew over and he could head for the border."

"And Raul came running."

Jody sighed. "Of course. And that was my mistake—a whopper. Raul would know as soon as he got here that Peaches was dead, and what would I do then? Kill Raul?"

Joaquin said nothing. I saw Jamie's free hand slide behind his back. I knew he carried a sheathed hunting knife on his belt.

"I wouldn't," said Jody. Jamie slowly raised his hand to show it was empty.

"Did you?" Joaquin's voice was soft.

Jody recognized that tone. Her shoulders tensed. "Did I what?"

"Kill my brother."

"No. When it was safe, I told him the truth. He already knew I'd killed two men."

"But you weren't going to take the fall for Peaches."

"Why should I? He was the only one who ever loved me . . . except, maybe, Paul. But brothers don't count." She picked up the saddlebags, signaling the discussion was nearly over. "Anyway, my plans changed. I needed to leave the country. Unfortunately I couldn't escape with Dad, and I couldn't leave him here to be arrested for killing Peaches."

"A dilemma," Joaquin agreed.

"I actually talked it over with Raul. It was all very surreal." Jody laughed softly. "Raul asked about my plans for Dad, and for Hoodoo. He was trying to reassure me that Dad would be okay. Instead, he made me realize that Dad had to die first for my will to be effective. He would never have acknowledged Paul."

"Paul *Cruz*?" Joaquin said.

"You didn't know? Raul guessed years ago." She shook her head. "I don't know which is worse—growing up with a father who had no concept of love, or growing up without a father at all."

The rhetorical question, and the pain and history behind it, silenced Joaquin. Jody walked to an elk hide hanging on the north wall. "I've left a note asking Paul to bury Dad's ashes in the family cemetery. As for Peaches—"

"We'll call his sister," said Joaquin. "Jody, in case something goes wrong . . . where's Raul?"

Jody paused, considered. "By the still, of course."

A ghost went by me in the dark, making no more sound than the wind in the grass. Charley, heading upcanyon.

"Look, Joaquin, I'm sorry, about all this. Wish it could have been . . ." Jody didn't finish the thought. Turning abruptly, she pushed aside the hide and disappeared. I heard the faint creak of leather, a few muffled hoofbeats, fading away.

Teresa met me at the front door. "I'll take care of the guys," she whispered, "and follow Jody through the tunnel."

"Good. I'll call Cruz and check on Nate."

I tried my cell as I ran past the barn and corrals, heading for the main house. No signal. I'd have to call Cruz from the house phone.

I took the veranda steps two at a time, flung open the screen door. The back door was locked. I bounded back down to the dirt yard and hustled around to the side window, the window in Nate's den. I'd break it if I had to. But I wanted to be quiet in case Jody had lied about where she was going—in case she doubled back downstream from the still, took the ranch truck, and headed for the border. It's what I would have done.

The dim light in the parlor beyond was enough to show me that the side window was open. I smelled urine and feces. I tugged off the screen and crawled inside, knocking a stoneware bowl from the table next to Nate's recliner. My hand brushed human skin and I yelped. Nate was in his chair.

I turned on my flashlight. His face looked asleep. His mouth sagged open. I knew, even before my fingers failed to find a pulse in his neck, that he was dead, had been dead for hours.

The bowl held the remains of cookie dough. Two empty bottles of trazodone hydrochloride were on the floor—one of them, the bottle I'd seen in the cabinet yesterday. Jody'd drugged Nate's favorite food.

I ran to the office and called Cruz. He said he was ten minutes away.

"Jody killed Bruder and Ron Talmadge—and Nate. Peaches is dead. She has Raul. I'm going after her." I hung up before he could say anything.

I ran back and reached under Nate's chair for the revolver Cruz had stashed there yesterday. It was loaded. From behind Nate's chair, I took a box of ammo—the right caliber, I hoped—and tucked it in my pocket. Then I unlocked the front door and went out the back. Might as well make it easy for Cruz.

The socks I'd worn over my shoes had disintegrated. I tore off the shreds and dropped them at the foot of the steps.

The eastern sky was turning from midnight to navy as I raced up the road past Peaches' cabin. I'd been gone only a few minutes, but it seemed like hours. I should be able to make better time outside than Jody, Teresa, Joaquin, and Jamie did inside the tunnel. I wasn't sure where the still was, but Charley'd be up ahead somewhere.

The canyon narrowed quickly. Pale tuff beds covered the ridges. I tried to be quiet, knowing I must soon reach the place where the old mine adit breached the canyon wall. That was where they'd had their still, and where the tunnel opened. A still meant a nearby source of water—a spring or stream. No water flowed beside the road, but that might be due to the drought. I sniffed the air, hoping to scent water or the verdant plant life that crowds a spring. Nothing.

I turned a corner. It was pitch black in the canyon, though the sky was perceptibly lighter. Here, even the moonlight didn't reach. But I didn't dare use my flashlight. The dirt road showed as two pale stripes. I followed the right-hand one, hoping I didn't run into a rattler. This was their time.

A few feet ahead, I could see the road curving to the left, to circle a bulwark of rock. I stopped at the outcrop, breathing hard. A voice—Jody's voice—not bothering to be quiet. I peered around the outcrop.

"Here's the key," she said. I heard the ping of metal

against rock. "By the time you get those off and go back for your brother, I'll be two miles upcanyon." A horse stamped nervously and champed on his bit. "Shhh, boy. It's okay."

"That's Peaches' horse." Raul's voice echoed slightly. He must be just inside the adit.

"Peaches doesn't need him anymore." Leather creaked as she swung into the saddle. I heard a quick intake of breath, almost a groan, as if the movement hurt her.

I weighed trying to hold her there at gunpoint, but Raul was still a hostage. Better to let her go. Cruz—or Charley—could catch her later.

"Adios," she said, and took off up the road at a canter. She hadn't gone more than fifty yards when I heard rocks trickling from the cliffs above the adit. Something crouched there, dark against the lightening sky. Charley?

The shape gave a hoarse cry that wasn't human.

Peaches' horse reared in fright. Jody lost her grip and fell with a thud to the road. The animal sprang, landing somewhere near her. Jody's faint scream was cut off.

The terrified horse bolted, galloping past me back toward the stable. On my right, not far away, Raul was swearing.

I ran toward Jody, gun in one hand, fumbling for my flashlight with the other, trying to sort out what was happening on the black canyon floor. The beam caught a jaguar, mouth clamped on Jody's head. She wasn't fighting. Blood covered her face.

I aimed close enough to scare the cat, but not to hit Jody. Fired once, twice—the cat dropped its prey. Crouching, it stared at me, eyes reflecting the light like glowing coals. Jaguars shy away from people. This one must be starving.

"Go," I yelled to Peaches' jaguar. "Don't make me kill you."

The jaguar hesitated, then turned and bounded up the slope as Charley appeared out of the darkness of the road ahead. We converged on Jody's still form.

"Sorry, I passed the adit in the dark," Charley said.

"I would have shot the cat." Raul crouched down and went to work on Jody. Somehow, during the commotion, he'd managed to unlock his cuffs.

Teresa, Jamie, and Joaquin burst from the adit to find Charley and Raul trying to staunch the bleeding by the light of two flashlights. Jamie and Joaquin were still cuffed together. Teresa must have broken the ladder to free them.

"Key's in my breast pocket," said Raul. Seconds later the cuff dropped to the dirt. Jamie took Charley's place helping Raul.

"I can't move." Blood bubbled on Jody's lips. She lay awkwardly, her head at an odd angle. The cat's canines had punctured her temples. The fall had broken her neck. "Charley?"

"Yes?"

"I tore up your check for the grulla. I don't need the money now. She's a gift. Sorry about Raul . . . and Peaches . . . Sorry." She coughed.

I handed the flashlights to Teresa. "I'm going for Cruz," I said.

But at that moment he came around the corner, flat out, on Peaches' horse. He was off the horse before it slid to a stop. The sky was now light enough to pick out the dots of trees on the ridges—and Raul's truck, parked in the tall grass at the side of the road.

"Paul?"

"I'm here, Jody." Cruz was on the ground, kneeling beside her. He looked at Jamie, who shook his head.

Jody's eyes were closed. She opened them a slit, enough to see the shocked expression on Cruz's face. She struggled to form words, to make herself understood. "Hoodoo Ranch is . . . yours."

"I never wanted—"

From somewhere she found a burst of strength. "Shut up. Carolina was the only mother I ever knew. And you were my only brother. Just take it." She coughed. "It's not enough . . . It could never be enough . . . I'm sorry. Tell Carolina—just tell her . . ."

"I'll tell her."

Sirens blared in the distance. "Peaches . . ." Her voice was a thread of sound. Her eyes closed.

"Turn off the damn sirens," Paul said into his radio. The sirens went out with a blip, one by one. "Talk to me, Jody." No answer. "Jody?" No answer. Jamie began doing chest compressions. Raul was counting.

I ran back to direct the rescue vehicles. Above, the sun

kissed the ridgecrest, pale gold against a cloudless sky.

The fire trucks and SUVs, lights flashing, sirens silent, drove into the ranch yard as I reached the barn. I hitched a ride back with the first vehicle.

"She's still breathing," Cruz said, as we reached them.

"No, Paul, she's not," said Raul.

Paul Cruz touched her hand once, then stood and turned away.

38

It took four hours to settle accounts with the contingent from the sheriff's department. Since Cruz was next of kin, and beneficiary of Hoodoo Ranch, we had to wait for another detective to take over the scene. She arrived with the forensics team and took statements from all of us.

We'd found Jody's will and the equine ownership certificates for her horses, including Shoefly Jo, on the dining room table. The gun that Jody'd been holding in the cellar, a .38 snub-nosed revolver, was recovered from her saddlebags. A phone call to Enrique confirmed the serial number matched the one he'd sold to the woman at the Tucson gun show. Ballistics would prove whether it was the weapon that killed Ron.

The forensics team recovered Peaches' body from the graveyard. All three bodies were bagged and removed. Cruz and his cohorts would be doing paperwork for weeks.

Raul was thirsty, hungry, and sore. He had a lump on the head from Jody's gun. It had stunned him long enough for her to cuff him to a metal ring inside the adit. He had a headache, but no signs of concussion. But he agreed to an X ray in town, just to be on the safe side.

Interviews done and statements made, we'd gathered around the kitchen table. Outside, the wind was blowing, stiff and clean and strong. A soaptree yucca near the kitchen window had burst into bloom overnight. The creamy blossoms danced in the breeze like silent bells. The veranda door rattled. But now, the sound didn't cause alarm. It was only a door, flapping on the house of the dead.

As Cruz closed his notebook, I belatedly remembered Ron's puzzles and the printouts Wyatt had given me, the messages concerning Bruder's life in Africa. I handed them to Cruz, along with my word list for the African puzzle. He wasn't happy that I'd torn a page out of Ron's notebook, but he didn't press it.

"Goma, again," he said, looking at the list. "Like in Talmadge's sketchbook. Must have been a real nightmare."

"One that didn't end," I said. "Yet Bruder wasn't killed because of Goma."

Exhaustion from the past few days had eroded deep furrows on Cruz's face. "Yes, he was."

Charley, Joaquin, and Raul stopped talking. Jamie and Teresa, in their own little world at the end of the table, straightened up. We waited.

"Indirectly," Cruz added. "Chapin called me as I was heading out of town last evening. Had something he'd neglected to give me. I doubled back. It was the contents of Jody's DUC file."

"The empty file I found in her office?" I said.

Cruz nodded. "Didn't have much in it—just a letter and a clipping." Cruz took an envelope from his coat pocket. Opening it, he spread the contents on the table. "These are copies, of course."

The first page, a photocopy of a newspaper article from an Albuquerque paper dated more than two years ago, detailed the court battle between the Lufkins and environmental groups over grazing rights and wilderness designation for their New Mexico properties, including Strong Ranch. Jody was pictured. Peaches stood behind her left shoulder. Two other small photos showed Byron Locke and Ron Talmadge. The article said Ron lived in Paradise, Arizona.

"Jody sent a copy of the article to Chapin, knowing DUC had been buying up mineral rights in the area. She offered to sell DUC the mineral rights to Strong Ranch if they'd help with the court fight. Chapin showed it to Bruder. He took one look at Talmadge's photo and agreed. Chapin didn't ask what the story was. Bruder was pretty closemouthed about his past. But that day, Bruder hired a PI to check out Talmadge. A week later, he asked Prebble to visit Paradise on his next trip to Arizona."

"Prebble confirmed this?"

"Talked to him last night. Bruder asked him to go to Talmadge's home. He wanted to know the layout—and he wanted to know more about the boy."

"*More?*"

"The PI had done his work."

"That was before Nadine died."

"She'd just gotten her diagnosis. Prebble stopped by to talk to Talmadge, ostensibly to find out if there was common ground between the Lufkins and the environmental groups. He saw Ronnie and Nadine. She sensed something was wrong, and asked who Prebble worked for. He told her, not knowing the history between her and Bruder. Prebble said she nearly fainted. Ronnie began throwing a fit. In the mayhem, Prebble slipped out. But he managed to swipe a Band-Aid that had fallen off a cut on Ronnie's arm."

"DNA?"

"Yup. It confirmed Bruder's paternity. Chapin saw the report."

"But Bruder couldn't have come here looking for Ronnie. He'd been dead—"

"Excuse me?"

I pointed to the top line of the wordsearch puzzles. "Ronnie never went to Tucson when Nadine was ill. That's why Toni couldn't find any trace of him. Nadine killed him."

Cruz sighed. His lips tightened. "Because Bruder knew where he was."

"And she was dying. She wouldn't be able to protect him."

"Like Jody and Nate."

I nodded. "I'll e-mail you my photographs of Ron's house." I explained how Ron had spelled out his son's name in flowers around the tree. "I think you'll find that Ronnie's buried there. And I'm betting Bruder figured out he was dead."

Cruz looked at the puzzles and then off toward Paradise, a mountain range away from where we sat. "You think Bruder came to kill Talmadge, the man who shot him in Goma—"

"And continued to use science to fight him in court," I

said. "Ron could have quit fighting when Prebble mentioned Bruder's name at his house. Ron could have run after Nadine and Ronnie died. But he didn't. Ron wasn't afraid of Bruder. He was probably the only person who ever stood up to him."

"Except Jody," Cruz said.

"But Bruder killed Locke instead of Talmadge?" said Joaquin. "It doesn't make sense."

"Not instead of," Cruz said. "First."

"You're saying Bruder planned to kill Ron after the meeting Friday night?"

"I'd guess Thursday night. Bruder didn't have a hot date. As soon as he got Jody's signature on the contract, he was going to drive to Paradise and kill Ron Talmadge."

"And Ron, anticipating that, was spending the night at Massai Point," I said.

Cruz nodded. "I think Jody was able to get the drop on Bruder because he was focused on what he planned to do later. Women weren't a threat to him. He never saw it coming."

"Sam Bruder dying at Massai Point with Ron just a few yards away," I said. "Do you believe in coincidence now?"

"I believe that some people's concern over unfinished business borders on obsession. The rest is just . . ."

I smiled. "Fate?"

"Greed. Opportunity," Cruz said. "Take your pick."

"Don't forget desperation." I felt tired, my energy reserves depleted. "It seems endless, sometimes—the violence."

"Circles within circles."

Joaquin picked up the battered straw Stetson that had been lying on the table in front of him and settled it on his head. The band held a fresh cigarette. He said, "If Jody hadn't killed Bruder, do you think Ron would have exposed him for what he did to Nadine in Goma?"

"Talmadge had a gun in his backpack. I think, this time, he would have killed Bruder."

Cruz's response stunned me. "Ron had a gun with him at the bridge?"

"Right."

"But he didn't try to use it?"

Cruz said softly: "Talmadge turned his back to Jody's truck. She fired from the cab at a stationary target. There was gunshot residue in the cab—and blowback on the truck door. She washed it down, but she missed a few places."

Jesus. Cruz was right. *Circles within circles.*

He folded up the photocopies and tucked them back in his pocket, along with the puzzles. Pushing his chair back from the table, he stood and said, "You can go now."

"May I take Shoefly Jo?" Charley said. "Or do I need to leave her?"

"Jody gave her to you, in front of witnesses. But would you board Peaches' gelding, for me? It'll be a while before this mess gets straightened out—and Peaches would want that."

"I'd be happy to," said Charley, accepting the two horse certificates and Cruz's handwritten note of authorization. "Come and visit him, anytime."

Cruz nodded, his emotions too raw for words.

"I'm sorry," I said. "About—everything."

"Me, too."

To save me the drive back to their ranch—and because she couldn't wait to embrace her sons—Rosa had piled the students and our gear into the van and driven to Willcox. Though Rosa and Charley were relieved that their children were safe and Teresa's wedding would go off as scheduled, they were shaken by the deaths of their friends. And by Jody's betrayal. They were shadows marring an otherwise happy reunion.

Charley treated us all to breakfast at Riva's Café, crowded this morning with families celebrating Mother's Day. Raul's wife, Cindy, and their girls arrived. Jamie had his arm around Teresa. Joaquin's was around Esme. Things were progressing quickly. As promised, he'd drive back to Tucson with us. It would give them more time together.

By ten we were saying our good-byes in the parking lot. "Did the Virgin melt?" I asked Rosa.

"No, but she wept. And I said a rosary that Philo would

return safely." She smiled. "I had plenty of time."

"I appreciate that." I hugged my other family. "See you in two weeks," I said, and closed the van door on my students.

"Got him!" Wyatt shouted behind me.

Harriet started, opened her eyes. I reached behind and put my hand on Wyatt's knee.

"Right," he said, only a little softer, and gave me a grin the size of Texas. "I'll use my inside voice."

He really was a sweetheart, I decided. They all were. It was amazing how we'd bonded in two short days.

At their request, I dropped off Wyatt and Vicente at Vicente's house. Wyatt wanted to see his friend's computer setup, and Vicente offered to drive him home later. "It's been real, Dr. MacFarlane," Wyatt said, as we unloaded their gear onto the driveway. "When will you post the grades?"

"Tomorrow," I promised.

"That was fun," Vicente said. "Call if you ever need Web searches. I'm pretty good at fixing computers, too."

"I will. Thank you both. We couldn't have done it without you."

I headed north again on Houghton Road. "Mind if we drop off my stuff on the way to campus?" I asked Esme, Harriet, and Joaquin.

"If you don't mind my using your bathroom," Harriet said.

A year ago, when my parents had returned from their sabbatical in England and my house-sitting term was over, I'd moved out of their Tucson home and into my grandmother Tyrrell's old house. She'd suffered a fatal stroke a few months earlier. Her will left me the house, free and clear, and enough cash to pay the property taxes for five years.

The brick home, with its small pool and one-bedroom guesthouse, sat on more than two acres at the east side of town. Most of the acreage had been left in its natural state—a forest of prickly pear, cholla, saguaro cacti, mesquite, ocotillo, and palo verde. In the back, near the pool, were two pepper trees and one obnoxious olive tree that littered the yard with black fruit. Granny Tyrrell had kept a tiny patch of lawn so her grandchildren and great-grandchildren could play tag and catch. And she'd planted hummingbird- and butterfly-friendly perennials around the perimeter. In a corner of the yard stood a terra-cotta fountain, my grandfather Tyrrell's last Christmas gift to his wife of fifty years. She'd outlived him by eleven.

I turned into my rutted gravel driveway. Jamie's MG had usurped the carport. I pulled the van into the shade of the olive tree. Harriet joined me on the brick walk. I opened the sagging gate in the picket fence and led her across the weathered flagstone patio, past the pool, and up the step to the guesthouse. I unlocked the door and used my shoulder to shove it open. The narrow rattan-covered entrance hall was dark. I turned right into the sitting room. The door closed as I reached to switch on the swamp cooler. It was already on. I could have sworn I'd left it off.

"Dr. MacFarlane? Frankie?" Harriet was standing in the hall, five feet away, her head turned toward the bedroom.

"The bathroom's right in front of you, Harriet."

"Yes, well," her voice shook slightly, "there's a naked man in your bed. He's got a gun—"

I turned, took two giant steps, shoved her in the bathroom, and screened the door with my body.

"Sorry," said the man, lowering the gun.

Words deserted me. I just stared, my limbs frozen.

"I'm Philo," he said to Harriet, who was peeking around my shoulder. "Philo Dain." He set the gun on the bedside table.

"Harriet Polvert," she said. "Pleased to meet you."

"Likewise. Frankie, if you'll close the door, I'll throw on some clothes."

"Don't bother on my account," muttered Harriet.

Philo grinned and swung his feet over the side of the queen-size bed that was far too short for his six-four frame. I regained the use of my limbs and closed the bedroom door.

"Yours?" Harriet smiled.

"He's not wearing a brand, and I haven't heard from him in ages, but yes, I suppose you could say he's mine." I said the middle part loudly enough to carry through the bedroom door.

Harriet chuckled as she closed the bathroom door.

"Is it safe to come out?" Philo opened the bedroom door a crack.

"You're the one brandishing a gun."

"I really am sorry, Frankie." The door opened all the way. "I didn't know where I was for a moment."

Philo had slipped into desert-pattern camouflage pants. No shirt. No shoes. He ran a hand over buzz-cut hair that had bleached out in the desert sun. Glints of gray shone at his temples. He hadn't shaved in a couple of days, and the light-brown stubble was touched with silver. His forehead was pale; his lower face, neck, and forearms were bronze. He was leaner than I'd ever seen him. Nothing there but skin, muscle, and sinew. The knuckles of his right hand were grazed. The gun was in a holster at his waist.

I tried to ignore the gun. "Fistfight?" I nodded toward his hand.

"Bumpy flight. I had an argument with some cargo."

"Turn around."

He turned. "Checking for new scars?"

"I'm looking for the reason you didn't call. I can see only a few minor scars—unless you were shot in the ass. And *that* shouldn't have rendered you incommunicado."

"My ass is fine, thanks." He paused. "And the new scars are on the inside."

Joaquin opened the front door a crack and poked his head in. "All unloaded, Frankie. Oh, hey, Philo." Joaquin set my backpack on the floor in the hall and shook Philo's hand. "Welcome home. When did you get back?"

"A couple of hours ago," Philo said. He looked at me. "Didn't you get my messages?"

"Last night. But they were pretty garbled. We were in the Chiricahuas."

"Frankie, why don't I take the van to school for you—leave you two to get reacquainted?" Joaquin said. "I'll bring your truck back after I take Esme home."

Esme stood in the doorway. "Oh, sorry," she said. "Didn't know you had company."

"Neither did I," I said, and introduced them. When Harriet opened the bathroom door, the already cramped hallway felt like the set of a Marx Brothers movie. Suddenly I was tongue-tied.

Joaquin, Esme, and Harriet slipped out, closing the front door gently behind them. I was alone with Philo. I said, "I'd pictured something a little more, um . . ." My voice trailed off.

"I didn't allow myself to picture it at all. There were times I was sure I wasn't coming home." He paused, trying to read my eyes. "You—"

"You—" I began at the same time. We laughed. Our timing was off. Couples felt the rhythm of conversation. We'd been apart too long. "You go first."

Philo took a step toward me. In this small space, his old limp was indiscernible. "You look—" My ears were ringing. "Cell phone." Philo pointed to my pants pocket.

I fumbled the phone out of my pocket and gave it to Philo. I didn't seem capable of speech.

"Hello," Philo said. "Yes, just got back. Happy Mother's Day." Even in my muddled state, I knew the caller couldn't be Philo's mother. She'd been dead for more than twenty years. "I'd love to join you for dinner. We'll see you at five." Philo handed me the phone. "It was your mother."

I tucked the phone in my pocket, but then wasn't sure what to do with my hands. "I'm hungry. Do you want to join me?"

His expression changed. There was a time I wouldn't have had to ask. I would have known he'd stay. He studied my face as if he'd never seen it before. "Stupid of me to assume everything's the same."

The implied question hung in the air. The three feet between us seemed as broad as the Atlantic. "Fourteen months, Philo. Fourteen months when I didn't know if you were alive or dead. I didn't even know where you were, not for sure."

"We moved constantly. Didn't you get my gift? A friend carried it out and mailed it."

"The burqa?"

He smiled the lopsided smile I remembered. "Did you like it?"

"It's six inches too short. The mullahs would thrash me for exposing my ankles."

"You've never been risk-averse."

"I'm rethinking that attitude. You have a bizarre sense of humor, Philo."

"That's the pot calling the kettle . . . You're wearing the ring."

I looked down at the carved carnelian-and-silver ring that I'd been wearing like a talisman.

"It's Afghani," he said. "The carving's a Muslim prayer for safe travel."

"I couldn't send you anything," I said. "I bought you presents—for Christmas, you know, and birthdays . . . I put them in the closet." I waved my hand in the general direction of the bedroom.

Philo reached out and ran a finger over my left cheekbone, then looked at his finger in surprise. "You're crying." He bridged the gap and wrapped his arms around me.

"I expected to meet your plane—at the base—and I'd be—" I grabbed tissues from the bathroom and blew my nose while I searched for words. "Well, *not* looking like this." I smoothed my grubby field shirt and pants. There was blood on my pant leg. Apparently I'd missed when I'd tried to wipe my bloody palms on my socks in the dark.

Philo smiled. He was no stranger to blood. "What *have* you been up to, Frankie MacFarlane?"

I surveyed the rumpled bed, then the semistranger before me. "I'll explain after I've had some food." My voice sounded strained. I took a step toward the one-butt kitchen.

Philo didn't move. "I'm sorry," he said softly. "I shouldn't have surprised you. But with Killeen and the family in residence at my place—well, I wanted to give them some warning before I showed up on the doorstep. They're going to need time to find a place of their own."

"Or not." I wiped my eyes, but couldn't yet manage a smile. "Are you home for good, then?"

"I hope so. Are you inviting me to stay?"

"I—I don't know. Yet. You've been gone a long time. You've changed . . . I've changed. It'll be awkward for a while."

"Or not." He reached for me and kissed me, a hungry kiss that was leading us to the unmade bed. I pulled away. "I smell of death."

"So do I."

"I need a shower."

"Thought you were hungry?"

"Not any more."

"How about a bath? I'll scrub your back, wash your hair . . ."

I reached around him to lock the front door. "In case any family members decide to drop by unannounced."

Philo was already out of his clothes and filling the bathtub. He set the holstered gun on the counter, next to the sink.

"You're right," I said. "Your ass is fine. So's the rest of you."

"Ditto," he said, helping me into the tub.

"But Philo?"

"Hmmm?" His eyes followed mine. "You want me to lose the sidearm?"

"If you can part with it. It's . . . distracting."

Philo and the gun disappeared into the sitting room. He was back a moment later, as I tossed a liberal handful of bath salts into the water. He slid into the tub behind me. The water level jumped to the overflow valve.

"Must have been some field trip." His voice came from just behind my right ear.

"I'll tell you my war stories if you'll tell me yours."

"Later."

Acknowledgments

My deepest thanks go to the following individuals for their aid during the research and writing of *Hoodoo:* Karen Sue Bolm and Robert J. Kamilli, USGS Southwest Field Office, Tucson, for providing geologic information on the Chiricahua Mountains and vicinity; geologists Frank and Eleanor Nelson and William and Pamela Wilkinson for discussing copper exploration in southeastern Arizona; Andy Brinkley, chief ranger, and the staff of the Chiricahua National Monument; Beth Brinkley, for serving as information conduit; Clark Lohr, Tucson, for guiding me through the world of gun shows and checking my gun facts; John Turner, DPS, retired, for advice on police vehicles; Robert Wm. Wagner, Chicago PD, retired, for advice on firearms and police procedure (Bob, I'll miss you!); Wynne Brown and Hedley Bond for volunteering their home in the Chiricahuas as a research base, and for leading botanical field trips to Rucker and Blumberg Canyons; Frances and Peter Grill, and the students of Goshen College, 2005, for facilitating the geologic field excursion to the Chiricahuas that helped spark this story; Deb Eichenlaub, Tucson, and the staff of the Myrtle Kraft Library, Portal, Arizona, for information on Nabokov's sojourn in Paradise, Arizona; Steven "Bear" and Hollie Pitts for donating a digital physiographic map of southeastern Arizona; Tom and Mary Judge Ryan for offering their cabin in the Catalinas as a quiet writing retreat; Jordan Matti and César Rascón-Padilla, for discussing computer game characters and for solving my computer glitches; and Jonathan and Logan Matti for their support and humor.

For their perceptive comments on part or all of the manuscript, I'm grateful to Hedley Bond, Wynne Brown, Elizabeth Gunn, William K. Hartmann, Lou Halsell Rodenberger, J. M. Hayes, Douglas M. Morton, and Liza Porter; and to Southwest Institute for Research on Women (SIROW) Scholars Elena Diaz-Bjorgquist, Mary Driscoll, Corey Knox, Beverly Lanzetta, Nancy Mairs, and Patricia Manning.

Lastly, I wish to thank Judith Keeling, editor in chief, and the staff of Texas Tech University Press for their continued support; and to copyeditor John Mulvihill, for his attention to detail.

About the Author

Susan Cummins Miller received degrees in history, anthropology, and geology from the University of California, Riverside. After working as a field geologist with the U.S. Geological Survey and teaching geology and oceanography, she turned to writing fiction, nonfiction, and poetry. She is a research affiliate and SIROW Scholar with the University of Arizona's Southwest Institute for Research on Women, and the editor of *A Sweet, Separate Intimacy— Women Writers of the American Frontier, 1800–1922*. *Hoodoo*, the fourth Frankie MacFarlane, geologist, mystery, follows *Death Assemblage*, *Detachment Fault*, and *Quarry*.